THE CONFIDANT

EDEN FALLS ACADEMY

CHERRY
BLOSSOM
ROMANCE

the confidant

JUDY CORRY

Also By Judy Corry

Eden Falls Academy Series:

The Charade (Ava and Carter)

The Facade (Cambrielle and Mack)

The Ruse (Elyse and Asher)

The Confidant (Scarlett and Hunter)

The Confession (Kiara and Nash)

Kings of Eden Falls:

Hide Away With You (Addie and Evan)

Rich and Famous Series:

Assisting My Brother's Best Friend (Kate and Drew)

Hollywood and Ivy (Ivy and Justin)

Her Football Star Ex (Emerson and Vincent)

Friend Zone to End Zone (Arianna and Cole)

Stolen Kisses from a Rock Star (Maya and Landon)

Ridgewater High Series:

When We Began (Cassie and Liam)

Meet Me There (Ashlyn and Luke)

Don't Forget Me (Eliana and Jess)

It Was Always You (Lexi and Noah)

My Second Chance (Juliette and Easton)

My Mistletoe Mix-Up (Raven and Logan)

Forever Yours (Alyssa and Jace)

Standalones:

Protect My Heart (Emma and Arie)

Kissing The Boy Next Door (Lauren and Wes)

For anyone who's found themselves at a crossroads and been brave enough to take a leap into the unknown.

PLAYLIST

"Paper Hearts" by The Vamps
"You Are In Love" by Taylor Swift
"Fall on Me" by Andrea Bocelli and Matteo Bocelli
"Friends Don't" by Maddie and Tae
"My Life" by Imagine Dragons
"Burn" by AJ Mitchell
"She's Mine" by Lauren Weintraub
"Favorite T-Shirt" by Jake Scott
"Give Me Some Love" by TYNSKY
"True Crime" by Taylor Acorn
"Missing You" by Lauren Weintraub
"Butterflies" by Abe Parker
"Dress" by Taylor Swift
"One Life" by Ed Sheeran

AUTHOR'S NOTE

Dear Reader,

Thank you so much for picking up The Confidant! I have wanted to write Scarlett and Hunter's story for several years, but since it is a deeply personal story, I waited until I was at a better place to tell it.

It is, of course, a work of fiction, and the characters and organizations within the book were created in my imagination. It deals with a cult-like church and religious trauma, which I know can be sensitive subjects.

My purpose is not to make anyone feel uncomfortable about their own belief system. Religion and spirituality are such a personal thing, and I don't want my readers to feel threatened by how the fictional religion in this book is portrayed or how my characters will interact with it.

In order to convey the trauma/tell the story, there are numerous religious details mentioned, but it was not written with the intent to persuade anyone to go against or for a particular belief, nor is it endorsing any at all. My intent is to set the stage for the issues that can arise when a friend or loved one steps away from a high-demand religion and how big of an impact these changes can have on their relationships.

The Confidant is still a best friend's romance at its core, but because of the subject, it is heavier/darker than my previous work. The emotions are very raw and real, and I tried to remain authentic to how the characters would react in given situations and circumstances. To say this book was tricky to write would be an understatement, but I hope that Scarlett and Hunter's journey is one that will stick with readers for a long time.

-Judy

PREFACE

When I was a child, my father lovingly cautioned, "Whatever you do, my darling, you must never open the tower door."

Well, my father had always been very good to me, keeping me fed and teaching me the right way to live, and so for many years, I followed his warning.

But one day, my curiosity got the better of me. I tiptoed up to the door and carefully drew it open...

And there, to my surprise, was sunshine, tall trees, and blue skies.

SCARLETT

"HOW'S THIS week's article coming?" I walked over to where my best friend, Hunter Blackwell, was typing at his computer station in the journalism classroom Monday afternoon.

The Eden Falls Gazette—our school's online newspaper—was set to go live Wednesday morning, and since I was the lead editor, it was my job to check in with the newspaper staff and make sure their articles were where they needed to be.

"I'm almost done." Hunter turned away from his computer to look up at me with his green eyes. "Just writing about the boys' basketball game on Friday night."

"Oh, good," I said, bending over to read what he'd typed into the word processor.

I didn't actually need to check in on what he was doing, since Hunter was one of the more responsible students in the class. But because I had so few opportunities to be close to him these days, I checked his article anyway.

My eyes scanned over the black text. As I read about the game against the New Haven Bulldogs, I resisted the urge to breathe in the scent of his delicious cologne—the cologne I'd bought him last spring when he'd gone from best friend to boyfriend for those few short weeks.

I both loved and hated that he still wore the cologne. Loved it because it was my favorite scent on earth—a scent that smelled especially amazing when mixed with his body chemistry. But also hated because it reminded me of how happy and delusional I'd been back then—to think that I could date the guy who'd been my best friend since sophomore year and not have things get complicated when my dad found out and made me break up with him.

"Is it okay?" Hunter asked in his deep voice, bringing me back to the present.

"It is," I said, making my gaze focus on the words again. "This is all really good. I think you just forgot to mention who made the winning three-point shot."

"Yeah..." He lifted his arm to run his hand through his chestnut-colored hair. "I might have left that out on purpose..."

"You did?" I asked. "Why?"

"Don't you think that would come off as bragging?" Hunter dropped his arm back onto his lap, and I tried not to notice how muscular his forearms looked with the sleeves of his shirt rolled up. "Since everyone will know that I'm the one who wrote the article?"

"It's not bragging if it's true," I said matter-of-factly.

"I guess..."

But when he didn't make a move to fix it, I slid the keyboard to the side so I could type: *With thirty seconds left on the clock, it looked like the New Haven Bulldogs would win the game. Not about to accept defeat, Carter Hastings stole the ball from the Bulldogs' point guard and passed it to Mack Aarden. Aarden then dribbled it halfway down the court before passing it to Hunter Blackwell. With just two seconds left on the clock, Blackwell aimed for a three-point shot and got nothing but net.*

When the final buzzer sounded, the Wolves claimed their victory with a final score of sixty-three to sixty-two.

"There," I said, standing up straight again. "Now it's more accurate."

Hunter looked over what I'd written. "You're the boss, I guess."

"Yes, I am," I said with a smile, probably a little too happy to use my power as lead editor.

But Hunter was way too humble for his own good and deserved to get credit for how well he played on the court instead of always transferring the accolades to our friends Carter and Mack.

"Hopefully, you approve of what I wrote about the girls' game on Thursday," he said.

"You didn't mention the part where I missed all of my foul shots, did you?" I mean, I believed in honest reporting and everything. And I prided myself on how accurate the school's newspaper was. But highlighting how I'd been way off my game last Thursday certainly wasn't necessary, right? Especially when my teammates had so many other great moments.

"Nah." He waved the thought away. "The only time I mentioned your name was when I talked about you stealing the ball from the other team and making it impossible for them to score the shot they needed to win."

"Okay, good." I sighed.

"And I assume you already have your article on the school musical written up and submitted?" Hunter asked with the crooked smile that I loved on his lips.

"I did that Saturday night." I returned his smile. "Gotta write it up while it's all fresh."

"Who needs sleep anyway?" He winked, referencing to how we'd already been up until midnight celebrating an amazing opening night of *The Phantom of the Opera* with our friends who were in the musical. "Sleeping in is what Sunday mornings are for, right?"

"Right..." I said, even though Sunday mornings weren't really for sleeping in. Not for me, anyway.

Not since my dad expected me to stream our church's Sunday service live at ten o'clock each week—dressed in my Sunday best, no less—so I could be ready for his interview immediately after.

The mandatory hour-long chat was my dad's way of testing me and making sure I wasn't skipping out on my weekly spiritual upliftment while away at boarding school.

Only once he got the spiritual quiz out of the way did he ask me how things were going here at school and if I was still on track to graduate as valedictorian.

Hunter used to join me for Sunday service in my room each week since his family belonged in my dad's congregation, and that had always made it more fun and less of a chore. But he'd stopped coming last spring—right around the time my dad made me break up with him.

At first, I had thought he stopped coming because things were slightly awkward during our transition to being just friends again. But even though we'd eventually gotten our friendship back to normal, Hunter still hadn't been joining me for church this year.

Maybe he just wasn't a fan of my dad now?

My dad could be a bit overbearing—very strict and set in his ways. But Hunter had always known all about that because even before we became friends, we'd been neighbors—he'd grown up just down the street from the church property where my dad, stepmom, and I lived in Manhattan.

Was it possible my dad had said something to Hunter that I didn't know about?

It was definitely a possibility.

Either way, things were different now. Instead of having someone at the school to complain to about how boring my dad's sermons were, Hunter was telling me about how nice it was to sleep in on a Sunday, or how beautiful his morning hike was when the weather was nice.

"Anyway," I said, pushing away my thoughts, "if you could email your article to Mrs. Donlan, she can proof it before we upload it to the website tomorrow."

While our journalism teacher was pretty hands off and let our class take care of a lot of the preparation on our own, she still proofread all the articles before I pushed the button to make the online newspaper go live on Wednesday mornings.

I left Hunter's station to check on what Ben and Casey were doing. Ben and Casey were the two senior guys in charge of the lifestyle and entertainment section. After last week's article on "How to Date Two People at Once Without Getting Caught" had been a huge embarrassment, I needed to make sure they'd come up with something better.

"We're still in the brainstorming stage," Ben said, the slight smirk he wore telling me he and Casey had been goofing off all period as usual.

"Yeah," Casey said. "We're just narrowing down all the options—" He cleared his throat. "The *many* options that we came up with over the weekend. But you can bet we'll have something epic by the end of the day."

"I hope so." I sighed. "Because I really don't have time to write your articles for you."

Again.

I was pretty sure Casey and Ben had only signed up for this class because they heard Mrs. Donlan was retiring and thought it would be an easy A. Which, yeah, she seemed to have checked out of teaching us anything about two months ago. But just because our teacher didn't care about the quality of the gazette anymore, it didn't mean I was going to let it crash and burn under my watch.

"We did come up with one idea, actually," Ben said, glancing sideways to his friend.

"You did?" I was skeptical of whatever these creative geniuses had come up with.

"Yeah." Casey nodded. "We were actually thinking that it would be cool if you asked the girl who writes *The Confidant* to post her stuff in the paper. Her stuff would fit in the lifestyle and entertainment category easily enough. Plus, you'd get the hottest column *and* wouldn't have her competing with the gazette anymore."

"And do you know how I might reach her?" I folded my arms across my chest. "Have you figured out her identity yet?"

"Well, no..." Casey ran a hand through his curly, blond hair. "But she has her email listed on the bottom of each post. You could probably email her and ask."

He thought I could just ask nicely and the person behind the most popular advice column I'd ever seen in a high school setting would hand over all her content to us?

I had no idea who was behind *The Confidant*, but whoever it was had to be a shrewd businesswoman. She'd started the online publication almost a year ago, giving advice to students who wrote her with their problems and doing a dang good job at it, too.

When it first popped up, I had been curious and even been a fan since this "Confidant" girl seemed to really know her stuff. But when the Eden Falls Gazette started getting less and less hits each week as *The Confidant* gained thousands of readers, along with sponsored ads from companies I'd actually heard of before, I knew the competition was steep.

"No, that's okay," I said, annoyed that they were trying to get out of doing their assignments. "I think I'd rather have you two actually write your articles and give our classmates something juicy enough to wipe out our competition."

The school newspaper might be a tiny publication in the grand scheme of things, but it was my responsibility. And I wouldn't have it failing because some know-it-all had suddenly decided to post her advice and thoughts on life at the boarding school for everyone to read.

I left Ben and Casey to their own devices and headed to the back corner of the room where our graphic designer, Addison, was sitting at her computer.

"How are things coming?" I asked, taking the empty seat beside Addison. "Were you able to fix the typo we found in the ad for the Valentine's dance?"

"Just fixed it." She clicked over to her photo-editing program and twisted her monitor so I could see it better. "It now says it's on February twelfth instead of the fourteenth."

"Perfect." I inspected the rest of the ad. It was a pretty simple design—a light-pink background with a silhouette image of cupid shooting an arrow at a big, dark-pink heart. All of Addison's designs were clean like that. Minimalistic but beautiful. "It looks great. And I really love the color scheme you used."

"Thank you," she said with a smile. "I just hope the typo from last week didn't mess up too many people."

"I'm sure it'll be fine. Most people expect the school dances to be on the Saturday before Valentine's Day, so I don't think it was too big of an issue."

"Hopefully."

"Are there any other designs you needed to submit?" I asked, even though I was pretty sure she'd already uploaded all the others. Addison was the opposite of Ben and Casey and usually had her work done days ahead of deadline. Which was why, aside from Hunter, she was the person I talked to most on the newspaper staff.

We'd actually been getting to know each other a lot better over the past month, since she'd taken the dorm room next to mine after the Cohen twins moved into their dad's house. She and her stepbrother were new to Eden Falls Academy this year. They had kept to themselves for the most part, but now that she was getting more comfortable around me, I could see her coming out of her shell and I was liking her more and more.

The fact that she was responsible and didn't need babysitting didn't hurt, either.

"I've gotten everything besides the ad for the Valentine's Grams done." She clicked back out of the program. "But I do have a question for you."

"You do?"

"Yeah..." She tucked a lock of her dirty-blonde hair behind her ear. "It's actually about the Valentine's dance."

"Uh, huh," I said, wondering why she seemed anxious to ask me about it. Was she worried I'd changed my mind about inviting her to join the group date with me and my other friends? Because I'd already cleared it with the other girls, and they were totally cool with Addison and her date joining us for the day.

"So..." She bit her lip and glanced behind us. My chest started to cave in, because based on whom she'd just glanced at, I had a good idea of what she might be planning to ask.

The question that everyone had been asking me lately— about whether I was going to ask Hunter to be my date to the dance.

"What did you want to ask me?" I sat up straighter, bracing myself.

"Well..." She looked down and smoothed her hands across the red-and-blue plaid skirt of her school uniform. "I—" She seemed to swallow before meeting my gaze again with her crystal blue eyes. "I was wondering if you were planning to ask Hunter to the dance?"

Yep.

I'd spotted that question from a mile away.

I glanced back at Hunter, my heart panging in my chest the way it did every time I thought about not being able to ask him to the Valentine's dance because of the stupid deal I made with my dad.

The deal was that if my dad allowed Hunter to be my escort for the debutante ball that took place last December, then I would agree to go to the next school dance with a guy of my dad's choosing. That guy being Xander Pierce—the college senior who had done an internship with my dad over the summer. Also known as the guy he'd been trying to set me up with for months.

So, since I'd been able to enjoy the debutante ball with Hunter and pretend for a night that things were different between us, it was time for me to fulfill my end of the bargain.

And like it or not, I'd be celebrating the holiday all about love with a guy who, while he seemed nice enough and was admittedly extremely attractive, I still didn't feel I knew very well.

But I guess that was why my dad kept insisting I spend time with Xander on this date. So I could get to know him better and see that there were other good guys who would make good future husbands besides my best friend.

I'd avoided telling my friends—especially Hunter—about this arrangement because I didn't want to accept that my dad had so much control over my love life. But with the dance less than two weeks away, I needed to fess up.

Even if that meant officially relinquishing any claim I had on my best friend.

After taking a deep breath, I said, "I'm actually going with someone else this time."

"You are?" Addison furrowed her brow, a shocked expression covering her face. "Y-you're really not asking Hunter?"

"No." I peeked back at my friend who was bent over his keyboard with his tongue poking out the side of his mouth like he was in deep concentration. "My dad has been trying to set me up with this other guy he knows, so I'll be taking him."

Did I think it was weird that my dad was setting me up with a college senior who probably had way better things to do than take an eighteen-year-old to her high school dance?

Yep.

But for some reason, Xander was on board with this idea that our dads had schemed up and had even texted me yesterday to say that he was looking forward to seeing me again.

Maybe the dating scene at Yale just wasn't everything I'd imagined it would be, and he was desperate for a date?

That was honestly hard to believe because Xander was gorgeous, wealthy, smart, and charming—things most people wanted in the those they dated.

But perhaps his family was like mine and had rules about only dating people with similar life goals—one of those being to marry someone who was a strong member of our church.

It made sense. You marry who you date. And things were a lot easier if you married someone whom you shared similar values with. Someone on the same path. Someone who'd want to raise your future children in the *right* way.

It was why I'd never really looked at anyone besides Hunter, since he was the only guy in our whole school who had all the qualities I needed in a future husband.

But while I'd had tunnel vision on my best friend this past year, my dad had apparently sought out Xander to be that someone for me instead.

Someone he deemed more worthy of his only daughter.

Someone who wouldn't break my dad's rules and try to steady date or kiss me before I graduated from high school.

Yes, I'm not perfect and only made it to spring of my junior year before I fell to the temptation of the beautiful boy with turquoise-green eyes and the kind of body that had maybe made me think slightly impure thoughts the couple of times I'd caught him doing pushups without his shirt on.

But it wasn't like we'd *done* anything wrong. Surely a few make-out sessions on the common room's couch, and a few more hours of kissing in Hunter's car, weren't high enough on my dad's list of sins that it made any future relationship with Hunter impossible.

You know...if Hunter was even interested in trying again after graduation—after the threat of my dad pulling me out of the school and bringing me back home because I'd broken his rules was gone.

But my dad had been touchy every time I talked about hanging out or studying with Hunter lately—as if he suddenly had something against Hunter after eighteen years of treating him like he was part of the family.

Maybe my dad had somehow found out that Hunter hadn't been watching the sermons with me anymore? Maybe the same person who'd told my dad that Hunter and I had started dating last spring had also informed him about that, too?

"Do you know if anyone else has asked Hunter then?" Addison asked, interrupting my thoughts.

"Oh, um..." I hesitated. "I-I don't think so."

He would have told me if someone had, right?

I might not have told him about Xander, but Hunter would have mentioned anyone asking him out, wouldn't he? We'd never kept secrets from each other before.

Addison chewed on her bottom lip as if still trying to get up the nerve to say something.

And the feeling of dread took hold of me again.

Because this was the moment I'd been dreading ever since last spring. The moment when someone else saw a door in the invisible bubble I'd kept Hunter in with me and was about to pull it wide open.

Addison pressed her lips together. I had the urge to bolt away before she could ask permission to do something I knew I had no right to control. But before I could run away, she asked, "Would you be okay if I asked him to the dance?"

Silence fell between us, a silence that I did not want to fill with the answer that I knew I should give.

Addison just stared at me with wide eyes, like she was scared of how I might react.

And I knew I must have looked jealous since I wasn't the actor my other friends were. But after a few heart-pounding seconds, I forced a smile on my face and said, "Of course." I patted her hand gently and smiled even wider. "Of course you should ask Hunter. He'd be so fun to go to the dance with."

"Are you sure?" she asked, like she knew I was internally screaming right now.

"You guys would be so cute together," I said, trying to sound enthusiastic even though I did not mean it.

"Okay, cool." She let out a long sigh, like she'd been holding her breath. "I just... He's been so nice, and I thought he would be a fun guy to go with."

"He is a great guy," I said. One of the best that I knew.

"Do you think he'll say yes?" she asked, a cautious look on her face.

"Probably." He'd gone to dances with other girls when they asked him last year. But those dates had happened *before* we'd dated. So this time would feel different.

This time would hurt a little more.

Seeing him dancing with someone else. Laughing with someone else. Being his sweet, gentlemanly self with someone else.

But it wouldn't be fair to expect him to remain single forever just because *I* wasn't allowed to be anything more than friends with him.

"When do you think you'll ask him?" I asked, knowing I'd need to prepare myself.

"I hadn't really gotten that far in my planning, actually," Addison said with a light laugh. "I mean, I wasn't sure where you two stood since you're always together, and I heard you dated last year. I was halfway expecting you to warn me not to go within ten feet of him."

Yeah...I kind of wanted to do that still...

"But since you're going with someone else," she said, "I guess I'll probably ask him after class."

And I would make sure to not be around to watch when it happened, so he wouldn't have to feel bad saying yes to someone else.

Would he prefer her blonde hair and blue eyes to my auburn hair and brown eyes? Her short, petite frame to my tall, athletic one?

Would that be his new type?

He'd never asked a girl out besides me, so I'd never had a chance to see what other types of girls he would gravitate to. And the girls who were interested in him before had never all looked the same.

Addison was gorgeous though, so he'd probably think she was attractive.

Why did everyone at this school have to be so beautiful?

"Well, I better go check on some other things," I said, needing to move. "I'll talk to you later."

"Okay," she said. "Thanks for your help."

"No problem."

Before she could say anything else, I went to my computer to see if *The Confidant* had any advice on how to watch your best friend date other people without turning into a jealous maniac.

2

HUNTER

"HEY, Hunter. Can I talk to you for a second?" a female voice asked from behind me after the final bell rang.

I turned around from where I was zipping up my backpack in the journalism room to find Addison Michaels standing behind me.

"Um, sure." I glanced at the clock on the wall, hoping she'd be quick. Basketball practice started in fifteen minutes, and I had to grab my gym clothes from my dorm room first since I'd forgotten to return them to my gym locker after washing them this weekend.

"Okay, awesome." She shifted the strap of her backpack on her shoulder. "I-I guess I'll just get right to it. So, I was wondering if you were going to be around on February twelfth."

"I think so..." I said, trying to calculate the dates in my head. Today was January thirtieth, so that date would be in about two weeks from now, right? "Unless there's an away game that day, I should be here."

"The twelfth is a Saturday," she said.

"Oh, then yeah, I should be around." I finished shoving my notebook into my backpack and pulled the zipper closed. "Why do you ask?"

"Well..." She bit her lip, a blush forming on her lightly freckled cheeks. "I was wondering if you...if you didn't already have a date to the Valentine's dance...if you'd go with me?"

She was asking me to the dance?

I cleared my throat, and out of instinct, I glanced behind Addison to Scarlett's table to see if she was listening to this. But instead of typing up a storm on her laptop with a pencil between her lips like she always did right up until the final bell rang, her seat was empty.

Was she talking to Mrs. Donlan? We always walked to the gym together since we both had basketball practice after class, so she couldn't be far.

"I know you and Scarlett usually hang out at these things," Addison added, as if sensing my hesitation. "But I just thought that since she was taking someone else, maybe you'd be open to going with me. If not, I totally understand..."

What...?

I looked back at her. "Scarlett told you she already asked someone?" Because this was the first I'd heard of it.

When had that happened? Who had she asked?

She'd been talking to Ben and Casey for a while during class. Had she asked one of them?

"Yeah, at least that's what I'm pretty sure she said when I asked her if she'd be okay with me asking you..." Addison said, her words trailing off.

She'd asked Scarlett if she could ask me to the dance?

And Scarlett had given her the green light?

Not that I needed Scarlett's permission to go on a date with anyone else. We weren't boyfriend and girlfriend anymore.

But Scarlett was taking someone else to the Valentine's dance?

"I'm sorry, maybe I shouldn't have asked..." I heard Addison say through the fog overtaking my brain. "I'll just go now."

She was turning to leave when my sense of shock wore off long enough to realize that I was being a complete jerk right now.

"No sorry, wait." I reached out to touch her arm before she could leave. "I'm just, I—of course I'd love to go to the Valentine's dance with you. Sorry, it's been a long day, and I think my brain decided to check out of school twenty minutes ago. But that sounds fun. And I'm free."

Apparently.

"Are you sure?" she asked, insecurity reflecting in her blue eyes. "Because if you already have other plans or were hoping someone else would ask you, I understand. I mean, I was originally thinking about, well..." She shook her head. "Never mind, but you don't have to feel obligated to—"

"I don't feel obligated," I cut her off before she could feel even worse than I'd already made her feel. "It'll be fun getting to know you better. And the dance sounds fun."

Since it appeared that my usual dancing partner already had found a new replacement for me, it was probably time for me to accept that after being in a stalemate with Scarlett for nine months, I needed to at least look like I was trying to move on.

And Addison was nice—a little quieter than my usual type, sure. But my usual type wasn't working out so great right now, so it would probably be good for me to try going out with a different type.

A second later, Addison's stepbrother, Evan, showed up at the classroom door with his backpack slung over his shoulder. I briefly wondered if he would be as overprotective of Addison as Scarlett's dad was of her. They were always together, and while Evan seemed like a pretty good guy, he was also huge—about the size of my cousin Arie who had been a bodyguard at one point.

I shook those thoughts away. It was just a date to a school dance. I didn't need to worry about every relative of the girl I was going out with having huge reservations about me dating their daughter or sister or whatever. Even if I was a lot different than I'd been a year ago—different in ways Pastor Caldwell found unacceptable to date his daughter—I was still a good person.

But it did suck that the reason Scarlett and I couldn't date was because I'd made some changes to my life plans that her father didn't approve of. To not be with the person I'd always expected to end up with—not because we didn't get along or weren't great together, but because I no longer believed everything Pastor Caldwell or the High Priest said as gospel truth.

He saw himself as an authority on the workings of the universe and didn't like to have his authority questioned.

"We'll go tubing at the ski resort during the day—I'll let you know the exact time when it gets closer," Addison said, giving me a few more details about our date. "And then dinner will be at The Italian Amigos before we head to the dance."

So we'd be going as a group with the rest of my friends? And I'd get a front-row view to watch Scarlett and her date flirt?

Yay...

"Sounds like a fun day," I said, trying hard to sound enthusiastic.

"I think it should be," she said, not seeming to realize how potentially awkward this group date could be.

She gave me one last smile, and then with a quick wave, she

walked out the door with her stepbrother to head to whatever after-school activities they had planned.

Once I was alone again, I blew out a long breath and tried to center myself.

This day had taken a sudden turn. Instead of going to another school dance with Scarlett as "just friends" like we'd been doing all year, she was moving on. And before I was ready, I was going on a date with someone new.

I pulled my backpack over my shoulder and glanced around the room one more time for Scarlett. But she still was nowhere to be found.

I headed toward her workstation to see if her things were still there, but they weren't.

So for the first time all year, I left the journalism classroom alone.

I just hoped this wasn't somehow an omen for more things to come.

3

HUNTER

"DID Ava say anything to you about who Scarlett's taking to the Valentine's dance?" I asked my friend, Carter Hastings, as we walked into the locker room after an exhausting practice.

His girlfriend Ava was on the girls' basketball team with Scarlett, and if Scarlett was telling people about whom she'd asked, Ava would probably be one of the first people to know.

I mean, as her best friend I'd assumed I would be the first to know about everything going on in her life. But apparently, I wasn't the only one of us keeping secrets right now.

"Scarlett asked someone?" Carter furrowed his brow and studied me with surprise in his blue eyes. "Someone that's not you?"

"Yeah, I guess so." I shrugged as we turned a corner and walked to the end of the hall where our gym lockers were. "Addison said something about it when she asked me to the dance today, and ever since then, I've been trying to figure out who Scarlett might have asked."

Usually my mind stayed pretty well in the present during basketball practice because exercise had a way of calming my brain. But since we'd been working on conditioning today, I'd had plenty of opportunities to stew over the question of who my best friend was trying to replace me with.

Was it someone I knew? Someone in one of our classes?

We mostly hung out with our core group of friends, and most of them were paired up with someone already. Our friend Nash was the only one besides Scarlett and me who wasn't currently tied up in a relationship—but he'd told me just a couple of days ago that he had a group of freshman girls fighting over who got to take him to the dance. So I was pretty sure it wasn't him. Plus, Nash was Carter's half-brother, so Carter would have told me if Scarlett had asked Nash.

Could she have asked Evan? He and Addison had been spending more time with us lately—eating dinner with us in the great hall since the rest of our friends were day students and usually went home for dinner.

I hadn't caught any vibes that Scarlett was crushing on Evan or anything, but he was a good-looking dude and had the more mature air about him that Scarlett liked in guys.

"Actually," Carter said as if just remembering something, "Ava mentioned something a while back about Scarlett's dad trying to set her up with a guy he knows. Maybe something happened with it, and she asked that guy?"

Her dad had been trying to set her up with someone?

And she'd told Ava about it but not me?

"So it might not even be someone who goes to our school?" I asked.

"I think this guy goes to Yale or something."

"Who goes to Yale?" Our friend Mack asked, joining us by our lockers after his chat with Coach.

"Some guy Scarlett's dad knows." Carter looked up at Mack. "We're trying to figure out if he's the guy Scarlett's taking to the Valentine's dance."

"She's not taking you?" Mack's dark eyebrows knitted together, like it was as shocking to him as it was to me.

Which I was grateful for, because it showed that maybe I wasn't as out of touch with everything as I'd thought. That maybe this really was coming out of left field.

I explained about Addison mentioning Scarlett taking someone else. And how Scarlett had apparently given Addison her blessing in asking me out.

"Well, that doesn't fit into the plans you had, does it?" Mack asked, sitting down to take off his basketball shoes. Mack was six-foot-five and the tallest player on the team. And even though I had just hit six-foot-one—thanks to a growth spurt this winter—my size twelve shoes always seemed kid-sized next to his. "Didn't you have some master plan to win her back as soon as we graduated?"

"Yeah." I sighed and opened my locker to grab my towel. "Though that plan won't work if she's dating someone else..."

Since Pastor Caldwell had threatened to take Scarlett out of Eden Falls Academy if she broke his no-steady-dating-while-in-high-school rule again, I'd been biding my time. I'd stayed close and tried to be okay with just being her friend while I silently counted down the days until graduation.

I'd assumed that if I wasn't allowed to be her boyfriend, then it meant no one else would be allowed to fill that spot, either.

But was it possible that her dad had changed his mind on that rule?

Since she'd turned eighteen a couple weeks ago, was he suddenly okay with her dating more seriously? Was he actually pushing for it, if it was with a guy he chose?

It wouldn't be too out of character for Pastor Caldwell. He'd always been strict but there were times when he'd definitely been wishy-washy before. Saying one thing was law—a commandment—and then turning around and changing things again as they suited his agenda.

And the church was known for pushing its members to marry pretty young...the no-sex-before-marriage thing going hand in hand with that.

Sadly though, if he *was* suddenly okay with Scarlett dating this Yale guy, that didn't necessarily mean he'd be okay with her dating just anyone—AKA me.

His requirements for the type of guy allowed to date his only daughter couldn't have changed much since the private meeting he'd called me to after the debutante ball—the meeting where he pulled the Pastor card and decided it was time for me to have a random worthiness interview.

I'd had worthiness interviews every six months since I turned thirteen and had always passed them with flying colors in the past. But this one was different. After asking a few questions about my beliefs and current level of activity in church-sponsored events, in the end, he decided that I was unworthy, considered a "threat to the church," and would be disfellow-shipped for my lack of belief.

I hadn't known you could be disfellowshipped for a lack of belief before. The only times I'd ever heard of people being disfellowshipped was because they broke actual command-ments—usually some sort of sexual sin—or breaking an actual law.

But Pastor Caldwell decided that my loss of belief in The Fold and its teachings was a big enough "sin" that even though I wasn't even attending meetings, I was officially forbidden from taking communion, singing the hymns, or saying prayers until I repented and humbled myself.

I left that meeting feeling dehumanized. Like my worth as a human was nothing compared to the members of The Fold if I didn't believe the same as them.

When I asked my mom if she'd ever heard of something like this happening before, she said she hadn't but also went on to tell me it was basically what I deserved for immersing myself in the anti-Fold lies. She even said that hopefully, this experience would help me see the error of my ways and come back.

Spoiler alert: it only cemented my feelings that The Fold was no longer a church I could be a part of. It pushed me to not just stop attending meetings but to also have my name officially removed from the records of the church—essentially cancelling my baptism and all the other rituals I'd participated in.

I wasn't planning to tell my parents about that last part, because it would only make them worry and fear for my soul even more.

But yeah, I was done. And since Pastor Caldwell had access to church records, he'd probably noticed my name was no longer listed with my parents on the attendance rolls at church.

"I'm sure it's nothing," Carter said, bringing me back to the present. "If it is that guy, she's probably just going to the dance with him to get her dad off her case."

"Hopefully."

I OPENED my phone as I walked to the great hall for dinner, and when I clicked into my email app, I saw that I had two hundred and twenty-seven unread emails.

Which was about eleven more than I'd had before practice.

Man, this is starting to get overwhelming.

When I started *The Confidant* last year, it had been an experiment to see if I could build a platform from scratch without using my parents' connections or place in society. To see if I was talented enough to gain a few subscribers and find readers interested enough in the words I wrote to come back to my blog week after week.

It was also a way to test if I could be self-sufficient enough to support myself off of my words. Because just like Scarlett's dad was able to control a lot of things in his daughter's life, my parents had a trust fund to hold over my head as well.

And after telling my parents that I didn't want to stay in the belief system that was so important to them, I no longer had the promise of a trust fund to rely on after college. They wouldn't financially support me if I wasn't "on the right path anymore."

So I'd taken my backup plan and ran with it.

The readership for *The Confidant* had grown slowly at first —each post only had a handful of hits the first month. But when I printed off a few columns and left them in random places around the school with the blog's URL at the bottom, it started to grow a little faster. And once more people started writing in and talking about *The Confidant*'s advice with their friends, it kind of snowballed from there.

It probably seemed presumptuous to assume that an eighteen-year-old guy would have enough life experience to hand out advice to his peers like some sort of expert. But I always made sure to leave the disclaimer that this was simply what *The Confidant* would do in each given situation if he was being his "best and wisest self."

And then I'd research from there.

Thankfully, the advice had been useful enough that people kept writing in.

There was another side effect that I hadn't expected, too. As more and more of my classmates wrote in anonymously, detailing some of the issues they were facing, it helped us all see each other in a more compassionate way.

Because on the outside, it seemed like the children of the country's most influential people would have it all—that all their problems would be minimal since money could be used to take care of most anything.

But once you read about *Wake Me from My Nightmare's* struggle with his mom's terminal illness and *Positive Test Distress's* anxiety over telling her ex-boyfriend that she was pregnant, it helped you see that even though people might look like they had it all together on the outside, it was highly likely they were dealing with huge difficulties of their own.

If only I had someone I could write to ask for advice for myself.

I slipped my phone into my pocket when I reached the great hall, deciding I'd figure out which emails to answer later. Then I got in the cafeteria line and loaded my tray with food. Tonight's menu included Swedish meatballs, mashed potatoes, and steamed broccoli—which was one of my favorite meals that they had in rotation at the school.

After adding a slice of chocolate tuxedo cake to my tray for dessert and grabbing a bottle of water, I headed toward the long, rectangular table where Scarlett and my roommate Asher were already seated.

"Hey Hunter," Scarlett said with a smile when I reached the table. "Have a seat."

And just like always, she scooted a little farther down the bench to make room at the table beside her.

So maybe everything is still normal between us and all my worrying over the past two hours was for nothing?

4

SCARLETT

"DO you know how many scouts have come to see you perform so far?" I asked my friend Asher as Hunter took the seat next to me at our table during dinner on Monday night.

Asher was one of the leads in the school's musical production of *The Phantom of the Opera*. He was crazy talented, and I had no doubt that he'd have offers from several of the country's most prestigious performing arts schools after they saw him bring Raoul to life on stage.

"Miss Crawley said there have been two so far—a scout from Juilliard and another from Carnegie Mellon. And I guess there are a couple more planning to attend this weekend."

"That's so cool," I said. "I bet they'll all be fighting over you."

"That would be pretty amazing," he said, his dark-brown eyes meeting mine from across the table for a second before sweeping over to Hunter. "But I'm trying not to think too much about who might be watching me or the possible scholarships on the line. Just trying to enjoy being part of the show that everyone has worked so hard on."

"Well, you guys are doing amazing. I watched it two nights in a row for a reason." Then, with a smirk on my lips, I added, "I mean, the chemistry between you and Elyse looks so real."

"Maybe that's because it is." He winked, and the huge smile on his lips showed just how in love he was with his real-life girlfriend who played his character's love interest on stage.

Elyse and Asher had just started officially dating a month ago and were so cute together that even though my love-life was currently a mess, I couldn't help but be happy for them. Asher certainly hadn't had it easy this past year and deserved to be with someone as sweet as Elyse.

Asher's phone buzzed on the table beside his tray. After turning it over to see who had texted him, he said, "Speaking of Elyse... She said that she just pulled into the parking lot, so I better head out." He slipped his phone in the back pocket of his school uniform slacks. "Do either of you feel like watching the show for the third time?"

"As much as I'd prefer that to homework..." Hunter chuckled beside me. "I really have to study tonight."

"Yeah, same," I agreed. "I have a test I need to study for if I want to keep my GPA up. Sadly, not all of us have multiple theater-school scouts after us and offering us scholarships."

"As if you have to worry about scholarships, Scarlett." Asher chuckled as he stood from the bench. "Didn't you just get offered full-rides to both Columbia and Yale?"

"Maaaaybe..." I said, drawing the word out. "But valedictorian is still up for grabs. And with Carter and your girlfriend in the running with me, I can't just sit back and twiddle my thumbs."

"Did Elyse finally let it slip that she's going for valedictorian, too?" Asher asked, surprised.

"Not exactly," I admitted. "But I might have caught a

glimpse of her transcript when I was helping her move into her dad's house last month. And yes, I also might have screamed when I saw that her GPA was exactly the same as mine." Like... down to the hundredths of a point.

"That's my girl," Asher said, a proud look on his face. "She's amazing."

"Well, if you feel like distracting her from her studies here and there, I won't hold it against you," I said.

"Nah." He bent over to pick up his dinner tray. "I think I'm gonna suggest even more study dates now that I know how close of a race it is. Maybe come up with a rewards system for every A she gets on a test. Possibly even bribe my roommate here to keep you distracted with non-scholarly activities." He winked at Hunter.

I couldn't help the blush that rose to my cheeks at the idea of Hunter and me doing what Asher was suggesting—of flirting or cuddling or kissing...all the things that people who liked each other did.

But then Addison and Evan stepped up to our table just in time to hear Asher's comment. The blood drained from my cheeks. From the way Addison was awkwardly looking down at her tray, I knew she'd overheard what Asher had said and also understood the implication that the feelings Hunter and I had been trying to ignore all year were still very much on everyone's radar.

Ugh. Why did friendship and dating at this school have to be so complicated sometimes?

Before Addison could feel bad or embarrassed about asking Hunter to the Valentine's dance, I hurried to say, "I'm pretty sure my dad has already added enough things to my schedule to keep me distracted."

"Oh hi, guys." Asher stepped to the side when he noticed

Addison and Evan. After a quick scan of everyone's faces, he seemed to pick up on the sudden awkwardness in the room because he looked at me and added, "I, uh, now that you mention it, I do remember Hunter saying something about your dad requiring you to attend some early morning church meetings before school."

"Um, yeah..." I glanced at Hunter who was suddenly interested in poking his Swedish meatball with his fork. "But there's also other stuff that my dad is keeping me busy with, too."

Asher's dark eyebrows furrowed together. "Does he make you attend those weekly youth meetings virtually, too?"

"No..." I frowned, wondering why my best friend had been telling Asher so much about our church. They'd only just become roommates at the end of November—months after Hunter stopped coming to church.

Why would they be talking about The Fold if Hunter wasn't even participating anymore?

Was it possible he was watching the Sunday sermons and early-morning Bible class in his room and just telling me he'd been sleeping in?

A swell of hope filled my chest with that thought. It would be so great if Hunter was still tuning in.

I'd been so worried that my friend was becoming lost.

I was about to explain that my dad was actually trying to keep me busy with dates and random dinners back at home with Xander, when Asher looked down at his phone and said, "Elyse just got backstage. I better run."

"Sounds like you better," I said.

"Break a leg tonight," Hunter called as Asher turned to put his tray away.

"Thanks!" Asher waved goodbye to all of us, set his tray on the table along the wall, and then rushed out of the great hall.

The table was quiet for several seconds after Asher left, and with what he'd said about Hunter and me still hanging in the air between all of us, I decided that it was time to visit the subject of who was going with whom to the Valentine's dance.

I cleared my throat and glanced at Addison, knowing I should probably say something about how excited I was when I heard through the grapevine that Hunter had agreed to go to the dance with her. But I was a terrible liar and a chicken, so I turned to Evan instead. "I heard that you got asked to the Valentine's dance in a pretty cool way yesterday."

"You heard about that?" He looked up from his dinner, seeming surprised that people had been talking about it.

"Yeah." I spread some gravy on my mashed potatoes with my spoon. "It's not every day that the cheer captain gathers the whole cheer squad together to flash-mob a guy and ask him to a dance."

"I guess that's probably true." He laughed his deep, throaty laugh. "It was kind of crazy. One minute, Addie and I were working on our chemistry assignment in the library, and then the next thing I know, there was loud music playing through a big speaker and a bunch of random people dancing in front of me."

"Did you have to do a dance to answer her back?" Hunter asked. "Because yikes, I couldn't do that."

"Thank goodness, no. Nobody wants to see me dance like that." Evan shook his head, his blue eyes going wide. "I just kept it simple and told her I'd love to go."

"Nice," Hunter said. "That's what I'd do, too. Dancing in front of other people is terrifying."

"I know, right?" Evan said. Then glancing back at me, he said, "And I'm guessing you probably heard that Hunter and Addie are going to the dance together."

I was about to say that yes, I'd heard of it when Hunter sat up straighter and said, "Oh, um...actually, I didn't get a chance to tell Scarlett that yet." Then he turned to me with a hesitant look in his eyes. "But I think you already knew about it, right?"

"I did," I said, hoping I sounded unbothered by the fact that the guy I wanted for myself was going on a date with another girl. "Addison mentioned she was planning to ask you. It sounds like you said yes."

"Yep," Hunter said. "It sounds like it will be super fun."

Super fun?

Did he really think that going to the dance with Addison sounded super fun?

Because if that was true, my heart just died a little at the thought of him looking forward to a date with someone else.

Was it possible that he was just saying that since she was sitting right across from him, and it was the nice thing to say?

Did it make me a bad person to hope that he was secretly dreading the dance as much as I was?

Addison picked up her fork and looked at me curiously. "I don't think you ever said who you were taking, Scarlett. Who is this mystery guy?"

Yeah... About that...

My cheeks suddenly felt hot as I realized it was time to tell Hunter and everyone about my arranged date.

Would it be weird to tell them that my dad had basically forced me to go with Xander?

Or should I make it sound like I was excited to go with him?

Hunter had said going with Addison sounded super fun... Should I keep the "super fun" parade going?

If only I could be sure that those words would come out of my mouth sounding believable.

But since I doubted my ability to seem that enthusiastic, I just said, "I'm taking a guy from my church. He did an internship sort of thing with my dad last summer and..." I picked up my water bottle, my mouth suddenly feeling dry. "And he seemed like a good guy to take to the Valentine's dance."

"It's someone who did an internship with your dad?" Hunter searched my face as I downed a big gulp of water, my face becoming more flushed under his scrutiny.

"So he doesn't go to our school then?" Addison asked, looking between Hunter and me.

"Yeah." I nodded and pushed back some stray hairs that were sticking to my clammy forehead. "He's actually in college right now. But his dad is good friends with my dad."

"You're taking *Xander?*" Hunter asked, putting all the puzzle pieces together. "That's who you're going with?"

"Uh huh..." I studied my best friend's face, trying to pick up on any clues as to how he felt about hearing I was taking Xander.

Was he just surprised? Or at all jealous?

Please be at least half as jealous of Xander as I am of Addison.

But Hunter was so good at hiding his emotions and keeping his expression blank sometimes that I couldn't tell how he felt— even after knowing him for most of my life and being his best friend for the past two years.

"So you're going with an older guy?" Addison's eyes lit up, seeming oblivious to the game of hide and seek I was currently playing with Hunter's body language. "That's kind of hot."

You think dating older guys is hot, Addison? Because if you want to trade dates, I'll do it in a heartbeat...

But since I couldn't really offer that, I just said, "He's a few years older than me and I don't know him super well, so I'm not sure how much we have in common, but I hope we'll have a good time."

I glanced back at Hunter, and when our gazes met, I tried

to tell him with my eyes what I couldn't say out loud. That my date with Xander meant nothing. That I didn't want to go with him.

That Hunter was still my number one...

5

SCARLETT

"WANNA STUDY IN THE LIBRARY TODAY?" Hunter asked as we walked out of the great hall after dinner. "Or should we risk the noise in the common room?"

"I think I'll need a quiet place today," I said.

If I was going to have a chance at memorizing everything I needed to know for my AP English test tomorrow, I needed to concentrate.

"So the library it is," he said.

We walked side by side through the school's halls, passing students headed toward the great hall for a later dinner. Our school was over a century old with stone walls, high ceilings, and two-story windows.

When I first came here my freshman year, I was used to being around old buildings since the church and parsonage I'd grown up in were pretty old, too. But where our cottage-like home on the church's property was just big enough for my dad, stepmom, and me, this school— with all of its classrooms, bedrooms, and other amenities for hundreds of students—felt more like a castle.

When we made it to the library, Hunter and I walked to our usual table at the back. Most evenings we had a few other friends join our study sessions, but since several of them were involved in the school play, we would most likely be on our own tonight.

Which was just fine with me. After today, I was feeling just a little territorial over my best friend.

"What classes are you doing homework for tonight?" I asked Hunter as we settled into the table. He pulled his laptop out of his backpack while I reached for the tablet and notebook in mine.

"I still have a few problems to finish for Calculus, and then I'll probably work a little on my research paper for Psychology."

"That sounds fun," I said sarcastically. While I enjoyed writing for the school newspaper, research papers were torture. All those rules for citing resources and quoting people were confusing.

"Yes. This paper is sure to be *super* fun." He chuckled and opened his laptop.

As I watched him put his pointer finger on the power button, I wondered if his use of the phrase "super fun" here could work the same way as when he'd talked about his date with Addison.

I pushed that thought away because it was stupid and probably a bit obsessive of me to try to dissect every little thing he said. So instead of wasting even more time worrying about a date that was almost two weeks away, I pulled up my AP English notes, put my noise canceling earbuds in, and settled in for an hour or two of studying.

"WELL, I think my brain is fried now," I said after coming out of my studying trance an hour and half later.

I glanced over to see how Hunter was doing, but he was still hunched over his keyboard. The look of concentration on his face told me he was still in the zone and hadn't even heard me.

His fingers clicked nonstop on the keyboard, so I figured he was probably in the groove with his research paper. But when I peeked at his computer screen, instead of it being open to the word processing software he usually used for his papers, I saw that he was actually typing away in his email application.

"Are you emailing someone a novel?" I leaned closer to get a better look at the few paragraphs he'd already written.

When my shoulder brushed against his, it brought him out of his emailing trance. He glanced at me with startled eyes. And when he saw that I was looking at his computer screen, he quickly clicked the minimize button to hide the window he'd been using.

"Uh, what did you say?" he asked, like he hadn't really heard me.

"I was just wondering what you were emailing. It looked long." I pointed to his screen that now showed the desktop photo he'd taken last year—the selfie of us sitting on the front steps of the school in our school uniforms, making silly faces for the camera.

"Oh that?" He glanced at the screen briefly. "It's just..." He stopped, as if trying to think of something else to say. But then, he shrugged and said, "I'm just emailing myself some notes, so I don't lose them."

"Notes?" I asked, hoping he'd expound. "Notes for what?"

"Just for a project I'm working on," he said.

A project he's working on? "Like for school?"

"No..." He shook his head. "Just something else."

Just something else?

Would this have something to do with the secret project he'd started working on last summer? The one that had him listening to all sorts of podcasts and reading tons of books and articles? The one he said had to do with a subject his older brother Sebastian had gotten him interested in?

Also known as the project he wasn't ready to talk about yet...because he wasn't sure what the results would be.

I'd assumed that whatever his summer project was had been completed months ago, since his nose hadn't been glued to his phone quite as much these past couple of months...but maybe he was still in the middle of it. Maybe he'd simply been working on it when I thought he was doing homework.

"Are you close to finishing this secret project of yours?" I asked, hoping he might tell me more if I went at it from a different angle.

"I'm not sure." He shrugged his broad shoulders. "I guess as long as it interests me."

I frowned. *As long as it interested him?*

He'd always been a deep thinker. Liked to really dig into various subjects so he could understand how things worked at an almost molecular level.

But that still didn't answer why he wouldn't tell me what this project of his was. Or why he wanted to keep it secret.

Was it possible this project was actually an online relationship with another girl?

A secret relationship could definitely fit in the category of a *project* you would continue to work on as long as it *interested you.*

That was usually how relationships worked, right? You stuck together until it didn't work, or someone lost interest and one or both of you wanted out.

Did Hunter have a secret pen pal he'd been writing to but didn't want me to know about?

He'd become preoccupied with his project about a month after my dad had made us break up.

Had he been having a secret relationship online ever since then and just hadn't told me because he knew it would make things awkward?

Maybe all those "podcasts" he'd been listening to were actually long voice messages from another girl. And the "articles and books" he'd been reading were really lovey-dovey emails or someone's social media feed with its eye-catching photos and videos.

My heart squeezed at the thought of him pining for another girl.

Because if he was secretly talking to someone behind my back, she was most likely gorgeous since Hunter himself was a level of hot that would put him on the cover of *People* magazine's "Sexiest Man Alive" issue. You know, if they broadened their research to include people who weren't already celebrities.

I studied his profile with narrowed eyes as he preoccupied himself with putting his laptop into his backpack.

His lashes were long and dark—the kind of lashes I wished I had, since mine were almost invisible if I didn't wear mascara. His jawline was no longer soft like it had been when we were freshmen—it had become more squared and defined as he'd matured into the eighteen-year-old man he was now.

His hair was short with a little bit of curl at the ends—the kind of hair I still daydreamed about combing my fingers through. And his eyes...my breath caught in my chest when he glanced up at me curiously, because his eyes were probably my most favorite thing about him. They were almost turquoise-green with a ring of gold around the iris.

"Why are you looking at me like that?" he asked, wiping his fingers across his chin like he worried he had Swedish meatball gravy stuck to his face.

"No reason," I said quickly, hoping he wouldn't notice how badly I wanted to take him into the library stacks and kiss him.

Just one more time so he would know what I couldn't tell him. That I still wanted him. That I just needed him to wait for me. To wait for just a few more months until I was free to date whomever I wanted.

"Is it because I'm emailing myself?" he asked. "Because it's not that crazy."

Oh yeah, that was why I'd been watching him at first. I'd just gotten a little distracted by his good looks and the things they did to my hormones.

"I've just never heard of anyone emailing themselves," I said.

"I do it all the time." He shrugged. "Helps me keep track of my ideas."

"Your ideas for your secret project?" I raised an eyebrow.

"Yes..." he said. "I mean, it's not like a *secret,* secret project. Nothing weird or anything like that. It's just something I'm doing for fun."

"So you're not emailing your secret girlfriend then?" I decided to just put it out there because I would only make myself crazy trying to dissect the half-answers he was giving me.

"What?" He pulled his head back, his eyes blinking rapidly, as if the thought of emailing some other girl would have never even occurred to him. "Who would I be emailing?"

"I don't know." I looked down at the pleats in my skirt. "A super hot Instagram model?" When he just stared at me like I was crazy to even suggest that, I added, "I just wondered if you didn't want me reading your email because you have a secret pen pal you haven't told me about."

"I think you've watched *You've Got Mail* a few too many times." He smirked.

"Whatever. It's impossible to watch a Meg-Ryan-and-Tom-Hanks movie too many times," I said, focusing on that so he wouldn't notice how relieved I was to learn he hadn't been emailing another girl.

"I don't know," he mused. "I mean, I get why you like *You've Got Mail*. I'm not too macho to admit it's not *pure* torture to watch it twice a year with you." A half-smile lifted his lips. We both knew he was the one who suggested it last time since it had been mid-October and *You've Got Mail* was made to be watched when the leaves were changing colors and the air became crisper. "But *Sleepless in Seattle?* Sorry, that one just didn't do it for me. They barely even knew each other. How are we supposed to believe that it's true love?"

"So you're an expert on romance movies now?" I asked.

"I don't want to brag or anything—" His green eyes brimmed with mirth. "—but giving my opinion on other people's love stories is just a gift of mine."

"You do seem to think you're an expert on quite a few subjects," I said. "I mean, you could probably give that girl who writes *The Confidant* a run for her money in the opinionated-advice arena."

"I take it she still hasn't turned you into a fan of the column yet?" He laughed. "At least, not in the sense of *liking* it. Since we both know you read everything she writes." He winked.

"I only read her column because she's my biggest competition." I wasn't about to admit that her writing was addicting. "That's what any good professional does. Research what people are reading so they can serve their audience better."

"Sure." He said it like he wasn't quite buying my excuse.

"And are you any closer to figuring out who she is?" He arched a dark eyebrow.

"No." I sighed and leaned back in my chair. "Probably just some nosy gossip who has a really high opinion of herself to be doling out advice to anyone that asks."

He laughed.

And since I knew that was mostly just my jealousy over *The Confidant's* success talking, I added, "But I guess she is actually okay at giving advice."

"Ah, so you *are* a fan." He gave me a crooked smile—my favorite smile of his because it showed the dimple in his cheek.

I couldn't help the blush that forced its way onto my cheeks when I met his gaze. "I'm just saying that even if she is the newspaper's competition, at least she's worthy competition."

"You still think *The Confidant* is a girl?" He gave me an inquisitive look, cocking his head to the side.

I shrugged. "Pretty sure, at least."

"Have you ever written to her?" he asked. "For advice, that is."

"No..." I hurried to say, suddenly feeling caught because I'd actually considered writing her this afternoon. "Have you?"

He got a funny look on his face for a split second before shaking his head and saying, "No. I, uh, I haven't needed her services quite yet."

Which made sense, since Hunter already had a pretty good gut-instinct about decisions.

"I figured you wouldn't," I said. "But were you listening during journalism today when Casey and Ben suggested we ask her to give us her column?"

"What?" He furrowed his brow. "They think that *The Confidant* would stop publishing on his or her website and let the Eden Falls Gazette post it instead?"

"I'm pretty sure they just wanted an easy way out of

writing their articles," I said. "But I doubt she'd do it since she actually makes money from her column."

Probably a lot from the amount of traffic she got to her blog and the high-level ads she had on there.

"But..." I picked up my pen and started drawing dots on the bottom corner of my notebook paper. "I was thinking this afternoon that maybe the school newspaper should come up with its own version of *The Confidant*."

"Our own version of *The Confidant*?" Hunter frowned, like he was confused. "But don't you think that would be against some sort of law? It has to be trademarked or something like that."

"No, of course it wouldn't be called *The Confidant*." I laughed. "You're so literal sometimes. What I mean is, maybe we could have our own version. Like, I don't know...*Dear Eliza*." I pulled the name off the top of my head. Eliza sounded like it could belong to a smart, wise person.

"And who would write it? Ben and Casey?"

"No, of course not them. They can barely write their own articles." I doodled the name *Dear Eliza* at the top of my notebook page in cursive lettering. "I was thinking I could do it."

"You'd have time for something like that?" He looked at me skeptically. "Don't you already have too much on your plate with basketball, the race for valedictorian, being our house captain, lead editor for the gazette..." He paused and seemed to hesitate before adding, "Not to mention all the things you do for church?"

"I could fit it in somewhere..." I said, not loving that he was doubting me. "Plus, I've got some pretty great advice."

He stared at me as if worried about my time constraints, but I just smiled at him and said, "I don't want our senior year to be known as the year that the gazette crashed and burned."

He pressed his lips together. After a long moment, he nodded slowly. "Then I think you'd be great at it."

"Really? Yay!" I sat up and gave him a quick hug.

"You're crazy, you know that?" He laughed and leaned into the hug for a second. "Only you would get excited about the prospect of having even more work to do."

"It's a Caldwell family trait," I said, pulling away again so I could open my tablet and go to my AwesomeMail app and see if the username *DearEliza* was still available. "You know my mom never stops working and my dad never stops serving his congregation."

"Which is why they got divorced, by the way," Hunter said. "Because they never saw each other."

"They stopped spending time together, and my mom started working more because they stopped liking each other," I corrected him.

Not that it mattered really. My parents' divorce had happened when I was seven. Which had sucked at first, of course. It felt like my whole world was falling apart when it happened.

But as the years went by and my dad found Megan, his new wife, and my mom fell in love with her personal assistant, Rodney, I got used to the fact that my parents could love other people and still love me.

"Plus," I said, typing in a password for my new email since the username was, in fact, still available, "it's not like my dad is going to change his mind about me having a boyfriend anytime soon. So my workaholic gene won't be interfering there, anyway."

"So you might as well run with this," Hunter finished my thought for me.

"Yep." I pressed the blue sign-up button at the bottom.

Within a few seconds, the screen opened up to a page that said, "Welcome to AwesomeMail!"

"Well, if this keeps you distracted from falling for Xander at the Valentine's dance, then I guess it would be in my best interest to tell you to run with this."

My heart stuttered as his words hit me. When I flicked my gaze to his face to see if I'd heard him right, he was staring at me with an intensity that made my insides melt.

"You don't want me to have fun with Xander?" I asked, needing to hear him say it. Even though we'd spent months hinting that our feelings were still there, just waiting on the sidelines until we were at a time when we could be open with them, he'd never actually voiced something like this before.

He glanced around furtively, as if worried that my dad had paid spies watching our every move. Then he leaned next to my ear and mumbled, "If I have my way, your favorite part of the night will be when I steal a dance with you."

So he was already planning to steal a dance with me?

"You don't think Addison will mind?" I asked in a breathy voice, reminding him that he wasn't the only one with a date that night.

He lifted a shoulder. "She's a nice girl, so of course I'll be a gentleman. But it's only natural to want to dance with the prettiest girl in the room."

I sat there dumbly for a moment, my mind racing a hundred miles a minute as I processed his words and their meaning.

He wanted to dance with me.

And he still thought I was pretty. He was still attracted to me that way.

Was this his way of reminding me that it still wasn't over then? That if we didn't have the threat of my dad taking me out of the school hanging over our heads, he might follow me into the journalism room right now, using the key Mrs. Donlan had given me, so he could press me against the wall and we could make up for months of lost time?

My mind buzzed, and I felt breathless just thinking about the possibility of being in his arms again after months and months of wanting and craving and pining and going crazy.

I looked back at him, my eyes searching his for all the hidden meanings behind his words.

It would be so easy to just let myself forget the rules and do what my heart wanted me to do.

To throw caution to the wind and cross the line I'd been hovering over for months—just waiting for the tiniest gust of wind to push me over and risk having to go back home and finishing my senior year online.

But since I couldn't do that, I just said, "Looks like there's a reason to look forward to the Valentine's dance after all."

"Looks like there is," he said in a low voice that had my gaze glued to his lips. I wanted to kiss those lips so badly.

Just for a second.

I watched the corner of his mouth quirk up into the smile he always got when he caught me checking him out.

After looking me up and down in a way that made me feel hot, he said, "Now you better hurry and make your little announcement in the gazette about *Dear Eliza's* future column, so we still have time for an episode of *The Office* before curfew."

"Y-you're right." I shook my head, needing to dispel the fog creeping in over my mind. Monday nights were the only nights we got to watch our show together since we had basketball games the other weeknights and hung out with the rest of our friends on the weekends. "I'll do that now."

"Good. I'll just take my stuff to my room and change into my pajamas."

"See you in a few minutes," I said.

I watched him head toward the library exit, allowing myself a moment to admire the confident way he walked. Once he was out of view, I forced myself to open my browser and sign into the gazette's website.

I quickly added a section to the draft for Wednesday's issue and typed in the words, "*The Confidant* doesn't have time for your questions? Just ask Eliza, the *official* advice column of Eden Falls Academy. New columns every Wednesday morning! Just email: DearEliza@awesomemail.com."

Once I had saved it, I shoved my things into my backpack and rushed to the common room so I could watch a funny show with my favorite person in the whole world.

6

HUNTER

"OKAY, wolf pack. It's time to hear you howl!" The cheerleaders called from the edge of the basketball court on Tuesday night.

The gym was packed with students and parents who had come to cheer on the girls' basketball team. We were playing against our rivals—the Sherman High School Lions—which was the public high school in Eden Falls. And from what I'd heard about each teams' rankings in our region games so far, it was sure to be an exciting game. The first five minutes of the first quarter had already proven that to be true, with the offense and defense for each team seeming to be evenly matched. I had my AP Chemistry textbook open on my lap with the intent to work on the assignment that was due tomorrow, but if things stayed this intense for the rest of the game, I might not make any progress on it.

Doing my homework in the middle of the crowded bleachers with students standing all around wasn't ideal, but since Scarlett and I always tried to make it to each other's home games and I had my sports column to write, it was the only way to do it sometimes.

"Hey, is this seat taken?" I heard a soft, female voice ask above the noise of the crowd.

I looked up. Addison was standing on the stairs beside me, pointing at the empty seat between my friend Mack and me.

I looked down at the spot, not sure what to say since it wasn't really an empty seat—more like a foot of space Mack and I had left between us so we weren't all up in each other's business. But saying no would make things awkward with our future date, and it was possible that someone as petite as Addison could squeeze in, so I said, "Uh, no, it's not taken yet."

"Can I sit there?" she asked.

"Sure..."

I was about to scoot closer to Mack, since it would be easier for her to just sit on the end, but she started stepping over my backpack to get to the spot, so I swiveled my legs to the side instead to let her in.

"I'm so glad I saw Mack and Carter's tall heads in the crowd," she said as she sat down beside me, sounding slightly breathless. "I didn't realize how big of a deal the game against Sherman High was, or I would have gotten here earlier."

"It's one of the biggest games of the year," I said, looking up at the backs and heads of the students towering around us since everyone else was standing while we sat. Once I finished my assignment, I planned to stand up with everyone else so it shouldn't be such a tight fit the whole time.

And what a tight fit it was. Even though I had half of a butt cheek hanging off the end of the bleachers to make room, Addison's hips and thighs were still pressed right against mine.

I hadn't sat this close to a girl in public since...well...probably since the last subway ride Scarlett and I had before breaking up last April. Even after our flirtatious moment in the library last night, Scarlett and I had still kept a few inches of space between us while we'd watched *The Office* from the large leather couch in the common room.

Would those few inches of space have been there if Scarlett wasn't paranoid that her dad had paid one of our classmates to keep an eye on us and report our every move back to him?

I liked to think that she would have cuddled up to me if that wasn't the case.

But just like always, she had hugged her end of the couch. So I tried to seem like I was completely fine with staying on my cushion as we laughed at the pranks the show's character Jim played on his quirky co-worker Dwight.

Sure, we could avoid the whole worry of classmates spying on our every move by watching the show in her dorm room like we had last year. But since we needed to "avoid the appearance of breaking her dad's rules," we now had our movie nights in the crowded common room.

"Working on your chemistry assignment?" Addison asked, glancing at my textbook.

"Yep," I said. "I have basketball practice in the afternoons, so I sometimes have to do my homework during the games."

"Want any help?" she offered. "Evan and I just finished our assignments before coming down to the game."

"Sure. That would actually be great."

I tilted my tablet toward her so she could see that I'd already completed the first thirteen questions in the online document.

Addison's blue eyes scanned the last two questions. "Okay, so this one was pretty simple. You just need to calculate the mass of iron, in grams, that reacted to generate the amount of heat calculated in the question above, and you should be good."

I nodded, looking at the table and formulas we'd been given. While I had a pretty logical brain, for some reason, chemistry just didn't come as easily to me as it did to some of my other classmates. In fact, the only reason I signed up for AP Chemistry was because Scarlett was taking it and I wanted to have another class with her this year.

Oh, the stupid things we do to spend time with the people we love.

I started working on the problem, and with just a little more input from Addison, who was apparently a chemistry whiz, I was able to finish the assignment before the first quarter ended.

***

ADDISON and I had been standing up with the rest of my friends in the student section for a few minutes when I felt my phone buzz in my pocket.

I figured it was probably just my mom sending me another article from one of The Fold's magazines, since she'd been sending those every few days in her determination to save my soul. But when I caught a glimpse of Mack from the corner of my eye and noticed him holding his phone and eyeing it like he'd just sent me something he didn't want to say in front of Addison, I realized that the text message must have come from him.

Hoping Addison wouldn't find out that the two guys on either side of her were texting back and forth, I fished my phone out to read what had come through.

Mack: **Not sure that you saw it since you were so busy with your homework...but Scarlett keeps looking up here and seems pissed that you're sitting with Addison.**

Sure enough, on the basketball court below, Scarlett was sitting on the bench and glaring in our direction.

When Scarlett noticed me looking her way, she directed her gaze to where Ava was at the free-throw line, shooting a foul shot. But just from that one look, I had a feeling that Mack was right.

I turned to Mack with wide eyes and texted him back: **What am I supposed to do now?**

He waited a bit to check his phone, but then as one of Sherman High's players rebounded the ball, a text came through that said, **No clue bro. But you better be careful.**

I was about to text him back again when Addison leaned close. Pointing down at Scarlett, she asked, "Do you know why Scarlett always wears a T-shirt under her jersey? I've been to a few games and noticed that she does that every time."

"Oh, it's just part of what she believes," I said, slightly surprised by the question. "Her church has specific guidelines about how they dress. They call it dressing modestly." I used air quotes around the word *modestly* since I knew it was a charged word that had different meanings, depending on someone's background and experiences with it.

"Dressing modestly?" Addison frowned, like she'd never heard of that phrase before. Which told me that even though Addison was Christian, her beliefs might not be as strict as mine had been.

"They're taught that their bodies are sacred and that they need to dress respectfully and in ways that show God and others that they know how precious their bodies are."

"So they do that by covering them?" she asked.

"Yeah." I shrugged. "That's essentially it. But obviously, they don't take it to the extreme that some other religions teach. Like, they don't have to wear prairie dresses or anything like that. But they do encourage the members to wear shirts or dresses with sleeves long enough to cover their shoulders. And shorts and skirts should come as close to the knee as possible."

Which was why the pleated skirts that Scarlett wore as part of her school uniform were always longer.

Sadly for me, since that girl had amazing legs.

"That sounds like it would be really hot in the summer," Addison said.

"It can be," I said, watching Scarlett who was dribbling the ball toward the basketball hoop. "But you get used to it."

"Why don't *you* wear a T-shirt under your basketball jersey? You're both in the same church, right?" She looked up at me. "Do guys and girls not have the same rules?"

"Well..." I rubbed the back of my neck. "Some of us are more extreme than others. For example, in my family, I was taught that it's okay to wear tank tops if I'm exercising. Scarlett's family is a lot more strict."

"Um...is it going to be a problem that I'm wearing a sleeveless dress to the dance?" She asked, her blue eyes widening. "Are you not allowed to dance with someone like that? Or since dancing can be considered exercise, maybe it will be fine?"

"No, it's fine." I chuckled. "I actually don't have a problem with that at all. I think it's fine for people to wear what makes them feel their best and comfortable in their own skin."

"So, you're a little more relaxed then?" She lifted an eyebrow.

"I am now..."

She looked at me like she wanted me to go on, so in a lowered voice, I said, "I'm actually not really involved with my old church anymore."

"Really?" she asked, seeming surprised. "Why not?"

I shrugged, hoping to make it seem like it wasn't a big deal even though it was actually one of the hardest choices of my life. "I guess it's because I came across some disturbing information when I was trying to help my brother come back to church."

"Disturbing information?" She frowned.

"Yeah..."

I scratched my neck, feeling somewhat uncomfortable since the last time I'd talked about this hadn't exactly gone well.

I cleared my throat. "Basically, I discovered that there were a lot of disturbing things that happened when the church was founded that I hadn't been told about. And I was also shocked by certain practices and beliefs in the church's past." *Some of the things the founder had done with teenage girls, all under the "command of God," were frankly disgusting.* "After learning about those things and seeing more of the full picture, I just couldn't believe everything like I used to."

"Is that why you and Scarlett broke up?"

"No..." I said. "I actually don't think she knows how I feel about the church. I mean, she knows I've stopped going to all the meetings and activities. But she probably thinks it's because I'm just being lazy."

"Really?"

I nodded. "That's kind of what everyone in The Fold assumes when people stop coming. That we're lazy or just didn't have a strong enough faith. Or that we were deceived by the devil."

My conversation with my mom during Thanksgiving break, where she'd basically told me I had been contaminated by Satan, still stung all these months later.

"But you stopped going because of some information that you found?" Addison asked curiously, like she hadn't ever talked to anyone about leaving a high-demand religion before. "Stuff that actually happened with your church? Things Scarlett probably doesn't know about?"

"Yeah, the church's founder did a lot of sketchy stuff." Stuff that had actually been validated and documented by church historians on the church's own website.

It was just difficult to find the information since they'd hidden it and whitewashed it so much that you had to click on the footnotes to get the real details.

"Learning that the founder essentially had a long history of being a conman got me questioning everything. And then, the more I dug, the more problems I found..."

I looked at Addison, wondering if she would think I was as weak-minded and easily fooled as my parents and Pastor Caldwell thought I was.

But instead of looking at me like she thought I had bad judgement, she said, "That actually sounds similar to something my parents went through."

"Really?" I raised my eyebrows, not expecting her to relate to my story at all. "Did it have anything to do with your religion?"

"No." She shook her head. "But they had a similar thing happen with a company they were involved with."

"Oh, interesting."

"Yeah..." She lifted a shoulder. "They were pretty invested in it. But it turned out to have a bunch of skeletons in its closet, and they realized they needed to get out."

"Which company is it?" I asked, curious if I'd heard of it since I'd just watched a documentary about an MLM with some pretty big issues.

She bit her lip, as if unsure what to say. "It's actually pretty crazy and—"

"We probably shouldn't be talking about this, Addie." A deep voice interrupted her from behind. When I turned around, I found her stepbrother standing on the row behind us.

Since when did Evan get here?

Had he been listening to us this whole time?

"Yeah, sorry. You're right." Addison's face paled. "I probably said too much already..."

Really?

When I looked concerned, she shrugged and waved her hand like it was no biggie and said, "It was basically just some business stuff gone wrong."

THE GAME ENDED JUST BEFORE nine o'clock, with Eden Falls barely squeaking by with a win—the final score being fifty-seven to fifty-six.

I took notes here and there to add into my sports update in tomorrow morning's newspaper, but when I wasn't doing that, Addison and I were chatting. She asked me how I'd liked growing up in New York City and about my interest in rock climbing.

She didn't say a whole lot about where she came from— only mentioning that she and Evan had come here from Arizona and that she had one other sibling, a brother who was four years older than her.

And even though my feelings for Scarlett weren't going anywhere soon, I had to admit that it was kind of nice having an easy conversation with someone whom I could have a fresh start with.

Most everyone else I knew at the school had known me as the religious zealot that I'd been our first three years. And since I hadn't really announced my faith transition to anyone, aside from my guy friends and now Addison, most people still assumed I was the same black-and-white thinking person that I'd been as a member of The Fold.

But with Addison, she was only interested in getting to know me, Hunter Blackwell. And it was kind of nice just being free to be the real me around her versus feeling like I needed to censor whatever I said—something I found myself doing around Scarlett a lot these days.

"I guess you're going to wait here to talk to Scarlett?" Addison asked as the crowd thinned and most of the students headed back to the dorms.

"Yeah," I said, feeling my cheeks warm. "We usually walk back to the dorms together after the games."

"Okay." She nodded, looking down briefly like she felt awkward. "I guess I'll see you tomorrow at breakfast."

"See you then," I said, feeling uncomfortable myself since we actually had a good time hanging out tonight. I wasn't sure what to think about it.

If my feelings for Scarlett weren't a factor in anything, I'd probably be stoked about the chance to go to the dance with someone as fun, smart, and pretty as Addison.

But I shouldn't want that, should I?

Two hours of great conversation with some laughs mixed in shouldn't threaten a friendship and bond that was years in the making.

But it would be nice to be with someone who is able to accept me for me.

Someone who didn't care about whether I believed the same things as her. Someone who didn't have a father who disapproved of our friendship so much that he promised to remove his daughter—one of Eden Fall's brightest students—from the school if I was open about what was actually going on with me.

I sighed as I watched Addison and Evan leave the gym together, feeling much more confused than I'd expected to be.

Once they were out of view, I pulled my tablet out of my backpack so that I could add the rest of my notes on tonight's game into the sports article that would go live in the morning.

My friend Carter scooted down from where he'd been seated on the other side of Mack and snuck a look at my notes. "You writing down the part where Ava threw a three-point shot right before the final buzzer?"

"Of course," I said. "You know, right after the part about Scarlett stealing the ball from Sherman High's point guard and passing it to her."

"Can't let Ava get all the glory for tonight's win, now can we?" Carter asked with a smirk. "At least, not when your *best friend* is involved."

"Just trying to be honest in my reporting," I said, ignoring the fact that he said "best friend" in the same way you'd say the words *mistress* or *secret lover*.

Which, yeah, since he was familiar about our history and I'd already told all the guys my side of the story, Carter knew that if I had my way, Scarlett and I would at least be closer to either of those things than me being stuck in the friend zone right now.

Okay, so maybe it was more like we'd be at a spot right in the middle of the friend zone and secret lovers, because even if I had completely re-thought my morals and what I believed was a smart level of intimacy for two eighteen-year-olds to have, I would probably still keep things at the steamy-kissing-sessions level for the time being.

Even if I no longer believed sex before marriage was a huge sin, like my previous self had thought, sex could still bring on a lot of complications and feelings that I personally didn't feel quite ready for.

"I think they're coming out now," Carter said, heading down the bleachers.

Sure enough, Ava and Scarlett walked around the corner a few seconds later, laughing about something one of them had said.

"You did so amazing tonight," Carter said to Ava, wrapping her up in a hug when they met on the basketball court. "That three-point shot was epic."

"Thank you," she said, beaming up at him.

As I watched their sweet moment, and then looked at Scarlett who stood just a few feet away from me, all I could think about was how I wished I could do the same. To pull Scarlett into my arms and whisper how amazing she is.

But since I was just her friend and not her boyfriend, I cleared my throat and said, "You did awesome tonight, too."

"Thank you," she said, her expression more cautious than normal.

We looked at each other awkwardly for a second as Carter and Ava took each other's hands and started walking toward the gym's exit.

Once they were several feet away, I said, "Ready to head back to the dorms?"

"Sure." Scarlett nodded, but there was a tightness behind her eyes that I hadn't expected.

Like she was upset about something.

"Is something wrong?" I asked as we walked up the stairs to the main level of the school.

She was happy that they'd won the game, right? She'd played really well tonight.

"I'm fine," she said. Then, with what I could tell was a forced smile on her face, she added, "We won, so that's awesome."

"Yeah..." I studied her expression. "You did..."

We made it to the top of the stairs, and I opened the door that led to the school's courtyard—our usual shortcut to the dorms. A foot of snow covered the lawn, but there was a narrow walkway that had been shoveled to make it easier to walk through.

We were about halfway across the lawn when Scarlett said, "It seemed like you and Addison had a good time tonight."

My heart thudded against my ribcage. After Mack's initial texts, I'd completely forgotten his warning about Scarlett looking upset at seeing Addison and me sitting together.

I'd been so wrapped up in our conversation and the exciting game that I hadn't realized Scarlett might still be watching us whenever she was on the sidelines.

"The game was fun," I said cautiously, worried that if I said the wrong thing it might make things even more uncomfortable.

"Yeah?" she asked, glancing sideways at me, her breath showing in the cold night air. "Did you and Addison talk about anything interesting?"

"Uh, not really." My heartbeat ramped up. "Just getting to know each other a little better."

Was it terrible that I could tell a girl I barely knew about the hard things I'd been going through the past eight months, but I couldn't tell my best friend?

Yes. It was terrible.

It sucked, actually.

I was dying to tell Scarlett what had been going on and why I'd stopped coming to church with her. But every time I thought about telling her I'd lost my faith, I just saw the same look she'd gotten in her eyes when I'd told her that my brother, Bash, was leaving The Fold.

The shock. The fear. The worry for my brother's soul.

The way she stayed away from Bash—not ever being alone in the same room as him if she didn't have to. As if apostasy was contagious.

How intense she'd been when she warned me not to listen to my brother about anything he had to say against The Fold.

How it was all just propaganda and lies—that looking into anything was like playing with fire.

"It's so crafty, Hunter," she'd said. "Even the most elite have been sucked in by it. Not the people you'd expect either. Like, really smart and powerful people have been pulled away by the anti-Fold lies. So it's better to just never even open the door a crack."

But I had looked through the crack in the door, and before I knew it, my whole world had been blown apart. And it had been impossible to shut that door again and ignore the things I'd learned.

Since there was no going back to where I'd been before, the only way to keep her from treating me like she'd treated Bash was to let her believe I was just being lazy.

Because if I was seen as lazy instead of an apostate—one of the most dangerous threats to the church—I could at least still be her friend.

Staying just friends with Scarlett was better than not having her at all.

7

SCARLETT

"JUST TELL your dates that we'll be heading up to the ski resort around nine o'clock and that they should be prepared for a full day of fun." I looked at my girl friends sitting around the table with me in Cambrielle's home library on Saturday morning as we finished up our planning meeting for the Valentine's dance. "Any other questions?"

"Do they need to bring their own snow gear?" Addison asked from her chair next to Elyse, her notebook and pen sitting on the table since she'd been taking notes the whole time. "Or is there a place up there to buy them?"

"Hunter should have a ski suit and everything he needs," I said, trying to sound neutral about *that* whole situation.

"Okay, cool," she said with a nod before jotting it down.

I probably should have just left things there, continued to pretend like I was Switzerland and didn't feel threatened at the thought of them spending even more quality time together soon. But before I knew it, my territorial side kicked in and I was saying, "Hunter and I go snowboarding all the time, so you can tell him to just bring his usual gear."

"Oh...okay." She seemed to gulp. "I'll just tell him that." When her cheeks flushed bright pink, I knew I was most definitely sending off the jealous-ex vibe.

But could you really blame me? She was going on a date with the one guy I liked.

The guy I would have asked to the dance myself if I hadn't made that stupid deal with my dad.

And he'd be wearing the lime green and black ski suit that *I* had helped him pick out—the one that brought out the color of his eyes and made him look like a snowboarding model.

"I can still buy my snow gear up there though, right?" Addison asked the group, interrupting my daydream of Hunter and me sitting on the ski lift and gazing into each other's goggle-covered eyes. "I'm from Arizona, so this whole snow thing is new to me."

"I totally didn't even think about that," Cambrielle said, thankfully sensing that I wasn't in the best place emotionally to answer Addison's questions. "Do you have any snow gear?"

"I have a coat and gloves..." Addison bit her plump bottom lip. "But I don't think my boots are the right type for playing in the snow."

"They do have a few shops at the resort," Cambrielle said. "But we're about the same size, so you can totally try on some of my boots and snow pants if you want. My mom and I may have gone a little overboard when shopping for new ski suits this year. I'm pretty sure I'll have something you'll like in my room."

"That would be awesome," Addison said, seeming relieved that Cambrielle was so helpful...*and that I wasn't the one talking to her right now.*

"Great." Cambrielle smiled. "We can just go up to my closet after this, if you want."

Elyse and Ava asked about the restaurants in the lodge and

whether we wanted to ask the guys for input on where to eat lunch or to just choose ourselves.

"There are several restaurants really close to each other," I said. "So I was thinking we could just pick whatever we're in the mood for that day, and then all meet up at the dining area they have on the rooftop."

"Perfect," Ava said.

"Is that everything?" I asked, ready to finish the meeting since I could already smell the lunch that Cambrielle's family chef had been making for us.

"I think so." Elyse seemed to look over the notes she had taken. "We're just going tubing in the morning, eating lunch at the resort, and then having dinner at The Italian Amigos before the dance, right?"

"Yep," I said.

"Then let's get some food so we can get the pool party started," Ava said.

A second later we were all racing down the hall to eat the delicious food we most definitely wouldn't be waiting a full hour to digest before jumping into the Hastings' amazing pool.

———

"YOU STILL OKAY having Addison join us for the dance?" Ava asked me a while later as we sauntered down the enclosed walkway that led from the main house on the Hastings' estate to the pool house. "Or do you think there's a conflict of interest because she's taking your ex?"

"I don't know." I sighed, adjusting the strap of the black, one-piece swimsuit that I'd just changed into after lunch. "I'd like to think that it will be okay. But ever since she asked him out and I saw them flirting at the game, it's just been hard to see them together."

"I bet." Ava's brown eyes met mine. "I never saw you and Hunter when you were dating, but just from seeing what you're like as friends, I can imagine you were really good together."

"We were." I tried to ignore the sinking feeling in my chest that was telling me the romantic part of our relationship may remain in the past tense if things kept going the way they'd been going this week. "Which is why I'm scared he's going to get distracted by this new thing with Addison."

"I think he's just trying to be friendly since they have a date coming up. I wouldn't worry too much."

"I'm trying not to," I said.

But it was hard not to get in my head about everything. Addison was cute, fun, and new while I was the "been there, done that," and "learned there was way too much drama to keep it going" girl.

My relationship with Hunter had been so easy last year. As natural as taking a breath.

But a lot of that ease and comfort had disappeared when we broke up. I couldn't help but wonder if Hunter, who was basically "Mr. No-Drama Llama," would choose to go with the new "Easy, Breezy, Beautiful, Arizona Girl" option instead of the "Lots of Baggage Best Friend."

Inside the pool house, the guys had already set up the volleyball net. Everyone in the water was dividing up into teams on either side of the pool.

Evan, Asher, Elyse, and Cambrielle were on one team. Hunter, Carter, Addison, and Ava—who had just slipped into that side of the pool—were on the other.

"You going to join us, Scarlett?" Carter called from the center of the pool with the volleyball in his hands. "You can be on our team."

But when I noticed Addison turn her back to Hunter and

lift her hair off her neck like she was asking him to help her remove her necklace, I waved a hand and said, "Nah, that's okay. I'll sit this one out, so the teams aren't uneven."

"Okay," Carter called. "Nash said he was planning to come a little late, so maybe when he gets here you can join in."

"Sure," I said.

Then before I was forced to watch Hunter bend down closer to Addison as he unhooked her necklace clasp, I headed to where Mack was sitting on one of the lounge chairs, looking like he was in about as good of a mood as I was today.

"Didn't feel like playing volleyball, either?" I asked as I sat in the lounge chair next to him.

"No." He propped one arm up behind his head as he watched everyone start the game. "Just having another one of those days again."

"Missing your mom?" I guessed.

"Yeah." He was quiet for a second, and I just waited, knowing from experience that it sometimes took him a little time to open up about his feelings. He scratched at a spot on his blue swim shorts, and then after sighing, he said, "It's like, I'll be just fine and happy and things are going well, and then out of nowhere I'll see something that reminds me of her, or I'll think of a funny joke that she would love... And then I remember she's not here and...I don't know... I just miss her."

"I'm sorry," I said lamely, wishing I knew how to make things better. But what could I say? I didn't know what it was like to lose a parent.

Even if I did sometimes think about what I'd do if I lost one of them, I saw things differently from my friend. Mack wasn't religious, and I didn't know if he had any real beliefs about what happened after this life.

I wanted to tell him that he could be with his mom again

someday. That if he was baptized into the church and had one of the priests bless him, he could live with his mom again.

But every time I thought about telling him about the great plan of the gospel, I remembered what had happened when I'd tried talking to his mom about it before she died.

How I'd told her that there was a way to see Mack and her husband again in the next life if she would just follow the plan the Lord had laid out for us—people going through trials always seemed more open to the Good Word.

But Mack's mom had just patted my hand and told me gently that she didn't see why any loving god would let differing beliefs about something as unknowable as what happens after this life to separate us from our families in the first place.

I hadn't really known how to respond to her after that, since in my experience, it wasn't unknowable at all. It had been revealed to the High Priest Samuel Williams back in 1838, during one of his many visitations with Jehovah.

But she hadn't been interested when I'd tried to tell her. She'd only said she was glad that my church brought me happiness, but she was happy with her own spiritual path.

I'd felt sad that she still couldn't see what I could. But after having other similar experiences with the people at my school, I stopped trying to push the gospel onto my friends and acquaintances. I'd learned from my own experience of trying to get my own inactive mother to join me for church, that I couldn't force them to listen if they didn't want to.

The volleyball game ended, and Mack went to join Cambrielle in the hot tub. When I noticed Hunter heading for the hot tub too, I stood to join them. But when Addison followed him, I realized the hot tub actually looked a little over-crowded and sat back down.

Did Hunter like Addison? I wondered as she sat on the

edge, with just her legs hanging in the water next to him. Did he like how she looked in her two-piece suit? It was more modest than the bikini Ava wore, but it definitely revealed a lot more skin than my one-piece bathing suit did.

In our church, a lot of the youth encouraged each other to dress in the guidelines the High Priest had given us for dress and appearance, saying that "Modest is Hottest."

I'd always liked the phrase, since modesty was important to me. It always made me feel good to think that other guys in the youth program would find it an attractive trait when so many other non-members around us dressed so differently.

While I'd never actually heard Hunter use the phrase himself, I'd hoped that he would appreciate how much effort I put into finding clothes that fit the church's standards.

But who knows, maybe he actually preferred the way Addison dressed.

Maybe not going to church for half a year had made him care less about those kinds of things.

I pulled out my phone and opened it to the email account I'd set up for *Dear Eliza*. Maybe reading about other people's problems would help distract me from my own. But as I tried to read the most recent email, my mind refused to focus on the paragraph that *He's My Best Friend's Ex* had written about her forbidden crush. The chatter and laughter from the hot tub were too distracting.

After reading the same two lines several times, I set my phone on my beach towel and headed back to the main house for a glass of water.

Hunter looked up in my direction as I walked past the hot tub and mouthed, "Are you okay?"

To which I nodded and gave a half-hearted smile before continuing on my way.

I used to get lost in this huge house when I first became

friends with the Hastings' back in sophomore year. But after hanging out here most weekends for the past two and a half years, it was like a second home away from home.

I grabbed a glass from the cupboard by the Hastings' industrial-sized fridge, filled it with chilled water, and then walked to the large windows they had in the dining area to look over their backyard.

I was lost in my thoughts, watching the snow lightly falling on the terrace, when I heard footsteps behind me.

I turned to see who had joined me and was both relieved and nervous when I saw it was Hunter. A few water droplets glistened on his chest like he hadn't quite taken the time to dry off before coming in here, but he had a towel wrapped around his waist to keep him from dripping too much on the Hastings' marble floors.

"Why haven't you gotten in the pool?" he asked, coming to stand near me, his abs on full display. "I thought you loved pool volleyball. It's why I suggested we set up the net."

"I just wasn't in the mood." I turned back to the window before my eyes could try to rake in his six-pack.

Even though we'd swam in the Hastings' pool more times than I could count, and we'd spent a week at their beach house in the Hamptons last summer, I still found it hard not to take him in every time he was dressed like this.

I liked to tell myself that the reason I was so curious about this shirtless image of Hunter was because I still wasn't used to the way he'd been transforming from teenage boy Hunter into this more manly and mature version of himself.

But I knew I was just fooling myself. Because if it were only mere curiosity, I should have stopped being so attracted to him long ago. I should be able to just glance at him the way I did my other guy friends and have no trouble looking away.

But apparently, my brain didn't always agree with the

"modest is hottest" thing, either, because yeah...shirtless Hunter was a look I definitely liked. And if I didn't have to worry about repenting for the unclean thoughts that I sometimes had about my best friend and myself—which involved fantasies of us kissing while his shirt was off and me running my fingers across his stomach to see if the muscles felt as good as they looked—I would probably commit this look of his to my long-term memory and revisit it over and over again as I lay in bed at night.

"Did something happen in your meeting this morning?" Hunter asked, bringing my attention back to the moment. "Is that what's gotten you down? Was there an argument about who gets to wear what color of dress to the dance?" he asked like he was trying to lighten the mood.

"Of course not." I rolled my eyes. "We all got our dresses weeks ago."

And everyone was going to look fabulous, what with Ava and Elyse's mom being a famous fashion designer, and Cambrielle's family being literal billionaires and her having a closet worthy of that status.

My dress looked good too, though. I had to search all over New York with my mom to find one with sleeves and a high enough neckline, but it was pretty and complimented my figure in a way that made me feel beautiful and feminine.

"If it's not that, then what's up?" he asked.

"I—" I stopped and sighed, knowing my next words would make me sound bad.

"You what?" he prodded.

And since open communication had always been what made our friendship so good, I decided to stay true to that. "I guess I just didn't like seeing you flirting with Addison today." I turned away from the window to look at him. "Like, I know I have no right to care since we're just friends but..."

"I know," he said in a low voice, his green-eyed gaze flickering to mine through his long lashes.

"You do?" My throat tightened.

"You don't think I ever get jealous of the guys you talk to at school?" he asked. "That even though you said you're only going with Xander because your dad arranged it, I'm not still jealous you'll be dancing with someone else all night?"

"You're jealous?" *Why does that make me feel so much better?*

He glanced down at the floor briefly, as if weighing whether to say something or not. Then, looking back at me with barely veiled pain in his eyes, he said, "I'm not the one who broke up with you."

My chest tightened and it was hard to breathe. After a few heart-pounding seconds, I swallowed and whispered, "I know."

Our gazes locked and we stared intensely at one another. It was just like that night last spring that started everything. The night when we'd been goofing around in his room, and I'd jokingly pulled out my phone to do the old TikTok trend where you recorded yourself kissing your best friend to see how they would react.

I'd turned on the song, "Electric Love," expecting him to run away when he heard it since we'd made fun of all the people doing the trend. But instead of telling me I was a dork and turning off the song, he'd pulled me close and kissed me like he'd been waiting just as long as I had for that moment.

Some people say there's no way that a simple kiss can change anything, but one kiss with my best friend had changed everything for me. It had told me what I'd always wondered— that Hunter had, in fact, been hiding his feelings under the surface just like I had.

And it had felt amazing at the time to have my feelings reciprocated.

I'd basically lived on cloud nine for the next few weeks as we started dating and found more moments to kiss and hold hands and do all the things that people our age did when they liked each other.

But we'd been so naive—so delusional to think that we could start steady dating while at school and keep it from my dad who lived an hour away.

If I could go back in time and tell myself that our fling would only last three weeks and it was better not to even start it, would I?

It would certainly make watching him talk to other girls easier. Make it easier for me to go out with other guys.

But those three weeks were the happiest weeks of my life, so even though I knew how it ended, I still wouldn't go back and give it up.

And things are fine now.

Mostly.

At least we'd managed to still be friends...

"What are you thinking about?" Hunter's question broke me from my memories, his pinky tracing lines across the veins in the back of my hand.

I knew I should probably make something up—to keep the past back where it was supposed to be. But as the chills raced up my arm from his soft caress, I found myself saying, "I was just thinking about the night I tried to do that best-friend challenge."

"You were?" He gulped, his voice more froggy than usual.

I nodded.

He studied me for a moment, his eyes darting back and forth between mine like he was searching for something. He must have found whatever he was looking for, because he cleared his throat and said, "Do you think about that night very often?"

I looked down at our hands, to where our fingers were now brushing lightly against each other. I wanted so badly to curl my fingers with his.

When I lifted my gaze to look at him again, there was a hunger in his eyes that made my face burn and my stomach twist in knots.

I think about that night every single time I look at you.

But before I could actually say it out loud, Nash walked into the house with his new fan club of freshman girls. As they all giggled at something Nash said and their voices grew closer, I knew I needed to step away from Hunter before we could draw any attention.

You never knew who might be watching.

I held my breath as I waited for someone to ask us what we were doing standing so close together when we were supposed to be just friends, but instead of coming into the kitchen, Nash and his posse walked down the hall toward the pool.

Once it was quiet again, Hunter cleared his throat and said, "We should probably get back to the party."

Even though going back to the party with everyone was the last thing I wanted to do, I nodded and said, "You're probably right."

8

HUNTER

"HEADING OUT ALREADY?" my roommate Asher rolled over on his bed to watch me as I slipped my coat over my shoulders Sunday morning.

I typically liked to sleep in on the weekends because it was the only time I didn't need an alarm, but my mind was alert and ready to go at seven fifteen, so I figured I might as well get a jump start on my plans for the morning—AKA working on *The Confidant*'s column for next Sunday.

"I'm just headed to The Brew," I told him as I reached for my backpack. "Want me to grab you something on my way back?"

"Nah, I'm good," Asher said with a yawn. "I'll just grab something from the great hall when I'm ready to actually be awake."

"Sounds good," I said. "Just get back to dreaming about all the scholarship offers you'll be getting after last night's performance."

"Will do," he said, a sleepy smile lifting his lips as he rolled back to face the wall opposite my side of the dorm room.

After the pool party yesterday, we'd all gone to the final performance of *The Phantom of the Opera*. And even though I'd been super impressed the first two times I'd watched my friends perform the musical, they had somehow done even better last night. The cast had been so in sync with each other that I wouldn't be surprised if Nash, Elyse, Asher, and even Cambrielle were offered full-ride scholarships to performing arts schools. The evening had been flawless.

Well...the *performance* had been flawless, at least. Things had been slightly awkward for me in the audience, sitting between Scarlett and Addison.

Yeah, that was kind of a mess right now. My attempt to be friendly to Addison at the pool party yesterday had certainly backfired with Scarlett. And I had a feeling that until the Valentine's dance was over with and I didn't have the pressure of being a good prospective date hanging over my head, things wouldn't be getting easier any time soon.

I could only hope things would get better once next Saturday had passed.

I sighed as I shouldered my backpack and walked out of my dorm room. Six more days and our dates with other people would be over with and where they belonged...in the past.

MY CAR—A matte black BMW X5 M—was covered with a few inches of freshly fallen snow when I made it outside, so I started the defroster and brushed off what I could.

The road was basically empty as I drove down the tree-shrouded road toward town. Our school was located a couple of miles from the actual town of Eden Falls, built on property that had once belonged to the Hastings family—who was one of the founding families—over a century ago.

The roads were a little slick, not having been plowed after the snowstorm last night, so I drove carefully down the winding road. A few minutes later, I passed the "Welcome to Eden Falls" sign and all the little mom-and-pop shops came into view.

When I'd first come to school here, it'd been quite a change from the rush and noise of Manhattan—the only home I'd known up until that point. But after a few weeks, I adjusted to the slower pace and actually came to love the small-town life.

Depending on what I ended up doing in the future—if I made a career out of being a writer like I hoped—I wouldn't mind settling down in a quiet place like this.

I passed the gas station with the soda shop Cambrielle and Ava were obsessed with, then drove past the quirky Mexican and Italian restaurant called The Italian Amigos. Once I made it to the end of the next block of shops, I pulled along the curb and parked.

The black-and-white sign for the coffee shop glittered with the first rays of sunshine when I stepped inside.

The coffee shop was officially called The Brew of Life—a play on the tree of life in the Garden of Eden, since Eden Falls loved playing into the title of "Connecticut's Own Garden of Eden" and caffeine seemed to be everyone's favorite life-source these days.

But to all the locals, it was simply referred to as "The Brew."

I walked onto the light-gray wood floor and warmth spread throughout my chest as I breathed in the smell of freshly brewed coffee. I glanced around at the industrial interior design that Mack's mom had helped make cozy with vibrant colors, mismatched tables and chairs, and inviting lighting before she passed.

"Hi, Hunter." The barista with dirty-blonde hair and

brown eyes greeted me with a smile when I stepped up to the counter. "What can I get for you today?"

The barista, Kiara, was here every Sunday morning, so we were on a first-name basis now.

I glanced up at the menu written on a large chalkboard behind Kiara out of habit, even though we both already knew what I was going to order.

Yes, I ordered the same thing every time I came in here. Why mess with a good thing?

"I'll have a large chai latte and the Rise and Shine sandwich," I said.

"Would you like your latte hot or cold?" Kiara asked, just like she did every time as she typed in my order.

"Hot, please."

I paid and after Kiara handed me my drink, I found a table in the back corner to set up shop for the day.

As I opened up my email account for *The Confidant* and took my first sip of my latte, I couldn't help but feel grateful that I was able to be here, doing this on a Sunday morning.

Back when I'd been a member of The Fold, I never would have been caught dead working on my column in a coffee shop on a Sunday. Shopping on Sundays—even for something as necessary as food and drink—was strictly forbidden. Writing in my column was also considered breaking the Sabbath because it made me money and working on Sundays was against the rules.

But even if the old version of me would have shaken his head at what I chose to do with my Sunday mornings these days, the current version of me loved the freedom to take things slow and have a relaxed morning doing the work and activities I enjoyed.

When I was first leaving The Fold, I felt like such a rebel not going to Pastor Caldwell's sermons. It had been thrilling coming to The Brew or going on a hike with Mack, Carter, and Nash instead of sitting in the chapel—or going to Scarlett's room to watch the tiny screen of her laptop for church.

It hadn't been all fun and excitement, though. There had definitely been some growing pains as I experimented with new options. Even though I was doing what most people outside of The Fold would consider completely normal, it had been difficult to manage my feelings and anxiety at times because my old thinking patterns and religious conditioning didn't just disappear overnight.

Like, even though I had such a great time out in nature that first Sunday, when I got back to the school and had time to reflect back on my day, the guilt and fear I'd been conditioned to feel when "breaking the commandments" would kick in and I'd have to fight off a panic attack. Part of me had still worried that by stepping away from the church, I was dooming myself to eternal damnation or putting my life at risk.

Those stories I'd heard growing up about people hiking or climbing on Sundays and ending up in fatal accidents because God was punishing them for their disobedience didn't just go away all at once.

Even though I logically knew that accidents that happened on Sunday had no extra meaning behind them compared to an accident that took place on a Tuesday, it was sometimes a struggle to separate my old beliefs from reality. And once my thoughts started spiraling, it usually took talking to my brother, Sebastian, or going to the ExFold support group on Reddit to feel safe again.

It took months to get used to my new routines. But now, whenever I did perfectly normal things that The Fold had special rules against, the feelings of guilt came less and less because I was learning that I could actually trust myself.

"Here's your sandwich," Kiara said as she set my scrambled-egg sandwich with green chilies, onion, tomatoes, and mixed greens on the table.

"Thanks," I said, scooting my computer to the side to make room.

"Working on your column again, I see," she said, her gaze going to my laptop.

"As always." I glanced around the small coffee shop to make sure no one I knew was in here before adding, "You still haven't told anyone about my secret yet, have you?"

I might have been a little too careless when I was here two weeks ago and accidentally left the dashboard for *The Confidant*'s website up on my screen at the exact moment she had come to offer me a refill on my latte.

If she'd never heard of *The Confidant*'s column, it wouldn't have been a big deal. But since *The Confidant* had over three hundred thousand subscribers at that point, it had been wishful thinking to hope that a high school senior from the very town that *The Confidant* claimed to reside in wouldn't know about it.

Even if Kiara went to Sherman High instead of Eden Falls Academy, it was a mystery a lot of teens in the area wanted to figure out now that the mystery of where Bailee Vanderbilt had disappeared to last year had been solved.

Bailee was a girl who went missing without a trace last year, and my roommate Asher was suspected of being involved in her disappearance until her whereabouts were discovered.

"I haven't breathed a word," she said, pulling a few napkins from her apron and setting them next to my sandwich.

"Thank you," I said, my shoulders relaxing a little.

"Though I'm still waiting for you to answer my email."

"You emailed *The Confidant*?" I asked, surprised.

She shrugged. "Maybe."

"What was your email about?" I asked, curious what Kiara would want advice about.

"If I wanted you to know which question was mine, I would have just asked you when you came in here," she said with a half-smile.

"I guess that makes sense," I said. "Though now I feel bad that I didn't help my favorite barista out when she's been so good at feeding my chai latte addiction and keeping my secret."

"Well..." She laughed lightly. "Maybe I'll have to send my question in again sometime."

"You should," I said. "This time though, maybe add a part that says something about me promising to answer your question so I don't miss it."

"I'll keep that in mind," she said with a wink before walking to a table a couple of spaces over and clearing the dishes a previous customer had left behind.

The next hour and a half passed quickly as I worked through more of the emails that had come through this week and typed up a few replies from *The Confidant*.

Since the column I was working on today would be posted next Sunday—the day before Valentine's Day—I decided to focus on questions that related to the topic of love and relationships.

The first email I answered was from a guy who wanted advice on how to build up his self-image after getting dumped by his girlfriend for a taller, more classically attractive guy. The next came from someone who wanted to know how to fix his reputation after getting caught stringing girls along for a bet he'd had going with his friends. And the third was from a girl who wrote:

Dear Confidant,

I'm starting to like a guy I rejected a few months ago. I didn't know him well back then and was interested in someone from back home. Is it reasonable to hope he might give me a second chance? How would you go about this?

    Thanks in advance,

    I Changed My Mind

I skimmed through the response I'd brainstormed Monday evening when Scarlett had caught me emailing myself in the library. I always liked to get some of my initial thoughts written down so they could simmer for a bit before I typed them into my word document. Usually, my gut-instincts were pretty solid though, so I didn't need to change a ton. After reading through my initial ideas, I ended up with:

Dear I Changed My Mind,

    I think a big part of whether you'll get your second chance or not depends on how you rejected him in the first place. Were you rude about it? Or were you able to let him down gently and remain on good terms? If it's the former, you may have an uphill battle. But if not, I'd suggest just opening up communication with him again.

    Talk to him and try to feel things out. Don't assume that just because he had feelings for you in the past that they still linger. But if the communication is good and he seems to be on friendly terms without hard feelings, then I suggest just having a conversation where you explain where you were and ask him out. Putting yourself out there is scary, but it's the quickest way to find out where you stand.

    Wishing you the best,

    The Confidant

I chuckled to myself as I wrote that last part because putting yourself out there after rejection was *much* easier said than done.

But luckily for me, I was simply the one handing out advice and not the person who had to actually put himself out there each time.

I FOUND Scarlett in the common room when I got back to the school after sending my column to my brother Bash to proofread.

"Hey," she said, eyeing my backpack and seeming to note that I was just getting back from somewhere.

"Hi," I said, feeling the tension tighten in my body because I knew she was wondering in what way I'd broken the Sabbath this morning. "How has your morning been? Do anything fun?"

It wasn't the best question to ask, since I knew exactly what she'd been doing the past two hours. But I wanted to at least pretend like things were normal between us and we didn't have several huge elephants standing in the room with us.

"Just the usual," she said with a shrug. "Church. Talk to my dad. Regular Sunday morning stuff."

Regular Sunday morning stuff for her, anyway.

She looked like she wanted to say more—to possibly ask where I'd been and why I'd missed church once again. But after a few seconds, she just pressed her lips together and left it alone.

I didn't offer an explanation of why I'd skipped, either.

I knew I needed to tell her eventually where I stood. But I just didn't want to—once it was out, I couldn't take it back. And if I said something in the wrong way, I couldn't stop her from writing me off for good.

Sure, it sucked having her think that I wasn't showing up at her room on Sunday mornings because I was lost or being lazy.

But once I told her I wasn't planning to ever come back, it would change things between us. Make her see me differently.

I'd go from being lazy and lost to being dangerous and fully in Satan's power—in the way my parents and her dad now saw me.

I just didn't want to see that hint of sadness in her eyes every time she looked at me quite yet.

"Did you eat lunch?" I asked, deciding to bring up a less polarizing subject.

Good food always made people happy.

"I was just headed there," she said. "Want to join me?"

"Yes," I said. "Let me just put my backpack in my room, and I'll be right back."

I dashed up the stairs that led to the boys' dorms, dropped my backpack inside my door, and then hurried back to Scarlett.

As we walked through the gothic colonnade that connected the dorms to the main part of the school, I asked, "Has *Dear Eliza* gotten many emails yet?"

"There were a few sitting in my inbox when I checked yesterday."

"That's awesome," I said, glad that she already had interest. When I'd first started *The Confidant*, I had to make up my own questions to answer since no one knew the column existed for several weeks. "Have you had time to answer any yet? I bet people are excited to see the new column in the gazette this week."

"I started to yesterday." She waited for me to open the door that would lead back into the warmth of the school from outside. "But then I got distracted by the party and everything else. So even though I stayed up super late to do homework after the play, I never got back to it."

I opened the large wooden door and held it for her. After

stomping my wet shoes on the rug just inside, I asked, "How late did you stay up?"

"I don't know, like two a.m." She brushed some snow off her coat sleeves as we walked past a few students sitting on a bench along the long corridor. "When I kept falling asleep on my laptop and found I'd typed, like, twenty pages of the letter L, I gave up and went to bed."

"It was the letter L this time?" I asked with a slight smile since Scarlett falling asleep at the computer wasn't anything new.

"Yep, that was the winner last night."

"Did you get most of your homework done, though?" I asked, a little worried that this *Dear Eliza* thing would be the burden I'd expected when she decided to do it.

But she just shrugged and said, "I'll just wake up at five tomorrow morning to finish."

I wanted to tell her she should just do her homework this afternoon and not sacrifice sleep, but Scarlett was even more paranoid than I'd been about keeping the Sabbath day holy back in the day, so I kept my mouth shut.

We filled our trays with food when we got to the great hall —today's lunch consisting of Malibu chicken, rice pilaf, and a green salad. I grabbed a bottle of water and a stack of napkins, since I was notorious for being a messy eater. No one from our friend group was to be seen among the crowd of Sunday lunchers, so we found an empty table for ourselves.

"Want me to help you pick which emails you'll answer this week?" I asked as I cut into my chicken.

"I don't know," she said, a hesitant look in her eyes. "I should probably wait until tomorrow or something."

"Why?"

She looked at me like her reason should be obvious before saying, "Because it's Sunday, Hunter. You know I don't work on Sundays." She poured ranch over her salad, her expression telling me that she was trying to figure out how to add more time into her schedule tomorrow. Then she set the small cup of ranch back on her tray and shrugged. "I'll just wake up at four a.m. tomorrow instead."

Oh no, she wouldn't.

And since her phone was currently poking out of the top of her back pocket, I quickly reached down and grabbed it.

"What are you doing?" She gasped, as if shocked I'd get so close to touching her butt.

Not that it would be the first time, since she certainly hadn't minded when I had run my hands across her back pockets during one of our make-out sessions in my car last spring.

I swiped up on the screen and held the phone in front of her face so the facial recognition technology would unlock it. As I searched for her email app, I said, "This isn't homework. It's an extra service that you provide to the students of Eden Falls Academy. Helping people is fine on Sundays, right? It's service, and Jehovah was all about serving people, wasn't he?"

She chewed on her lip, looking like she wanted to protest my logic. But after a moment, she sighed and said, "Okay, yeah. I guess that's true."

She took her phone back from me and opened the app herself. "Wanna go through these with me then? Maybe help me think of advice?"

"I'd be honored," I said. Then just because I should, I added, "Not sure how good my advice will be. But I can take a crack at it."

She clicked on an email, and as it loaded, I leaned closer so I could read it with her.

"Is that a new shampoo?" I asked, realizing too late that I'd just made it obvious I'd sniffed her hair.

But instead of looking at me like I was a weirdo, she nodded. "It's one my mom sent me for my birthday."

"I like it."

When she blushed at my compliment, it took everything in me to read the email she had open instead of staring at her.

The first message was from someone who called himself, "Can't Catch a Break," who wrote about the trouble he was having with a teacher.

This particular teacher used to be one of my favorites, and I managed to get A's on all my assignments and tests at the beginning of the year. But when I went home for Christmas break, I found out that my dad had moved out while I was away and that my parents were getting a divorce.

It was a shock because they had always seemed so happy. But ever since then, I've had a difficult time concentrating and keeping up on my studies.

I'm still showing up to my classes and working hard, but it feels like the drama at home messed up my brain and I'm not sleeping well anymore and zoning out all the time.

Anyway, I completely failed a test last week, and when I asked this particular teacher for a way to make it up, she didn't seem interested in helping.

I really need to get my grades up since I'm in sports and hoping to get a scholarship for baseball. But if I can't get my GPA up, I won't even be allowed on the field.

Thank you in advance,

-Can't Catch a Break

"Oh, that's rough," I said when I finished reading the email.

"I know." Scarlett nodded and set her phone down on the table. "And that teacher sounds like a jerk."

"She probably has no idea what's going on," I said, trying to give the teacher the benefit of the doubt. "But I get where this guy is coming from. It's hard to keep up with everything when it feels like your life is falling apart or you're going through huge life trauma or grief."

"So what do you think Eliza should tell him to do?" Scarlett looked at me with wide eyes, like she expected I'd have a good answer.

I pursed my lips and thought for a moment. "I'd probably start off by telling him to be gentle with himself and keep doing his best. And also suggest that he try talking to the teacher again and explain what has been going on. Maybe also talk to a trusted friend or therapist, if possible, since it helps to be able to talk things out sometimes."

"That's really good advice," Scarlett said, looking thoughtful. "I was so young when my parents divorced that I didn't have that understanding, but I think what you said is perfect."

"Thanks." Warmth radiated in my chest at her compliment.

I'd had pretty good feedback on my previous advice from the readers of *The Confidant,* but this praise felt a little different—better—since it was coming from someone I cared about.

She picked up her phone again like she was going to draft the response now. "Did you read that advice somewhere?" she asked as she typed into her phone.

"No."

I lived it.

Trauma and grief could come from many sources, but the way our body and mind react to various types of trauma is similar. And even though my trauma came from a different source —my previous religion instead of a divorce—I'd gone through, and was still going through, the grief cycle. My grades from the first semester would definitely signal that something had been going on with me during that time.

I finished my chicken as Scarlett typed a few notes into her phone. When she was done, she pushed it over to me and said, "Think that sounds okay?"

I set my water bottle down and took her phone to see what she'd written, but just as I started reading it, a text notification popped on the top of the screen from someone I hadn't expected her to be texting: Xander Pierce.

Her date for next week.

As my eyes scanned over the text, my heart plummeted in my chest.

Because, what the heck?

9

SCARLETT

"UM, what exactly is Xander asking to see?" Hunter asked after I took a big bite of my salad, his voice full of concern.

"Huh?" I looked up from my food, confused at what he was talking about.

He handed my phone back to me. When I looked at the screen, I saw that I'd just received a text from Xander.

Xander: **I think I need a video of you showing me that.**

I read the text again, my stomach jumping to my throat because it took me a moment to remember the context of our conversation from earlier.

A context that Hunter didn't have, which was why he was currently looking at me like I had a double life going on inside my phone.

This looked so bad.

"It's not what it looks like, I promise," I hurried to say before he could think Xander was asking me to send an inappropriate video or something. "We were just texting earlier about something funny that happened during my dad's sermon.

When I told him I had perfected my impersonation of that expression my dad gets when he's upset but trying to keep it together in front of the congregation, Xander said he didn't believe that my face could look like that."

I thought he might have been trying to flirt since his actual words had been, "You're way too pretty to look anything like that," but telling Hunter that part would only make things worse right now.

"So he just wants to see your face?" Hunter narrowed his green eyes, like he didn't believe me.

"Yeah..." I cleared my throat. "Of course." I opened up my messaging app so he could see my whole text thread with Xander if he wanted.

But instead of trying to read any of the texts I was scrolling through, he just asked, "So, do you guys text regularly then? For some reason I thought everything was set up by your dad."

"He texted me a few times last summer when he was interning with my dad at the church and needed something here and there," I said. "But that was basically it until this week."

He nodded and seemed to be thinking things over. "Did something happen during your dad's sermon that was really funny?"

"Yes," I said, my chest still feeling like it was full of little pop rocks fizzing against my ribs. "The organist, uh, I mean Sister Moss's phone went off while my dad was talking about something really spiritual and it took her, like, a full fifteen seconds to grab her purse and silence it. Normally, my dad would just chuckle and be understanding, but the song was 'I'm Sexy and I Know It.' So, it was just a really funny and cringeworthy moment."

"Oh, I bet you're dad looooved that," Hunter said sarcastically.

"He didn't look happy." I shook my head, remembering the way my heart had stopped as I watched my dad's reaction through the computer screen. "Pretty sure Sister Moss's job is on the line now."

I said it lightly, but with how strict my dad was, it could definitely happen.

I doubted my dad was even familiar with that song. Most of the music he listened to was put out by the church. But since the song used the word "sexy," which was a big no-no word at my house, it had actually been kind of scary to watch my dad's reaction and wonder if he would call Sister Moss to repentance right there in front of everyone.

"It sounds like Sister Moss has some positive affirmations going with that song, at least," Hunter said, thankfully seeming to find the humor in the scenario instead of focusing on the fact that Xander had texted me.

"I think so," I said. "And they must be working too, because she totally showed up at the church Christmas social with a silver fox."

"Sister Moss is back in the dating game?" Hunter's dark eyebrows rose.

"Yep." I smiled. "And they looked *very* happy."

"Good for her." Hunter's eyes brightened, seeming genuinely happy for the woman who had been a long-time member of our congregation. "I'm kind of sad I missed seeing that."

Yeah...me too...

The church Christmas social just hadn't been the same without Hunter this year. I'd played Mary in the nativity as usual, but instead of having Hunter there to be Joseph, they had to ask twelve-year-old Austin Smith to take the role.

It was a seemingly small thing. A few missed church socials. An hour on Sundays that he wasn't there. The early morning Bible study where we'd text each other complaints about how tired we were and how boring Brother Rodger's object lessons were getting.

I missed having him in that part of my life. We'd had so many inside jokes. So much shared history since we were the only ones in the entire school who understood what it was like to grow up in the way that we had. Hunter knew just how difficult it could be to navigate the teenage years where we had to live in the world with friends who didn't understand our beliefs sometimes and why we lived life in a way they found peculiar.

I mean, I couldn't think of anyone else in the whole school besides me who wore T-shirts under her basketball jersey and was forbidden from having a steady boyfriend before she graduated.

Standing apart from our peers and being an example to those around us wasn't always easy, but at least I'd always had Hunter by my side when things got tricky.

I studied him as he picked up his napkin and patted his lips. He caught me watching him out of the corner of his eye, and I worried for a moment that he might be able to read my thoughts on my face.

But instead of asking what I was thinking, he said, "Speaking of songs going off at the wrong time, do you remember that time at Brother Henson's funeral when everyone knew his much younger wife was a gold-digger? And her phone went off during the eulogy with the song 'Bye Bye Bye?'"

"That was epic!" I laughed, remembering that particular funeral well. "I just wish I could have seen her face when she found out that he willed all his money to his kids, and she didn't get a dime because he knew she was a gold-digger all along."

"Talk about karma," Hunter said with a smile.

"Except she turned around and married his oldest son," I said.

Hunter shook his head. "Some guys are idiots when it comes to beautiful women."

"They really are," I said, feeling only a little jealous that he'd just implied that Sister Henson was beautiful because she looked way more like Addison than me.

"Though," he said. "I guess if they're both okay with each other's shallowness, it can work out okay."

"I guess."

Hunter looked thoughtful for a second, like something just occurred to him. "Hmmm, I wonder..."

"You wonder what?" I asked, curious what had popped into his mind now.

"Do you think your dad arranged this date between you and Xander because Xander's dad just hit billionaire status last year?"

"What?"

"You said your dad is the one who arranged this whole thing, right?" He angled toward me on our lunch bench. "So I'm just wondering why Xander is his top pick when he's, like, four years older than us?"

"It does seem a little strange to set up a high school senior with a college senior," I allowed.

Hunter nodded. "Especially when he's been so against you dating *anyone* in the past."

"Yeah." I sighed. The subject of whom I was allowed to date was slightly uncomfortable since Hunter had somehow landed on my dad's blacklist. "I guess part of me wondered about the billionaire thing when he first told me. But I would hope that my dad isn't that shallow, you know?"

Though if he was, hopefully it was just his way of making

sure I was financially secure if I wanted to be a stay-at-home mom when I was older.

"So maybe it's just because he knows Xander a little better after working so closely with him last summer?"

"Maybe." I shrugged.

10

HUNTER

"ARE YOU READY FOR THIS?" Addison asked me as we walked toward our friends standing in the parking lot in their snow gear early Saturday morning.

"So ready," I said, trying to sound enthusiastic despite my worries that today could either be really fun or really awkward.

The past week had been busy with school, advice columns, and basketball. So while I was definitely a bit anxious about balancing being a good date for Addison while juggling whatever feelings might arise while I watched Scarlett go on her date, I hoped it would be a good day.

"Hey guys," Mack greeted us when we joined the group. "We were just about to load into the vehicles, and you two are riding with me."

"Sounds good," I said.

"It's going to be kind of a tight fit, though. Evan and his date have asked to join us," Mack continued. "So if you have any extra stuff, you can just put it in the back."

I hadn't brought anything besides the snow gear I was

already wearing, so I just waited for Addison to tell me where to sit. We ended up climbing into the third row of seats in Mack's gray Land Cruiser. While we buckled in, I asked, "Did you know Evan was planning to come today?"

The last thing I needed was another overprotective family member of the girl I was on a date with, watching my every move.

But Addison just said, "He asked if he and his date could join us a few days ago, since they didn't have a day date planned and wanted to try tubing."

"You don't mind your stepbrother tagging along?" I asked, still so curious about the dynamic they had. They were literally together all the time.

"Not really." She shrugged, her ski jacket rubbing against mine with the movement. "He's not too bad."

"Have your parents been married very long then?" I asked. "For some reason, I thought I heard that they had just gotten married this past summer or something like that."

"Oh yeah," she said. "Th-they did just get married recently, but um, Evan and I have known each other since I was, like, ten. He and my brother were pretty good friends growing up."

"Oh, that's cool." And kind of explained why they were so comfortable with each other.

There had actually been a couple of times when I'd wondered if there was something more between them than the stepbrother-and-stepsister stuff...but maybe they were comfortable being so close to each other because they had history.

Kind of like Scarlett and me.

"Speaking of my stepbrother..." Addison nodded toward the door we just climbed through.

"You guys got enough room for me back there?" Evan ducked his head inside to look at Addison and me.

"Sure," I said. Though with how big and muscular he was, it was definitely going to be a tight fit and would probably be better for him to sit in the middle row with his much more petite date than sitting by Addison.

"Great," he said.

And just like I'd expected, when he sat on the other side of Addison, we were squished in there like sardines.

"Where's your date?" I asked, looking around at everyone who was still standing outside.

Cambrielle and Mack were just climbing into the front. Ava, Elyse, Carter, and Asher were walking over to Carter's truck, which was parked in the row of cars in front of us.

The only person still outside was Scarlett, who was on her phone like she might be calling Xander for his ETA.

"Oh..." Evan waved his hand. "She texted me a few minutes ago to say that she was running late. But she'll probably be here in a couple of minutes."

"And all of her cheerleading buddies weren't doing a day-date activity?" I asked, still thinking it was a little weird that they'd decided to join us for our date.

"No, we're just doing dinner and the dance with them," he said.

Cambrielle and Mack closed the front doors, and just as the engine was roaring to life, a Bugatti Chiron in dark blue drove into the parking lot and parked a few spaces away from us.

"Now *that* is a beautiful car," Evan said, his jaw dropping as he seemed to take in its sleek lines and expensive rims.

A moment later, the door opened and out stepped a tall guy with brown hair whom I hadn't seen since last spring when he'd stopped by Scarlett's house looking for her dad.

Xander wore sunglasses and a black parka lined with fox fur. And even though beneath the sunglasses and coat there *could* be a completely unthreatening, homely-looking dude, I knew that there was actually a smooth-talking alpha male with the type of athletic body and blue eyes that most of the girls at my school would die over.

That was, if they didn't die over the fact that he was the only heir to his father's billions of dollars first.

My parents may be wealthy socialites with eight-figure bank accounts... but that was small potatoes next to the Pierce's fortune.

I watched as Xander strode toward Scarlett on the lightly snow-dusted parking lot, looking like he could be a model for Gorski's winter line. And even though Scarlett had told me their date was set up by her dad, it didn't stop the pit of jealousy from forming in my stomach when Xander took off his sunglasses and greeted Scarlett with his charming smile followed by a hug.

"Is that Scarlett's date?" Addison gasped, like she hadn't been expecting good-girl Scarlett Caldwell to be set up with someone so magnetically attractive by her overprotective pastor father.

"Yeah, that's Xander," I said, feeling even more uptight now that Addison had basically confirmed that Xander was hot.

"And he's from her church?" Her eyebrow arched when she glanced at me, as if she'd thought only homely-looking people liked to feast on the Good Word of The Fold.

"He goes to Yale right now, but yeah, Scarlett's family met Xander's family through their church."

"Well, good for her," Addison said. "No wonder she was okay with me asking you."

Which meant what? That I was chopped liver when compared to Xander?

Evan cleared his throat loudly, which must have made Addison realize how her words were coming across because she got a bashful look on her face and said, "Sorry, that didn't come out very well. I'm not trying to compare you guys at all. I mean, you're great. I asked you for a reason..." She stopped, shook her head, and then added, "I just pictured Scarlett's date differently when she described him."

"It's fine." I was hoping to sound unbothered since being offended that she found Xander attractive when I myself was having a hard time not staring at Scarlett, who looked particularly cute in her pink ski suit with her hair pulled up in a high ponytail, would be super hypocritical. "I'm secure enough with myself that I can admit Xander is a good-looking guy."

"Well, that's good," Addison said, relief showing in her eyes. "Because I really don't want to screw up today before we even get started."

I was about to tell her that she hadn't screwed up anything when the door in front of me opened and Scarlett peeked her head inside. After glancing at me with an expression I couldn't read, she looked toward Mack and Cambrielle in the front and said, "Hey, I just wanted to let you know that Xander and I decided to take his car up the mountain. So we'll just meet you guys up there."

"Does he have an extra seat in his car?" Mack asked in a light-hearted tone. "Because that car is amazing."

"I think you might need to drive still." Scarlett chuckled. "You know, since you have a carload of people in your own vehicle."

Mack nodded at Cambrielle. "You can drive them, right, babe?"

"Sorry, but I don't really feel like having my boyfriend ditch me for a car." She smacked his arm playfully. "You dork."

"Fine." He sighed dramatically and turned back to Scarlett. "I guess I'll stay with these commoners."

Says the guy dating the daughter of the seventh wealthiest man in the United States.

"Drive safe, guys," Scarlett said. Before I could say that she better tell that to the guy with the fast sports car, she shut the door and walked arm in arm with Xander back to his Bugatti.

Should I just give up all hope of her still wanting me now? Or wait until he proposed with a ten-carat rock?

Because yeah...if Scarlett's father was trying to hook her up with Xander because of his daddy's money, I was in trouble. Even with the recent success of *The Confidant*, there was no way I'd ever be able to compete with someone like that now that my trust fund was gone.

"Hey Evan." Mack turned to face us commoners all the way in the back. "Is Lissa still planning to come?"

"I think so..." Evan frowned. "Let me see if she texted me."

He pulled out his phone and seemed to scan through his recent texts. "Ah, dang," he said. "It looks like she had a family emergency and won't be able to make it tubing after all."

His look of disappointment seemed slightly exaggerated to me.

"Oh that sucks," Cambrielle said, turning back with a sympathetic look. "I hope it's nothing serious."

"Hopefully not." Evan slipped his phone back into his pocket. He paused for a moment, and then asked, "Do you guys mind if I still come?"

"If you don't mind being the only single guy up there, it's fine with me," Cambrielle said. To Addison, she asked, "You okay with that?"

"Sure." Addison shrugged. She angled her face toward me and asked, "You don't mind having my stepbrother tagging along with us, do you?"

"No, that's just great," I said, even if there was a slightly paranoid part of me that wondered if this had been their plan in the first place.

But I tried to push that thought away. Because how likely would it be that I was destined to go out with not just one but two girls in the past year with super overprotective family members keeping a close watch on my every move?

11

HUNTER

"I THINK I'm ready to head back to the lodge for some lunch," Addison said after we'd made it back to the top of the hill again with our snow tubes. "What about you?"

"Sounds good to me," I said. My stomach was literally growling, since it apparently thought going down a hill and being pulled back up it again a dozen times was enough of a workout to burn through my breakfast.

We'd been at the Eden Falls ski resort for the past two hours and it had actually been a lot of fun so far. I'd never been tubing here before, since I usually went snowboarding when I came with my friends, but it was definitely something I'd have to do again.

Maybe I could convince Scarlett to make a quick stop here next weekend before we headed back to spend President's Day weekend with our families in New York.

"Should we wait for everyone else?" Addison turned back toward the group of our friends who were just making it to the top of the hill again. "Or just tell them to meet us down there?"

"I'm good with either," I said.

She'd planned the date, so I was just along for the ride.

Though...in all honesty, I wouldn't mind a few minutes where I didn't have to watch Xander flirting with Scarlett.

Like, I knew they were on a date, but did they really have to go down the hill on the same snow tube?

I wasn't sure whose idea it had been to go down the hill together, but it had taken everything in me to keep my jaw from dropping at the sight of Scarlett on the lap of some guy she barely knew.

At least, I *thought* they barely knew each other. That was how Scarlett had made it seem, right?

But who knew, maybe they had a secret summer fling while he was spending twenty hours a week at the church on the same property as her house, and I just hadn't noticed anything because I'd been too distracted by my deep dive into church history.

Everyone ended up walking back to the lodge with us. Addison and I were at the front of the group and everyone else trailed right behind us, with Scarlett and Xander bringing up the rear.

Which was probably good, so I wouldn't have to accidentally overhear their conversation.

"What type of food are you in the mood for?" Addison asked when we made it to the top floor of the lodge where all the restaurants were located.

"I usually like the sandwiches at Amelia's Cafe," I said, pointing to the small cafe across the way from us. "But if you want more of a hot lunch, then The Hot Pot is really good, too. Their pho is amazing."

"I think everyone wanted to meet on the rooftop to eat, so let's go with the sandwiches."

We walked over to Amelia's café, and we'd only been in line for thirty seconds before I regretted not suggesting another choice. Because Scarlett and Xander stepped right behind us just then.

"Hey guys," Addison said, turning back to look at them.

"Hi," Scarlett replied, her gaze going briefly to me before returning to Addison. "Did you have fun tubing?"

"It was so fun," Addison said with a smile. "What about you guys?"

Scarlett and Xander glanced at each other before he spoke for both of them, saying, "It was really fun. In fact, I think we might need to try it again."

I flicked my gaze to Scarlett, to try and get a read on how she felt about going tubing with Xander in the near future, and my heart sunk a little when she blushed under his gaze.

So maybe she did like riding on the same snow tube as him.

"I don't think we've been officially introduced yet," Addison said, bringing my attention back to her as she spoke to Xander. "I'm Addison, and this is my date Hunter." She gestured to me.

"It's a pleasure to meet you, Addison." Xander offered his hand for her to shake, a charming smile spreading across his lips. "I'm Xander Pierce."

"It's so nice to meet you, Xander." Addison took his hand, and I tried not to notice how she, too, flushed under his gaze.

Yep...I was basically chopped liver today.

Xander offered his hand to me next. "You look really familiar. Do we know each other?"

"Yes," I said, making sure to keep my handshake firm. "We went to the same church, growing up."

I didn't like bringing up The Fold in normal conversation, because it was a part of my life that I wanted to keep in the past. But since it was actually where we knew each other from, I couldn't exactly say it any other way.

"Hunter is Sebastian Blackwell's younger brother," Scarlett

said, offering clarification. "You were in Sebastian's Bible class, right?"

"Oh yeah," Xander said, further recognition showing on his face. "Sebastian and I go way back. And now that you mention it, you and your brother look so much alike."

The line moved as some people got their orders, so we took a few steps forward.

"So Scarlett said you go to Yale?" Addison asked Xander, keeping the get-to-know-you session going. "What are you studying?"

"I'm working toward a dual major. One in History, and one in Religious Studies," he said.

Which really shouldn't surprise me. Only people with the kind of money Xander had in his future could study something that had such a small chance of becoming a lucrative career path.

Though, I guess I really couldn't talk since I was hoping to study Creative Writing and Psychology.

"What made you pick History?" Addison asked, seeming intrigued by that for some reason.

Xander shrugged his broad shoulders. "I've always enjoyed learning the stories of how we got to where we are now. I also really like studying the lives of the great leaders in the past and seeing what commonalities they had."

"Do you want to become a leader of something someday?" Addison asked.

Xander nodded. "I actually did an internship with Scarlett's dad this summer and would love to possibly become a pastor someday. Which is where the Religious Studies comes in."

"What made you interested in that?" I couldn't help but ask since there wasn't usually a lot of money in church leadership.

Well, unless you were at the top—the High Priest and his Elders certainly had a nice stipend provided by the church.

But pastors like Scarlett's dad didn't bring in much more than they could live on. Scarlett's investment banker mother was the one who'd pushed and paid for her daughter's expensive boarding school education.

But again, Xander probably wouldn't ever have to worry about making any real money from his passion projects.

"I've just been so blessed by the church that I want to help more people find what I've found," Xander said, his voice deepening like he was feeling emotional talking about this. "I just see so many people who would benefit from inviting Jehovah into their lives and want to do my part to help them find him."

"Oh cool..." Addison nodded slowly, her voice raising in pitch at the end, like she was worried about the turn this conversation had suddenly taken.

And I knew that deer-in-the-headlights look well—the one that said, *that's cool you like your beliefs, but please don't try to convert me since I'm actually happy where I am.*

Yeah, I might have seen that look several times in the past when some innocent person would ask me what I did over the weekend, and I would instantly go into "convert the non-members" mode and try to get them to go to church with me.

"Hey, it looks like it's almost our turn to order," I said, touching Addison's arm to save her from the conversation she'd unintentionally walked into. "Do you know what you want?"

"Oh, I haven't even looked at the menu yet." Relief showed on her face when she turned back to me. "What do you like from here?"

I glanced at the menu. "I usually like the French dip sandwich or the BLT."

"A BLT sounds amazing," she said. "I think I'll get that." Then stepping closer and linking her arm through mine, she whispered, "Thanks for saving me. I literally thought I was about to be invited to welcome their version of Jesus into my life."

"No problem." I patted her arm. But since I couldn't resist having a little fun of my own, I bent next to her hair and whispered, "Though, if you want to go to church with me tomorrow, I think that could be a romantic second date."

Addison took in a sharp breath and looked up at me with an expression that told me she was about to bolt away.

"I'm kidding." I held up my hands, unable to hold in a chuckle.

To which she responded with a quick elbow in the ribs. "Not funny, Hunter."

"Except it kind of is." I shot her a playful wink.

Man, it was cathartic joking about the things I used to take so seriously.

It was our turn to order a moment later. While Addison told the guy at the counter what she wanted, I allowed myself a quick glance back at Scarlett and Xander just to see how things seemed to be going.

But instead of being happily engaged in conversation like they'd been most of the morning, I found Scarlett glaring at the back of Addison's head.

Like, she thought that little back-and-forth we'd just had was our version of flirting.

Which...I guess it could have been...

12

SCARLETT

"JUST TWO MORE HOURS AND this will be over with," Ava whispered to me as we stood on the edge of the great hall where the Valentine's dance was taking place. Our dates had just gone to throw away the cups and plates—we had heart-shaped cookies and pink "love potion" punch—so Ava and I had a few seconds to ourselves. "You doing okay still?"

"I'm hanging in there," I said, trying to sound more cheerful than I felt.

Because in all honesty, I was not doing well.

The day had started out fine. I'd started out the morning fully intent on being a happy and bubbly date for Xander since he'd taken the time to drive here from New Haven. I mean, it had to be slightly awkward for him to be spending the day with a bunch of high school kids, so I figured I'd have to make things as enjoyable as I could.

But even though I'd been putting forth my best effort to be present and in a good mood for him, having Hunter and Addison's date right there in my face had started to really wear on me as the day went on.

"I bet Hunter is feeling just as off about everything today as you are," Ava said, rubbing her hand across my back in a comforting way. "And come tomorrow, things will go back to normal."

"They better." I sighed heavily. "Because if I'm losing him..." I stopped, knowing I couldn't finish that sentence without my voice breaking.

If he and Addison decided to go on a second date, then a third and a fourth—

I closed my eyes, not even wanting to picture a future where he ended up with someone that wasn't me.

"You're not going to lose him." Ava looked at me with an assurance in her light-brown eyes that I didn't feel. "He wouldn't lose all of his feelings for you after just one date. I bet it's just as hard for him to watch you with Xander as it is for you to see him with someone else."

"I hope so," I said.

Though even as I said it, the flame of jealousy inside me was instantly lit even hotter because Hunter and Addison decided to walk onto the dimly lit dance floor in that exact moment—him leading her by the hand.

He was holding her hand? My heart cracked with the thought.

"Does he not realize I'm standing right here?" I wondered aloud as he pulled Addison into his arms for a slow dance beneath the twinkling lights.

Because he either knew I was standing ten feet away and just didn't care that I had a front-row seat to everything, or he was too preoccupied with falling in love with perfect little Addison to notice me.

"Just stop watching them," Ava said when she noticed the way I was trying to burn Addison's perfectly curled blonde hair to a crisp with my jealous glare. "It's only going to make things worse."

But despite knowing I should do what my friend suggested, I couldn't make myself look away.

Because if Hunter was going to fall in love with someone else, seeing it firsthand would make my current feelings of denial harder to lean into later.

"Look away, Scarlett," Ava said more firmly when Hunter bent close to Addison's ear to say something.

What was he whispering to her?

Was he telling her she looked beautiful in her sleeveless maroon dress and that he liked the way it hugged her every curve?

Was he pressing his hand more firmly against her back the way he always did to me when we danced...his way to silently signal that he was still attracted to me even if we couldn't say the words aloud or make it too obvious to people around us?

"Scarlett." Ava touched my elbow to get my attention.

But when I didn't look away, she physically took my arms in her hands—using more strength than I thought she had—and swiveled me around so that my back was to the dance floor.

"Carter and Xander are on their way back here," Ava said in a soft voice. "And you owe it to yourself to have a good time."

"Yeah, like that's possible." I snorted.

"Fine, then don't have fun." She lifted her hands in the air. "I mean, I'm sure you and Hunter are above playing mind games with each other. But if I were in your shoes, I'd at least try to make it *seem* like I was having a good time. Let Hunter see that you're not just going to sit around and be sad as he flirts with someone else."

"Huh?" I furrowed my brow, not following.

"You're on a date with a freaking billionaire, Scarlett. One who is crazy hot and older, too," Ava said, like it should be obvious. "I bet Hunter is already sweating but just hiding it better than you. You know how he is. He is, like, the king of looking chill under pressure."

"You think so?"

"Yes," she said. "You're a freaking catch, Scarlett. If he's not already thinking that, it's time for you to *remind* him of what he can have with you."

"But how is that supposed to help anything?" I asked. "It's not like I can actually even date him right now." I glanced around us to make sure no one was eavesdropping before lowering my voice and saying, "Even if I could make him jealous of Xander, it's not like anything could happen with Hunter. My dad still has his rules."

"We graduate in less than four months. That's not that long, and you're worth waiting for," Ava said. "Focus on that tonight, and then we can set up plans for sabotaging Hunter and Addison in the morning if we need to."

———

"THIS IS A GREAT SONG," Xander said as we danced to "Lady in Red" by Chris DeBurgh thirty minutes later. "Don't you think?"

"Yeah, I like it," I said. The DJ was playing love ballads from the past several decades to go along with the dance's theme of "Romance Through the Ages." It was a song I'd only heard a few times before, but it was nice and had a great slow beat that was perfect for slow dancing.

And despite things being somewhat rocky the first hour at the dance, things were going a little better now.

Partly because of the plans Ava had suggested, where I stopped acting like a jealous ex and instead twist things around so that Hunter would assume I was having a great night, too.

And also partly because Xander was actually fun to talk to.

He was smart and witty, an engaging conversationalist. We had a lot of things in common—New York, The Fold, and the insatiable drive to be high achievers—so that gave us plenty of things to relate with.

The fact that he was also really attractive and had half the girls in the room turning their heads to steal glances at him might have also helped me feel slightly better about the night.

"I think this is actually the song my parents danced to when they got married," Xander said, bringing my thoughts back to the music we were swaying to.

"Really?" I asked, surprised a guy in his early twenties would even remember something like that.

"Pretty sure, at least." He lifted one shoulder in a shrug. "So it's kind of cool that we're dancing to it tonight."

"Well, that's cool you know that about your parents," I said. "I have no idea what song my parents danced to at theirs."

They hadn't exactly stayed married long enough for me to get to an age where I would even think to ask them such a question.

"Megan is your dad's second wife, right?" Xander asked.

"Yeah, they got married when I was ten," I said. "So she's been my stepmom for a while. But my mom lives just down the street from them since she wanted to be close by."

She actually lived in the same building as Hunter's family. And while Hunter and I hadn't been friends until coming to school here, it made it really nice now for hanging out together when I had my weekends with my mom.

In fact, Mr. and Mrs. Blackwell were actually the ones to tell my mom about Eden Falls Academy, since their oldest son Sebastian had attended the school and enjoyed it.

"I don't think I've met your mom," Xander said, his brow narrowing thoughtfully. "Did she stop attending our congregation when your parents divorced?"

"It was a little before that," I said, flushing a little since my mom's church inactivity was a little embarrassing to talk about. "She became inactive a year before they split."

Which was a big reason why their marriage had fallen apart. It was difficult to make a relationship work when you were on two different paths.

"Is that why they divorced then?" Xander guessed before quickly adding, "I only ask that because from what I hear, it's difficult to have a mixed-faith marriage."

"I think there were other reasons, but yes, it was a big part of it," I said.

There had been a lot of heated arguments late at night where my dad tried to get my mom to come back to The Fold. He'd say that my mom choosing to be a career woman was putting worldly thoughts in her head. It was making her selfish and conflicted with the example she was supposed to set as a pastor's wife—the example of a godly woman who knew that the most valuable thing she could pursue here on Earth was to raise me and help build up the kingdom of God.

Most of the women in The Fold were housewives—at least while their kids were young. So that was what he'd always planned for my mom to do. But she'd gone back to school when they found out they couldn't have any more kids, and she found she really enjoyed working outside the home.

But instead of those conversations bringing my mom back into strong activity like my dad had hoped, they had only pushed her further away. Further from him and further from the gospel.

I would like to think that deep down my mom still knew the church was true, but that run-in with the patriarchy had left her with a bad taste in her mouth for our religion.

And yet, I was still holding out hope that she'd return someday, because the thought of not having her with me in the next life was just something I couldn't accept.

"So your dad mentioned that you got accepted to Yale," Xander said, changing the subject. "Is that true?"

"It is." But before he could think that was the only school I was considering, I quickly added, "I was also offered a scholarship to Columbia, so I'm still trying to decide where to go."

I was leaning toward Columbia, since it was closer to home, and I liked knowing Hunter and Mack would be there. But I was also giving myself a little time to make sure before sending in my official decision.

"Well, if you don't mind hearing my totally unbiased opinion," he said with a wink.

"Since we both know someone who already attends Yale is unlikely to have a bias," I said with a smile.

"Naturally." He chuckled. "But I'd have to tell you that Yale is a great option. And aside from having great professors and some of the best courses, I think I heard there's also a pretty cool guy named Xander who goes there, too."

"Xander, you say?" I asked, playing along. "I think I might have heard that name before. But I thought for sure he was a senior this year. So I don't think that's much of a selling point because he'll be gone before I even get there."

"But didn't you hear?" he asked.

"Hear what?"

"That since he added Religious Studies as a second major, he's actually not going to graduate until next year. So he could definitely still show you the ropes."

"I guess I didn't realize that," I said. And even though we'd just been talking theoretically, I was suddenly worried that he was asking me to pick Yale because he was there.

I mean, we were getting along fine, but I didn't want to pick a college just because a cute guy my dad actually approved of went there.

If cute guys had any weight on my college decision at all, then Columbia would already have the acceptance letter from me because Hunter was going there.

"Do you have any ideas on what you'd like to major in?" Xander asked, not seeming to notice my hesitation.

"I've been thinking about journalism," I said. "Since I already have experience with the school newspaper and I'm pretty good at it. But I've also considered studying something like Family Life and Human Development. I figured something like that would be useful for raising a family."

"So you want to be a mom?" Xander's blue eyes lit up.

"Yeah." I shrugged. "I mean, don't most girls dream of that?"

"Not a lot of the girls I've been talking to lately. I mean, they talk about wanting a family later on. Like once they're settled in their careers and, like, thirty years old or something. But it's never in their plans for the near future."

"Don't they realize that they can't have more than one or two children if they start that late?" I asked.

"I don't think they want more than that. Which is why it's so refreshing to hear you're already planning for it."

Anyone listening to our conversation would think we were crazy. Talking about plans for our future families when we were only on a first date.

But since you dated to get married, it made sense to get expectations and future plans laid out from the start, so you didn't waste time falling in love with someone on a different life path.

Not that I was actually considering dating or falling in love with Xander. I was still hoping Hunter would be the next guy I dated.

And even if my hopes for Hunter and me didn't pan out the way I wanted, I was still in high school, obviously, and planning to wait until I'd at least finished my first year or two of college before settling down.

But maybe Xander was interested in pursuing me?

He did seem to have a pretty good idea of what he wanted in a future wife.

"Are you hoping to have a career like your mom does?" he asked. "Or do you think you'd rather be more like Megan and focus more on things at home?"

Did he have a list of questions memorized and was just checking them off?

Because if so, no wonder my dad had picked him as the guy for me to ask to the dance. Xander would be an ideal patriarch for a good family.

"Let me guess, you want the best of both worlds?" Xander asked when I didn't immediately answer his question.

"Not necessarily," I said. "I'm just thinking. These questions are a little deeper than I expected for a school dance."

"I guess you're right." He chuckled like he only just now realized how deep he was getting. "Sorry, people tell me I can be a little intense sometimes."

"It's okay. I actually prefer depth over small talk."

"So, what do you think?" Xander asked. "Career woman, stay-at-home mom, or a mix of both?"

I bit my lip. If he was trying to get my answer based on him being part of that future scenario, then me bringing in an income was something that would simply be for fun. I'd be working because I loved my job, not because I needed money.

But if he was asking just in general, if I were picturing myself married to someone else... Someone not quite at the billionaire level, then...

I sighed. "I think most people would expect me to say that I

want to be a career woman like my mom, since I've always been
pretty driven to succeed—"

"I'd expect nothing less than the best from a Caldwell,"
Xander agreed.

I nodded. "But I'm actually not sure what I would choose."
It was a question I'd wondered about a lot since I liked to be
challenged and feel like I was working toward something. But
you could do that as a mom too, right? Raising kids the right
way seemed like a big job all on its own.

Especially if you were going to have more than one or two.

Growing up, I'd always heard my dad say it was best to start
a family as soon as you could and have as many children as you
could feasibly manage so that they could be raised in a good
home with the gospel.

Putting that off until you were settled into a career was
considered selfish, since the Lord would always provide.

God was all about families, and even if my mom had set a
different example for me, the High Priest always said that the
most valuable thing a woman could do was to bear and nurture
her children.

Being too distracted by selfish and worldly desires would
just set a family up for disaster.

Hunter used to be on the same page as me with all of this
stuff, which was why I'd figured we'd be a good match.

But just last month, Hunter had mentioned something
about how his cousin Arie had said that waiting a few years to
have kids had been great for him and his wife's marriage. And
then there was that post he'd accidentally forwarded to me
when he'd been scrolling through some online forum—the one
from a woman with six kids who talked about having a difficult
time coming to terms with the fact that her family and religion
had pressured her into having six kids. Because now that she
had left whatever church she'd belonged to, she felt tricked

into taking on more children than she would have had otherwise.

But those people were all raising their children outside of the gospel, so I wouldn't actually put a lot of trust in their judgement regarding something like that.

"How many kids do you think you want?" Xander asked, bringing me back from my thoughts. The song was coming to an end, so he probably wanted to get all his questions out before a faster song started and we went to hang out with my friends.

"I think maybe three or four," I said. "That way, they can all be best friends."

"Sounds like we have similar ideas," Xander said with a wink. "Maybe we're more compatible than we knew."

My body warmed with his words, and as I studied his face, I briefly wondered if he had gotten even better-looking over the past few minutes.

Was it possible that having so many things in common was helping to knock down some of the walls I'd had up earlier? That after opening up a little, I was actually able to see him for who he was versus seeing him for who he wasn't—my current best friend.

The song came to an end. As Xander escorted me to where my friends were gathering in the middle of the dance floor, I allowed myself to wonder if my dad had some better insights about my right match than I'd originally given him credit for.

The night continued to go well as I let myself just live in this moment and not worry about where any of us would stand after tonight. Hunter and I made eye contact a few times across the circle, and there were some moments when I wondered if he was going to steal that dance he'd talked about stealing. But whenever a new slow song would start and our dates pulled us away to dance, I figured it was probably for the best.

Hunter and I didn't have to dance at *every* dance our senior year.

When the DJ announced that he'd be playing the last song of the night and "You Are in Love" by Taylor Swift started playing through the speakers, my stomach twisted up in knots and my mood instantly shifted.

Because just like Xander had talked about his parents' wedding song, this song belonged to Hunter and me.

Just stay in the moment, Scarlett, I told myself as Xander pulled me close to him. *Don't think about anything.*

But even though I tried to keep myself in the present, right here at the dance with Xander, as the intro played and Taylor started singing the gentle lyrics of the first verse, I couldn't keep the memories from streaming back.

It was like a music video was ready to instantly play in my mind whenever this song came on. And before I could stop them, all my favorite moments from last year's spring break started flitting across my mind.

The movie nights cuddled up with Hunter on my mom's couch.

The long walks in Central Park where we held hands and chatted about our dreams for life after high school.

The breathless dash to the private rooftop above Hunter's penthouse where we made-out for hours after keeping our hormones in check all day.

So many amazing memories passed through my mind before stopping on the one memory specific to this song—the night Hunter and I had lain side by side on his bed and he told me he had a song he wanted me to listen to.

I could still see everything so vividly. Knew exactly what clothes we'd been wearing as he pulled out his phone and opened it to a playlist he'd titled *Scarlett and Hunter.*

Yes...he was the type of guy to take the time to do something like that.

He'd scrolled down the playlist, through several songs that we'd listened to together, and then clicked on one I wasn't familiar with.

But even though I'd never heard this song before, as Taylor sang just the first few lines, I knew it was perfect. It was calming and romantic—a song about small moments that might seem ordinary to anyone not paying close attention, but when put all together made up a beautiful love story.

Hunter and I had just lain there, watching each other as we listened to the melody and lyrics that completely captured the slow and steady growth of a friendship blooming into a romance.

And as the song detailed all the different experiences the couple had together that told them they were in love, I also knew it was the same for Hunter and me.

Because even though we never got the chance to say the words aloud before breaking up, I knew it had been love.

I blinked my eyes shut, urging the memories to just stop. To wait until I was back in my room, so no one would see the way this song made me want to cry.

But the memory of how Hunter had looked deeply into my eyes before pulling me close and kissing me on the forehead only became more vivid with my eyes closed, so I forced myself to open them again.

That was a mistake. Because when I looked past Xander's shoulder and saw who was dancing right behind him, I found Hunter staring right back at me.

When our eyes locked, my heart squeezed hard in my chest because he was looking at me the same way he'd looked at me that night on his bed.

Like he loved me.

I knew I should look away, to not add any more memories of Hunter to go along with this song. But since this was the first time all night where neither of our dates could see Hunter and me watching each other, I just let myself stare—to hungrily rake in the beautiful boy with chestnut-brown hair and green eyes who looked amazing in his navy-blue suit and tie.

For just a moment, I let myself imagine it was Hunter with whom I was dancing. That it was *his* jawline that my temple rested against. *His* hands that wrapped around my waist. *His* shoulders my hands rested on.

And as his gaze only seemed to get more intense as Addison pulled herself closer to him, I wondered if he was doing the same in his mind. If he was imagining it was me he was holding, and we were back to that night in his room.

He had to be feeling the same things as I was, right?

It had to be just as hard to see me dancing with Xander as it was for me to see him with Addison. I couldn't be the only one feeling this.

The music swelled as the final chorus played. Hunter pressed his lips together, like he had something he wanted to say to me.

What does he want to say? I wondered, holding my breath.

After three more heart-pounding seconds, he met my gaze again and mouthed what looked like the words, "*I wish...*" before stopping and closing his mouth again.

Even though my heart had been pounding hard before, it now felt like it was going to beat right out of my chest because I wanted to know what he had almost said.

Did he wish he was dancing with me?

Did he wish we could be together?

Or did he wish we'd never dated in the first place because everything was so much harder now?

I watched him as he looked down at the wooden floor, like he just might need a moment to think over the words.

Words were powerful, and Hunter was someone who knew that better than most people.

After studying the dance floor for a few seconds and giving his head a slight shake, Hunter met my gaze again and mouthed, *"You look beautiful tonight."* Then after a short pause, he added what looked like, *"And I wish I'd stolen that dance with you."*

Even though I knew that I shouldn't, I clung to those words. I repeated them in his voice in my mind so they could be burned in there forever. Because after the long and confusing day that I'd had, I needed to know that he still found me beautiful.

And since I didn't want him to be the only one to be vulnerable tonight, I mouthed back, *"I wish you'd stolen it, too."*

13

HUNTER

"WHICH GIRL ARE you ordering flowers for today?" Asher asked, breaking the silence in our room and startling me from my deep thoughts. "Addison or Scarlett?"

I looked behind me, surprised that Asher was awake this early on a Sunday morning. It was nine o'clock on the day after the Valentine's dance, and I had just finished writing up *The Confidant's* column in our dorm room—opting to skip my trip to The Brew since I'd needed some extra sleep this morning.

"I was thinking about getting a Valentine's Gram for Scarlett." I glanced at the online order form that I'd just brought up on my computer. Today was the very last day to order them since tomorrow was the actual Valentine's Day and the florist would need time to put together the last-minute orders. "But I'm trying to figure out a way to do that without offending Addison."

I actually wanted to take Scarlett on a real date with dinner and some other romantic activity—something that might make up for not stealing that dance last night—but since that wasn't allowed, I figured flowers were the next best thing.

"So, I'm guessing that wistful smile I saw on your face during the last dance wasn't because of your date?" Asher asked.

"No." I sighed, my mind going back to the last song where Scarlett and I had seemed to have a moment as we'd danced with other people. "That particular smile was for someone else."

Someone who I hoped would be happy to get things back to normal now that the Valentine's dance was in the past.

"Addison and I had a good time together," I added when he looked confused. "But I don't see us being anything more than friends."

In fact, I might be crazy, but I was pretty sure I'd caught her staring at Evan quite a few times last night.

Which was kind of strange.

Like, I knew they were just *step*-siblings—so not blood-related—and she'd said that he'd been best friends with her brother before their parents got married. But it would be weird if she had a crush on him, right?

I pushed the thought away. Maybe I was imagining it.

Or maybe there was something else going on there that I didn't know about.

"You could send the flowers anonymously," Asher suggested, sitting up straighter on his bed and combing a hand through his tousled dark-brown hair. "Maybe use a code name that only Scarlett would understand. That way, if she gets them delivered during a class she has with Addison, Addison might not figure out who they're from and feel bad."

"You think that would work?" I asked, skeptical of his idea since pretty much everyone at school knew my history with Scarlett well enough to guess that I would be the one sending her flowers anonymously.

"It might." He stood from his bed and pulled a white T-shirt over his head like he was getting ready to head down to the great hall for breakfast. "Or you could just deliver them yourself."

Which would bring me back to my first problem of trying to avoid doing things that would make Scarlett's dad think we were sneaking around behind his back again.

We still didn't know who had reported us to him.

"I'll probably just send them from 'Anonymous Cool Guy' or something like that," I said.

"Good plan," Asher said. "Though, it might make her think they're from me since I'm clearly the coolest guy at our school."

"Obviously." I chuckled. "Which will only get people further off my trail, right?"

"Right." He smiled for a second, but then got a thoughtful look on his face. "You know what would throw even more people off your scent?"

"No."

"If I changed the name on my order for Elyse to 'Anonymous Cool Guy' too." He smirked. "Then everyone will wonder which scoundrel is going after both of our girls."

"Oh the drama." I laughed. "And now you have to do it."

"I think I will," he said. "Gotta keep the romance alive somehow."

I doubted they needed any help keeping the romance alive. From what I'd seen of them together the past month and a half, things seemed to be going very well. But I could understand wanting to add a little fun into the mix from time to time.

After he left, I turned back to my computer to look over the different bouquet options on my screen. The first option was for the traditional long-stemmed red rose. You could either order a single red rose, a bundle of three roses, or a bouquet with a dozen. Most people would probably pick one of those options because roses were a symbol of romantic love and what most girls would hope to receive on Valentine's Day.

But I had actually been eyeing a different kind of bouquet. One with a mix of pink peonies, white carnations, and lavender. In the past, Scarlett had preferred the variety ones rather than the traditional red roses, so I figured they would be what she'd want out of these options.

They were also offering boxes of chocolates as an add-on, but since I didn't want to go too overboard, I just added the flowers to the cart and checked out.

Now I just had to wait and see how she would react to receiving flowers from 'Anonymous Cool Guy' after going on a date with a super-rich billionaire heir.

"SO HOW MANY girlfriends do you have right now?" I turned to my friend Nash after taking my seat in AP Chemistry the next day.

Nash sat directly behind me. From the *one, two, three, four, five...six* red roses and three boxes of chocolates he had sitting on the table in front of him, I guessed that his fan club had only grown larger over the past week.

"None, officially," Nash said, glancing down at his spoils for the day. "But it probably doesn't look like that."

"It definitely looks like you have a lot of options, at least," I said. "When you're ready, that is."

"I guess so," he said, sounding less enthusiastic than I thought someone with so many admirers would be.

But when his gaze drifted over to the other side of the room where Elyse and Asher were sitting, I realized why he might be feeling a little down.

Apparently, the feelings he'd had for Elyse hadn't quite disappeared when she picked Asher over him in December.

"Just pretend you didn't see that, okay?" Nash said, seeming to realize that he'd been wearing his emotions on his sleeve. "As far as everyone is supposed to know, I got over that crush a while ago."

"I didn't see a thing."

How could I think of him being unable to flip a switch on his feelings after a month and a half as a bad thing when I was still holding out for Scarlett after almost a year?

Speaking of Scarlett...

I sat up straighter when I noticed her step into the classroom. I hadn't seen her since second period because she had a house-captain meeting during lunch. But man, she looked beautiful today. Her auburn hair was down and curled. And while she wore her usual school uniform—the girls were wearing the pink and beige ones today in honor of Valentine's Day—there was something different about how it looked on her compared to everyone else. The pink tones next to her reddish hair made her glow just a little more.

"Hey," she said, taking her seat beside me and setting down her things.

"Hi," I said.

I noticed something red out of the corner of my eye, so I turned to see what she had just placed on the table.

In addition to coming in with the bouquet of flowers I'd sent anonymously—which must have been delivered to her sometime between second period and now—she also had an oversized bouquet of red roses.

Someone else sent her flowers?

"You got two bouquets?" I asked, feeling slightly threatened and jealous as the blood drained from my face.

"I did." She nodded, her cheeks turning a darker color of

pink. "The pink bouquet is from someone who calls himself 'Anonymous Cool Guy' and the other is from Xander."

"*Xander?*" My voice came out sounding strangled.

How did he know about the Valentine's Grams? Had she told him about it and hinted that she wanted flowers from him?

I knew we hadn't really had a chance to talk after the dance —she'd been with her mom yesterday and we had a test in our class this morning—but I'd thought for sure that our little moment during the last song had meant something.

"That's what the card said, anyway." She tucked a lock of hair behind her ear. "He must have seen one of the posters on the wall," she said, her brown eyes wide. "I think there was one by the bathrooms. Maybe he thought I'd like some flowers and ordered one from that?"

"I guess that makes sense," I said, hating that I wasn't better at hiding my jealousy. "Looks like he ordered the biggest one, too."

"He did..." she said before quickly adding, "But as pretty as they are, I think I like the pink bouquet better." She cleared her throat. "I know red roses are supposed to symbolize romance and love at first sight or something like that. But..." She met my gaze, a meaningful look in her brown eyes. "As you know, my favorite color is pink, and so this bouquet means a little more because only someone who really knew me would know to send it."

My body warmed slightly with her words. "Yeah?"

"Yes." She lifted the bouquet I'd given her and inhaled the scent. "They smell better, too."

"I'm glad you think so."

I glanced around the classroom to make sure Addison wasn't sitting in her seat already and possibly overhearing our conversation.

Neither she nor Evan were at their usual table yet, so I

lowered my voice and said, "I know doing something tonight is probably out of the question. But..." I swallowed, my heart pounding hard in my chest because I hadn't thought this through enough to find an eloquent way to say it. "But I was wondering if you wanted to go to dinner and a movie this Saturday."

I hadn't exactly planned to ask her that, but if Xander was trying to move in on her, I needed to do something now. Waiting and being patient was no longer an option.

I might lose her for real if I kept doing what I'd been doing all year.

"Dinner and a movie?" she asked, her expression somewhat startled. As if she hadn't expected me to ask her to do something so date-like after so many months of just "hanging out." "Like, at a restaurant and movie theater back in New York?"

"Yes." I nodded. When she got a hesitant look in her eyes, I added, "Your dad only said you couldn't *steady* date, right? Steady dating typically means going on several *consecutive* dates with the same person—not that you can never go on a date with someone. As long as they're not consecutive dates..."

I held my breath as I watched her work through this new go-around that I was offering. This loophole would work if she went on a date with someone else in-between our dates...

It wasn't ideal, but she'd given me all the signs that she still wanted something with me, right?

I hadn't been reading things completely wrong, had I?

She bit her lip, and I could see the way she was rationalizing everything in her head.

"If your dad asks where you're going, you can just say we are hanging out," I offered, my chest feeling tight as I worried she might turn me down.

Though...if he was still holding onto the same feelings that he'd had after our last interview, just knowing Scarlett was hanging out with an apostate with no other friends around would probably have his guard up.

Maybe that was why she was hesitating? Maybe she knew her dad put up with us hanging out at school because we had the whole forced-proximity thing going, but when we were back in New York, he wanted her to keep her distance...

Addison and Evan walked into the room a second later. When Addison looked at me for a moment and smiled, Scarlett seemed to reflexively reach for the bouquet I'd given her.

Like she was feeling territorial over the flowers and worried Addison might try to snatch them away from her.

I smiled back at Addison in as friendly of a way as I could, while reminding myself at the same time that I shouldn't feel guilty for sending Scarlett flowers and asking her on a date two days after the dance with Addison.

I mean, it wasn't like Addison even needed to know about it right now, anyway. With the way things were with Scarlett's dad, I was sure she'd be fine keeping a possible date on the down-low.

Addison and Evan walked to their seats kitty-corner from us, and the bell rang. Just before Mr. Park could start teaching today's chemistry lesson, Scarlett leaned close to my ear and whispered, "I would love to go on a date with you this weekend."

14

SCARLETT

"STILL OBSESSED WITH *THE CONFIDANT,* I see."
Hunter leaned closer to look at my phone screen on Saturday
morning. We were riding the train home, and I was doing some
catching up on *The Confidant*'s column from last week.

"I'm not obsessed with her," I said, gently bumping my
shoulder to his. "I just think she has good ideas."

I'd been so busy with school and basketball all week that I
hadn't had a chance to check her column for last Sunday until
now. And when I saw that she had done a column completely
dedicated to love advice in honor of it being Valentine's week, I
was jealous that I hadn't had the idea myself.

Sure, I was only a couple of weeks into writing as *Dear
Eliza*, so I couldn't be too hard on myself for not coming up
with all these great ideas when I was still learning how to even
run an advice column. But it would have been nice to feel like I
was somewhat closer to beating her in this competition she
didn't know I was in with her.

"Whatever," Hunter said, pushing back against my shoulder. "I think you have a big ol' journalistic crush on her."

"Okay, fine, you got me." I laughed. "I have a big crush on *The Confidant*."

Though not as big as the crush I have on you.

Which was getting way harder to ignore since he'd asked me on a date tonight.

Yes, I had an actual date with Hunter, and I barely stopped smiling all week because of it.

"Speaking of your crush." Hunter raised an eyebrow, and for a terrifying moment, I worried I might have just spoken my thoughts aloud. But then he said, "Are you any closer to figuring out who she is?"

I calmed down. He was talking about my journalistic crush and not my real-life, love crush.

"Not really." I slipped my phone back into my pocket and swiveled on my seat to look at him better. "I've been trying to narrow it down, though, and I've decided that she has to be at least a sophomore since she started writing the column last year."

"That's probably a good guess," he said, a thoughtful look on his face. "And you still think it's a girl?"

"Pretty sure." I shrugged. "I mean, no offense, but I don't think many high school guys are in tune with their emotions enough to give the kind of advice that she does."

Not most of the guys I'd met, anyway.

"*...she says to a high school guy,*" Hunter narrated in a sarcastic tone. I realized he thought I was including him in that generalization.

"You know I wasn't saying that about you." I gave him an apologetic look. "Like, we both know that if any guy *could* be *The Confidant*, it would be you."

Seriously. With how helpful he'd been with *Dear Eliza*, I was pretty sure he could take the reins from me and be every bit as good as *The Confidant*.

Maybe even better, actually, since he was just amazing and insightful like that.

"Well, it's good to know that you find me superior to all the other high school guys that you know," he said with a wink.

Normally, I wasn't a fan of the whole flirtatious wink thing, but from Hunter?

Yeah, it was hot.

But I was pretty sure he could be rolling around in a puddle of mud right now and I'd still find him overwhelmingly attractive.

And I have a date with him tonight! Eek!

Sure, I was slightly paranoid that my dad would somehow find out tonight was a date instead of just two buddies hanging out, but I hadn't looked forward to something like this for sooo long that even if I did get in trouble, it would be worth it.

"So you've narrowed down your suspects' list to include only the female population at our school," Hunter said, narrowing his green eyes at me. "But have you figured out what grade she'd be in? Aside from being at least a sophomore?"

"Most likely a senior," I said with a shrug.

Again for maturity level reasons.

"Ever wondered if it's a teacher?" He arched a dark eyebrow.

Hunter had nice eyebrows. Dark and just the perfect size and shape for framing his beautiful face.

Eyebrows were probably a weird thing to be attracted to. But I loved his and how he was always so expressive with them.

Like how he's looking at me right now, like I've completely zoned out.

Which yep, I'd gotten so distracted by his handsome face that I forgot what we were talking about.

"What did you say again?" I asked, feeling a little sheepish.

The half-smile on his face told me he knew he'd just

dazzled me again. "I just wondered whether you've ever considered a teacher actually being the mastermind behind *The Confidant.*"

Oh, that's right.

"I've never considered that," I said before I could get distracted by the slight dimple showing on his face. "But that would be kind of hilarious. And also a really big possibility, since it's definitely someone more mature than a lot of the kids at school."

"Might need to add all the teachers' names to your list then," he said. "And maybe also consider a few of the more *mature* guys, too..." He winked again. Man, he might need to stop doing that if we wanted all the people on the subway to think we were just two friends headed home on a school break.

"Let me just get my notebook." I pretended to pull a notebook and pen from my invisible backpack and jot down a list of names.

He asked, "Do you think anyone is wondering about who *Dear Eliza* is in the same way you wonder about *The Confidant?*"

"I hope so," I said, forgetting my imaginary list of suspects and looking up at him. "Because if we can cause as much of a mystery around that and make people wonder who she is, we might have a chance at dethroning *The Confidant.*"

He looked like he wanted to say something about my plans to dethrone the advice-column queen, but then the subway pulled to a stop and there were suddenly a dozen people getting on and off the train.

I turned my legs to the side to let people pass by. The subway doors closed again, and we were just about to head to the next stop when Hunter noticed an elderly woman standing a few feet away, looking for a seat.

I glanced around to see if there were any available spots, but all the seats were taken.

Hunter must have seen the same thing because before I could say anything, he was standing up and offering his seat to the woman.

And even though it looked like she was trying to refuse him at first, the relief on her face told me she was grateful for his kindness.

Hunter helped her to the seat, and when the train started moving again, he grabbed the handrail a few feet away to steady himself.

And even though he was wearing a baseball cap with his letterman jacket over his white hoodie, he might as well have been wearing shining armor right then.

HUNTER and I made eye contact and faces at each other for the rest of the ride. When it was time to get off at our stop, I took a chance and looped my arm through his just because I wanted to be close to him.

I never did things like this at school because I was always worried someone would report us to my dad. But since this was New York City—one of the easiest places in the world to blend in—I left my usual reservations behind and just let myself do what I actually wanted for a change.

When Hunter covered my hand with his and looked down at me with a quiet smile on his face, it felt better than Christmas morning.

It felt like the good parts of spring break all over again.

Hunter walked me to my dad's house. After planning to meet him outside the church gates at six—we didn't want to risk getting caught together—I spent the afternoon playing board games with my dad and Megan.

My dad and Megan were both in their sixties—my mom had been much younger than my dad when they'd gotten married. So he and my stepmom lived life at a slower pace than the rest of the world—yet another reason why things hadn't worked out between him and my modern-thinking mom.

"I heard from Xander a couple of days ago," Dad said after moving his game piece—the shoe—around the board and dropping it on Boardwalk. "He told me you two had a good time at that school dance of yours."

"He did?" I asked, trying to keep my face neutral as I picked up the dice.

My dad didn't know about my plans with Hunter tonight, so if I didn't want to tip him off to anything, I needed to be careful with my reactions.

"Did you have a good time with him?" Dad asked, his brown eyes seeming to be searching my face for clues across the table from me.

"It was fine," I said with a non-committal shrug. I knew my dad probably wanted me to say that the date had been fantastic since he was the one who had arranged it.

But I was still living on a high from walking arm and arm with Hunter this morning and had felt nothing like that from a whole night of dancing with his billionaire intern, so my dad was just going to have to be fine with disappointment.

I picked up my game piece—the thimble—and counted seven spots on the Monopoly board to land on Pennsylvania Avenue.

"That will be fifty-six dollars," Megan said after checking the amount of rent I owed for landing on her property.

I pulled the blue and white bills out of my cash stash to pay her, and after organizing the money in her own stockpile, she took her turn.

As Megan made her way around the board, my dad cleared his throat and said, "Well, I hope you will take the time to get to know the lad better. He comes from a really good family and has a really good head on his shoulders."

"Sure," I said, even though I didn't really have plans to continue getting to know Xander.

He went to Yale; I was leaning toward Columbia. It wasn't likely that we'd have a reason to spend much time together in the near future.

Dad took his turn. After seeming to think for a moment, he said, "I should probably tell you that I've invited Xander to Sunday dinner tomorrow."

"What?" I looked up from the board.

Dad nodded. "He's in town for the weekend, just like you, and I thought it would be a good chance for you to continue the friendship you've started."

"Why?" I asked. Why was it so important to my dad that I get to know Xander better?

Dad got the stern and serious look in his eyes that he sometimes got. In a low voice, he said, "Because it's time you started spending more time with people on the right path, Scarlett."

"What do you mean by that?" I asked.

Dad sighed. "You've been spending a lot of time with the non-members at that school of yours, and while I have always supported you being a good example to those without the gospel, there does come a time when you need to surround yourself with other like-minded people."

"My friends aren't bad people," I tried to say. They might not believe the same things as me, but they all had great hearts and were about doing good things.

"I know they have been good friends while you've been at

school," Dad said. "But you need to look to the future. You'll be graduating soon. Getting married. Starting a family. You know just as well as I do that you won't find someone among your current circle who can give you the life you want and need."

Which meant, he probably knew Hunter was skipping church and Bible class if he was including him among the group of people who couldn't give me that life.

Which also means that I really can't let him find out that I'm going on a date with Hunter tonight.

"So will you give Xander a chance to get to know you better?" Dad asked when I didn't say anything.

And since I was all about keeping the peace when it came to my dad, I nodded and said, "Of course."

Just let me have one night where I didn't think about any of that stuff first.

15

SCARLETT

HEY, *Dad. I just had a friend from church invite me to hang out at her house. Be back at eleven?*

I practiced the words in my head as I paced around my room. It was five-thirty and I'd changed into a pink blouse with textured polka dots that I knew was Hunter's favorite.

I'd also curled my hair and took extra care on my makeup.

I'd even given myself a spritz of the perfume Hunter always complimented me on.

The only thing I hadn't done to get ready for my date, though, was to get the actual go-ahead to leave the house.

When I was at school, I could basically come and go as I pleased on the weekends, as long as I was back by curfew. But even though I was technically an adult at eighteen years old, whenever I was staying at my dad's house, I was back to needing permission to go anywhere.

I paced the rug in my upstairs room some more.

Hey Dad, I practiced again, *so there is this really cool new movie that I wanted to see—it's rated G, of course—so I'll just see you guys later? I might also grab dinner while I'm out. Be back by curfew?*

He'd believe I would go see a movie by myself, right?

My phone buzzed with a text from Hunter. **Excited to see you. Still okay to meet me at the gate at 6?**

Ah! That was only thirty minutes away.

Me: **I still haven't told my dad about my plans for the night...**

Hunter: **You might need to get on that then...**

Hunter: **That is, if you're still up for everything.**

Me: **I'm up for it.**

Seriously. I hadn't been so excited for a Saturday night in months.

Me: **Just trying to find a way to word it without lying...**

Hunter: **You can't go with the "hanging out with Hunter" plan?**

Me: **Probably not.**

Not after what my dad said about spending my time with people on the straight and narrow—

"Scarlett?" Dad called from the other side of my door, followed by a light knock.

"Yes?" I asked, my voice coming out at a higher pitch than usual.

"I just got a call from Brother Morris," he said. "Sister Morris is going through a hard time and has asked for a blessing."

I opened my bedroom door and saw that my dad had changed into a white shirt and tie.

"You're heading out?" I asked.

Don't look too excited. Act cool. Nothing to see here.

"Yes. Megan wanted to come along, too, since she and Sister Morris are close."

Even better...

"Okay." I nodded.

"We might be gone for a couple of hours. Will you be okay without us?"

"Um, sure." I glanced around my room like I was trying to come up with something to do...even though I was obviously way more dressed up than I'd been during board games this afternoon. "There's actually a new movie that I was hoping to see while I was in town. So I think I'll find out what time it's showing and head out. Maybe grab something to eat."

That didn't sound suspicious, right?

My dad studied me, like he thought there might be more that I wasn't saying. But since I'd never been one to get into trouble, he said, "Just be back by curfew."

"Will do."

He took a step away from the door. Just when it looked like he was going to leave and I could relax again, he turned back and said, "You know, if you wanted someone to go to the movies with, you might try Xander."

Man, my dad was set on something happening with his summer intern, wasn't he?

"Oh, um," I said, scrambling for a way to say that I wasn't interested in that option. I couldn't exactly say I was already going with someone after making it seem like I was going alone. After a few heart-pounding seconds, I settled with, "It's kind of a really girly movie. I'm not sure a guy in his twenties would be too excited to watch something like this."

"You never know." My dad shrugged. "Xander might surprise you."

"I'll think about it."

Dad hovered in the doorway for a few seconds longer, like

he wanted to say something else. Then turning back to me he asked, "Are you taking your pepper spray?"

"It's in my bag." I gestured to my crossbody bag on the bed. "So I'll be safe."

The pepper spray was a gift that my anxiety-prone dad had given me for my eighteenth birthday, since the streets of New York could be dangerous at night.

The small aerosol can had basically sat at the bottom of my bag ever since I'd put it there last month, because I was usually with Hunter when I was out and about.

But it was nice to have it there just in case.

"Good." He sighed, seeming relieved. "And you know how to use it?"

"I think so." It was pretty intuitive, but I'd watched a few YouTube videos on it anyway.

My dad nodded at my bag and said, "Well, be safe then. And enjoy your movie."

HUNTER WAS WAITING for me by the church gates at six just like he said. Instead of the hoodie and baseball cap he'd been wearing earlier, he had a maroon T-shirt on that I'd never seen him wear before, and jeans.

The kind of jeans that made his butt look way too good.

Stop thinking about his butt.

I made my gaze move back up to the upper half of his body, and then I noticed that his reddish-brown hair was shorter than it had been this morning.

"Did you get a haircut?" I asked, inspecting the short, trendy new hairstyle he had. He never let his hair get too shaggy—he had sensory issues with his hair touching his face—

so there wasn't a huge difference. But since I'd been staring at him all week, it was noticeable to me.

And it looked good.

Hot.

Dare I say, sexy?

Okay, no, I wouldn't dare say the word *sexy* aloud since I was still afraid of getting my mouth washed out with soap for saying no-no words like that. But he looked good. Really, really good.

"I thought it would be nice to clean things up a bit." He pushed his hands into the pockets of his jeans, seeming bashful. "Does it look okay?"

"It looks great," I said. And because I wanted today to be different from just two best friends hanging out, I added, "You look really handsome, actually."

"Handsome?" The word sounded as weird coming out of his mouth as it had from mine.

"Too old-sounding?" I asked, scrunching up my nose.

"Just a bit." He chuckled. "But I'm glad you think I'm handsome." He let his gaze travel the length of me, and after making my body grow warm everywhere his gaze went, he said, "You look really good tonight, too."

Even though this wasn't the first time he'd ever complimented me on how I looked, butterflies took flight in my stomach with the way he said it and with how he was looking at me.

"Shall we go?" he asked after I continued to remain speechless.

"Y-yes," I said.

"This way then." He gestured to the sidewalk outside the church gates.

And as we strolled down the sidewalk toward The Imperial

Grill—my favorite Indian restaurant within walking distance—
Hunter slipped his hand into mine.

"This okay?" he asked, looking down at our intertwined
hands briefly before meeting my eyes.

"It's perfect," I said, feeling breathless for some reason.

Tonight was going to be perfect.

"THAT WAS SO GOOD," I said to Hunter after we left the
restaurant with our stomachs full.

"They always get me with the naan, so I felt bad that I
couldn't finish my entrée," Hunter said. "But it was amazing as
usual."

When we'd first gotten to the restaurant, I'd been slightly
anxious since a couple from church were sitting just one
section over from us—I was worried I might get caught on my
forbidden date with Hunter.

I didn't think most people at church knew exactly how
strict my dad was about me steady dating anyone while in high
school, but if they happened to see me and Hunter together,
they might mention it to my dad at church tomorrow and I
would be in so much trouble.

They left about halfway through our dinner without
seeming to notice us though, so I'd been able to relax and just
have a good time chatting and laughing with Hunter after that.

"So, what movie are we going to see?" I asked as we walked
toward the movie theater down the street. "Did you already
have one in mind? Or is it supposed to be a surprise?"

"I thought about ordering our tickets beforehand, since you
know I can read your mind and know exactly what type of
movie you're in the mood for." He winked. "But I wasn't sure
how long dinner would take and I didn't want to feel like we

were in a rush, so I figured we could just pick a movie when we get there."

"Works for me."

We walked into the movie theater on the corner a few minutes later. After scanning over the list of showtimes, we decided on the latest Justin Banks movie.

"How can I help you?" the guy behind the ticket counter asked when Hunter and I stepped up.

"We'd like two tickets to *The Resident,*" Hunter said.

The movie theater employee tapped on the screen in front of him. After checking it over for a second, he frowned and said, "Looks like we only have a few seats left in this showing and they aren't together."

"Really?" Hunter asked.

"Yeah," the ticket guy said, swiveling the screen around so we could see it for ourselves. "There's a seat on row J and another right behind it. But that's the closest I could get you."

"Dang." Hunter looked at me apologetically. "Guess I should have ordered the tickets earlier after all."

"Do you want to pick a different show?" the ticket guy asked. "Or wait until the next showing at nine fifteen?"

"What do you think?" Hunter asked me. "Does anything else look good?"

I scanned the list again. The only shows that would be coming up in the next thirty minutes were rated R—which I wasn't allowed to watch—or little kid movies.

"I'm not really interested in any of the other movies," I said.

"Do you want to come back for the nine-fifteen one then?" Hunter asked.

"I have to be home by eleven, so I don't think I'll have time to watch that."

Hunter sighed, seeming disappointed that things weren't working out for the movie. He turned to the theater employee and said, "I guess we'll just have to try again another night. Thank you."

"Sure," the guy said. "Enjoy the rest of your evening."

"So what should we do now?" I asked as we walked toward the exit.

"If you're still in the mood for a movie, we could go back to my house and watch something there," he said. "My parents are at a charity event tonight, so it will be just us..."

Just us, alone at Hunter's parents' house?

Um, why hadn't he mentioned that option earlier? Because watching a movie alone with Hunter—where no one would be watching us, and I could relax and sit close—maybe, just maybe a kiss might happen.

"Let's do that," I said, the words coming out a little too eager.

"You like that idea?" he asked.

I nodded. "Yes, that sounds great."

16

HUNTER

"IS THERE a particular movie you'd like to watch?" I asked Scarlett as we rode the private elevator that would take us up to the top floor of our building. "You know, aside from that Justin Banks one we were too late to see."

"I'm kind of in the mood for a classic. Maybe *You've Got Mail*," she said, biting her lip as she met my gaze. "Does that sound okay?"

"That sounds good."

I squeezed her hand and tried really hard not to read into the reasons why she would suggest a movie we'd both seen a dozen times.

Well-loved movies were the perfect set up for doing other things. You already knew the movie well enough that you usually didn't mind missing parts if you suddenly got distracted by something...

I shook my head. *Don't get your hopes up, Hunter.*

Just because Scarlett agreed to a date and we were going to actually have some time where we were finally, completely alone without other eyes around to report our every move, it did not automatically mean that she was planning to kiss me again.

I needed to just chill and be okay with whatever happened tonight, instead of setting myself up for disappointment.

Because really, just standing close and holding Scarlett's hand right now was a win.

The elevator stopped and opened up to my parents' penthouse. I flicked on the lights in the small entryway and we both sat on the bench to take off our shoes. Then I asked, "Do you want any popcorn?" Even though I wasn't hungry at all.

At least...not hungry for food. I was definitely craving something else, though.

"I'm good," Scarlett said. "I am a little thirsty after that walk. Could I have a glass of water, please?"

"Sure." As I led her down the tiled hall toward the kitchen my parents had just had completely redone, I tried not to think about how I'd been thirsty in a different way for about ten months.

Don't get your hopes up, Hunter.

We each drank a glass full of water in the kitchen. After refilling our glasses, we carried them into the open living area that was attached to the kitchen and dining room.

"When did you say your parents would be back?" Scarlett set her glass on one of the coasters my mom had bought on a recent trip to Spain before taking a seat on the cream-colored couch.

"They usually don't get back from these charity dinners until after midnight." I set my glass next to hers and grabbed the TV remote from the drawer in the cocktail table.

"So we have a couple of hours then," she said.

"Yep."

To watch a movie. You're only counting on watching a movie...

I stayed standing while I turned on the TV, trying to figure out in my head how close I should sit to Scarlett on the couch.

She was sitting on the middle cushion, which was where she usually sat when we watched movies at my house in the past. But should I hug the arm rest like she usually did whenever we watched *The Office* back at school?

Or should I just kind of plop down right next to her?

"You planning to sit?" She looked up at me expectantly.

"Yeah, of course." *I'm just over here overthinking everything because I don't want to mess this up.*

But when she patted the cushion next to her, I made the split-second decision to just sit in the middle of that cushion.

Not too close to the arm rest, not close enough to Scarlett.

"So you said *You've Got Mail?*" I asked, hoping to sound nonchalant as I opened the movie-streaming service.

"Unless you were hoping to watch something new."

"You know I can't get enough of that banter between Kathleen Kelly and Joe Fox."

"Me either." She smiled, and even though we'd already spent an hour and a half together, I still couldn't get over how beautiful she looked tonight.

Man, I really hoped I didn't mess anything up.

17

SCARLETT

THIS IS PERFECT.

Hunter and I were about halfway through one of my all-time favorite movies. At first, we had sat stiffly next to each other during the first ten minutes, but then Hunter put his arm around me and we settled in comfortably on the couch.

It was so nice being close to him like this again. He felt good. Smelled good.

We were walking the tricky line between friendship and possibly going back to something more... and it felt amazing.

Like I was finally back to where I was supposed to be all along.

Next to Hunter, cuddled up on his parents' couch as he lightly traced patterns along my arm.

I'd forgotten how much I enjoyed his light touch and how it sent chills racing all the way from the top of my head and down to my toes.

He stroked his finger along the back of my left arm, and when I shivered with pleasure, he asked, "Is this okay?"

"Yes," I said, relaxing my head even more against his chest

so I could listen to his heartbeat. He drew in a quick breath as my arms went around him, like he hadn't expected me to pull myself closer. But after a second, he seemed to relax.

At least, anyone looking at him would probably think he was relaxing, but since I could feel his heart beating against my ear, I knew he must be just as highly strung as I was right now.

This wasn't necessarily brand-new territory: us cuddling on the couch during a movie. But it had been almost a year since we'd allowed something like this to happen, so it felt new.

Exciting.

Right.

Like I was back home after a much too long vacation.

I listened to his heart for a moment, and when it continued to race as fast as mine, I couldn't keep a smile from my lips.

Because this was happening.

We were together on a date, and he was holding me close again. Holding me like I was his girlfriend and not just a friend.

It was like time had simply held still for the past ten months and we were just now picking things up from where we left off.

And if that was what we were doing—if we were right back to where we'd been before—it also meant there might be a chance I could kiss him again—to press my lips to his and see if he tasted and felt the same as I'd remembered.

He wanted that too, right?

Everyone knew that the only reason you choose to watch a movie you'd both already seen a dozen times was because you really were hoping to do something else.

I just needed one little sign from him, and I could tilt my head back a little and kiss him.

But since I wasn't sure how he'd feel about me doing that, I tightened my arms around his torso instead and said, "Your heart is beating so fast right now."

"Yeah?" he asked, his voice low and throaty.

"Yeah." And just because I didn't want him to feel like he was alone in having nerves, I added, "Mine is probably beating just as fast."

"You think so?" he asked.

"Want to feel?" I sat up a little. Taking his hand in mine, I placed his palm on the side of my neck.

He looked at his hand on my neck for a moment, as if surprised to see it there. But then his eyes focused and he seemed to lock in on the tempo of my heartbeat.

"It's pretty fast, too," he whispered. He let his fingers slowly trail down my neck, leaving a path of fire where he touched my skin. And when his eyes locked with mine, my whole body swelled with heat because that look was familiar. The look I'd reimagined so many times over the past year—the one I'd been hoping to see tonight.

Because it was the look he used to get right before he kissed me.

"Scarlett, I—" he started to say.

"Yeah?" I licked my lips, anticipation thrumming in my veins.

He slipped his hand farther behind my neck to cradle it, and just when he was tracing his thumb across my jawline, the elevator doors opened and soft footsteps sounded on the floor.

"*Crap!*" I muttered under my breath right before launching myself to the other end of the couch—the place where someone who was just supposed to be Hunter's best friend would be sitting.

When I glanced back at Hunter, hurt and confusion flashed across his face for a second. But then, whoever had just come in the door threw his or her shoes in the closet, and Hunter's eyes widened, coming to realize there was someone else besides us in his family's penthouse.

"Hey guys," Hunter's brother Sebastian said, glancing up

from his phone when he walked into the living room a second later.

Sebastian was a senior at New York University and lived in an apartment close to campus. He and Hunter looked a lot alike, with the same tall, athletic build, the same strong jawline that could cut glass, and the slight curl to their hair. The only real difference between the two brothers was that Sebastian had their dad's darker brown, almost black hair, along with their mom's infatuation with designer clothes.

Which, based on what I'd heard from Hunter a few months ago, was becoming a problem for Sebastian now that his trust fund had become more of an "if he gets it" thing instead of a "when he gets it."

All depending on if he decided to follow the parable of the prodigal son and come back to The Fold.

Sebastian slipped his phone into the back pocket of his jeans. "When did you guys get back to town?"

"We rode the train in this morning," Hunter said, scooting closer to the armrest on his side of the couch, as if he, too, was worried his brother might suspect we were on a date. "We don't have school on Monday so we're home for the weekend."

"Nice." Sebastian took a seat on the chair next to Hunter. He nodded at the movie that I'd long since forgotten. "I see you're watching your favorite movie again."

"We are." Hunter chuckled. "Though the self-preserving side of me feels the need to clarify that it's *Scarlett's* favorite movie and not mine."

"Just keep telling yourself that, Hunter," Sebastian said, teasing his brother. He shifted in his seat. "Mind if I finish it with you, though? My roommate is throwing a party, so I decided to hang out here tonight."

"S-sure." Hunter glanced at me with a look that said he

wasn't sure how I would feel about his brother joining us. "That okay with you, Scarlett?"

No! Go back to your apartment, Sebastian, so I can kiss your brother.

"Totally fine with me," I lied as I slipped what I hoped was a believable smile on my lips. "As long as you don't make fun of it like you did the last time you watched it with us."

Sebastian chuckled. "I'll keep my thoughts to myself."

18

HUNTER

"SORRY BASH DECIDED to intrude on our night," I told Scarlett in a low voice as we were putting our shoes back on by the elevator after the movie ended. "That was not how I expected the evening to go."

Especially not when things had been about to take a much more exciting turn right before my brother had walked in and scared Scarlett clear over to the other end of the couch.

"It's okay." She pulled her boots onto her feet. "We said we wanted to watch a movie, so that's what we did."

That we did.

Watched the whole dang thing.

Which was about forty minutes more than it should have been.

Should I say something about that? Bring up the fact that I'd almost kissed her?

Or just leave it be and hope another opportunity arose in the near future?

"It was fun, though," she said. "I had a good time with you tonight."

"Well, that's good," I said, still feeling lame for basically failing at the date.

I mean, not only had we skipped the movie theater because I hadn't ordered the tickets ahead of time, but we'd also ended up with a third wheel.

A very vocal third wheel because Bash was, like, the loudest person to watch a movie with—always finding a reason to comment about one thing or another.

I grabbed Scarlett's red wool coat from the closet. After helping her put it on, I pulled on the hoodie that I'd worn this morning and added my letterman jacket over it.

"Ready to go?" I asked once she'd buttoned her coat and pulled her knit gloves over her hands.

"Ready."

"Is your mom in town this weekend?" I asked Scarlett as we headed down the elevator, passing the fifth floor where her mom lived.

"She and Rodney went to visit his family in Georgia," Scarlett said. "That's why she came to visit me last weekend."

"I bet it's nice to escape the cold for a few days."

"That's what they were thinking."

The elevator made it to the main level, and we walked out into the cool February night. And despite the traffic being busy, the lightly falling snow made it seem calmer.

Definitely not like the quiet that came on a snowy evening in Eden Falls, but nice.

Scarlett and I headed toward the parsonage that was about a five-minute walk from my house. As we made footprints in the snow that would most likely be melted by morning, I allowed myself to think over tonight's events.

Despite Bash coming in and ruining the moment I'd almost had with Scarlett, it had been a pretty good night. We'd enjoyed each other's company. And even though I hadn't gotten the kiss I'd been craving, I had been able to hold her in my arms for a few minutes.

Which was something I hadn't done in way too long.

Hopefully, it wouldn't be another ten months before it happened again. Hopefully, tonight was just the first of many dates—non-consecutive if need be.

"It's so nice out here," Scarlett said, stopping briefly under a streetlight and looking up. "Kind of makes you miss living here during the winter, doesn't it?"

"A little, I guess," I said.

"You sound unsure about that," she said, chuckling. "Does that mean you like Eden Falls more?"

"It's grown on me." I shrugged. "What about you?"

"I do like Eden Falls. A lot more than I thought I would since I was pretty homesick my freshman year."

"You were homesick?" I asked, never having heard of that.

She nodded. "I didn't really have friends that year. Partly because I was a little too intense about everything—sports, grades, church..." She looked up at me. "And partly because I felt like no one really understood me."

"You had a hard time connecting with our classmates back then?" I asked.

"I grew up so differently from a lot of the people at school," she said. "Most people would probably say my world was very small since even though I came from one of the biggest cities in the world, I only really spent time with members of The Fold."

"Me too." My life, like Scarlett's, had revolved around the church. Before going to Eden Falls Academy, I had a handful of friends from school and sports that came from other faiths or none at all, but they were all more at the acquaintance level. I never did things with them outside of those activities, though. If I was going to hang out with a friend after school or on the weekends, it was usually one of the guys from my youth group.

"But you seemed to do fine when we got to Eden Falls," Scarlett said. "You made friends with Carter, Mack, and Nash pretty quickly and were able to fit in. Where I—" She sighed. "—I was always fighting with my roommate because she wouldn't stop throwing crosses at me and telling me I was brainwashed and part of a religious cult."

"Wait, she actually said that?" I asked, surprised. Despite being quite the fanatic for my previous religion, no one had ever done anything like that to me.

Scarlett nodded. "Yeah, I think she was in one of those religions that goes around talking bad about The Fold. The ones that travel to the church pageants so they can hand out those anti-Fold pamphlets to people."

"Yikes," I said. "That was not a good pairing on the school's part."

"It was a rough year." She looked ahead as we passed a couple walking down the street. "Which is why I told my mom that if she was forcing me to come back to school the next year, she would have to get me a single room."

"You almost didn't come back?" I raised my eyebrows.

How had I not known this?

"I basically spent the whole summer after freshman year begging my parents to let me switch to a school closer to home. Or at least let me switch to online school because I didn't want to go back."

"I had no idea." I thought back to my impressions of Scarlett before we became friends. "I remember thinking you were always by yourself because you were so focused on studying to get straight A's and didn't have time for friends."

"That's what I wanted people to think," she said. "But yeah, I had to make it look like I didn't have time for friends because it made it seem like a personal choice, rather than the fact that no one wanted to be friends with the super strict, religious girl."

"What made you decide to come back?" I asked. "Were you just forced by your parents? Or was there something that changed your decision?"

"It was actually you who changed my mind." She stopped in front of the bakery next to the church and looked up at me with her big brown eyes. "You made me think I could come back."

"Me?" I put a hand to my chest, surprised by her answer. "How? We weren't friends until sophomore year."

She nodded. "Do you remember the church social that summer? The one right before school started where they rented the bouncy houses and had a big potluck dinner in the courtyard?" She pointed toward the path that led to a private courtyard within the church grounds—the spot where members enjoyed sipping their coffee and chatting after church when the weather was nice.

"Is that the social where Brother West tried to convince everyone he had a vision that he was supposed to be the High Priest and bring back more of the traditions they had in the early church?" I asked, remembering the quirky man who I'd thought was just a really crazy dude...until this past fall when I realized he had probably just been researching church history and saw the ways The Fold had changed to blend in a little better with the mainstream religions and wanted to go back to the "true order" of things. "Didn't he start his own break-off sect after that?"

"He did," she said. "Apparently, there was a lot of drama that my dad had to deal with because of it, too." She shook her head and sighed. "Anyway, Mr. West aside, it was at that party where I got the little bit of hope I needed in order to come back to school."

"And you say it had something to do with me?" I asked, trying to remember what I might have said or done that night to convince her to return.

"You probably don't even remember it." She started walking down the sidewalk again, letting her glove-covered fingers drag against the pickets in the wrought-iron fence. "But we were paired up to run the fishing booth for the little kids. While we were back there putting the prizes on the ends of all the little kids' fishing poles, we started talking about school." She looked up at me again. "Do you remember that?"

"A little," I said. An image of a blue tarp with laminated fish and seaweed duct taped to it so it resembled the ocean came to mind. "I think I remember asking Mrs. Jones to assign me to that particular booth because I saw you were there. I was hoping it would give me an excuse to talk to you."

"Really?" She gasped, her eyes lighting up. "You asked to be put there?"

I nodded, feeling my cheeks warm up. "I might have had the tiniest crush on you back then, but was too afraid to talk to you."

"You liked me back then?" Her voice went higher and her eyes widened, like she had no idea how long I'd had a crush on her.

"I told you this, didn't I?" I asked, sure I'd said something about it last year.

But she just shook her head. "I thought for sure you saw me as this super nerdy girl. Which was why I was so excited when hot, athletic Hunter Blackwell was actually talking to me instead of ignoring me behind that tarp."

I laughed. "Glad you thought I was hot, even back then."

"I've always had extremely good taste," she said with a big smile.

"Same." I winked. And for a few heart-pounding seconds, we just looked at each other with goofy smiles on our faces.

Man, I'd missed this.

Missed being open and able to tell Scarlett about all the moments that had made me fall for her.

We started walking again. When we were about twenty feet from the gates where I would be leaving her for the night, I asked, "So was it something that I said that night? Or did you just decide to come back to school because I was cute?"

"Probably a little of both." She grinned and looped her arm through mine. "But basically, you were just talking about how excited you were to get back to school and see your friends again and...I don't know, you made it sound fun—so much different from how my freshman year had gone." She leaned her head against my shoulder. "And I guess it gave me hope that if I tried to be more normal and tried to find the things I had in common with everyone instead of always seeing the things that made us different, that maybe it could be okay."

"Well, I'm glad you decided to give Eden Falls Academy another try."

"Me too."

We made it to the stone arch that the church gates were attached to. As she unlocked the gate and swung it open, I found myself wishing we'd walked slower on our way here just so I'd have a few more minutes with her.

Because even though we spent so much of our days together, I could never get enough.

Scarlett was the bright sun among the indistinguishable clouds. The one person whose company I never grew tired of.

If I could stay next to her all day and all night, I would.

"Well," Scarlett said, turning back to me. "Thank you for a wonderful evening." She tucked a lock of hair behind her ear. "I had a really great time."

"Thank you for coming." I took a slight step closer to her beneath the arch. "We'll have to find a way to do this again."

"I'd like that," she said with what seemed like a hopeful smile on her face.

We stood there just looking at each other for a moment, like we were both trying to figure out what came next.

A hug or a kiss?

I knew what I wanted.

But apparently, I'd lost all my courage when Bash ruined the moment earlier, because after we both just looked at each other for a while, like we were both waiting for the other to make the first move, she lifted her arms at her sides and said, "Hug?"

"S-sure." I cleared my throat. "Of course."

I stepped closer and wrapped my arms around her waist, and she stood on her tiptoes to rest her arms around my shoulders. And for a moment, with our bodies pressed together, we were one.

I expected the hug to only last a moment or two, but when she didn't step away after several seconds, my heart started to race.

Because this was familiar.

This lingering hug.

This was exactly like the hug she'd given me when we'd been in my room last spring, listening to the song "Electric Love."

Is it? Is it? Is it? My mind chanted as her arms slipped lower and her hands slid along the sides of my hoodie just beneath my jacket.

Just go for it, Hunter, I told myself. *She wants it, too.*

"Is your heart beating fast again?" she asked, her breath hot on my ear.

"Yeah," I said, my voice coming out all husky-sounding. "What about yours?"

"Uh huh." She nodded.

I dipped my head low as I breathed in the scent of her shampoo, her cheek resting against mine.

She breathed. I breathed.

She stepped half an inch closer. I stepped half an inch closer.

We were still waiting for the other to make the move. To cross the bridge we'd been standing on the edge of for ten months.

The bridge that would take us from just friends to something more...

Not boyfriend and girlfriend, since that was still against the rules, but possibly to friends who kissed at the end of an amazing night.

Her hands slipped up my sides again, making warmth spread across my ribcage until she slid her palm over my heart.

She held still for a few seconds before she whispered, "I can't feel your heartbeat. I think you might be dead."

"It's definitely beating fast." I chuckled quietly. "You just can't feel it through my sweatshirt."

Because if she could, she'd probably call nine-one-one since it was beating heart-attack fast right now.

"I guess I'll take your word for it," she whispered back.

We stood there for a few more seconds. I knew that if something was going to happen, it needed to happen soon. Moments like this didn't last long and who knew when we'd find a chance to be like this again.

It was also getting close to Scarlett's curfew, and for all I knew, her dad might come out at a minute past eleven to go looking for her.

In fact, he could be watching us right now...

I quickly glanced around to make sure Pastor Caldwell wasn't hiding behind the bushes just beyond the gate.

"Is something wrong?" Scarlett asked.

"I'm just making sure your dad isn't out here."

"Oh, good idea." She pulled her head back so she could scan the area as well.

"I don't see anyone," I said, releasing the breath I'd been holding.

"Me either," she said, sounding as relieved as I felt. "And if he or Megan did look through the windows, I don't think they'd be able to see us inside the arch."

"And he wouldn't have a reason to walk over to the church this late at night, would he?"

"No," she said.

"Okay, good." I sighed, feeling less anxious about that, at least.

"So if we were to stand here a little longer," she said, her voice going higher, "I don't think he would notice."

Okay, she was definitely hinting that we should be kissing right now, right?

We both looked at each other for a moment. I was just trying to remember if I was supposed to turn my head to the left or the right when she whispered, "Unless you think I should go inside..."

"*No.*" I tightened my arms around her waist before she could assume I didn't want to be here. "Don't go in yet." I pulled my head back so I could meet her eyes. "Sorry I'm—" I sighed. "I'm just nervous. It's kind of been a while and..."

"I'm nervous, too," she whispered.

"You are?" I asked, surprised since she'd always been so much better at things like this than me.

She nodded, her gaze seeming to go to my lips before she met my eyes again. "I just don't want to mess anything up or..."

"Have things get weird like they did last time?" I finished for her.

She nodded.

And I was reminded again of just how fragile relationships could be if you weren't careful.

Or if you were keeping secrets from the other person.

Don't think about that right now.

This was just one night. One date.

One kiss.

We weren't promising each other forever tonight, so I didn't need to worry about whether she could see herself ending up with someone like me yet—if she was willing to navigate life with someone who saw the world in a different way than she did.

We could have that conversation later.

When the time was right.

So before we could lose *this* moment, I slipped my hand to the back of her neck and whispered, "Do you want this right now?"

"Yes." She said the word quietly as she searched my eyes.

"Then how about we stop worrying about any obstacles in the future and just enjoy this moment tonight?" And without overthinking anything else, I leaned my face back down and kissed my best friend.

The kiss was slow and careful at first. Like we both needed a moment to get used to breathing the same air and sharing the same breath again.

We took our time, testing the waters and tasting each other's lips. Our lips brushed against each other once. Twice. And then again and again—the rhythm increasing as we got used to the movement.

"You still taste like mint gum," she whispered between kisses.

"And you still taste like strawberries," I whispered back.

Her lips were softer than I remembered though, but they fit perfectly with mine. And as our mouths met for a long, slow kiss, I knew she wanted this. That she cared about me and had been patiently waiting for this moment just as long as I had.

"You're so tall now," she said as she ran her hands up my arms and pressed her body closer.

"I am." I leaned against the brick arch behind us, pulling her with me. "Is that good or bad?"

The last time we'd kissed, I'd only been an inch or two taller than her since I hadn't yet reached my latest growth spurt then.

And while I'd always loved kissing her, it was somehow even better now. The five inches I had on her made me feel more masculine, like I could have a chance at protecting her if I needed to.

"Definitely good." I felt her lips curl up into a smile against my lips. "I like having you tower over me."

"I like towering over you, too." I chuckled, unable to keep from grinning. "It's so much hotter, right?"

She giggled. "So hot."

And then, we were kissing again. I smoothed my hands behind her back and slid them along her spine. She wore a wool coat, so it wasn't as intimate of a touch as I would have liked, but she felt good in my arms. When I tangled my fingers in her hair, it was just as soft as I remembered.

"That feels so good," she whispered when my fingertips slowly grazed against her scalp.

"Yeah?" I asked.

"Yeah." She sighed against my lips.

And when I combed my fingers through her hair again and she shivered with pleasure, my stomach flooded with heat because I liked that I could make her feel good this way.

I wanted to make her feel good all the time.

"This is so much better than I remember," she said, pulling away slightly and kissing my cheek and then the spot just below my jawline.

"I know," I said, letting my head fall back to expose more of my neck for her to kiss. "So good."

She kissed her way down my neck, causing blood to rush everywhere she kissed.

And all I could think was, *Holy crap, this feels amazing.*

So good yet so much different from our first kiss last year.

We'd been so timid back then. Nervous as we both experienced our first ever kiss and jumped into the unknown.

But even though we'd both been experiencing the pre-kiss jitters just a few minutes ago, they had apparently been a fleeting thing because there was nothing timid about this kiss now. It was hot and fierce and stirred feelings I hadn't experienced since our last kiss—the kiss during spring break where we'd taken the huge, exhilarating risk of making out on her dad's couch while he was working on his sermon at the church next door.

Also known as the kiss that had made me worry I might not be worthy to take communion the next Sunday, because it had to be a sin to feel as amazing as that kiss had made me feel.

Thank goodness I didn't see sin and worthiness the same way now, or I might have to stop this soon.

And I definitely did not want this to stop. I wanted to keep going. To keep kissing Scarlett. Until my toes were numb and my lips were swollen.

We had so much time to make up for.

I was suddenly wishing we were in a more comfortable and private spot because I would love nothing more than to pull her onto my lap again and kiss her back in a way that no innocent bystanders happening to walk by this late at night should see.

"Is there some place we can go?" I asked, my voice sounding rough and deep to my own ears. "Some place we can sit?"

Because I was already standing on shaky legs, and they might give out completely if she kept kissing me like this for much longer.

"There's a bench just inside the gates," she said, sounding breathless—like she was feeling the same things I was right now.

"Take me there."

Without second-guessing anything, she grabbed my hand, pulled me through the gates, and led me to a bench that had thankfully been placed in just the right spot that there was almost no snow covering it.

I immediately sat down and pulled on Scarlett's arm so she could sit sideways across my lap.

"Is this okay?" she asked, looking down at her legs, like she was worried it might be uncomfortable for me to have her sitting there.

"It's perfect," I said, before pulling her mouth to mine and kissing her again.

We kissed slow, we kissed fast. We clung to each other and kissed until my heart felt like it would explode.

We told each other with our kisses what we couldn't say out loud.

That the feelings were still there.

They hadn't disappeared when her father broke us apart.

That even though we were really good at being best friends, we were even better at being more.

And what could be better than being best friends with your soulmate?

I didn't know.

Probably because such a thing didn't exist.

Not in my world, anyway.

I didn't know how long we sat there, wrapped around each other on that bench, but my toes were just beginning to feel numb when something started sniffing at my legs.

I pulled away from Scarlett long enough to see the creature who had joined us and found the Caldwell's Pembroke Welsh Corgi standing on his hind legs to greet me in his favorite way—by humping my leg.

"Archie!" Scarlett said in a hushed tone. "Stop that!" She glanced at me with an apologetic look and said, "Sorry my dog is so weird."

"He just missed me, that's all." I chuckled and bent over to pet the little fur ball. "Right, Archie? You missed me so much."

I used to come to Scarlett's house every time we were home from school, but tonight was the first time I'd actually been on the church grounds since my last interview with her dad.

"I wond—" Scarlett started to say when the light on her house's front porch turned on.

A second later, Pastor Caldwell appeared in the door and called out, "Come back here, Archie! Time for bed."

"*Crap!*" Scarlett jumped off my lap. "My dad and Megan must have just gotten back from the Morris's house." She smoothed her hands over her hair, as if attempting to tame the tangled mess I'd made of it. "You need to get out of here before Archie rats us out to my dad."

"*Right.*" I glanced around the church yard, not wanting to come face to face with Pastor Caldwell quite yet.

The exit through the archway was about twenty feet away, and while the path over there was layered in trees that I could dart behind, her dad would probably notice something if he looked this way.

"Just hide in that corner." Scarlett pointed to a spot behind us. "I'll take Archie with me, and hopefully, my dad will think I was just late getting back from the movie."

"Okay."

I was about to step behind the bench to hide when Scarlett gripped my arm and said, "Thank you again for tonight. It was amazing."

"Yes, it was," I said, the high I'd been feeling all night coming right back.

"*ARCHIE!*" Pastor Caldwell called again.

"I'll talk to you tomorrow," Scarlett whispered before standing on her tiptoes and giving me one last kiss. "Be safe walking home."

"I will. Good night, Scarlett."

"Good night."

As she picked up Archie and carried him back toward her home, I slipped behind the bench and pressed my back against the fence.

That was close.

I drew in a deep breath, hoping it would help calm my racing heart as I watched Scarlett walk away through the moonlight.

And then, I couldn't help but smile. I had finally taken a step forward with the girl of my dreams. We were no longer living in limbo.

Scarlett headed inside the house with her dad. When their front door closed, I quickly stepped out from my hiding place and dashed through the trees. I briefly paused under the big elm tree I used to climb as a kid, my gaze lifting to the giant cathedral hulking thirty yards away.

Even though the sight of that church used to be a place of comfort—a happy place I could come to each Sunday morning —instead of feeling any warmth, I felt nauseous and cold.

Along with a sense of dread and betrayal.

Because for seventeen and a half years, I'd been raised believing in and dedicating my life to a church built on a sandy foundation of lies.

Don't think about that right now, I told myself, forcing my gaze the other way. *That organization doesn't need to ruin another night.*

It had already taken so much.

So instead of dwelling on the past, I looked away from the shadows of the church and slipped through the gate, closing it and the past behind me.

Tonight, I would allow myself to be happy. Tonight, I would live in the bliss of kissing my best friend.

I'd find a way to talk to Scarlett about everything else some other time.

19

HUNTER

I SLEPT WELL THAT NIGHT, and when the sun peeked through my windows the next morning, I found myself smiling. I rolled onto my side and reached for my phone, figuring I'd send Scarlett a "good morning" text.

Should I be daring and send a photo of me waking up with bed head and a smile on my face?

Or would she think that was weird?

Maybe I should put a shirt on first? That way she wouldn't think I was trying to make this a sexy thing.

I mean, I wouldn't mind having our relationship turn into something more serious like that eventually, but since we were still at the very beginning of figuring things out, I didn't want to push anything or make her feel uncomfortable.

I grabbed a shirt from my dresser and lay back in bed to pretend like I'd just woken up. Except, when I reached for my phone on the nightstand, I found that in my love-drunk state last night, I'd forgotten to set it on my wireless charger and so it was completely dead.

Guess I'll try that some other time.

I set my phone back down, this time making sure it was where it needed to be in order to get a full charge. Then I climbed out of my king-sized bed for the second time.

After taking a quick shower and giving my chest a spritz of the cologne Scarlett had given me last year, I headed down the hall to whip up a chai latte using the special house-made blend my mom bought by the gallon from the local coffee shop.

My parents should be heading out to church any minute, so I figured I could use the time they were out to work on *The Confidant*'s next column.

I'd received a bunch of really great questions this week, so if time and inspiration permitted, I might try answering a few more than I usually did.

But when I walked into the kitchen, instead of finding my parents rushing to get out the door for the ten o'clock Sunday service they were never late for, they were sitting at the table sipping their coffee.

And they were wearing regular clothes instead of my dad wearing his church suit and my mom wearing one of her Sunday dresses.

Had the three-day weekend messed up their schedules and they thought today was Saturday?

I checked my watch to make sure I wasn't the one who'd mixed up the dates. But as I expected, the date at the top corner said it was Sunday, February twentieth.

What was going on? Were they late getting ready because they'd been waiting to give me some sort of a spiritual intervention first?

It wouldn't be too shocking if that was the case, really, since one of them—usually my mom—insisted on having some sort of "please come back to The Fold and leave the path of darkness" conversation with me whenever I was home.

I considered sneaking back to my room and pretending I

was sleeping in until noon, but my dad looked up from the business book he was reading and said, "Oh, hey Hunter. We were just wondering when you'd be up." He marked his page with a bookmark and set his book down on the table. "Did you get in late last night?"

"Not too late," I said. "About eleven-thirty."

Which I was pretty sure was before they did, since I'd heard them laughing about something when they got home from their charity event around one o'clock.

"Do anything fun last night?" Mom turned in her chair to look at me.

When people saw me with my parents and brother, they always said I took after my mom because we had the same chestnut-brown hair and green eyes while Bash took after my dad with his dark brown, almost black hair, and blue eyes.

It used to bug me growing up—to be compared to a woman since I very much identified as a male. But now that I'd finally hit my growth spurt and had inched closer to my dad and Bash's height of six-foot-two, I didn't mind it as much.

In fact, I was pretty sure I'd only appreciate it even more the older I got. My mom had what her other socialite friends called "magic genetics" and still didn't have a single gray hair or need plastic surgery and Botox to take care of the signs of aging that most image-conscious women nearing fifty like my mom did.

"I hung out with Scarlett," I said.

"Of course," Mom said, a smile on her lips. "You two are basically tied at the hip."

"I guess," I said with a shrug, hoping my parents wouldn't be able to tell how excited I really was about the time I'd spent with my best friend last night.

They were good friends with Pastor and Sister Caldwell,

and I couldn't have them saying anything to them about Scarlett and me being on a date last night.

I looked at the clock on the wall, wondering when my parents would realize how behind they were on their morning. Mom followed my gaze to the large clock, and when she saw it was nine-forty-eight—just twelve minutes before their church started—she got an uneasy look in her eyes before glancing at my dad.

Was this the moment right before they jumped into their *"Let's save our son so he can be with us in special heaven"* chat? Or were they planning to hit me again with their *"Do you really want to be on your own without your trust fund after college?"* bribe?

I hoped this wasn't the beginning of one of those conversations because I really didn't feel like getting into any of that with them right now. It was exhausting, and their attempts to bring me back to church never turned out well, no matter how many times they shared their testimonies or tried to put the fear of God in me.

I still had a whole day and a half to get through with them before I'd be heading back to school. I didn't want to spend the majority of that time feeling triggered or like none of the people I cared about would ever understand me.

So instead of standing there looking like I was waiting for them to start that conversation, I turned to the fridge and pulled out the whole milk and chai latte concentrate. I grabbed one of the silver pitchers from the cupboard, and after pouring equal parts of each liquid into it, I took it to the espresso machine to steam and froth it.

Once my drink was ready, I poured it into my mug. I was just thinking about sneaking back to my room to work on my column when Mom said, "So Hunter..."

"Yeah?" I looked at my parents, bracing myself again.

"Your father and I were just wondering what you'd like to do today."

"Umm..." I started, not quite sure what I should say. "I guess I was planning to do some homework this morning. Why?"

Was this some sort of set-up? If it sounded like I was just planning to lie around while they were at church, would they use that as an excuse to get me to go with them?

"Well..." She looked at Dad for backup to whatever she was about to say. "I guess we were thinking about doing some family stuff today. Maybe play some card games or watch a movie before going to lunch."

Going for lunch?

On a Sunday?

They really must not know what day of the week it was.

Even though I didn't want to bring the big elephant into the room, I asked, "Don't you have church, though? It's Sunday, right?"

They always had church. Even when we were on vacation, or they were on business trips, they still found a way to attend their church meetings.

"About that..." Dad sat up straighter and cleared his throat. "I guess now is as good of a time as any to tell you that your mother and I...well—" He glanced at Mom briefly then back at me. "I think it's probably time for us to tell you that this past month or so, we embarked on a similar journey that you and Bash took and..." He paused for a second before finishing with, "We actually stopped attending church three weeks ago."

"Wait. What?" I took a step back, not sure I'd heard them right. "You stopped going to church?"

"Yes," Mom said. "We did."

"But...?" I shook my head, my mind reeling with what they were saying. "How? How is that even possible?"

Hadn't she just been telling me that I'd been contaminated by Satan? And that I deserved to be disfellowshipped because she hoped it would help me get back on the right path?

I was disfellowshipped around the end of December. It wasn't that long ago.

But they stopped attending in January?

"How about we all sit down in the living room to talk about this?" Dad suggested.

We walked into the living room where Scarlett and I had watched the movie last night. My parents sat on the couch together while I took the chair.

"We'll just start from the beginning, okay?" Mom said, pulling one of the throw pillows on her lap like she needed it to ground her.

"Okay." I set my mug on one of the coasters on the cocktail table, so confused and curious.

It had taken me four months of intense study before I really felt okay not going to church. And another four months after that before I removed my name from the records.

But I'd only been raised in the belief system for seventeen and a half years. My parents were almost fifty and had been members of The Fold their entire lives.

They'd done so much, served so many hours—paid millions of dollars in tithes to the church over their lifetime.

And suddenly, they were out?

I mean, if this was true, I was probably going to throw a party because the idea of having my parents understand and accept me was something I hadn't dared dream of. I thought for sure they'd continue believing I was #TeamSatan until they died.

But how was it possible for them to go from "all in and planning to live their eternity without their sons by their side" to suddenly quitting church cold turkey?

All within the timespan of six or seven weeks.

It sounded way too good to be true.

Unbelievable, really.

Mom blew out a long breath. Then swiveling on the couch cushion, she looked at me and said, "It all started when you told us about your meeting with Pastor Caldwell."

"It did?" I was so confused because she hadn't exactly been very sympathetic to my painful experience at the time.

"I know I responded horribly in the moment, when you first told us. I said a lot of really stupid things because I was so confused that my smart and wonderful boy would even land in that kind of a situation." She shrugged. "But after a few days, your dad and I realized that along with the pain we were feeling over losing yet another son, we were also disgusted. Disgusted that our sweet boy, who had never done anything wrong aside from losing his faith, would be treated in such an un-Christlike way by someone who was supposed to be God's servant."

"You didn't see it as being for my own good then?" I asked, surprised at this one-eighty.

"Obviously, I reacted terribly at first." She looked down at her hands. "I responded really harshly in the heat of the moment, and I said a lot of things that I'm really embarrassed to have said." She glanced at the large family photo above the hearth. When she wiped at the corner of her eye, I realized she was becoming emotional.

"It's okay, Mom," I said, reaching over to touch her shoulder. I hated seeing Mom cry. "You were just doing what you'd been taught."

Even though some of the things she'd said had hurt at the time, I'd known it was just her religious programming talking. I knew she only said those things because she loved me and was just worried about losing me.

"I know," she said, her voice quiet and full of emotion. "But that doesn't make it right."

Dad nodded and sat up straighter. "We feel terrible for how we treated you and Bash. Back then, we weren't at a place where we could understand the pain you were going through and be there for you. You must have felt so alone during that time."

He took off his glasses and wiped at his eyes. I had to grab a tissue from the corner table because I was suddenly emotional, too, thinking about how hard it had been trying to tell my parents about what I was going through—essentially having an existential crisis—and not having them even get close to understanding me.

Having them tell me I was making my research up and just looking for things to be upset about.

"How sad is it that we couldn't even have an open and honest conversation with our own children?" Mom shook her head and scoffed unhumorously. "That we put an organization above our own boys? Trusted it blindly." She met my gaze again, sadness in her green eyes. "I'm so ashamed of that."

"You lived in a bubble for fifty years," I said, looking at my mom and then my dad. "It's hard to see things objectively when you've been warned your whole life not to even look."

That if you crack open the door, you'll find darkness and misery and lose the ability to discern what's truth and what's made up.

"It's just ridiculous they had us so scared that we couldn't even look into anything. We couldn't even listen to our own sons," Mom said.

"Fear is a powerful tool," I said.

"That it is," Mom said with a sigh. "Fear of things that can't actually be proven is how they keep you in."

She looked to Dad in a way that told me she was remembering what they'd been through the past weeks and months.

"So how did everything actually go down for you guys?" I asked, so curious since different things brought different people out of The Fold. "You said it was my interview with Pastor Caldwell that pushed you over the edge?"

"Yes," Dad said. "After you told us about it, I was upset and confused. Then I remembered the email you sent your mom and me after our first conversation about you leaving." He shook his head. "And I clicked that link to the essay you told us about—the one that had so much research compiled in one place."

"You read the *Questions for The High Priest?*" I asked, surprised he'd even clicked the link to the document I'd come across in my research that outlined so many of the dark parts of the church's history: the secret blood oaths and rituals, the way Samuel Williams manipulated multiple women to have sex with him, the real reasons why the early church had always been in trouble with the government.

"I was scared to open it at first," Dad said, "since I knew it had to have some disturbing information in it—I'd heard whisperings of it at church before. But I pushed that fear aside for an hour or two, and let's just say, it was quite the eye-opening experience..."

"It's a lot, isn't it?" I agreed.

"It is," Dad said.

And yet, at the same time, it still only scratched the surface of all the ugly parts of the church's history and ways it had lied to and controlled its members.

"I basically didn't sleep for a week because there was just so much to research. Your mom noticed something was off, and after I told her that I wasn't sure God was even real anymore, she decided to look into it."

"I basically had nothing to lose at that point." Mom shrugged. "My sons and my husband were all out of the church —three men whom I knew to be thoughtful in all the other areas of their lives—so I decided I'd better see what this thing was actually all about. And..." She stopped and blew out a big breath. "Talk about getting TKO'd out of the church."

Dad nodded. "We went to church two more times after that, just to give it a chance to convince us back." He placed a hand on my mom's knee and looked at her for a moment, like he was remembering the journey they'd gone on together. "But as I'm sure you know, once we realized we couldn't trust the founder—when we found out Samuel Williams was basically just an experienced conman, pulling off the biggest con of his life—we knew we'd been duped, and everything unraveled pretty quickly after that."

Which was how it had been for me, too. Once you saw the man behind the curtain, you couldn't just unsee everything.

"Does anyone at church know why you stopped attend-ing?" I asked, curious how that had all gone down since my parents had been very prominent figures in the congregation.

"We had a short conversation with Pastor Caldwell at the end of January where we asked him to take us off all of the committees we served on, explaining that we wouldn't be participating in any church-sponsored events anymore."

"How did he take it?" I asked, my jaw dropping at how bold my parents were.

"He was shocked but said he hoped we would reconsider," Dad said.

"And that he'd pray for us," Mom added.

"I guess that's nice of him," I said.

"We told him we hoped he and Megan would still consider us friends. But..." My dad drifted off.

"They haven't invited you to a game night recently," I

guessed, knowing from the online support groups I was in what usually happened when people came out about their faith transition.

"We haven't seen them since then," Mom said. "We haven't really seen anyone from church. But I guess that's normal. We don't have our beliefs in common anymore, and The Fold keeps everyone so busy that a lot of them don't have time to socialize outside of church functions."

"But it's fine," Dad said. "We know what it's like because we've been in their shoes before."

"Yeah," Mom agreed, looking at my dad in a way that was actually really sweet. "I'm just thankful I'm on this side of things now. It's been so hard, of course, and I'm sure it will continue to be really difficult since we still have to rebuild our world view and support system. But I'm glad we're on this journey together." She looked at me. "And I'm glad I don't have to worry about my sons so much. My family is all I really care about—knowing that I'm not going to spend eternity without you and Bash by my side has given me more peace of mind than you could know."

"And now that we're away from it," Dad added, "it's just like, how in the world did we ever believe so many of those crazy things?"

I nodded. "It's amazing how hard it is to see anything from within the bubble."

But if my parents had been able to see through the fog The Fold had them in, maybe there was a chance that Scarlett might see through it sometime, too.

I just had to find the right way to bring it up to her.

Hopefully, her dad wouldn't put his spin on my story first.

20

HUNTER

BASH JOINED my parents and me in the living room around eleven—they'd already told him the news of their faith transition a couple of weeks earlier. We spent the rest of the morning and early afternoon talking about all the things we'd discovered in our research and just connecting in a way that I never dreamed Bash and I would be able to connect with our parents.

After grabbing a bite to eat at the French cafe down the street where I had an amazing filet mignon and some fancy potato dish, I went upstairs to my room to work on my column. But before I could answer the first email, my phone buzzed with a notification. I then realized I hadn't checked my phone all morning.

Hoping it was Scarlett, I retrieved my phone from the charger and saw that I actually had a few missed texts from her. As I read the messages that started with her asking how I was and if I wanted to meet on the rooftop above my parents' penthouse, my mind took me back to last night with Scarlett, making my stomach flap with butterflies.

Sorry I didn't see your texts until now. I quickly

texted back before she could think I had decided to ghost her after such an amazing night. **But I can meet you at the rooftop anytime.**

The text went to "read" immediately, and I held my breath as I waited for her to respond.

It only took a few seconds for her reply to come through.

Scarlett: **I can come now. See you on the rooftop soon.**

IT WAS chilly when I made it to the rooftop a few minutes later, so to make it more comfortable—a place where Scarlett and I would want to spend hours sitting up there if the mood permitted—I turned on the fire pit table, grabbed a few blankets from the basket by the door, and poured two insulated tumblers high with hot chocolate.

I was just sitting down on the patio furniture when Scarlett walked onto the rooftop wearing the same red wool coat she'd worn last night, with her hair down and curled in the way she always did it for church.

"Hey," I said, standing to give her a hug as she walked closer. "I'm glad you texted."

"Hi," she said, returning the hug briefly before looking around at the cozy area I'd set up. "Did you do all this?"

"Yeah," I said, feeling my cheeks flush, hoping it wasn't too much. "I thought it would be nice to stay warm."

"It looks nice," she said. "Very cozy."

But instead of sitting right next to where I'd been on the couch, she sat in the patio chair.

So maybe this wasn't the type of rendezvous I'd been thinking it was?

I sat back down. When I looked at her, I realized something was off about her energy today. Instead of acting excited or like she was anticipating what might happen between us, she was agitated.

"Everything okay?" I asked.

Was she having second thoughts about last night?

Or had her dad seen me hiding in the corner and had pulled her aside to talk about what he knew about me?

We sat in silence for a few more seconds. When she cast her eyes down at her hands, like she was feeling uncomfortable and didn't know how to talk about whatever was making her feel weird, I knew something had to be up.

"What's going on, Scarlett?" I asked, bouncing my knee up and down. "You're scaring me."

"Sorry, I'm just—" she started. When she looked up, there was sadness in her eyes. My heart instantly jumped into my throat because her expression told me everything I needed to know.

Something was indeed wrong.

And she was here because of it.

Please don't tell me you regret last night.

She sighed. "There's no delicate way to put this, I guess," she said, glancing at the hot chocolate before lifting her gaze to mine. "So I'm just going to put it right out there."

"Put what out there?" I asked, my whole body tensing and preparing for the blow.

"I was at church today and..." She paused, her eyes welling up. "And I heard that your dad was cheating on your mom."

Wait. What?

Had she just said what I thought she said?

"Sorry, what did you just say?" I asked. Because my mind was clearly taking whatever words she'd just said and turning them into something else.

"I'm so sorry," she said, her tone apologetic. "This is probably something your family didn't want anyone to know about. I mean, that's the only reason why you wouldn't have told me about it yourself, but I was talking to Leandra after church today and she told me all about it. She said your parents stopped coming to church a few weeks ago and it's because they're getting a divorce and can't stand to see each other at church anymore."

So I *had* heard her right.

"Leandra said my dad cheated on my mom?"

"She told me all about it." Scarlett nodded. "She said it started happening over the summer and that was probably why you started acting so weird and stopped coming to church, because you knew about it and felt guilty for keeping it from your mom."

"She said I knew my dad was cheating and that I..." I put a hand to my chest. "That I was in on the secret and didn't come to church because I was keeping it from my mom and felt guilty?"

What in the crazy-twisted-stories was this?

"Yeah, and I just—" She looked at the fire and shook her head, like she actually believed this pile of crap. After a second, she turned back to me with hurt in her eyes and asked, "Why didn't you tell me about this?"

"Because none of it is true." I leaned forward and met her gaze, so she'd know I wasn't hiding some dark secret about my parents. "What Leandra told you is completely false. Like, it's not true at all."

"It's okay if it is, though, Hunter." She scooted closer and rested her hand on my knee. "I know you're a different person from your dad. I won't judge you for what he did. It's not your fault he started looking at porn and decided to cheat on your mom with the new girl at his office."

"She said he's looking at porn? And that it led to him cheating on my mom?" I asked, so confused at where all of this was coming from. "My dad isn't addicted to porn. He isn't sleeping with someone from work. My parents are fine. Better than ever, actually."

They were literally downstairs together right now, taking an afternoon nap in their room.

"Then why aren't they coming to church anymore?" Scarlett asked, like the only logical reason for a whole family to quit coming to church was if the dad was addicted to porn and having an affair. "Why did *you* stop?"

And here we were.

At the conversation I'd been avoiding for months.

"Why aren't you coming to church anymore, Hunter?" she asked, her voice soft and sad, like me not going to church anymore was literally breaking her heart.

Because it's not true, Scarlett, I wanted to say. *Because Samuel Williams—the beloved High Priest—was really great at duping the superstitious people who first joined his church. People who lived in a time when they couldn't fact check or effectively warn each other about how they'd been swindled by him since the Internet wasn't a thing back then.*

He'd used the same skills he'd been building since his forgery days as a teen to create his biggest con of all—to create a religion that gave people answers to the big questions they had and promise them all the things they wanted. He gave them hope in a world that was harsh and dark at times—all while basically naming himself king.

All it took was dedicating your life to the church and ten percent of your income, and you could receive all of the blessings of eternal life and happiness.

Funny how I hadn't even seen tithing as buying my way into heaven until *after* I left—no matter that the church already had billions of dollars that sat in their overstuffed bank accounts, gaining interest instead of being used to help those in need.

"We stopped attending because our beliefs have changed," I said, finding nicer words.

"But how? How could your beliefs have changed?" She furrowed her brow, looking hurt and confused. "You guys were so strong—one of the strongest families in the whole congregation. How did this happen?" She shook her head and glanced down briefly before looking back at me with so much sadness in her eyes. "Were you guys just faking it this whole time? Did you ever even believe?"

"How can you even ask that?" I pulled my head back, her words hitting me like I'd been kicked in the gut. "Of course we believed, Scarlett." I sighed heavily, my chest sinking in because I could feel that I was already losing her. "Do you think I would put so much time and effort and tears and sleepless nights into figuring this out if I didn't actually believe? You think I could pretend for seventeen and a half years, go to all the meetings, do all the things...just for show?"

Of course she couldn't know everything I'd done to fight for my belief in The Fold, since it wasn't something I'd felt safe or comfortable talking to anyone about while I was going through it. But there had been so many nights where I'd just pleaded with God to make me feel something. To send some sort of sign that would tell me that everything was okay. That I hadn't been tricked. That the version of God I believed in and had felt to be real actually existed.

That somehow this was all just a big misunderstanding and everything I'd discovered could be explained away with one simple piece of information that I was missing. That if I just looked hard enough, I could find it and all would be well.

I could go back to the safety of believing the same things as my tribe and not worry about being discovered in my disbelief and shunned.

But instead of being comforted whenever I prayed, I had felt nothing. There was only silence.

It wasn't until I took a step back and stopped trying to fit everything into my "the church has to be true" box that I was able to see how everything had actually come together.

How piece by piece the great High Priest had built his kingdom. How he'd put a mirror here, added some smoke there, and built a beautiful shiny fortress that would distract the trusting members from what was actually going on within its walls.

He'd done a fabulous job of duping my ancestors who'd sacrificed so much for what they believed in—and the generations after that who continued down the same path because they'd been indoctrinated from birth, and it was the only thing they'd known.

But the blind obedience would stop with me. I would not be passing the spiritually abusive traditions of my ancestors down to my future children.

"Well, how did it happen?" Scarlett asked. "Did Sebastian get to all of you? Did he show you some of that anti-Fold material? Did you get caught up in all the lies?"

"Bash didn't show me anything," I said, offended she so easily latched onto the rhetoric The Fold gave her about people who stepped away. "I did my own research."

"Sounds like you got some pretty faulty information." She crossed her arms. "I can't believe you're throwing it all away. Throwing away your eternal salvation because of lies."

"It's not lies, Scarlett," I said, growing more and more frustrated. "And just so you know, my research started on The Fold's own website."

"What?" The blood drained from her face.

I nodded. "I read all of the church history essays. Every single one of them. I thought they would make things better and satiate the questions I had, but they only brought up more questions. So then I started looking at all the footnotes in the essays, reading all of the source material. And I found out that a lot of The Fold's history had been whitewashed. It had been made to look pretty. But the truth wasn't nearly as pretty as what we've been taught. And that led me down the rabbit hole.

"You know how I was always reading something on my phone over the summer and during downtime this fall, and you teased me about having a secret social media addiction?"

She gave a small nod.

"That was just me researching The Fold," I said. "I spent so much time reading everything. I've never read or studied so much in my life. For six months I ate, drank and slept church history. Read biographies of Samuel Williams and the other High Priests after him. Journals from the people in the early church. It was basically an explosion of new information. And the more I learned, the more questions I had."

"The more lies you read," Scarlett cut me off, her body trembling from how upset she was becoming. "It's so crafty, Hunter. Satan is crafty and he got you. He got your whole family."

"No. That's not it at all..." I tried to say, but she wasn't listening anymore—the cognitive dissonance was too much to allow her to actually hear me through.

"Stop trying to lie to me, Hunter." She stood from her chair and took a step back, like my disbelief was a contagious thing. "You got your parents, but you're not going to get me."

Before I could say or do anything that might salvage this conversation, she turned and walked away. And all I could do was sit back on the bench with my shoulders slumped and think that this conversation had not gone how I wanted at all.

But it was impossible for someone to hear the truth if they had been warned their whole life not to listen to people with opposing views.

Just like Mark Twain had said, it was so much easier to fool someone than to convince them that they'd been fooled.

Leaving The Fold was like running from a burning building and trying to tell your friends and family that it's on fire.

But it was usually pointless. They rarely ever listened.

Because all they could feel was its warmth.

21

SCARLETT

I RAN ALL the way back home, barely able to keep the tears at bay. And instead of stopping to help Megan set the table for our Sunday dinner with Xander like I said I would when I got back, I ran right past the dining room and up the stairs.

When I shut the door to my bedroom and threw myself onto my bed, all I could think of was: *I've lost him.*

I'd been worried since last summer that something was wrong with my friend. I'd known something was off and that he was acting differently around me. Keeping secrets.

But I didn't think it was this bad. I'd assumed he was just taking a break. Relaxing a bit since senior year was busy and there was only so much free time to go around before all the responsibilities of adulthood hit.

But he was done?

Finished?

A defector? An *apostate*?

If I had talked to him about it sooner, would there have been a chance to get through to him?

Was it too late now? Was he too far gone and entangled in Satan's grasp?

I was in the middle of spiraling and sobbing into my pillow because I couldn't imagine living in a world where Hunter fully cut ties with the church when a text came through.

I sat up and wiped at my eyes so I could read what my phone said.

Hunter: **Sorry that didn't go well. I'm sure it shocked you. I wanted to tell you in a different way.**

I wish he'd told me sooner, like when he was first looking at anti-Fold material. That way, he wouldn't be so far down the path. His heart wouldn't be so hardened, and it would have been easier to bring him back.

But maybe it wasn't too late? He was still trying to have this conversation at least...

I typed back my response with trembling fingers. **Can you just read *Visitations with Jehovah* again and pray about it? Actually read and ponder it?**

If he could just read more about Samuel Williams visits with Jehovah, surely he would be able to feel the spirit and see through the cover of darkness he'd put himself in.

But instead of sending anything that made me feel better, he simply texted back: **I've read it ten times, Scarlett. I know what it says. I don't need to read it again.**

Me: **Please.**

Hunter: **I read it a few months ago when I was trying to figure everything out. It won't do anything.**

But it might. People shared experiences all the time about how reading *Visitations with Jehovah* changed their lives and helped them get on a better path. If it worked for them, it could work for Hunter.

Me: **Can't you read it just one more time? For me?**

For us.

For the future and the family we could have together someday.

I held my breath as I waited for him to respond. When the next text came through, I almost dropped my phone from how jumpy I was feeling.

Hunter: **If I agree to read it one more time, will you read the essay at this website? questions-forthehighpriest.com It's about a two-hour read.**

Me: **Is that anti-Fold material?**

Was he trying to get me to visit an anti-Fold website? Did he think I'd actually fall for something like that?

Hunter: **It's an essay that a Pastor wrote to the High Priest when he was having a hard time making sense of the things he came across while studying for his sermons. It's a compilation of everything I researched, but all in one spot and much more condensed. But it has all the basic info and details. A lot of the unwhitewashed church history, along with the anachronisms from *Visitations with Jehovah*.**

Anachronisms?

I'd never heard that word before.

After a quick search in the online dictionary, I found that the word referred to situations when an object, event, or custom was attributed to a time period it didn't belong to.

The example the Internet gave me was: "Like Abraham

Lincoln using a cell phone to update his wife on the Civil War."

Cell phones didn't exist back then, so a story mentioning something like that would obviously be made up.

I didn't know what kinds of anachronisms he believed were in *Visitations with Jehovah*. Probably things that Samuel Williams had just written down wrong when transcribing what Jehovah told him during one of his many visitations.

A human error was bound to come up here and there in a three-hundred page book.

But that was beside the point. One or two mistakes couldn't discount all the truth and goodness that came from the gospel.

It was like he was trying to say that the church was purposely trying to hide things from us. That's what he meant by "whitewashed history," right?

Me: **So you're saying that the Elders and High Priest lied to us? That my dad lied to us?**

What had this research done to Hunter?

Made him paranoid and mistrusting of everyone?

Hunter: **I'm not saying that. I know your dad and the other leaders are good people and just doing and teaching what they believe is true. But there are a lot of things that were hidden from the church members by some of the early leaders. Things that they weren't proud of and that hurt their agenda.**

Me: **The church is good, Hunter. It teaches us to be good people. It doesn't tell us to do bad things. The only "agenda" is helping people be happy and follow Jehovah.**

Hunter: **I know. I was one of you. I was a good person too when I believed it.**

Me: **But you don't believe it anymore?**

Three dots showed on the screen, and I held my breath as I waited to see how he would answer my question. He had to believe at least some of it still. He had to know deep down that it was true, and he'd been led astray.

He couldn't actually deny it when he'd had so many spiritual experiences that witnessed to him that the church was true.

But then his text came through. **No. I don't believe it.**

No?

I know he'd said as much earlier, but this was just so *final*.

And with that simple confirmation, it felt like my heart was fissuring in my chest.

My stomach dropped down to the floor as I thought about all the plans I had for Hunter and me after high school. How we'd go to college together. Be able to actually start dating. Fall deeper in love.

He'd ask me to marry him. I'd say yes. We'd get married in the church, buy a home, have children, raise a family in the gospel together. Build a life.

But none of that could happen if he wasn't a believer.

I couldn't tie my eternal salvation to someone who didn't share the same values as me.

My mom and dad had failed to make things work when my mom dissented. Plus, I didn't want to only have the promise of living with my husband and children in *this* life only. I wanted to marry someone I could be with *after* this life, too. Forever.

I wiped away the tears that were streaming more quickly now, and with trembling fingers, I typed: **Can't you just stay for me? Please? Do it for me? For us.**

I held my hand over my heart as I waited for his answer, sure that it would break into a million pieces if he said no.

After another thirty seconds where I felt like I couldn't breathe, he replied: **I can't live a lie, Scarlett. I was taught to live with integrity, and it wouldn't be fair to you or to me to pretend to believe and support something that I just don't.**

After reading those final words from my best friend, I covered my mouth to stifle a huge sob.

He really was lost.

22

HUNTER

I DIDN'T HEAR from Scarlett all Monday. And instead of riding back to school together like we'd planned on Monday afternoon, she texted at the last minute and said that Xander had eaten dinner with her family on Sunday night and had offered to give her a ride to the school since it was on his way back to Yale.

Me: **Xander ate dinner with your family on Sunday?**

Scarlett: **My dad heard he was in town and thought we should continue to get to know each other better.**

Me: **Cool**

Not cool.

Scarlett: **Yeah.**

Our text conversation died after that, and I didn't see or hear from her until breakfast in the great hall on Tuesday morning.

I headed over to the table with my tray, determined to smooth things over enough that she would realize I was still the same person I'd been all year. That I still cared about her and wanted a lot of the same things still.

But when I walked up to my usual spot next to her, instead of scooting closer to Asher to make room for me on the bench like she usually did, she didn't budge.

Was it possible she didn't notice me standing behind her? Should I say something?

I was about to open my mouth to address her when she glanced briefly at me before turning back to her conversation with Asher.

Okaaaay. This was awkward.

I glanced at Addison and Evan to see if they had noticed what was going on, and after giving me a compassionate look, Addison patted the spot next to her and said, "There's space right here for you, if you want."

"Thanks," I said, my chest feeling hollow with this whole weird situation.

Was Scarlett going to just pretend like I didn't exist now?

Apparently, she was planning to keep being weird about things, because when Addison asked me questions about my weekend, I noticed Scarlett looking at us and listening but pretending like she wasn't each time I looked directly at her.

We had our regular classes together, but each time I tried to talk to her, to apologize for not telling her everything sooner and for coming across so harshly, she'd turn around to start a conversation with someone else.

By the time school was out, I was so fed up that I pulled her aside before she could leave the journalism room and said, "So, are you never going to talk to me again? Is that what you're trying to do here? Is that why you've been ignoring me even though I've been next to you all day? Are you, like, not even going to be my friend anymore?"

"I don't know," she said.

"You don't know if we can still be friends?" I asked. "Because I don't know what you see me as now, but I'm still the same person I was before this weekend." I stepped closer and lowered my voice, desperation making me add, "I'm still the same person you kissed on Saturday night."

She shivered, like she was remembering the kiss. But instead of softening with those words and the memory of Saturday night, she crossed her arms and said, "Yes, I know you're still the same person you were last week. It's just now I know the truth. I know that who you are and who I thought you were are two different things."

"And you can't be friends with me anymore because I believe differently than you?" I looked around to make sure the classroom was empty aside from us. "Because you've been fine being friends with everyone else at this school when they haven't wanted anything to do with your church."

She flinched and took a step back, as if my calling it "her" church instead of "our" church physically hurt.

I cleared my throat and tried to speak in a calmer voice. "I don't want things to change," I said, taking her hands in mine and rubbing my thumbs across her knuckles.

"But they did change," she whispered and looked up at me, pain etched in her brown eyes. "You changed, Hunter. You changed everything."

"So you can't accept me anymore?" I let go of her hands, my shoulders slumping as I took a step back.

"If I only saw you as a friend, it would have been different," she said, her voice breaking as more sadness seeped into her expression. "But I saw you as more than just a friend, Hunter. More than a best friend. You know that. You..." She looked down and sighed momentarily before meeting my gaze again. "We may have never spoken the words, but we both know that even though my dad made us break up, we still both planned to be together after high school."

"I know..." I said, feeling hollow and scared, like I was actually going to lose her for good.

"I can't tie my future to someone who doesn't share my beliefs, Hunter," she said. "It's too important. The church and God are too important to me, and I can't sacrifice my eternity..." She glanced down at her shoes for a moment, and then meeting my gaze, she whispered, *"Even for you."*

And it felt like I just got acid poured over my skin before being stabbed in the heart.

"Just being with someone who loves you in this life isn't enough?" I asked, feeling so broken.

When pain etched deeper in her eyes, I realized what I'd just said.

I'd just told her that I loved her for the first time.

"You said before that you can't stay just because you care about me," she said as tears pooled at the corners of her eyes. "It's the same for me. I can't sacrifice eternity because of how much I love you."

Screw The Fold.

Screw the stupid belief system that taught Scarlett she couldn't be with her husband and children after this life if they didn't believe and obey every single commandment she'd been taught.

I suddenly understood why Bash said he flipped off the church every time he had to go past it.

It was destroying everything.

Scarlett looked like she was going to leave—to head out to basketball practice like my heart wasn't bleeding out at her feet.

But before she got two steps away, she turned back to me

and said, "I want to stay friends and remain in each other's lives. But I..." She sighed. "I'm going to need some time to get over you, Hunter. Just a little space, okay? Until I can be normal."

And all I could do was clench my jaw, bow my head, and say, "Okay."

23

SCARLETT

"ARE you going snowboarding with us this weekend?" Ava asked me during lunch one day. "From what Carter says, it's one of our last chances to go, since the boys' basketball finals are the next weekend."

It had been two weeks since Hunter and I had broken up. Two weeks since we'd said more than a handful of words to each other.

And even though two weeks shouldn't seem like a very long time, it felt like a lifetime.

Basketball season had ended for me—the girls' team had our last game last Thursday, and while we'd done our best this season, we hadn't had what it took to make it to the playoffs.

It sucked because it was my last year and it would have been cool to go all the way to the state finals, but it just hadn't been in the cards for us this year.

Unlike with the boys' team who were basically a shoo-in for the state championship—thanks to the triple threat that was Hunter, Carter, and Mack.

"I wish I could go snowboarding with all of you," I said,

untwisting the cap from my water bottle. "But I'll actually be checking out Columbia with my mom this weekend. So I'll be heading home after school on Friday."

It was getting down to where I needed to decide between Yale and Columbia. Visiting those campuses over the next two weekends would give me the perfect excuse to get out of town and away from everyone.

"You sure you're not purposely scheduling all these things so you won't have to see Hunter and Addison together on a ski lift?" Ava asked, her gaze going to the other end of the table where Hunter and Addison were huddled together, chatting about something.

"I'm trying not to think about those other reasons," I said, looking away before the green monster of jealousy could rise up within me again.

I was eighty-nine percent sure Addison and Hunter had more of a friend-vibe going, since I hadn't caught them holding hands or cuddling on the common room couch together yet. They only did things with the rest of the group, or at the very least, with Evan close by. So I doubted they were sneaking off to make out in the library stacks before study sessions.

But who knows, maybe they were just really good at sneaking around. Maybe Hunter had been able to turn off all his feelings for me—what he'd claimed to be *love*—the moment I told him I could only be friends going forward and he'd instantly jumped into a relationship with a girl whom things could be easy with. A girl who had already shown interest in him by asking him to a dance.

I knew it wouldn't be fair of me to be mad at him if he was moving on, since I was the one who'd told him we couldn't work.

But couldn't he at least make it look like he was as miserable as I was?

Couldn't he look a little rumpled in the mornings at break-fast—like he didn't have the energy to comb his hair properly or had bags under his eyes because he hadn't been able to sleep?

Couldn't he pretend like he was unable to eat more than a few bites at each meal because his nervous system was so messed up from the heartbreak that it made his stomach a jumble of nerves any time he saw or thought about me?

Couldn't he look like this was at least half as hard for him as it was for me?

I mean, I knew I was the one who'd had to draw the line in the sand and make the hard choice to do what was best for myself in the grand scheme of things.

But couldn't he be pining for me, just a little?

Show just an ounce of suffering?

But no, he was all smiles whenever I looked at him, and I was the one left wondering if I could have said or done anything differently to have kept him in The Fold.

Why hadn't I said something sooner? Why hadn't I done something the first time he missed church?

If I'd made him feel more needed and like he made the church a better place, would he have come back? People liked to be valued, and maybe being away at school and only getting his spiritual bucket filled through online sermons hadn't been enough for him.

Maybe he'd needed the in-person connection to stay strong.

While he said he made his choice based on some research that he did, maybe if he'd felt more valued, he never would have had motive to start looking for reasons to leave in the first place.

24

HUNTER

I WAS RIDING home on the bus after a playoff game on Wednesday when Mack and Carter asked me what was going on with Scarlett and me.

"Things have been weird the past two weeks," Mack said from his seat across the aisle from me. "You're usually joined at the hip. But Cambrielle and I have noticed that you two have been sitting at opposite ends of the lunch table and barely talking during any of the classes we have together."

"I've noticed that, too," Carter added from the seat in front of me. "And she's been skipping study sessions to be on her own."

I figured people would notice things were off.

It was just like last May all over again.

Only worse since there was no hope of a future this time.

"We're just going in different directions." I shrugged.

"Does it have anything to do with you breaking up last year?" Carter asked. "Has it just been too hard to get back to normal?"

"It's been tricky," I said. "But that's not it. We were good for a while again. And we actually went on a date on President's Day weekend."

"You did?" Mack's dark eyes went wide.

"Yeah," I said. "I was going to tell you guys about it. But..." I drifted off, hating that I had to say the next part because I hated that it was real. "She found out I don't plan on returning to church, and because of that, she decided she needed space."

"So she's not allowed to date someone who isn't a member of her church?" Mack frowned, confused.

"Kind of," I said. "Mixed-faith relationships can be tough in general—but they're nearly impossible in high-demand religions. When you believe that families can only be together if the husband and wife and children remain strong and *worthy* according to The Fold's standards..." I did air quotes on the word *worthy* since it was such a loaded word for me now. "So me already choosing to step away, with Scarlett and her father thinking it's important for her to end up with someone who stays in, causes issues."

"And here I thought secretly dating my best friend's sister had been complicated," Mack said, running a hand over his black curly hair. "I knew things were more strict for you guys and that there were more rules. But I didn't realize just how deeply they affected all of your choices."

"Being part of The Fold is a way of life," I said. "If you're a true believer—someone who literally believes the High Priest speaks to and for God—you can't help but feel like you need to do everything he says in order to be saved from eternal torment after this life."

"Saved from eternal torment?" Carter asked, his blond eyebrows knitting together. "So, since Mack and I don't believe, does that mean we're, like, doomed in their mind?"

"Sort of," I said with a shrug. "It's actually better for you than it is for me, though. Because in their eyes, I had the truth and threw it away whereas you two never had the truth. So while you still don't get the highest level of heaven, you can still go to, like, mediocre heaven. And since I'm now considered an apostate, I'll be booted to Hell and the land of fire and brimstone."

"Yikes," Carter said.

"Yeah..." I nodded.

"So right now, in Scarlett's mind, you're, like, gonna be living with all the murderers and rapists and terrorists in her religion's version of the afterlife?" Mack asked.

"I don't know if she has quite put me in that place," I said. "But that's definitely where the doctrine puts me."

"That's rough," Mack said.

It was. It sucked.

"Is there a way to—pardon me if this is offensive—" Carter said, "—but, like, how do you get through that kind of indoctrination? Can we have an intervention? Is there something that just works and clicks someone out of that reality?"

"Yeah..." Mack leaned closer. "Because you've literally done nothing wrong. It's dumb that a religion can come between two people as perfect for each other as you and Scarlett."

"If there is a way, I don't know it," I said. "It's literally impossible to reason with some believers because of how closely they identify with the church. All of their defenses go up and they feel personally attacked when you say anything bad about The Fold." I remembered the way Scarlett had cut me off and fled the rooftop when I started to explain my research. "They literally can't listen. Their brain tries to protect them from the information that will disrupt their whole nervous system. And then there's the whole talk of how you always need to be on your guard because Satan is always trying to get you on his side."

"But something worked for you, right?" Carter asked. "And your brother and parents, too?"

I nodded. "If the person is ready or has had enough things happen to put cracks in their beliefs—like maybe they had a family member defect whom they knew to be a good person—or maybe they came across some disturbing or confusing information here and there and they put it on their proverbial spiritual shelf. Once there are too many issues on the shelf, it all comes tumbling down. Sometimes, another sort of traumatic thing can trigger a change that can help you snap out of the mind fog."

"So if we just tell Scarlett about all the issues you found, it might help get her out?" Mack asked like it could be a relatively simple process.

"It might...if you could get her to even listen," I said. "But also, a faith crisis is a major traumatic event that I wouldn't wish on anyone. Like, it's hard to understand if you haven't gone through it, but it's like getting tossed off a boat and suddenly finding yourself lost at sea with no life preserver. The Fold is a huge safety net for a lot of people and having it suddenly dissolve can be terrifying because you have to rebuild everything after that.

"For me, I believed it so much that my whole world view basically revolved around what I'd been taught. How I thought the world had been created. What I thought the purpose of life was. How I should live. It played a part in every single decision I made. It was everything. And losing that, along with initially losing my parents' support..." I shook my head, remembering the darkness and how alone I'd felt and all the days I'd spent lying on my bedroom floor, trying to make sense of the universe and the purpose of life. "It sucked."

"I had no idea what you were going through," Mack said. "I wish you'd been able to help us understand better so we could be there for you."

"You were dealing with your own stuff," I said, thinking about how his mom had been in her last few months of life while I was going through the thick of it. "And actually, you guys did help me. Seeing that there were actually really great people out there, who didn't have any strict religious beliefs, helped me realize that The Fold didn't have a monopoly on good people."

Helped me have hope that everything would be okay.

"But you don't think we can just have a straightforward conversation about all this with Scarlett?" Carter asked.

"I don't know," I said. "You can't always tell how someone will react. Some people are completely fine and move on quickly and easily. While other people are traumatized and go spiraling into making a lot of unhealthy and unsafe choices."

"And you think Scarlett may be more of the trauma and spiraling type?" Mack asked.

"Maybe." I shrugged. "If she did break free and come to the same conclusion that I did, I think she'd feel a huge sense of betrayal and go through the stages of grief like I did. But maybe not."

"And maybe she'd still stay in, even after learning the things you learned," Carter surmised.

"Yep." I sighed. "There are entire websites and podcasts dedicated to explaining away a lot of the issues with The Fold and how if you look at them at just the right angle they can all still be fine. People will do a lot of mental gymnastics to stay in the safety of their belief system. So who knows, she could end up saying the extra information only made her faith stronger. It just depends."

"Which is why you haven't really tried to push it with her?" Carter asked.

I nodded. "If she wants to look into things, it's something she'll have to do on her own."

"You're a more patient man than me," Mack said. "I'd be doing that intervention pronto if I were you."

"I probably would, too," Carter agreed. "If Ava got mixed up in an organization that tried to keep her from me, I wouldn't be able to keep from doing everything in my power to get through to her."

"Same with Cambrielle," Mack added.

Carter chuckled and looked at Mack. "It's still weird hearing you say that about my sister, by the way."

"Probably almost as weird as seeing my sister walk through the door last night with her hair all messed up and knowing that my best friend was responsible for it," Mack said.

They both laughed.

But what they were saying did make me think.

If Scarlett was as important to me as my friends' girlfriends were to them, shouldn't I be trying harder to fix things?

Ugh, but it was so hard when neither Scarlett nor I could compromise our beliefs.

I certainly wouldn't be willing to live a lie or raise a family in an environment that could be dangerous and spiritually abusive.

Scarlett didn't see any of those things yet, of course. But there had to be a way for me to at least try.

I mean, it wasn't like things could get much worse from where they were right now.

25

SCARLETT

MY TOUR of Columbia went well on Saturday. My mom and I made a whole day of it, and it was fun seeing her favorite hangout spots on campus from back in the day.

"I always kind of regretted not finishing my degree here when I had the chance," she said as we walked past the Butler Library—a ten-story, neoclassical-style building that had an amazing colonnade with the names of famous writers, philosophers, and thinkers inscribed above the twelve columns. "It's not every day that you get accepted to an Ivy League college, you know. And while I had so much fun my freshman year, I always felt like I missed out on some of the college experience when I married your dad, got pregnant right away, and had to drop out."

"Do you sometimes wish you hadn't gotten married so young?" I asked, curious since I knew a lot of that had been influenced by my dad and the church. And now that she was inactive and divorced, it would make sense if she was upset about those things the same way that the lady whose story Hunter accidentally emailed me about did.

"Would I recommend it to you?" she asked, looking at me with her brown eyes that matched mine. "Probably not. Just because when you're young, there is so much to experience and so many opportunities. It was hard taking care of a baby and figuring things out with a husband who was so much older than me when I hadn't quite figured out who I was as a person."

"So it was hard?"

"It was hard for *me*." She nodded. "I didn't think so at the time, but I was a lot more immature back then and had no idea what I was getting into when I married your strait-laced, pastor father."

"You were immature when you were nineteen?" I asked with a teasing glint in my eyes, since my mom had always been more of a free spirit, despite being an extremely successful investment banker.

Her motto was that she worked hard so she could play hard. She thought I should be better at adopting that motto myself, always commenting on how I needed to loosen up and have a little more fun instead of stressing so much about the future.

"I know it's hard to imagine I was ever immature, since I've always been such a fabulous mother to you." She chuckled like she'd just told a joke. "But those first few years of motherhood were rough, and there were many occasions when I felt envious of all my friends who were able to just get their degree done all in one go without the complications of a husband and family."

"So you regret having me so young?" I asked, trying not to feel hurt at being seen as a complication.

"It's not that I regret having you. It's definitely not that." She put her arm around my shoulders. "I would never give you back in a million years. You've always been such an amazing daughter."

"But you would have waited a few years if you had to do it all over again?" I asked.

"Probably," she said. "Sure, there are positives to having kids young. You have more energy then. And because I was only twenty when you were born, it totally means I'll be a cool, hip grandma when you have kids..." She squeezed me closer. "In, like, ten years—after you've had a chance to figure out what you want to do, right?"

I responded with a non-committal shrug.

Waiting until after college was probably smart, but I also knew from what I'd learned at church that even if I did have a baby before the time my mom recommended, the Lord would provide a way since he always did.

My mom must have seen something in my eyes, because she looked at me sideways. "You're not planning to elope with Hunter right after graduation, are you?"

"What? No." I took a step back and shook my head. "I mean, H-Hunter and I— We're not like that."

"You're not?" She raised an eyebrow, like she didn't believe me. "I know I don't always see everything that goes on, since you spend most of your time away at school. But I could have sworn you two were an item and just pretending to be friends because your father has that stick up his butt about steady dating in high school."

"It probably looked like that," I said, somewhat surprised that she'd thought I'd gone behind my dad's back and had been okay with it. "But Hunter and I—well, we're actually barely even friends right now."

"What?" Mom gripped my arm and stopped in the middle of the walkway, forcing the people who'd been walking behind us to quickly step around us. "You and Hunter are having problems?"

I nodded, hating the fact that just thinking about Hunter caused tears to prick at my eyes. "Things got tricky a couple of weeks ago and—" My voice wobbled, and I dabbed at the corners of my eyes with my fingertips. "And I don't think they'll ever be the same."

"Did he hurt you?" Mom furrowed her brow. "Because if he did, I'm going to march right up to the Blackwell's penthouse tonight and tell them they need to talk to their son."

"He didn't do anything to me," I hurried to say. "It's complicated and..." I drifted off. When my mom had been an active member of The Fold, she'd been more of a cafeteria member. She'd been raised by very nuanced parents and had been taught that it was okay to pick and choose which commandments and teachings she wanted to apply to her life—throwing out the things she didn't connect with or want to believe in.

She never understood that things actually were black and white and that it was important to follow all of the commandments the High Priests had revealed to us if we wanted to have all the blessings in the next life.

So if I told her that Hunter and I were having problems because I couldn't see a future with someone who was on a different page with his beliefs, she wouldn't understand.

I mean, she was dating Rodney—a guy who was agnostic and claimed that the spiritual workings of the universe were unknowable. She couldn't care less that the guy she considered her soulmate wanted nothing to do with religion, even though she'd always told me that she would "probably come back to church someday."

It just wasn't something that was important to her right now.

"Is it complicated because he's stepped away from The Fold?" Mom asked when I didn't finish my thought.

My eyebrows knitted together. "How did you know about that?"

She started to walk down the sidewalk again. "His mom came by a few weeks ago to ask me why I stopped attending church. I guess they came across some disturbing information and were wondering if I'd heard about it, too."

"What did you say?" Had my mom read whatever Hunter and his parents had read and just not ever said anything about it?

"I told them that I'd never heard of the things they were talking about." Mom looked at me. "I guess they were having issues with Samuel Williams and the early church—along with some of the things they thought the church was behind the times on."

They wanted the church to shift its doctrine to fit in with the ever-changing world? Didn't they realize that God made the rules, not man?

"Anyway," Mom continued, "I told them I stopped going mostly because I didn't fit the mold of a pastor's wife or even as a regular member of the church. That I've always been wired differently since it wasn't giving me the spiritual upliftment it seemed to give everyone else on Sunday."

"Is that all you talked about?" I asked, curious what else they may have said. "Did they ask you to read the anti-Fold material they were reading?"

Had they seen the chinks in my mom's belief and tried to pull her further away?

"They know I never knew enough about the doctrine to really care about any of that stuff." Mom shrugged. "But I guess they've been doing a ton of studying—Hunter, too—which is why I wondered if that was the reason you two were having a hard time. Has he been pushing you to research the church the way he has and it's making you uncomfortable?"

"He sent me a link to a website when I asked him to read *Visitations with Jehovah* once more," I said. "But nothing since then."

"Did you read what he sent?" she asked, sounding simply curious and not like she cared whether I had or hadn't read it.

"I knew better than to open it."

"I wouldn't blame you if you looked. It sounded like some pretty interesting stuff." Mom shrugged again. "But like I said, a lot of what they were saying was over my head. I just told them that I saw The Fold as a good place to raise a family. I've always been fine with your father taking the reins in your spiritual education—it's what he does for a living, after all—and I've focused more on making sure you were getting the best education for everything else." She glanced sideways at me. "As well as trying to keep you from burning yourself out." She paused and seemed to remember why we'd started talking about this stuff in the first place. "But it's too bad that this has come between you and Hunter."

"Yeah..." It sucked.

"And you don't think there's a way to reconcile?" she asked. "Because I may be out of touch on a lot of things, but I know that boy cares about you. A friendship like yours doesn't come around every day. Your father and I were never really friends, which is another reason why we didn't work out. And I know that you see things differently than me, but I just figure that you only get one life that we know of. You might as well make the most of it. Stop worrying so much about the future and focus on what's right here in front of you. Because if you ask me, what you and Hunter have is worth figuring out."

"Too bad that is much easier said than done." It seemed pointless now when we were basically on opposite ends of things. He wanted nothing to do with the church, and I knew it was something I could never leave.

We made it to the restaurant where we planned to eat dinner, and as we waited to be seated, my mom said, "I do know that this whole experience has been quite hard on

Hunter. Having his parents so against his choice initially and taking away his trust fund had to make him feel so alone."

"His parents took away his trust fund?" I stared at my mom, consciously having to keep my jaw from dropping.

"He didn't tell you?" Mom frowned, like she assumed Hunter had told me all the details of what brought him to where he was now.

"I didn't really know anything about this until a few weeks ago," I admitted. "Not until after I confronted him about why his parents stopped going to church."

Why hadn't he told me any of this?

"I wouldn't take it too personally." Mom patted my back gently. "I'm sure he didn't say anything about it because he needed time to figure things out before announcing such a big change. From what I hear, it has been quite the process. Hundreds of hours of study. And with a family as strong as the Blackwells, I'm sure it was something he didn't want to take lightly."

"Possibly," I said, thinking about what my mom was saying. Hunter definitely was the type of person who made choices carefully. So I guess it was possible he'd actually put in a lot of time and effort into his decision.

He was thoughtful about everything he did.

"Plus," Mom continued, "after what happened with his parents, he probably didn't want to rock the boat and risk losing you, too."

I nodded. "You're probably right."

And if that was the case, I'd done the exact thing he'd been trying to avoid.

I'd completely iced him out when he needed me most.

Man, I was a crappy friend.

I GOT to church early the next day. After shaking my dad's hand—something he did with everyone as they walked through the front doors—I walked into the back of the chapel and found Xander standing there, chatting with Brother and Sister Morris.

Did he come here every Sunday? I thought for sure he attended the congregation in New Haven while away at school.

I was just looking for an empty seat near the front when Xander seemed to notice me. He flashed his dashing smile, and after finishing his conversation with the Morrises, he stepped up by my side and said, "What a pleasant surprise this is to see you here. I didn't realize you were in town."

"I came to check out Columbia with my mom yesterday," I said. "And since the closest congregation to Eden Falls is in New Haven, I figured I'd catch today's service in person before heading back to school."

"Well, it's good to see you."

"Good to see you, too," I said. And I didn't know why it happened, but for some reason, I blushed every time I was around him.

Okay, so my blush probably had something to do with the fact that he was super hot and older, and I still didn't understand why he'd agreed to go to the dance with a high school senior like me.

He must have noticed my blush because he said, "I forgot to ask, but did you ever get those flowers I had sent to you after the dance?"

"Oh yes, I did," I said, realizing that I'd totally forgotten to thank him for the Valentine's Day flowers in my excitement to go on a date with Hunter. "I can't believe I forgot to say anything, but thank you. They were so beautiful."

"Beautiful flowers for a beautiful girl." He winked.

I wasn't sure how I felt about his flirtatious wink—it didn't feel the same coming from him as it did from Hunter. But I managed to smile anyway.

A few more families entered the chapel. As the pews started filling up, Xander asked, "Mind if I join you for the sermon? I noticed you sitting alone a few weeks ago and was hoping you'd like some company."

"S-sure," I said, even though I wasn't sure about it. But when he walked to the pew that was front and center in the chapel, I followed and sat next to him anyway.

The service started the same as usual. There was an opening hymn, followed by a prayer, followed by another hymn to help us prepare for communion. The Lord's Supper—small pieces of bread and juice—was then passed around on trays by church officials. We each took the offering, and for the next few minutes, I pondered on the meaning behind this tradition and thought back to the sins I needed to repent of from this past week.

I hadn't done anything huge. I was pretty good at staying away from the *big* sins.

But I probably should have turned off one of the songs I'd listened to on my train ride from Eden Falls since it had cursed a few times and the message of the song had been hovering right on the line of promoting lustful thoughts.

I probably also shouldn't have watched those last few episodes of *The Office* either, with some of the characters really pushing it with their suggestive jokes as well.

If only it wasn't such a funny show and they hadn't hooked me with Jim and Pam's storyline, I could have quit watching it a long time ago.

Everyone had their vices, and apparently, PG-13 TV shows and songs were mine.

I'd just have to try to do better next week.

Once everyone had received communion, my dad made his

way to the pulpit to introduce the special guest who would be addressing us today.

My dad did the sermons three-fourths of the time, but at least one Sunday a month was reserved for one of the special leaders of The Fold.

When one of the Elders stood by my dad, I realized why Xander was here today instead of in New Haven. "Did you come home this weekend because you knew Elder Radley would be speaking?"

He nodded as he unbuttoned his suit coat. "Your dad mentioned it while we were chatting on the phone earlier this week, so I changed my plans to be in town for it. Elder Radley's talks have always been my favorites."

"I usually like his, too."

The Elders—the men who were in the office just below the High Priest in our church's hierarchy—frequently traveled to the different congregations in the church district they were in charge of, giving the members inspired messages for our day. So it was always a special treat to have one come.

"Any idea what he'll be talking about today?" I whispered as Elder Radley pulled an iPad, which probably held the notes for his sermon, out from his suit coat.

"Not sure." Xander shrugged, his shoulder rubbing against mine with the movement and wafting some of his expensive-smelling cologne my way. "But I'm sure it's a good one. He was actually scheduled to talk somewhere else before the High Priest asked him to change plans and come here today."

"Good thing I brought my notebook then," I said.

I always jotted down notes here and there during the sermons so that I could reference them in my interview with my dad afterwards. I doubted my dad would grill me too much today—after all, he could see me on the front row and know whether I was paying attention or not. But if this was going to be a special sermon that the High Priest had felt inspired for Elder Radley to give, I might be transcribing the whole thing.

I loved that our church had continued revelation. It was always fun anticipating what new, groundbreaking news the High Priest and the Elders had to share with us since the revelation came to them directly from God.

Would he have a more accurate timeline for when the Chosen One would be born? We were told we were living in the last days before Jehovah and Samuel Williams's return to Earth, so it would make sense that more would be revealed soon in order for us to prepare.

Or maybe there was another revelation that wasn't even on our radar...

But Elder Radley began explaining the importance of staying on the straight and narrow path instead and making sure we were careful of whom we associated with.

"We're living in the last days where Satan and his Henchman are increasingly cunning," Elder Radley said boldly into the microphone. "Even the most valiant are getting caught up in the twisted web of lies that they are weaving. We cannot be lazy learners. We cannot let our guards down for even a second. I know there are a few, once beloved members of your own congregation who have become victims of this. They were not vigilant in nourishing their faith in the gospel. They were not cautious with the material they allowed to enter their minds and it has damaged their ability to discern between truth and fiction."

He paused for a moment, and I was pretty sure he glanced my way before looking out at the rest of the congregation again. "We can be polite to those who have gone astray, but it is imperative that we do not let them pull us down the path of darkness and misery with them. I exhort you all to be diligent in keeping the commandments and immersing yourself in the teachings of our beloved High Priest and the words of Jehovah, so you don't find yourself caught up in the bondage of the adversary and headed down the same path that our once valiant friends have chosen."

Is he talking about Hunter's family? I wondered as a chill raced down my spine. Because from the way he'd looked at me, the pastor's daughter who was known to have been close with the Blackwells, it definitely seemed like it.

Seemed like this whole sermon might actually be a form of damage control for the disruption their absence had brought to the members of my dad's congregation.

And if it was about them, I couldn't help but think that Elder Radley was being really dismissive and almost like he was trying to turn the whole congregation against them instead of encouraging us to help them back.

I mean, isn't that what Jehovah said we should do? To reach out to the lost sheep?

Even though I might not be on the best of terms with Hunter at the moment and I had said some careless things about his level of belief in one of our last conversations, I knew that he had been a true believer before this year. And he'd most definitely been a better student of the gospel than me if he'd read *Visitations with Jehovah* a dozen times like he'd said he had.

I didn't understand exactly what Hunter and his family had been through to push them out of the church, but they had not been lazy learners. If anything, it sounded like their doubts had made them study more than most of the members I knew.

As Elder Radley continued to talk, instead of being an uplifting sermon that made me want to be a better person, he went on a rampage of telling us how much better the members of The Fold were than the non-believers without the gospel.

He talked about how when we were baptized into The

Fold, we were given the special gift of the spirit that helped us seek out and discern the truth—something those without the gospel weren't worthy to have.

I'd probably heard dozens of sermons like this before, but now that I had a friend on the other side, I was hearing it with different ears.

I also didn't love the way he spoke as if we were superior to the non-believers. The way he was actually demonizing them.

I mean, what if one of them happened to come in here today? Hearing them being talked about like this wouldn't make them want to come back.

People came to church to hear uplifting messages. Not to hear fear-inducing talks like this.

By the time he was finished and the closing hymn started, I was ready to get out of the chapel. I needed some fresh air to clear the conflicting thoughts going through my head. So I pretended like I needed a bathroom break. I walked out the chapel doors and went outside to sit on one of the benches.

I didn't know why I was so upset after hearing Elder Radley's talk. He really hadn't said anything I hadn't heard before.

Was I just projecting my own thoughts onto his sermon? Was it possible he wasn't even talking about Hunter's family being the "valiant friends" who left the church?

But having Hunter's family in my mind just made the words sting a little more, because it made their choice seem so final and scary.

It also made things confusing because the way Elder Radley talked about apostates and how their countenances became dark and loathsome without the gospel didn't exactly fit, either—Hunter still looked and acted the same as he had before.

He was still a good person.

I mean, he gave his seat up for an old woman on the subway just because that was who he was. He did good things like that.

And now that I knew he hadn't even believed in the church at that point in time, I also knew he'd simply done that out of the goodness of his heart. Not to get extra brownie points from the angels watching our every move from heaven.

"Is something wrong?" Xander asked, his voice startling me from behind.

"I just needed some fresh air," I said, not sure I wanted to talk about it.

"Are you upset about Elder Radley's talk?" He stepped in front of my bench, inspecting my face with his piercing blue eyes.

"Kind of."

He took the seat next to me. With a sigh, he said, "Elder Radley does come off really strong sometimes."

"He did today, at least," I said. Which seemed to be a popular quality in church leaders since my dad came off strong a lot of times, too.

"Are you upset because of your friend Hunter?" Xander asked in a gentle voice.

"Yes..." I furrowed my brow and looked at him. "How did you know?"

"Your dad mentioned something to me about his family leaving." Xander swept his gaze over the courtyard before adding, "I guess it caused quite the stir among the members here."

"It did."

A lot of rumors too, I thought as I remembered the story Leandra had told me about Hunter's dad getting addicted to porn and cheating on his mom.

"And I'm sure it hurts a little, doesn't it?" Xander rubbed

the back of his neck. "To have your friend reject something that is so important to you."

I nodded, feeling the pain of the last few weeks well up in the form of tears.

Don't cry, I tried to tell myself. *You made it through that whole stupid sermon, you don't need to tear up now that Xander is asking you about it.*

I must not have been very good at hiding my emotions though, because Xander wiped at a tear just trickling out the corner of my eye. Leaning close, he said, "I know how hard it is to go through something like that."

"Y-you do?" I asked, frowning.

He nodded. "I had a good friend leave The Fold when we got to college." He sat back against the back of the bench. "It was rough seeing someone I cared about—someone who had been so strong—just toss his beliefs out the window."

"Were you able to remain friends?" I asked, leaning back beside him.

"No." Xander shook his head and draped his arm behind me on the bench. "He started partying and just living a really wild lifestyle, so I had to distance myself. It was really sad, actually. He became an addict and really went spiraling after that."

"That's too bad," I said, not really knowing what else to say.

"It is." Xander nodded. "Sadly, that kind of thing happens all the time when people leave the church. Which is most likely why Elder Radley was so aggressive in his talk today."

I hadn't really known anyone who stopped coming to church besides my mom and Hunter's older brother Sebastian before this month. And they'd been able to avoid too much spiraling.

But were they just the exception to the rule?

Was Hunter only okay right now because it was just the beginning and we were still in high school?

I really hoped he wouldn't go wild like Xander's friend and get involved in drugs and alcohol or do something reckless like sleeping around.

Which made me realize that I had no idea if he even planned to keep his oath of chastity anymore now that he didn't believe everything else.

Would he stay pure before marriage? Or had all of those standards disappeared with his faith?

I didn't know. I hadn't thought to ask him any of those questions.

I RODE the train back home after dinner, still thinking through the events of the day. I didn't typically get upset by the sermons. I was usually cheering whenever they talked on the more hard-hitting topics since being a member of The Fold wasn't supposed to be easy. With this life being a testing ground for the next one, we needed to prove we deserved the blessings the Lord wanted to give us.

But the way Elder Radley had singled out the Blackwells bothered me. Sure, I got that they had been led astray and could become dangerous if they tried to spread the lies they'd read among the members of the congregation. But Hunter was also my friend—estranged or not—and I didn't want to just stand by and watch his family's reputation being smeared by a person whom many people looked up to.

Elder Radley was a powerful man with a lot of influence. The words he said held a lot of weight with the members of the church.

When I walked into the common room around seven, it was full of students sitting at tables, catching up on this weekend's homework or watching a scary movie on the big TV.

Usually, Hunter and I played card games at a table in the corner or joined in on the Sunday movie night since they usually picked fun movies that I hadn't seen before. But I would probably be on my own tonight.

I was thinking about heading to my room to write in my journal when I spotted Hunter out of the corner of my eye, sitting alone at a table with a stack of cards.

Had he been waiting for me?

Was this my chance to try and clear the air with him?

To tell him that while I still couldn't see things working out romantically in the future, it would be nice to get back to being best friends again?

I drew in a deep breath, gearing up to walk over there, but then Addison headed straight for Hunter's table with two mugs of hot chocolate in her hands. And when Hunter smiled as she approached, my chest fell.

He was waiting for her... not me.

He held out his hands for one of the mugs, and when she sat down, they started playing a game of slap jack.

So it was just like every other Sunday night to Hunter. The only thing different was the person he played his card games with.

"Want me to make room for you on the couch?" Evan's voice sounded through the fog that had suddenly filled my head.

I turned around. Evan was sitting on the nearby couch, watching me with a worried expression. Like he knew I was seething with jealousy right now and worried I might make a scene.

Should I pretend like I was fine? That I didn't care that Hunter had decided to move on without me?

Because like it or not, I was probably going to have to get

used to this. I couldn't expect Hunter to stay single forever. Not when he was mega-hot and smart and amazing.

I pushed those thoughts away.

"I actually think I'll just hang out in my room tonight," I told Evan instead, hoping I sounded somewhat believable.

"Okay, cool." When his gaze went over to Addison and Hunter, I couldn't be sure, but it almost looked like he was clenching his jaw. As if he, too, was upset that they were sitting together.

But that wouldn't make any sense, would it? For him to be jealous of his stepsister hanging out with Hunter?

Maybe I was just seeing things because I didn't want to be the only person seething with jealousy tonight.

"Have a good night, Evan," I said before I could imagine any other weird things.

"You, too."

I headed up the stairs to the girls' dorm and checked in with our house mom, Heather, so she'd know I made it back from my weekend away.

Once I was in my room and changed into my pajamas, I pulled out my journal to write out my jumble of thoughts. But when I saw my entry from a few weeks before where I'd complained about how much time *Dear Eliza*'s column was taking from me, I had an idea enter my head.

I seemed to be at a loss for what to do with Hunter. Maybe I should contact someone who always seemed to know what to do.

So before I could rethink the impulse, I grabbed my laptop and opened it to the junk email account that I'd set up freshman year.

As I typed out my email to *The Confidant*, I just prayed that she would have some insights for how I could get out of this mess I was currently in.

26

HUNTER

I WOKE up early on Monday, my body still used to getting up by five-thirty after years of early morning Bible class. I tried falling back asleep, since I actually hadn't slept that great last night. But after fifteen minutes passed and I only became more and more alert, I figured I might as well grab an early breakfast and sort through some of the emails *The Confidant* had sitting in his inbox.

I got dressed in the dark so I wouldn't bother Asher who was still asleep. With my backpack over my shoulder and my phone in my hand, I headed down to the great hall to see what the school's cooks had whipped up for us today.

I was the first person in the great hall for breakfast—apparently, no one else was hungry this early—so I had the first pick of ingredients to add to my bowl from the oatmeal bar. I got a huge scoop of steel-cut oats, topped it with some blueberries, almonds, and a teaspoon of mini-chocolate chips to make it interesting and sweet. Then I filled a mug with some of the filter coffee they had at the coffee-and-tea station and went to the table I usually sat at with my friends.

I started sorting *The Confidant*'s emails into my Yes, Maybe, and No folders and gave a star to a few of my favorites. I didn't know why I even had the "No" folder. I should probably just delete the emails I sent there right then, instead of saving them for my weekly purge. But I kept the folder as a safety net anyway, just in case I changed my mind later.

I found a few emails that I thought would be good for my next installment. There was one asking for advice on how to decide which college to attend the next year—college-decision day was coming up fast.

Another asked how to set a boundary with a friend who continually pressured this reader to allow them to copy their homework week after week.

And then there was another that I'd starred when I first sat down because it struck so close to home for me.

I opened the email again and took a bite of my oatmeal as I read.

Dear Confidant,

My friend and I had a huge fight recently. Like, an epically bad fight. We've been best friends for years and have never had a disagreement like this before. But recently, things shifted. He's decided to take a different path with his life, and we aren't able to see eye to eye on some really important things.

I don't know how to fix it. I'm also really worried about him and what might happen if he doesn't get his life back on the right track.

Any advice on how to stay friends even when you have big differences?

-I Just Want My Best Friend Back

This had to be Scarlett, right? Like, who else could it be? Sure, *The Confidant* received emails from people all over the United States now, so it was possible that it was someone else. But...it had to be her. Especially since it came from an email address that Scarlett would totally pick: futurevaledictorian@awesomemail.com.

Scarlett was all about using her goals as passwords and other things like that.

I thought about responding to the email right away, because if it was Scarlett, I also wanted to figure out how to be friends again. But the great hall was just beginning to populate, and since I'd rather not have anyone looking over my shoulder and figuring out my secret identity, I decided to head out to the library with the hopes that I could find a quiet corner.

I had just turned the corner of the hall that would lead me to the library when I found myself suddenly walking straight toward Scarlett. I looked at the time on my watch, and just like I expected, it was seven o' five and she must have just finished her early morning Bible class.

As we stepped closer toward each other, my heart beat faster. Even though I knew nothing would ever happen between us now, I couldn't get over how beautiful she was. Her auburn hair was pulled back into a high ponytail—such a simple look on most girls. But on Scarlett, it got my heart pumping every time because it showed off her long neck. And as my gaze landed on the simple gold chain with a tiny star charm, I was instantly taken back to the first time she'd let me kiss her neck.

We'd gone to a party at Mack's house the Friday before spring break, and instead of heading straight back to the school, we'd ended up pulling over to the side of the road and kissing in my car for three hours.

I could still feel the softness of her skin on my lips. Remember the way she'd smelled. The way she'd sighed and let her head fall back as I'd kissed my way along her jaw and down her neck.

It had all been so new and exhilarating, and even though I'd always thought it would be easy to keep my oath of chastity, that was the first night I'd realized it was actually possible to get into a headspace where you wouldn't want to stop.

I'd felt so guilty about our kissing session the next Sunday when Scarlett's dad gave a special sermon to the youth and spoke about the need to stay watchful that our passions didn't get the better of us and lead us down the slippery slope to breaking our covenants with God. All I could think of the whole time he was talking was that if he knew what I'd just been doing with his daughter two nights earlier, he'd probably never let me within twenty feet of her again.

Scarlett had apparently felt guilty enough about it, too, because as soon as we left the youth meeting that night, she'd pulled me into the back of the church courtyard so we could come up with a plan that would keep us in check. And that was when we came up with the "three-kisses rule."

The three-kisses rule being our agreement that we would only kiss each other three times each night so we wouldn't be tempted to take things too far again.

Our three-kisses rule only lasted two days though. By day three, we were desperate and clever enough to find a work-around our own rule—deciding that each kiss only counted as a separate kiss if our lips separated.

So as long as we didn't pull away long enough to catch our breath, a single kiss could go on for ten minutes or longer—depending on how much rationalizing we did.

By the next Friday, we abandoned the whole idea completely. I ended up pulling her onto my lap while we watched a show on her dad's couch so we could make out through several episodes of *All-American* while her dad and stepmom were out of the house.

We probably would have kissed for several episodes more if Xander hadn't knocked on the back door, hoping to talk to her dad.

Hmmm. That's interesting.

We'd been making out on the couch in the family room, and from the right angle, someone from outside could have seen us there.

Was it possible Xander had been the one to tell Pastor Caldwell that we'd moved away from just being platonic friends?

That would be an interesting twist, wouldn't it...

Her dad had found out about us steady dating just the next day, right?

I'd always kind of wondered if he had nanny cams or paid a fellow classmate to keep an eye on Scarlett and make sure she stayed "pure."

I cringed, thinking of the word and how damaging purity culture was to me now.

But maybe there hadn't been any hidden cameras or student spies at all. Maybe Xander was the secret mole...

Scarlett and I were only a few feet away from each other now, and when she seemed to notice me, I tried to figure out what to do.

What I wished I could do was to turn around and walk with her so we could chat while she ate her breakfast like we used to do.

But instead of doing that, we both gave each other an awkward smile and a wave.

And then she was gone.

I turned to watch her from behind, and when she was a few

feet away, her shoulders seemed to sag—like she, too, had been disappointed that we'd just passed by each other.

Man, I needed to fix this. And since she'd already reached out to *The Confidant*, I would try to use that to make it happen.

27

SCARLETT

I WAS JUST SCROLLING through *Dear Eliza*'s emails on my phone, waiting for first period to begin on Monday morning, when an email notification popped up at the top of my screen from TheConfidant@awesomemail.com.

Wait.

What?

I clicked on the notification, which took me to the inbox of my junk mail account, and sure enough, I had a response to my email from last night.

Dear I Just Want My Best Friend Back,

I know you probably expected me to respond in my weekly column, but I didn't feel I had enough info to give you very good advice.

First off, I'm sorry to hear things are rocky with your best friend. That must be hard to have such a big disturbance come to a relationship you've had for so long. You say you don't see eye to eye on some important things? That you're worried for him?

It's hard to know what things you might be referring to without the details. But I'm guessing these are changes he is making and not you. He has broken the status quo that you wanted to keep, and it has you worried for him?

Have these changes brought negative things into his life? Or are you just preemptively worried about what might happen based on what you've heard about people in these circumstances before?

Trying to understand so I can better advise,
-The Confidant

Does The Confidant *email everyone back?* I wondered, surprised that she'd even seen my email.

She most likely didn't have time to respond to all the emails she got, since she had to receive hundreds of them each week. But this was cool of her to take the time to clarify before advising. Which just went to show why she was the best at what she did.

I checked the clock on the wall as a couple more of my classmates trickled in. We still had about ten minutes before the bell would ring, and since Hunter hadn't joined me at my table yet, I quickly pulled out my laptop so I could type out a quick response.

———————————

Dear Confidant,

Thank you for your email. I appreciate you taking the time for me since I know you must be extremely busy.

So to answer your question, I haven't really noticed anything, like, bad happening yet. Just that well...I guess it might be hard to understand if I don't go into the particulars...

I THEN PROCEEDED to give some of the details about how we'd grown up in the same church. Believed the same things. Wanted the same things out of life.

How we'd both been on the right path: the straight and narrow path.

Then I talked about how Hunter had jumped off the boat recently and that because of what we'd been taught, I was worried that he would become lost and lose his faith in God completely and be in Satan's power and led down the path of darkness.

I explained a little about what Xander had told me about his friend and how we heard talks in church all the time about people who left and started living recklessly because of it and only found happiness again when they came back to The Fold.

My friend still seems okay for now. He hasn't completely lost the light in his eyes...but his countenance has dimmed a little.

Hunter walked into the room then, looking like he'd just run all the way here from wherever he'd been going when I'd seen him before breakfast. As he stepped closer, his eyes going to the back of my computer, my heart jackhammered in my chest because I couldn't have him see what I was writing.

So with trembling fingers, I finished my email with a quick: *I hope that makes things a little more clear. Thank you so much for your response again.*

There was no time to type out my long pseudonym, so I simply pushed the send button.

Once my computer made the swooshing sound that told me the message had been sent, I closed my laptop and tried not to look like I was internally screaming over the fact that Hunter almost caught me emailing *The Confidant*.

That was way too close.

"Hey," Hunter said, a cautious look in his eyes as he sat next to me.

"Hi," I said back.

I almost expected that to be the extent of our conversation since that was basically as far as we'd gotten the past few weeks. But instead of distracting himself with opening his backpack and pulling out his notebook and things, he surprised me by asking, "D-did you have a good weekend?"

"It was fine," I said. "I visited Columbia with my mom. Went to church."

Saw you flirting with Addison and made a desperate move to write The Confidant.

"That's cool you went to see Columbia," he said, his eyes lighting up like this was the first he'd heard of it.

Which, I guess it could be if Ava hadn't told him that was why I wasn't snowboarding with everyone this weekend.

"Are you any closer to picking a school now?" he asked, a hesitant look in his eyes, like he himself wasn't sure which place he wanted me to choose.

He'd already confirmed his decision to go to Columbia months ago and had been all for me joining him there at that point. But maybe his hesitant look was because he wasn't so sure he wanted to go to the same college as me anymore?

"I have a tour of Yale on Saturday, so I think I'll be ready to make my decision after that," I said.

"This Saturday?" His dark eyebrows knitted together. "Are you not coming to the basketball finals?"

"That's *this* Saturday?" I asked, realizing that in my desperation to get out of town on the weekends and away from the awkwardness of everything here in Eden Falls, I'd completely overlooked the fact that Hunter would be playing the most important game of his high school career this weekend.

He nodded. "If we win our playoff games this week, that is."

"Which you will, since you guys are amazing," I said, trying to figure out how to be in two places at once.

Even without any real advice from *The Confidant* yet, I knew that if I wanted to fix things with Hunter and be friends again, I needed to actually start acting like a friend.

"I already scheduled things for Xander to show me around the campus that morning," I said, trying to figure out the problem aloud. "But maybe we can finish early enough that I can still make it."

New Haven was only an hour away from the arena in Uncasville, so as long as I didn't stay too late, I could probably make it.

But before I could say that out loud, Hunter asked, "Xander is giving you a tour of Yale?"

"Yeah...he is..." I tucked some hair behind my ear, trying to think of how to explain why I was looking at a college with the guy I'd taken to the Valentine's Dance and not have him think it was more than it was.

"Have you been hanging out with Xander a lot then?" He looked like he was trying to play it cool, but from the way he clenched his jaw and his posture stiffened, it made me wonder if he felt the same about me spending extra time with Xander as I'd felt about seeing him with Addison last night.

Which was probably dumb because we both knew it was in our best interest for each of us to date other people.

But to avoid more weird feelings, I quickly said, "We haven't really been hanging out."

"But he's showing you Yale?" Hunter narrowed his eyes like he thought I might be lying to cover up something.

I nodded. "I saw him at church on Sunday, and we chatted for a little while afterward." *Talked about you, actually.* "And when he heard I was checking out Yale, he offered to show me around."

"Okay," he said, seeming like he was somewhat relieved.

"I think it's more of a favor to my dad than anything," I added even though I probably shouldn't.

I didn't need to explain why I was hanging out with another guy.

Especially not when he was hanging out with Addison.

But there was another awkward pause, so I hurried to ask, "But what time is the game on Saturday? Maybe I can get my tour in the morning and then head to the arena afterward."

28

SCARLETT

STILL NOTHING. I sighed, slipping my phone into the back pocket of my jeans as I followed Xander into the cafe where he'd suggested we have our late lunch.

I'd been glancing at my phone all week, hoping each time it vibrated that it would be an email back from *The Confidant*. But so far, I'd received nothing in response to the last email I'd sent.

Had I weirded her out when I told her that my issues with my best friend were because of our different religious views? Religion could be a touchy subject with some people, and there were a lot of people who found my particular religion weird for some reason.

The Confidant had always seemed so open-minded in her responses to everyone else, though, so hopefully it was nothing like that.

Maybe she was just busier than usual this week.

"What would you like to order?" Xander turned back to me as the line at the cafe moved forward.

"I'm in the mood for a sandwich, but I'm not sure what

kind." I looked up at the menu boards above the barista's head. There was a board with sandwiches and salads. Another with breakfast foods. And two more listing all the drinks that they offered. "Is there anything you recommend?"

"Everything I've tried here is really good," Xander said. "But I think my current favorite is the turkey chipotle club. Their special sauce really elevates the sandwich."

"I guess I'll try that then," I said. I considered making a joke about billionaires probably needing everything in their life to be elevated, but since Xander and I weren't exactly at that level of friendship, I left it at that.

"Do you want a drink, too?" Xander asked, his blue eyes meeting mine again. "Their cold brew is pretty good. But if you want something hot, I'd have to recommend the Mexican Mocha. It's amazing."

"You had me at mocha," I said, my mouth already watering as I imagined taking a sip of it. "I'll get that, too."

He smiled. When the people in front of us moved to the side, he stepped up to the counter and placed our orders.

I studied his back and shoulders as he spoke to the barista. I was used to seeing Xander dressed in a suit and tie, since we usually saw each other at church things. But today he wore a charcoal sweater—the sleeves rolled up to reveal his muscular forearms—along with a pair of jeans.

His clothes were obviously designer and had most likely been tailored to fit his tall, athletic frame perfectly. But even though he still had the air you'd expect the son of a billionaire to have around him, if you didn't look too closely at the Rolex on his wrist, he could almost blend in with the rest of the college students today.

He paid for our food, and then we went to a table near the back to wait for our order.

"What do you think of the school so far?" Xander asked, pulling out a chair for me. "Does it feel like home at all?"

"It's really cool." I sat in the chair he offered me and scooted in with his help. "But I might need to see the dorms before I can officially make my decision."

"We can head there next if you like." Xander took the seat across from me. "My dorm is just across the street actually, so we can just pop right over there."

"Did you just say that you live in the dorms?" I asked, not sure I'd heard him right.

He furrowed his brow. "Where else would I live?"

"I don't know," I said, trying to think about where I'd imagined him living. "I guess I figured you probably lived in a big apartment off campus or something."

Something with a maid service and personal chef—kind of like what the Hastings family had.

Xander shook his head. "I've thought about getting something like that, but I actually really enjoy life at the dorms. There's always something going on, and if I lived off campus, it would be harder to stay in the loop and get the real college experience."

"I guess that's probably right." I'd heard so much about how exciting dorm life could be. How the parties were crazy and there was always something going on.

I didn't necessarily want to go to tons of parties next year, since I wanted to focus on getting my degree in two years instead of four. But it would be fun to have parties to drop in on once I'd gotten my studying for the week already done.

"Do you have a shared room?" I asked. "Or a single?"

"I've had my own room the past three years," he said. "But I shared one with that friend I was telling you about my freshman year."

I nodded, remembering the friend he'd talked about who had left The Fold and gotten into a lot of trouble because of it.

"And since that turned into quite the fiasco by the end, I decided to go with a single room after that."

"Sounds like we had similar issues that year," I said, remembering the difficulties I'd had with my roommate my first year at Eden Falls. "It's hard when you don't know what you're getting into."

"Yeah," Xander said. "Or when people suddenly change on you."

He met my gaze across the table, and I realized he was referring to the other thing we had in common.

The best friends who left our church.

The barista brought our drinks to the table. After thanking her, Xander took a sip of his cold brew and said, "It's interesting how much you and I have in common, isn't it."

"It is." I picked up my own drink and took a sip. And I didn't know what I was expecting, since I'd never had a Mexican Mocha before, but it was good.

So good that I'd have to add this cafe to my list of reasons for why Yale was a good university to attend.

"So, are there girls' dorms right across the street, too?" I asked, wondering how close I could possibly live.

"Yeah, the one I live in is actually gender-neutral housing, so I'm sure I could talk to the manager and arrange for you to get a room in my building if you wanted."

"Really?" I asked. "You could do that?"

"Of course," he said. "I know you're still deciding between Yale and Columbia, but if you come here, I'll make sure you're taken care of."

THE REST of lunch was nice. Xander told me more about his favorite classes and professors, recommending which general education courses to take and which professors to avoid. And even though I'd been leaning toward Columbia after my tour with my mom, the more Xander talked about Yale and his experience here the past four years, the more appealing Yale became.

We finished our food. When he reached for my hand to lead me across the street and toward the dorms, I briefly wondered what it would be like to do what my dad had been encouraging me to do all year.

To date Xander.

He was cute and smart, and we were getting along great.

He was also a really good guy who wanted the same things out of life as I did. Which was so hard to find these days.

I hadn't gone to college yet or anything, so I couldn't really be sure what the dating pool was like there. But there weren't a ton of guys in The Fold in New York or Connecticut. Most members of The Fold were concentrated in Pennsylvania where it had been originally founded.

But I was starting to think that if I couldn't have Hunter, Xander wouldn't be too bad of a second choice.

Xander showed me around the common areas in his dorm. And because I told him I'd most likely be getting a single room since I didn't want to run into the same issues I'd had my freshman year of high school, he took me up to the third floor to get a tour of his room.

When I walked inside, I could see why he had been okay staying here instead of getting an apartment on campus. His room was huge.

"Are all the rooms this big?" I asked as I looked around the open-room plan. He had a big living area with a couch and a loveseat. Along with a full kitchen.

This was nothing like the dorms they showed on all the college movies I'd seen.

Xander chuckled and tossed his wallet and keys on the counter. "My dad had this room renovated just a little when I moved in." When I stared at him with my mouth hanging open, he added. "This is one of my dad's buildings."

"Oh." I nodded slowly, looking around the room again and seeing it more clearly. "So this isn't actually what my room would look like if I moved in?"

"It would be about half this size," he said. "This used to be two rooms before I moved in."

"Well, it's nice." My gaze went to the tall bookshelves on the far wall. He had so many books in here. And I was immediately curious about what types of books Xander read in his free time.

Did he read a lot of classics? Or nonfiction? The books all looked old, so I couldn't imagine they were any of the recent bestsellers.

"Do you read much?" He took a seat on the arm of his couch as he watched me look over his book collection.

"A little," I said. "It's mostly for school right now. But in the summer, I read a lot more fiction."

I ran my fingers along the spines, seeing many of the classics.

"Are these first editions?" They all looked so old and in various levels of condition.

"A lot of them are." He cleared his throat. "I started collecting them in high school, but it's kind of gotten out of control since then."

"It's really cool."

Hunter would love to have a library like this.

He loved browsing the rare book collections in the libraries of New York and had talked about needing a library as big as the Hastings' to hold all the books he'd have when he was older.

A library that I'd imagined sharing with him someday.

I pushed the thought away. I didn't need to think about things that made me sad right now.

I finished scanning the row I'd started on before looking at the books on the next shelf over. That was when I saw a book with a faded maroon spine that actually looked kind of familiar —like I'd seen it in a museum somewhere or something.

I turned the familiar-looking book over in my hands. When I opened it up, instead of printed typography inside, the contents were actually written in old-fashioned cursive.

"Is this someone's journal?" I looked back to Xander who was watching me with interest.

"It is." He stood from the armrest and walked closer to me. Then taking the book into his hands, he opened it to the very first page. "It's actually one of Samuel Williams' journals."

"What?" I gasped, not sure I'd heard him right.

Had he just said that this was the first High Priest's journal?

Sure enough, when he pointed to the name written in the top lefthand corner of the cover, my jaw dropped. Because there it was, the name Samuel Williams—written in the beloved High Priest's own handwriting.

"How do you have this?"

How did a college student have such a precious artifact from our church's history?

Sure, he was a billionaire's son, so that definitely came with special perks. But things like this were usually kept in the church's vault.

Or at least in the Church History Museum in Pennsylvania.

"It's from my dad's private collection," Xander said. "He

has all sorts of church history stuff since we're descended from Samuel Williams."

"Wait." I pulled my head back, my eyebrows squishing together. "You're one of Samuel Williams' descendants?"

He nodded. "Didn't your dad tell you?"

"No." I shook my head, suddenly not sure how I should act in the presence of Samuel Williams' actual bloodline since they were like church royalty. "My dad never said anything about it."

"I guess that's probably good," he said. "We don't typically like to spread that around. People sometimes get weird about it."

"I bet."

He narrowed his eyes at me, seeming to pick up that I didn't know how to react to him myself. "Are you going to get all awkward on me now, Scarlett?"

"No, of course not," I hurried to say.

Act cool. Act normal.

Instead of acting cool, I found myself saying, "But it's no wonder why you want to be a pastor now."

"It is?"

I nodded. "Spreading the gospel is literally in your blood."

"I guess it is." He chuckled, like he'd never thought about it that way before.

"So have you read this journal?" I asked, so curious about what kinds of things Samuel Williams might have written in it. "Is it from the time that he was the High Priest? Or is this one from before that?"

"He started writing in this one a few years after the church was founded." Xander walked to the side table near the window and set the journal down. He opened the old book carefully and turned a few pages. "Most of the entries in this particular journal are from the time period that his spiritual partnerships started."

"His spiritual partnerships?" I walked over to his side to look at the journal with him, never having heard that term before.

Xander nodded. "He wrote a lot about his partnerships with other women. Women you may have heard of, like Helen Partridge and Patty Huntington."

"Huh?" I frowned, not recognizing the names of those women who must have lived close to two hundred years ago. Most of the people I knew about from the early church were men, since they had always been the leaders.

Xander looked at me carefully. "I'm sure you're familiar with Melissa Walker though, right?"

"Of course. She was Samuel Williams' wife," I said. Growing up, I'd heard all sorts of stories in Bible class about Samuel and Melissa's marriage. How he'd fallen in love with Melissa when he'd been an apprentice at her father's printing press and how they'd eloped because they were so in love that they couldn't wait to be married.

Their marriage had always been painted so beautifully. Samuel had been so in love with Melissa and treated her like a queen. Wrote her beautiful love letters whenever they were apart.

They'd had their difficulties, of course. Lost several children. Had their first printing press burned down by a mob. But they'd always had each other's backs, and it had been a really inspiring love story for me.

"So as we learned in church," Xander continued, "Melissa Walker was Samuel's first wife—and the only woman they really talked about Samuel having a relationship with, right?"

"Uh huh." I nodded.

He'd probably courted other girls when he was younger,

but since those had never been anything serious and had been before Samuel knew he was a High Priest, it was normal for those relationships to never be talked about.

"But you just said that she was only his *first* wife?" I asked, picking up on the way Xander had worded things.

"Yes..." He looked at me carefully, like he wasn't sure how to continue. After a moment, he shrugged and said, "But I found out, through this journal and from a few other sources, that he had several wives after her. Or I guess *Spiritual Partners*, as they were called."

"He had other wives?" I scrunched up my nose, not believing what Xander was trying to say.

I mean, did Xander actually expect me to believe something like that? Was this just some kind of weird joke?

But Xander nodded and said, "It's hard to know the exact number because there aren't records of everything from back then." He turned a few pages in the journal, and after seeming to read one of the entries for a moment, he pointed to a sentence and said, "But since he wrote about it himself, it seems pretty legit. Just read this..."

I looked down at the paragraph and read the words that said: *And despite much tribulation and prayers to the Lord, I followed his command and took Flora Wadsworth to be my first spiritual partner.*

My eyes widened, and I read over the sentence again.

The handwriting did look old, and it did mention spiritual partners, but...there was no way this was actually legit. They would have said something about it in church if it was.

My dad would have at least said something to me about it since reading the scriptures and studying the church was his job.

"Are you sure this is one of Samuel's actual journals?" I asked. "Because I just don't know how he could have been married to anyone besides Melissa when no one ever talks about it at church."

"I'm pretty sure this is an actual journal of his," Xander said, gently turning a few pages. "There are quite a few of his revelations written down in here, too, which have been documented to go along with the time period as well."

"So you believe that he had a few spiritual partners to go along with Melissa?" I asked, still waiting for the punchline.

"I've read several books about this by church historians," Xander said. "And there are about twenty-seven women that the different experts have all agreed as being his actual spiritual partners."

"T-twenty-seven women?" I stuttered, completely shocked. "Like, he was married to almost thirty different women?"

I'd heard of that happening in other cultures and religions before. But Xander was saying Samuel Williams did that?

In the United States during the 1800's?

"They weren't legally married," Xander said. "It was against the law by the time God revealed the practice."

"But they...acted like they were married? They were—" I paused, not sure how to word my question since I always felt uncomfortable talking about this. "Like, he had intimate relationships with these women?"

"We can't be sure how intimate each relationship was," Xander said. "But yes, he is assumed to have been the father of Lucinda Beaman's first child. And Sylvia Kingsley's second child because the son looked so much more like Samuel than her first husband."

"Did her first husband die right before she got pregnant?" Was that why it had been a question of whose child it was?

"No." Xander shook his head. "Her first husband was still alive. But he was sent on a mission to Europe during that time."

"Huh?"

"Samuel took spiritual partners who had living husbands. It's called polyandry." Xander furrowed his brow, his eyes searching mine. "You've really never heard about any of this? I thought your dad would have told you at least something by now."

"My dad never said anything..." I shook my head, confused.

"That's interesting that he's taking so long," Xander said. Then, as if talking to himself, he mumbled, "Which doesn't leave us with very much time."

I was about to ask him what he meant by that when he picked up the book again and offered it to me. "Here, you can actually borrow this if you want to learn more about it."

"Oh, um..." I stepped back. "I don't know if I should."

It could be some kind of forgery, and I didn't want to get any lies in my head. It could lead me down the path of doubt, which wouldn't be good.

But instead of being deterred, he held the journal out to me again and said, "It's actually a pretty interesting read."

"N-no. That's okay..." I held up a hand to reject his offer, my heart pounding so hard.

Was this what it was like to be offered anti-Fold material?

Was he going to try to force something else on me? Tell me other wild stories to confuse me?

I'd thought Xander was safe. He had interned with my dad; he wanted to be a pastor someday.

Someone like that should be fully invested in the church and not look up weird, counterfeit stories.

"I think I better head out." I glanced around the room, suddenly worried that he might try to keep me trapped here and force me to listen to more twisted stories.

He must have sensed my alarm because he put the book back down on the table and gently said, "Sorry if I startled you with this. I know it sounds crazy—I honestly thought it was really crazy when I first came across it." He sighed and shrugged. "I just thought your dad would have mentioned it to you by now."

"Well, he didn't."

"I can see that." He drew in a deep breath and seemed to think before saying, "Maybe just ask your dad about this. You talk to him every Sunday, right?"

I nodded.

"I promise I'm not making up stories," he said. "I really just thought you'd be interested in the journal so you could have the background of everything that's supposed to happen with us..."

What was he talking about?

I was still so confused at what was even happening, but I walked closer to the door and said, "I'll ask him about it. But I really should head out."

Before he could say anything else, I quickly left, heading down the stairs to go find my car.

29

HUNTER

"DID you find Scarlett in the crowd yet?" Mack asked breathlessly as we walked off the court and into the locker room for our halftime pep talk from the coach.

We'd been neck and neck with the Jefferson High Knights for the first quarter, but managed to pull ahead by six points before the buzzer rang for halftime. If we could just do what we'd been doing in the second half, we might win Eden Falls Academy's first state boys' basketball title in over twenty years.

The first one since Mack, Asher, and Carter's dads had played for the school.

"I tried looking for her when I was out of the game for a few minutes, but I didn't see her," I said, my shoulders slumping a little with the thought.

I knew she had her tour at Yale this morning, but I really had hoped that she'd make it.

But maybe I'd just been extra hopeful after those emails she'd sent to *The Confidant*. Or maybe she'd changed her mind.

Or maybe she hadn't come because The Confidant *totally*

forgot to send the drafted email that strongly suggested she start spending time with me again.

Crap! How had I forgotten to send that through?

I'd discreetly read through the email when I'd been sitting next to her in class Monday morning, and I'd written the response after practice that evening. But before I could hit send, Scarlett had walked in the library. And I'd apparently been so busy with school and the playoff games this week that I'd completely forgotten to go back in and send my response.

Looks like I know what I'll be doing when I get back to the school tonight.

"Maybe she's just running late," Mack said, patting me on the back.

"Maybe," I said.

Everyone else was here, though. My parents and Bash had made the trip and were sitting in the seats just behind our team with the Hastings and Mr. Aarden. And the student section was completely full since most of the student body from my school had come on busses to cheer us on.

But no sign of Scarlett yet.

Had she gotten distracted by Xander? She'd said he was just giving her the tour as a favor to her dad, but what if it was actually more than that?

The coach went over our strategy for the last half of the game and soon we were headed back out to finish. Coach put Carter, Mack, and me on the floor with Edgar and Dallas. I was completely immersed in the game until the other team called a time-out and I happened to look out at the crowd at the same time that Scarlett walked through the doors and sat in an empty seat near the top.

Her gaze seemed to go in my direction briefly, and I felt breathless for a reason that had nothing to do with the exercise this game was giving me.

She came.

She made it.

We all played our best for the rest of the game, and when the final buzzer sounded, Eden Falls Academy was in the lead, 59-53.

The Eden Falls fans roared with a cheer, and before I knew it, the whole basketball court was filled with students and parents all congratulating my teammates and me on a game well played.

My dad hugged me and told me what a great job I'd done and said that as soon as I was showered and ready, they wanted to take me out to dinner to celebrate.

"Just be thinking about where you want to eat tonight and we'll go there," Mom said, giving me a hug. "I'm so proud of you, honey. You did such a great job out there."

"Thanks," I said, returning her embrace. "It was a good game."

I pulled away from her a second later, and that was when I saw Scarlett standing behind Bash, looking like she might be waiting to say something to me.

"Hey," I said, not exactly sure what to do.

"Hi." She looked down, her hands wringing together. Then meeting my gaze again with her beautiful brown eyes, she said, "Y-you played so well tonight. Congrats on the win."

"Thank you," I said, feeling my cheeks warm a little because I was still unsure of where we stood. "I'm glad you could make it."

"Me too." She nodded. "I got stuck in traffic so I was late, but I'm glad I got to see at least half of it."

My mom stepped up by my side. She turned to Scarlett and said, "Have you eaten yet? We're planning to head out to dinner after this, and if you aren't in too big of a hurry to get back to Eden Falls, we'd love to have you join us."

"Oh, um..." Scarlett glanced at me, like she wasn't sure what she should do. And I realized that I probably should have told my mom that things had been off between Scarlett and me lately.

But since it actually would be nice to have Scarlett there, I said, "I was thinking we should just stay close and eat at one of the restaurants in the building. You should come."

"Are you sure?" she asked, still looking apprehensive.

To which my mom said, "You're practically family, so of course you should come."

DINNER WAS DELICIOUS, and it was nice sitting by Scarlett again and actually talking. The dinner conversation started out somewhat awkwardly, since my parents had asked what kinds of things Scarlett and I had been doing together lately...which was hard to explain when the only things we'd been doing the past few weeks was simply existing side by side but not really talking.

But once the entrees came and Dad and Bash started telling jokes, we were able to loosen up enough that whenever our legs bumped under the table, I no longer felt like I needed to apologize for each accidental touch. By the end of dinner, I was able to relax and think about how comforting it was to celebrate the end of an amazing basketball season with the beautiful girl whom I'd known for most of my life.

"How did you get here?" Scarlett asked me as we walked out of the building later.

"I rode the bus to the game with the rest of the team," I said, hitching my duffel bag higher on my shoulder as we stepped into the car garage.

"So you didn't bring your car?"

"No." I pointed my thumb over my shoulder to where my parents and Bash were walking behind us. "I was planning to get a ride back with my family."

Eden Falls wasn't too far out of their way on their drive back to Manhattan.

"Do you want to ride back with me?" She glanced up at me, meeting my gaze in the dim lighting. "It would save your parents from having to backtrack to Eden Falls on their way home."

"You don't mind the extra company?" I asked, just to give her a way out in case she was simply offering to be nice.

But she shook her head and said, "It would be nice to have the company." She bit her lip and seemed to search my eyes. "Nice to talk to you again."

And even though she was only talking about taking a simple car ride together, my heart was racing at the thought of finally being alone with her again.

To finally have the chance to clear the air and get one step closer to friendship again.

"That would actually be great." I cleared my throat. "Let me just tell my parents."

She nodded and waited for me as I told my parents about the change of plans. After hugging my parents goodbye, I put the duffel bag with my basketball stuff in the trunk of the white Lexus Scarlett's mom had bought her for her eighteenth birthday and climbed in the passenger side.

"Thanks again for coming to the game today," I said as Scarlett drove us toward the parking garage's exit. "I know you had other things going on, so it means a lot that you made time to come."

"Of course." She glanced at me, the overhead lights scanning across her face as we drove. "I'm glad you reminded me about it. I would have regretted missing it."

She pulled onto the main road that would lead us out of Uncasville and toward Eden Falls. When "Paper Hearts" by The Vamps started playing through her car speakers, I had to turn it up because it was one of my favorite songs.

"You like this song, too?" I asked.

"Yeah," she said.

"How did you hear about it?" I asked, surprised that she had it on her phone since The Vamps were a British pop band and I hadn't heard of any of my friends listening to their music.

"It was on that playlist you shared with me last year."

Oh.

I'd forgotten I'd shared my *"Scarlett and Hunter"* playlist with her when we'd started dating—the playlist I'd been compiling since sophomore year when I was trying to get up the nerve to tell her how I felt.

Man, I'd had a crush on Scarlett for so long. And that playlist was probably over a hundred fifty songs long by now because I was still adding new songs to it when they made me think of her.

"Do you listen to that playlist very often?" I asked, curious how much insight she had into my feelings for her.

"Sometimes..." She sighed and tapped her thumbs on the steering wheel before glancing back at me. "I like to check in on it every once in a while to see if you've added anything new."

Did that mean that she'd seen the songs I'd added after she told me we couldn't ever be more than friends? The angsty songs like "True Crime" by Taylor Acorn that talked about a girl who'd imagined spending her life with the guy she was dating, only to have the rug pulled out from under them.

Or had she seen "traitor" by Olivia Rodrigo, which didn't actually speak directly to my feelings toward Scarlett at all but had simply been added because there were two lines in the chorus that talked about feeling betrayed and how the betrayer would never feel sorry for what they did.

Those particular lyrics actually fit my feelings toward The Fold more than anything since it was the real villain in mine and Scarlett's story. The villain that never apologized for any of the damage it caused even when it was proven to be wrong.

"Does it bother you that I still listen to the playlist?" Scarlett asked in a quiet voice when I didn't say anything. "Because if you want me to stop listening to it, I can. I just like to see where your head is..."

Why did I like hearing that so much?

Probably because it showed that even though she couldn't see a way to be with me, she still cared.

Scarlett still cares about me.

"No, it's fine." I cleared my throat because it was suddenly froggy. "I mean, I don't mind if you keep listening."

Speaking my feelings had never been my strong suit, so this would actually be a much easier way for me to communicate things with her.

Music always captured things like that so well.

The song ended, and when another song from the playlist began, I asked, "Are we listening to that playlist then?"

She bit her lip and seemed embarrassed when she said, "I've been listening to it a lot this week."

"You have?" My arms and legs tingled at the thought that she'd been missing me as much as I'd missed her.

"Seeing you spending so much time with Addison made me want to remember how things used to be with us." She paused before adding in a softer voice, "Even though I know I probably shouldn't."

"You know Addison and I are just friends, right?" I asked, my throat feeling thick for some reason.

"You are?"

I knew it was stupid for my chest to fill with hope at the way she said that. But I was stupid, and I still wanted her to like me.

Wanted her to want me enough that she could stop caring about the things she thought should keep us apart and realize that those things didn't actually matter.

"We're just friends," I clarified.

I wasn't the type of person who could just get over someone.

I didn't know if I'd ever get over Scarlett.

Not when I didn't actually *want* to get over her.

"Well, in case it seemed otherwise, Xander and I are only friends, too," she said.

"That's good to know."

We were quiet for a moment, each lost in our thoughts. Then she said, "Xander mentioned something interesting to me today, though."

"He did?" I asked, curious about what Xander may have said that she found interesting enough to bring up. "What did he say?"

"Well, it's actually a little weird," she started to say. "You see, I was looking at some of the old books that he had on his shelves when he was showing me around the dorms, and I saw one that looked interesting. It was old and maroon and didn't have a title on the spine like the rest of the books."

"I've seen a few books like that."

She nodded. "Anyway, Xander said it was one of Samuel Williams' journals."

"It was?" I sat up straighter, suddenly more intrigued. Even though I had stepped away from the religion Samuel Williams had founded, I still found the enigmatic leader to be quite interesting—always wondering why he really did all the things that he did.

"I guess Xander is one of his descendants or something like that," she said. "So his dad has quite a few of Samuel's journals and things in his collection."

"He's related to Samuel Williams?"

"That's what he said." She paused and swallowed before adding, "Anyway, he told me that the journal mentioned his spiritual partnerships." She glanced at me again. "Have you heard anything about those?"

"I've heard of them," I said, wondering why in the world Xander was telling Scarlett about Samuel Williams' spiritual partnerships since it was something the church didn't want members talking about. It was one of the things they had tried to sweep under the rug and wanted to keep there.

But if Xander was talking to Scarlett about it, then it meant that Xander had been researching things, too.

Had he, like me, been trying to make sense of the disturbing things in The Fold's history? And was he hoping Scarlett was a safe person to talk about it with since he'd probably heard about my family by now and knew Scarlett and I had been friends?

From my interactions online with other people who'd left The Fold, I'd learned that there were actually a lot of people who didn't believe anymore but still attended church just because they didn't want to disrupt their relationships or have a spouse file for divorce.

So maybe Xander was one of those people and was trying to spread the truth about the church's history from the inside?

"How did you hear about the spiritual partnerships?" Scarlett asked. "Did someone tell you about them?"

"I read a lot about them the beginning of summer."

"And you think they actually happened?"

I nodded. "I read tons of firsthand accounts of the women and the men who were involved in them."

"Really?" she asked like she still didn't believe they had actually been a thing.

"Yes."

"And it was, like, a commandment from God?"

"I guess." I shrugged. "Back then it was, anyway."

At least...that was how Samuel Williams had presented it. Like it was only happening because he'd been commanded by God to take multiple women and teenagers into his bed.

A flash of anger passed through me as I thought about the disgusting things that wolf in sheep's clothing had done in the name of God.

"That's weird that my dad never told me about them," Scarlett said, like she was actually considering that the story could be true despite never hearing about it in church.

"It's not exactly part of the history that The Fold is proud of," I said.

"Why did they do it?"

Because Samuel Williams was a married man and fell in love with his teenage foster daughter and wanted an excuse to be with her.

"He said it was a commandment from Jehovah," I said instead. "Something about building a stronger kingdom of God since the more women Samuel took as spiritual partners, the more his special, more righteous bloodline would continue."

No matter that this new "revelation" didn't even become known about until after he got caught having his first affair.

It was all extremely suspicious to me, but his excuses worked for a lot of the believers back then who had already been manipulated by the High Priest time and time again.

Once you learn you can swindle people, you tend to believe you're untouchable.

"They stopped doing it though, right?" Scarlett asked, like

she needed the reassurance that the modern church wouldn't continue to do something that was so obviously wrong.

"They officially denounced the practice."

Though there was evidence that even though they publicly denounced it, one of the later High Priests told his descendants to continue the practice in secret. Saying it was still the Higher Law and a way to ensure Samuel's bloodline continued so that the right High Priest was in office for the second coming.

This wasn't common knowledge among the members of The Fold, but there were break-off sects that formed here and there when the more stalwart believers came across this information and wanted to live the Higher Law.

But those sects weren't very big—not compared to the millions of members that The Fold had.

The people in the break-off groups mostly kept to themselves on the outskirts of society while members of The Fold were able to blend in more easily.

Sure, the Fold's beliefs were slightly peculiar to outsiders, but they weren't as obviously dangerous—the guilt and shame that came along with the current teachings weren't seen as dangerous, anyway. Even if constantly wondering if I was good enough to make it to the highest level of heaven hadn't been great for my anxiety-prone nature.

"Did you read about this on that website you sent me a link to?"

"Yes..." I said the word slowly, worried that she would automatically discount it since it wasn't a church-approved resource. "But I also came across this information when I was reading the church history essays. The footnotes and original sources actually have a lot of details about it."

"Okay..." She let out a shuddering sigh—almost like she was scared and didn't want to think that the church had been keeping secrets from her. "Do you think my dad knows about this?"

I nodded slowly. "I talked about it with him when I first started doing my research last summer." I'd hoped Pastor Caldwell who was so well versed in scripture would have some magic words of wisdom that could explain away all of the things I found so morally wrong about the church's founder. "I don't know how much he's actually looked into things, though."

He said that other people had come to him with difficult topics before. But in our conversation, it sounded like he had mostly read the pro-Fold historian's arguments to make it okay for him.

Which I understood. He was a pastor. His entire world revolved around this church.

His financial wellbeing. His reputation.

He'd been defending it for decades. It wasn't an easy thing to question when it literally affected every single aspect of your life.

Plus, sometimes it was easier not to pull back the curtain and see what was back there. Sometimes you just knew that what was hidden back there was ugly and that it could stir things up, and so you'd purposely decide to ignore it to maintain the status quo.

Most people didn't want to intentionally upend their lives or belief system. We already had so much to deal with in life without looking for more to trouble us.

The school gates appeared in front of us, and I realized we were back in Eden Falls.

Man, that past hour had gone by fast.

Scarlett drove through the gates and to the side of the school where the parking lot was. After she parked and turned off the engine, she looked at me in the moonlight and said,

"Can you just promise me you're not going to go all wild and fly off the rails?"

"I'm not planning to," I said in a low voice, somewhat hurt that she actually believed I would do something like that. But I told myself I shouldn't be offended when she'd been told her whole life that that was exactly what happened to everyone who left the church. "I'm still mostly the same person, Scarlett. Sure, I buy my chai lattes and breakfast sandwiches on Sunday mornings now and I see the world a bit differently than I used to. But I'm still Hunter."

To me, I was actually a better version of myself than I'd been before. I had been able to let go of my more judgmental side that always thought everyone was doing things wrong when they weren't living life the same way I was.

When Scarlett still looked like she needed reassurance, I added, "I still want to be a decent human."

"Yeah?" she asked, sounding hopeful.

I reached across the console to take her hand, tentatively running my thumb over her knuckle. "I'm still figuring out what I believe, but I still want to be a good person. I want to live a good life." I looked into her eyes. "If anything, I want to be even better now. If for no other reason than to prove that you can still live a meaningful and happy life without being a member of The Fold."

Her eyes filled with tears. She whispered, "I've just been so worried about you." She leaned closer and rested her forehead against mine. We both closed our eyes and seemed to breathe in this moment before she said, "I mean, I even emailed *The Confidant* for advice."

"I know," I said, my voice coming out all gravelly because being this close to her did funny things to me.

And then I realized I'd just told her that I knew she'd emailed *The Confidant*.

Crap!

But she didn't seem to pick up on that. She pulled away slightly, her brown eyes watery and searching mine as she asked, "You know I've been worried?"

"Yes, that..." I looked down and drew in a deep breath, trying to find the words to tell her that I was the one she'd been emailing this whole time.

But before I could think of the right words, a light-blue Honda Civic pulled into the parking spot beside us.

A second later, Asher had climbed out of the driver's seat in Elyse's car and was knocking on my window.

I pushed the button in the door to roll down the window to see what he wanted.

"Hi?" I said.

"Hey roomie!" He bent over to peek his head inside. And when he got a good look, he said, "I hoped that was you in there, Scarlett."

"Hi Asher." Scarlett waved.

Elyse came around from the passenger side of her car and said, "Sorry, I didn't realize anyone was in here or I would have asked Asher to park somewhere else."

"It's fine," I said, curious what they thought about seeing Scarlett and me together after the distance of the past weeks.

"So, are you guys friends again?" Asher asked. Then getting a devious smile, he added, "Or did we just interrupt a different kind of reunion?" He wiggled his dark eyebrows like he was suggesting we'd just been making out.

"Asher," Elyse chided.

"What?" Asher stood up straight again to look at his more reserved girlfriend. "We all know that's what they've been wanting to do all year, anyway."

Scarlett leaned over the console to look at Asher and Elyse better and said, "Hunter and I are just talking."

"Well, that's boring," Asher said before a half-smile lifted his lips and he added, "But I'm glad you guys are talking again."

"So am I," I said, glancing back at Scarlett.

There was a moment where Scarlett and I just stared at each other. It must have made Elyse uncomfortable, or maybe she could sense that we still had things to talk about because she cleared her throat and said, "Anyway, we'll leave you two alone. I was just dropping Asher off."

"I guess you'll have to catch me up on everything back in our room," Asher said before taking a step toward Elyse. But then he paused, turned back around, and ducked down by my car window. He whispered in a tone that everyone could still hear, "If you need to stay out past curfew, I'll cover for you," and ended it with a really obvious wink.

It was like he was getting payback for the time I told our house dad that Asher wasn't in our room one night because he had diarrhea.

My face was just turning beet red when Elyse grabbed Asher's arm and tugged him away, saying, "You need to go to bed before you say anything else, Mister."

Asher just laughed but let Elyse lead him toward the school entrance.

Once their image disappeared from the rearview mirrors, I let out a long sigh and said, "Asher seems to be in a really good mood tonight."

Scarlett smiled, thankfully seeming to find my roommate's antics more funny than annoying. "He definitely seems excited that we're talking again, at least."

"That he does."

We were both quiet for a moment, like we were trying to remember what we'd been talking about before the interruption.

Her phone dinged. I wouldn't be surprised if it was Asher

trying to rile us up even more with some nonsense. But Scarlett groaned and leaned back against the headrest. "These emails are starting to get overwhelming."

"What emails?"

"All the *Dear Eliza* ones." She showed me her phone screen. "I literally get, like, ten emails a day, which I'm sure is way less than what *The Confidant* gets, but there are so many that it feels like all I do during my free time is look through emails when I should be studying." She shook her head. "I thought once basketball was over I'd be able to fit it in better. But with all the school stuff and figuring out college stuff and trying to beat Carter and Elyse for valedictorian...it's just not panning out."

"It is a lot," I said, thinking about all the emails I had waiting in *The Confidant*'s inbox right now.

She narrowed her eyes. For an anxiety-filled moment, I worried she was going to call me out on being *The Confidant*, but then she said, "Do you think this is part of Asher's evil plan to make sure Elyse wins valedictorian?"

"Part of Asher's plan?" I frowned, wondering what these emails would have to do with Asher.

"I don't know." She shrugged. "Like, maybe he figured out I'm *Dear Eliza* and he decided to make a bunch of spam email accounts to send me random questions just to keep me distracted. He did say that he wanted to help Elyse win."

"I really don't think he'd do that." I laughed. "I don't think either he or Elyse are *that* cutthroat about her getting valedictorian." If any of my friends was going to be cutthroat about it, it was Scarlett. She was the most competitive of everyone.

"You're probably right." She slipped her phone into her back pocket. "Maybe I should just shut the column down. I feel bad getting all these emails and not really having the time to give the column the focus that it probably needs."

"You could do that," I said. "Or, if you wanted, I could help you with it."

"You could?" she asked, her voice sounding hopeful. And it was probably a good thing that she didn't know just how much I would be willing to do to make her happy. "Do you think you'll have enough time? Because we have most of the same classes, so you're probably just as busy as me."

"Now that basketball is over, I have a few extra hours in my week," I said. "Plus, I have time before school that you don't have."

"Oh... right..." Her expression fell a little. "I guess not having Bible study every morning or church on Sundays freed up some time."

"The church did keep me busy, and so yes, I've had a few extra hours freed up that I can fill in with other things that are meaningful to me."

"It's not all a chore," Scarlett said, her tone defensive. "I mean, I know some people find the lessons boring or get overwhelmed with everything we're supposed to do. But there is a lot of good that comes from it, too. There's a lot of peace that comes from the gospel."

"I know," I hurried to say, not wanting the truce we'd reached tonight to suddenly disappear because I'd offended her. "I know a lot of people love it and that's great. I was just saying that *I* can use that time differently now. I can use it in ways that mean more to *me* specifically."

I watched her cautiously, not sure how she would accept my next words since for so long, spirituality had been defined by my religion more than being catered specifically to me. But it was important for me to be more authentic than I'd been previously.

I added, "Something that means a lot to me and helps fill my spiritual bucket is writing and also trying to help people. So helping with some of the *Dear Eliza* stuff really isn't a problem since I enjoy it. Knowing I'm helping my best friend out is an added bonus." I searched her eyes. "Supporting you in accomplishing your goals and dreams is important to me."

"You care about my goals and dreams?" she asked, like she wasn't sure she believed me.

"Of course." I took her hand in mine again. "I know you might feel differently about me now. But I still care about you and want you to have all the good things in life."

She intertwined her fingers with mine. Looking at me through her lashes, she said, "I want you to have all the good things, too."

I wanted to say more, to tell her that I wanted so much more than that.

That I still wanted *her*.

But since we had already made so much progress tonight and I didn't want to risk ruining the moment, I just kept those thoughts to myself.

As long as we were still talking, we might just have a chance.

30

SCARLETT

I SLEPT in on Sunday morning, needing more rest after staying up so late talking to Hunter the night before. So instead of grabbing breakfast and having time to get dressed for church before my dad's sermon started at ten, I just watched the meeting online at my desk in my pajamas.

But as my dad started talking about the story of David and Goliath and how we can apply it into our lives today, my mind wandered back to what Xander had said about Samuel Williams' spiritual partners and how Hunter had actually confirmed that those things really did happen in the past.

Maybe I should have borrowed that journal from Xander after all. Just to see what it had said.

I pulled up my phone to text Xander and tell him that maybe I would like to look into that journal, but when my eyes landed on my text thread with Hunter, it gave me another idea.

I scrolled through the last few messages. Which were very few, since we hadn't texted in weeks, and clicked on the link he'd sent me.

It opened up to a page on my browser that had a single

photo—an image of a couple sitting together on a bench—along with a hyperlink with the words *Questions for the High Priest*.

My pulse thrummed hard and fast as I hovered my finger over the link.

Did I dare click it?

Should I do it?

It's just a simple essay, right? One little document couldn't hurt a faith eighteen years in the making.

I had a good head on my shoulders, and I would be able to see past any lies...

I closed my eyes and held my breath as I tapped my finger on the screen. When I opened my eyes again, I saw a page with a light teal block at the top and a quote from one of the well-known church leaders.

I released a shaky breath. *It's just a quote from a church leader. It can't be anything bad.*

But as I started to read the quote that talked about the importance of finding truth, even when it came from unexpected places, an overwhelming feeling of darkness crashed over me.

I shouldn't be doing this. I shouldn't be reading this essay when I knew it had led so many church members astray.

Before I could get curious and read any more, I quickly exited out of the page, locked my phone, and tossed it onto my bed like it had burned me.

Okay. So that didn't work.

But Hunter had said something about reading some essays on the church's website, right?

Reading those should give me the answers I was looking for, shouldn't they?

With my dad's sermon still playing in the background, I opened a new tab on my computer and typed in www.the-fold.org. I typed in the words *Spiritual Partners* along with

Samuel Williams in the search bar, and a few articles popped up. The first one was titled, "Spiritual Partners of Samuel Williams in Chester, Pennsylvania."

I scanned through the essay, checking in with how I was feeling as I looked it over. My heart was still beating fast. But since this was the church's website, I told myself that it would be okay. And even if whatever I found could be new and something I hadn't known before, it would all be okay because the church was true and God worked in mysterious ways.

The first few paragraphs mostly described the practice as being difficult for the members to accept at first—having multiple wives and husbands wasn't accepted in western culture like it had been in biblical times and in other places around the world. Then it said that the first spiritual partnership happened with Samuel's foster daughter, Flora Wadsworth, who was not yet fifteen.

Not much was known about this relationship, but it didn't last very long and was done in secret. Samuel knew it went against the norm and it was a hardship on Samuel's first wife, Melissa.

The practice was so sacred, though, that the revelation wasn't even written down until five years later in 1846 when Samuel was commanded by the Lord to continue the practice with Margaret Johnson—a girl of seventeen who was the daughter of his close friend.

I did the math in my head. Samuel was born in 1812, so he was twenty-nine years old when he was commanded to be with a fourteen-year-old? And then thirty-four when he was partnered with a seventeen-year-old?

Why were they so young?

I frowned and continued reading.

Margaret refused Samuel at first because she was in love with someone else. But Samuel came back a few days later, saying that an angel had threatened to kill him if he refused to obey the Lord's commandment. He also said that Margaret's whole family would be in danger of God's wrath if the partnership wasn't consummated...

So to spare his life and to spare her family, Margaret accepted.

I frowned. *That doesn't seem right.*

The Lord wouldn't ask that of someone my own age, would he?

It would be like me being told to marry someone the same age as my mom's boyfriend, Rodney.

Gross. I shivered with the thought.

The essay talked about the upheaval in the area during this time and how non-members didn't accept or understand the peculiar practice, persecuting Samuel for taking so many young brides. Samuel had apparently written in his journals that he too had gone to the Lord in earnest, trying to understand why he was being asked to do this, and the Lord told him it was to continue his more spiritually pure bloodline and build the kingdom of God on Earth.

Just as Jehovah was born to a virgin, Samuel Williams was also told to have these spiritual partnerships with women who were virgins as well.

But hadn't Xander said there was a woman who had already been married when Samuel Williams approached her? Had the commandment been changed for her?

I felt sick as I continued reading. None of this felt right. He was already married before any of this started happening. Why couldn't he just continue his bloodline with Melissa, his first wife?

But then I remembered how Melissa had a hard time bearing children and having them live past infancy. They had a daughter at the time Samuel took his first spiritual partner, but five other children had died during infancy at that point. Having babies and keeping them alive was harder back then.

And since the priesthood could only be passed through men, and the High Priest had to be a man, Samuel needed more chances to produce male posterity to fulfill those roles.

Melissa was able to have two male children survive into adulthood. The oldest, Jethro, becoming his father's predecessor after Samuel's death in 1896, making the spiritual partnerships apparently not necessary.

But...even if it didn't make sense, it was something that tested the faith of the early church members. And those involved had their eternal salvation ensured because of their willingness to sacrifice their will for the Lord.

The practice was discontinued in the early 1900's when it was revealed that the need for the practice had been fulfilled.

I leaned back in my chair when I finished reading the essay, slightly stunned that this was an actual part of the church's history. It was just so weird with how the church worked today. Having sexual relationships with multiple women was a major sin now. Grounds for excommunication from The Fold even.

But maybe it wasn't as weird in the 1800's as it was now? Maybe girls got married younger back then?

I *had* been raised knowing that it was important not to wait too long to get married. When the time was right and you found the right person who you could trust to stay strong in the church, you didn't hesitate.

It wasn't abnormal for girls from my congregation to get married a year or two after high school. Many of them having babies before they even graduated from college.

Even *I* had daydreamed of marrying Hunter right after high school. Which was only a couple of months away. I'd just celebrated my eighteenth birthday in January. I'd been seventeen just a short time ago...so maybe it was fine that Margaret had only been seventeen when she was commanded to become Samuel's spiritual partner?

Sure...Samuel had been almost old enough to be her father...but the Lord worked in mysterious ways... And God's ways were not our ways....

The sound of the organ started playing through my computer speakers, breaking me from my thoughts. I'd completely missed out on most of my dad's sermon. Hopefully, he wouldn't notice if I just mentioned what I'd heard during the first few minutes.

The service ended, and about fifteen minutes later, my dad FaceTimed me from his office at the church.

He asked me how I've been, and after telling him that I'd had an interesting weekend, I said, "Actually, I heard about some interesting things that Samuel Williams did and got distracted by reading one of the essays about it on the church's website."

"What got you interested in that?" My dad's graying eyebrows dipped together in concern. "Did Hunter mention something to you? Because that boy promised that he wouldn't talk to you about anything he was reading."

Wait, what?

My dad had made Hunter promise not to talk to me about the church's history?

Was that why Hunter had never said anything about his change of beliefs until I came to him with the church gossip? Because my dad had forbidden him?

But I said, "Hunter's not the one who brought it up. It was actually Xander. He mentioned some things about the early church when he was giving me my tour yesterday. He had this journal..."

"Oh..." My dad drew the word out, almost like he was realizing Xander would have been the one to bring it up. "And did you look in this journal?"

"No," I quickly said. "I didn't want to look at anything that might be anti-Fold."

"Okay. Good girl," he said. "I'm glad you're being careful about the information you consume. It can definitely get tricky to navigate things like that."

"That's what I thought," I nodded.

Though, it did make me curious what types of things the anti-Fold material would mention if the church's own website talked about such an obscure practice like spiritual partners.

"Times were just so different then," my dad said. "It's hard for people of our time to understand all the things the early church members did, so it's better to just leave the history in the past and put those questions on the shelf." He paused and rubbed the back of his neck. "We are here to be tested, and there were a lot of things in the early days that tested the faith of the members."

"But why did they need to be tested in such a weird way?" I asked.

"There are many things we can't understand," he said. "We weren't there during that time."

But if it wasn't okay for a twenty-nine-year-old man to be with a fourteen-year-old girl now, why would it be okay back then?

God was unchanging, wasn't he? And he wouldn't have commanded them to practice something that his own church had taught me to find morally wrong, right?

"I actually do have some things to discuss with you the next time you're home," Dad said, clearing his throat. "You're still planning to come home in two weeks, right?"

"I think so." The High Priest was planning to visit our congregation and since it was such a special occasion, and I'd assumed I'd still be avoiding Hunter when I'd made the plans, I'd agreed to be there.

"Great." He looked like he was going to say goodbye and end the call, but then he said, "Just... I think it would be prudent for you to spend less time with Hunter. He and his family are lost now, and I'm not sure I'm comfortable with the influence he may have on you."

"He's a good person," I said, feeling prickly at the thought of spending less time with Hunter when we'd just barely managed to patch things up last night.

"He *was* a good person," my dad said way more dismissively than I liked. "But even the most elect will fall, Scarlett, and I don't want to risk losing you."

I bristled at his words. He wasn't going to lose me. I wasn't going anywhere.

I'd already tried staying away from Hunter and it was miserable. I couldn't just turn around and do that again when Hunter hadn't even done anything wrong.

Even last night when I asked him about the spiritual partnerships, he hadn't pushed anything on me. He'd simply answered my questions and told me where I could find more information if I wanted it—referring me to the church's own website.

He was respectful.

Spending time with him would be fine.

And if my dad had a problem with that, I just wouldn't tell him.

I was eighteen now after all. He shouldn't get to choose my friends for me anymore.

31

HUNTER

"YOU PLANNING to come rappelling with everyone?" I asked Scarlett as we walked out of the journalism room together on Monday afternoon.

"Of course." She slipped her backpack over her shoulders and looked up at me. "Why wouldn't I?"

"You've just missed a few things lately, so I wanted to make sure," I said, hoping she wouldn't be offended that I was still unsure about where we stood after our talk on Saturday night.

She'd had church yesterday, along with her interview with her dad, so I couldn't know if something was said to make her second-guess being friends with an apostate like myself.

"I'm not planning to avoid you anytime in the foreseeable future," she said, giving me a meaningful look. "So I'm coming."

"Good to know." My shoulders relaxed. "Because the last few weeks sucked."

"They really did." As if to prove her point that she wouldn't be avoiding me, she looped her arm through mine as we made our way through the sea of students headed toward the dorms.

We made it to the common room a few minutes later. After

agreeing to meet back there in a few minutes so we could drive together in my car, I ran up to my room to change out of my uniform and into clothes that would be more comfortable to rappel in.

"Hey!" Asher yelped when I opened the door. "Maybe knock first so everyone in the hall doesn't get a look at the goods?"

"Sorry." I quickly stepped inside and closed the door, realizing my roommate had been in the middle of pulling his jeans over his boxer briefs. "Didn't know you were in here."

"It's fine." He finished buttoning his jeans and pulled a T-shirt over his head. "I just noticed some freshman girls in the hall with Rushil earlier and didn't want them to get distracted by the fact that I never skip leg day."

"I see that getting voted Best Physique in the Senior Class hasn't gone to your head or anything." I chuckled as I dropped my backpack on my bed.

"Heavy is the head that wears the crown," Asher said in his dramatic theater voice. "But the people have spoken, so I guess it's my cross to bear." He shrugged.

"And you carry it with such grace and modesty, too."

"Why thank you, dear peasant." He patted me on the shoulder. "I do try."

"Are we about to enter a scene that you're practicing for the spring play?" I raised an eyebrow when I sensed that Asher was about to go from cocky gym rat to theater nerd on me.

"I almost did." He grinned. "But thanks for stopping me there. I need to save that for when Nash and I are stuck together on the cliff this afternoon."

"You guys still not getting along after everything?" I asked, sure they'd been mending things more recently.

"We're getting better." He shrugged as he stuffed his wallet and protein bars into his backpack. "But as long as we're still going after the same roles, there will always be some competition between us both."

"A little competition is good, I guess."

"It is," he agreed. "Keeps us pushing toward being the best at our craft."

"That it does." I removed my blazer and tossed it onto my bed before loosening my tie. "Are you riding with Elyse to the Hastings'? Or do you want to catch a ride with Scarlett and me?"

"You and Scarlett are driving together?" He cocked a dark eyebrow. "Does this mean you're officially together again?"

"Not quite." I slipped my tie out from under my collar. "But we're friends again, so she's riding with me."

"That's good," Asher said. "Do you think she's still set on keeping everything in the friend zone with the recent changes you've made?"

"Pretty sure." I tossed my tie onto the bed with my other things. "And as long as she still believes her church is the only path to true happiness, I don't see that changing."

"So everything really is super strict with her?" Asher asked. "Like, she can't just have a fun high school romance if it doesn't fit precisely into this life plan her church has for her?"

"We were taught that you date to get married." I shrugged. "Having a *fling* would just be wasting time."

Not that I'd be able to have a fling, either. It would be too hard knowing that no matter how great we were together, we'd eventually have an expiration date.

I mean, *I* would be fine figuring things out. If staying in The Fold was that important to her, I'd take her any way I could get her.

I just didn't know if she could bend her rules enough to be with someone on a different spiritual path.

"I guess that makes sense," Asher said. "At least you're friends though, right?"

"Yep."

Asher walked to the door like he was leaving.

"So I'm guessing you're driving with someone else?" I asked, realizing he'd never answered my first question.

"I'm hitching a ride with Elyse."

"Oh cool," I said.

"But I might take a ride back."

"Sounds good."

He left. I quickly changed into a dark-green T-shirt, jeans, and running shoes. If we were rock climbing today, I'd bring my climbing shoes as well since they were way better at gripping the rock. But because the whole group was coming today, we'd decided to stick with rappelling only, so my Altras would do just fine.

Scarlett and I drove to the Hastings' estate together. There were only a few hours before sunset, so we immediately went to the backyard where they had about a dozen ATVs parked in a big garage.

The cliff we'd be rappelling down was near the waterfall our town was named after. The quickest way to get there from their house was through the trails they had on their thousand-acre property.

"I think I want to ride in the side-by-side with Carter and Ava," Scarlett said as everyone started picking the four-wheelers they'd be riding on this afternoon. "Want to ride in the back with me?"

"Sure," I said. We'd spent so much time apart this month that I was all about staying close to her all afternoon.

I put my climbing backpack with my rope, helmet, and harness in the back of the ATV and was just about to climb in the seat next to Scarlett when Nash hopped into the back.

Scarlett looked at Nash and then at me, like she wasn't sure what to do.

"I'll just grab a four-wheeler," I said, not about to ask Nash to give up his seat when the vehicle belonged to his family.

"No, don't," Scarlett said. She bit her lip and seemed to think things over for a second before saying, "We can all fit if I sit on your lap." Then seeming to realize that it might be an odd suggestion, she quickly added, "Unless you think that's weird."

"No, that's...um..." I swallowed and looked around at everyone else, not sure exactly how I should respond. While having Scarlett so close sounded like heaven, I wasn't sure what our friends would think of us riding like that.

But I shouldn't care what everyone thinks, right?

I should just do what I wanted to do.

Even if my heart might regret it later.

So I cleared my throat and said, "I mean, that would be great."

"Yeah?" Her shoulders sagged as if relieved I hadn't turned her down.

I nodded. "Yeah."

She stood from the spot she'd taken behind the driver's seat, making room for me to climb in behind her. I slipped into the seat, and after I patted my legs, she sat down carefully and pulled the seatbelt around both of us.

"That okay?" she asked after buckling us in.

"Yes." And in a voice that was lower than usual, I whispered in her ear, "It's perfect."

She shivered, like I'd surprised her. But then she leaned back into me more.

We sat still for a moment, getting used to being close after so long. But when Nash leaned forward to chat with Ava about something, I allowed my arms to go around Scarlett's waist to pull her even closer to me.

"Is this okay?" I asked when she lightly gasped in surprise. But after taking a second to breathe, she quietly said, "It is."

"Good," I whispered back.

When she turned her head sideways and lifted her eyes to mine, I was pretty sure I saw desire reflected in them.

Did that mean she still wanted to be close in the same way that I did? Could she also feel the electricity sizzling between us?

Because even though she was simply sitting on my lap—something platonic friends did with each other all the time—it was clear that the sparks between us hadn't disappeared when she'd said we could only ever be friends.

We might have been ignoring them, but they were still very much there.

Carter climbed in the driver's seat a second later, and after making sure we were all ready to go, he backed out of the ATV garage. We drove down the trail toward our destination, and as we traveled down the tree-shrouded path, I just let myself enjoy this moment. Let myself breathe in the scent of Scarlett's shampoo and enjoy the weight of her body on mine.

Man, I'd missed this so much. Missed being close to Scarlett. Missed holding her.

"I'm glad the weather is nice enough that we could do this today," Carter said conversationally over the roar of the engine, looking back at Scarlett, Nash, and me through the rearview mirror. "You've been hoping to break in your new rope and harness ever since Christmas, haven't you, Hunter?"

"Yeah," I said, pulling my head back from Scarlett's hair so I wouldn't be yelling in her ear. "Bash talked about taking me climbing over spring break, so this will be a good maiden voyage for it."

My brother Bash was the one who got me into outdoor sports since he'd done a lot of climbing with the oldest Hastings' sibling, Ian, back when they were at the academy together. And it had been perfect when I'd become friends with Nash and Carter freshman year because they had just started climbing with their older brother, too.

"Has that cottage always been there?" Scarlett asked when the path turned and a little cottage appeared in the clearing in the woods. "I don't think I've ever noticed it before."

Nash looked to where Scarlett was pointing. He turned back to her and said, "It's been there since before I was born."

"Really?" Scarlett asked.

"Yeah." Nash nodded. "It's where Regina lives with her daughter." Regina was the head of staff at the Hastings' estate.

As if on cue, the back door to the cottage opened and the barista I recognized from The Brew—Kiara—walked out onto the back porch.

"Is that Regina's daughter?" Scarlett pointed at Kiara.

Nash glanced briefly toward Kiara before saying, "Yeah, that's her."

"She looks our age," Scarlett said. "Why doesn't she go to our school?"

"I think she goes to the public school in town," Nash said.

"Oh cool." Scarlett's hair whipped in front of her face when she turned to look at Kiara once more. "She's really pretty."

"Yeah, I guess." Nash shrugged before looking ahead at the trail.

"Did you bring anything for your hair?" I asked Scarlett when she continued to hold her hair back behind her neck after facing forward again.

"No, I forgot." She glanced back at me. "Am I going to need one?"

"It's a good idea," I said. "Just to keep your hair from getting caught in the rappel device."

She frowned, like she was imagining hanging from the cliff by her hair.

"I think I actually might have an extra elastic in my bag that you can use," I said, remembering that I'd put a few hair ties in there after going canyoneering in Southern Utah with Bash and our cousin Arie last fall. Arie's six-year-old daughter had gotten her hair caught for a minute after she'd lost her hair tie on the hike in. After that, I'd always wanted to be prepared just in case I found myself in that situation again.

I swiveled around to reach for my backpack and was able to slide open the zipper for the small pocket at the top. I felt around the little bottle of Tylenol, my extra Chapstick, and the small first aid kit I had in there, and sure enough, at the bottom were the hair elastics.

I used my fingers to pull one out and brought it to where Scarlett could see. "Ta-da!"

"Oh good." She sighed, relieved.

"Do you want it in a ponytail or a braid?" I asked.

"Oh, um," she said, like she hadn't expected me to help her. "Do you remember how to do a braid?"

"It's been a while, but I think so."

The last time I'd done a braid was when she'd taught me how to French braid her hair one Sunday evening last spring when we'd been bored in the common room.

She let go of her hair, and after some of it flew into my face, I separated her strands into three sections and started braiding them together.

It ended up being harder than I remembered—probably mostly due to the fact that my fingers were trembling with nerves over touching her silky hair like this again. But I managed to get the first half done without having to backtrack more than once, so that was good.

"That feels nice," Scarlett said, glancing back at me with

hooded eyes after I'd combed my finger against her scalp to pick up a new section.

"H-hopefully it looks okay, too," I tried to say lightly, hoping she wouldn't sense the way my pulse scrambled from the heat of her look before resuming a steady but faster beat.

"I'm sure it's great," she said.

I finished the braid, wrapping the black elastic around the end. And just as I was relaxing back against my seat, the trail merged with the main road that would lead us through a long tunnel.

"Here we go," Carter called back to us as he turned on the headlights. A second later, Ava squealed as we were plunged into the tunnel's darkness that I knew would last about a quarter of a mile.

As we traveled down the dark tunnel with only the lights from the ATVs in front and behind us beaming on the walls, I closed my eyes and let myself pretend it was just Scarlett and me in here.

Scarlett leaned back against me, and I allowed myself to slip my arms around her waist again and breathe in the light perfume on her neck.

She smelled so good today. Like something citrusy and fresh.

We rode like that for a few moments until she re-situated herself on my lap, turning sideways so her shoulder and hips pressed against my torso, her cheek resting against my brow.

I instinctively nuzzled her neck with my face, and she drew in a shallow breath.

Followed by another shallow breath.

Was she having a hard time breathing, too?

I let my fingers curl into the softness of her hips, and when she drew in another shallow breath like she was trying not to pant, I was reminded of another time we'd gone to the falls and had trouble breathing.

It had been a Saturday afternoon in early April. We'd gone to the waterfall for a picnic and a hike, but instead of going on the hike that we'd planned after lunch, I ended up pulling her behind the waterfall for a kiss.

It was only supposed to last for a few seconds—just to experience a moment she'd read about in a book once. But as soon as I pressed her against the cave wall and had her soft curves against my hard edges, time immediately disappeared.

Her lips had tasted like chocolate strawberries that afternoon, her auburn hair unbelievably silky when I'd tangled my fingers in its softness.

We had spent a lot of time kissing those few weeks that we'd dated—so much that I'd wondered if I'd ever be able to fill the insatiable craving I had for her. But after crushing on my best friend for so long, it was understandable. I had years of longing to make up for.

I never had a chance to discover whether the chemistry would have leveled out if we'd been able to continue dating. But I had a feeling that moments like that would have still happened a lot.

Because even now, a year later, our chemistry was still very much there.

Maybe even stronger, since we knew exactly how explosive it could be and fighting it was just that much harder.

Man, I needed to kiss her again.

I couldn't just accept that I'd never get to have stolen moments like this with Scarlett again, could I? Or that the differences in our beliefs would stop us from being together.

We made sense in literally every other way.

We were perfect for each other—knew everything there was to know about a future mate.

All the little things.

Everyone always told me that I should marry my best friend since friendship was a huge thing in any long-term relationship.

And I wanted to.

I knew we were only eighteen and probably too young to think seriously about something like that. But I also knew that if she would let me, I'd marry Scarlett in a heartbeat.

Because I knew her and loved everything about her.

Even during our slightly awkward stages—when we'd both been gangly and she had braces and I had acne—I had a huge crush on her.

Who wouldn't when she was smart, fun, kind, driven, and gorgeous.

Other girls could be great, but they weren't Scarlett. It was her as far as I was concerned.

It had always been her. And if we could just overcome the obstacles keeping us apart, it could *always* be her.

So if it came down to it...if I had to choose between staying true to myself and living the way I thought was right for me versus sacrificing my freedom and some of my integrity in order to have the possibility of spending the rest of my life with her, could I do it?

Could I go back to being a good sheep? Could I remain silent and forget what I knew?

Could I do the mental gymnastics needed to get myself back into belief in The Fold... if it meant being with her?

I didn't know.

But it was something I needed to figure out before it was too late.

Either way I would be a little tortured. And wouldn't it be better to pretend to believe in a church I didn't trust but still have the girl I loved by my side?

Surely that was a better choice than living a lifetime without her...

We drove out of the tunnel, and Scarlett turned to face forward like she'd been before we'd entered the tunnel.

We arrived at the rappelling area a few minutes later. As Scarlett climbed off my lap and out of the side-by-side, she said, "That was interesting."

And all I could do was swallow hard and say, "Yes it was."

32

SCARLETT

XANDER: **Your dad told me that you're coming home next weekend. I'll also be in town. It would be cool to see you.**

Does Xander, like, talk to my dad every day? I wondered as I read over Xander's text that came through during my Adult Roles class on Tuesday afternoon.

We were giving oral reports this week and Nash was currently standing at the podium, telling us all about the purpose of dating. I didn't have to present until next class period, so I got to just sit back and relax today.

"You and Xander still text a lot then?" Hunter asked in a low voice beside me, his gaze darting toward my phone which I was holding in between us to keep it from our teacher's view.

"Only when he texts me first." I sighed. "Which usually happens when he hears from my dad that I'll be coming home or need a tour guide."

"Sounds like he's into younger girls," Hunter said with a wink.

"Or he just has really great taste." I smirked, happy that

instead of turning this into a jealous thing, Hunter was able to joke about it with me.

"Only the best for the billionaires of the world, I guess," Hunter said.

"You know it."

He looked like he wanted to say more. Maybe something about how he had similar taste since we'd obviously had our own chemistry—yesterday's rappelling adventure was proof of it. But he stopped himself and turned his attention back to Nash instead.

But I really didn't want Hunter to worry that there was something going on, so I texted Xander right back with: **I'll be in town so I'm sure we'll see each other at church again.**

Sure, he was probably implying we hang out on Saturday or something, but even though I'd enjoyed the tour he'd given me at Yale last weekend, I just wasn't interested in making this into more than it was.

I mean, it was flattering that someone like Xander was interested enough to keep texting me. But I was still in high school and not quite ready for the kind of commitment that I sensed Xander was looking for—especially when I was back to wondering if I could find a way to make things work with Hunter...

"Thank you, Mr. Hastings," Mrs. Johnson's voice interrupted my thoughts after Nash finished his report. "That was very insightful." She looked down at the paper with her list of students doing reports today. Then looking toward my table, she said, "Mr. Blackwell, you're up next."

"Wish me luck," Hunter said under his breath as he scooted his chair back.

"Good luck." I set my phone back down on my lap, ready to give Hunter my full attention. I hadn't asked him what his presentation was about, but it was sure to be good since Hunter always did a great job at everything he did.

Hunter walked to the podium with his iPad. As he started talking about the power of non-verbal communication, using his hands as he spoke, my mind was instantly transported back to yesterday and the way he'd held me with those same hands in the side-by-side.

When I'd suggested we ride in the side-by-side together, I hadn't considered what sitting so close to him would feel like again. But it had felt absolutely incredible—even if my heart had felt like it might explode at a few points.

The whole afternoon had been amazing, actually. We'd laughed and joked around as we hiked to the top of the water-fall, which was something we'd needed again after so much angst the past few weeks. But even though we were joking one minute, as soon as he was helping me make sure my climbing harness was on just right, the sparks immediately flickered back to life.

I was probably weird for being so into it, but even as I lay down to sleep last night, my mind had still wandered to the way he'd tightened the straps around my waist and tugged on the loops to make sure I was secure.

And the way I'd felt when his hands had lingered on my hips before sliding across my lower back was probably sinful all on its own.

Mmmm. I closed my eyes for a second. I could almost feel his fingers grazing across the exposed skin on my back now. He'd only been doing it to adjust the hem of my shirt—making sure I was comfortably modest for my rappel. But yeah, I had a feeling that the innocent brush of his fingers would be playing over and over in my head until the next time I found an excuse for it to happen again.

Ah, I wanted to kiss him again so bad.

Even if it was just once.

Hunter kept talking, going into more depth about positive and negative non-verbal communication. And when he ran his hand through his hair as he tried to think of a word, giving it a slightly tousled look, I couldn't help but think that he looked super sexy today.

Like, how had I managed to keep things in the friend zone for so long when he was so unbelievably attractive?

I let my gaze follow the veins extending from under his rolled-up sleeves, admiring the way they wrapped around his strong forearms. I liked being in those arms.

I studied his jawline as he spoke, loving how strong and masculine it was now.

I watched his lips as he formed the words I couldn't concentrate on right now.

And then I shifted my focus to the turquoise-green eyes that lit me up every time they were looking my way.

How was it possible for someone to be so attractive? Like, every single thing about him was my exact type.

His eyes were perfect. His hair was perfect. His arms were perfect. His hands were perfect. His legs were perfect. His butt was perfect.

Yes, I was totally lusting after him, which was a sin according to one of the church magazines I'd read last month...

But man, God had really outdone himself when he made Hunter because he was perfection in human form.

Hunter kept talking. I must have had the devil rise up in me or something, because before I could think better of it, I was picking up my phone again and typing out a text that I knew would pop up as a notification on Hunter's iPad.

Me: **You look really hot today.**

I hit *send*. I knew the exact moment he read the text because his eyes dipped down to the podium, and in the second that it would take to read the flirty text, he suddenly started stuttering through his sentence like he'd lost his train of thought.

He regained his composure in a bit, but since I couldn't help myself, I texted: **You have sexy arms.**

And just like with the first text, his words stuttered for a moment before he swallowed.

When he shot me a bewildered glance, I knew I had to send another text to make my message clear.

He was hot and I wanted him.

So bad.

I texted without looking at my phone, just watching him since his reactions were making my heart pound harder.

Me: **You make non-verbal communication sound so hot.**

He sighed when the notification pushed through. And when he ran a hand through his hair and bit his lip, I knew he was getting my messages loud and clear.

I lifted my phone again to type another message, but he noticed what I was doing and gave me a pleading look, as if begging me to stop riling him up so he could focus.

I was having way too much fun though, so I just smiled sweetly back at him and continued typing.

But then he made a show of turning his iPad face down on the podium to apparently finish his presentation from memory.

Well, that's no fun...

A minute later, he concluded his presentation, doing impressively well without his notes. When he sat back in his seat, he scooted his chair close and pressed his thigh against mine.

And I loved that such a simple touch could make my nervous system go haywire.

He pulled his phone out of his pocket, like he was going to

text me back.

The three dots bounced on my screen until he hit the send button.

Hunter: **If you keep teasing me like this, I can't be held responsible for what might happen after class gets out...**

Goosebumps of pleasure raced across my arms and down my neck. When I glanced sideways at him, his eyebrow was raised in a challenge.

So I quickly texted him back: **Is that a promise?**

As soon as my text showed up on his phone, he licked his lips as if he, too, was imagining what it would taste like to kiss me again.

And when he mumbled under his breath, "It's definitely a promise," I knew I was in the best kind of trouble.

33

SCARLETT

THE FINAL BELL rang a few minutes later. As everyone around us packed up their things to head to their after-school activities, Hunter leaned close to my ear and asked, "Do you have the key to the journalism room?"

I sucked in a breath, surprised by his question. But before I could think too much, I said, "Yes."

"Then let's go there." His breath was so hot on my ear it made me shiver. "Right now."

"Okay." I gulped.

We stood, and Hunter was just reaching for my hand when Mrs. Johnson looked up from her desk and said, "Oh, Mr. Blackwell. Can I talk to you for a few minutes?"

Was he going to get in trouble because of my texts?

He gave me a look that told me he might be wondering the same thing.

"S-sure," he said. But before walking to her desk, he squeezed my hand and whispered, "I'll come find you."

I picked up my backpack and left the room on shaky legs.

Is this actually happening?

Were we going to be doing what I hoped we'd be doing in the journalism room?

Would I finally find myself in his arms after so much longing?

I hoped so.

I *really* hoped so.

In the journalism room, instead of switching on the lights, I just walked to the back corner. It had been a few hours since I'd had a chance to brush my teeth, so I did a quick breath check. Yep, I could definitely use a little freshening up.

I set my backpack on the table next to me and dug inside for a piece of gum. I was just throwing the wrapper in the trash can nearby when the classroom door opened and Hunter stepped into the dark room, making me jump.

"Scarlett?" he asked in a hushed tone. "Are you in here?"

"I'm just over here," I said, my voice squeaking, revealing how nervous I was.

"Oh good," he said with a sigh, like he hadn't been sure I'd be in here.

He shut the door, and as the room was cast in darkness once more, my whole body tingled with anticipation. His footsteps sounded on the tile floor.

A moment later, he was taking my hands in his and saying, "Hey."

"Hey," I said back, taking in a shaky breath.

We stood there for a few heart-pounding seconds before we both said, "So—" at the same time, followed by some awkward chuckling.

"So," Hunter said again, clearing his throat, "class was interesting."

"Yeah." *It was...* "Did you get in trouble because I kept distracting you?"

He shook his head. "Mrs. Johnson just wanted to tell me I did a good job."

"That's good." I tucked some hair behind my ear.

"Yeah." He nodded, his gaze tracking down to my lips for a split second. "So I wasn't in trouble."

Was he going to kiss me?

He was looking at me like he might be thinking about it.

"Y-you did a really good job, though," I said when the silence had stretched on too long. "Despite my distracting texts."

"Thanks." He took another step closer and tucked some of my hair behind my shoulder. "You certainly weren't making it easy for me."

"I know..." I glanced down briefly, biting my lip. "But I don't think too many people noticed."

Why was I suddenly so shy after acting so bold earlier?

Because dang, for all our flirting in class, and those moments during the rappelling trip yesterday, I was acting like I'd never been kissed.

But that was how Hunter and I always were. We were best friends who could flirt and text about how much we wanted to kiss each other, but when it came down to it, we were such chickens.

Probably because there's so much to lose if things go badly.

I pushed the thought away. I didn't want to think about things not working. I'd already had a taste of what it would be like not to be close to him. I wouldn't let that happen again.

"Are you worried about something?" Hunter asked, his brows furrowing as he lifted my chin to inspect my face.

"I'm just—" I sighed, not really sure I wanted to talk about it.

Talking about my fears for the future would be the exact

kind of mood killer that I wanted to avoid right now. I'd rather just not think about any of it.

Just go for it.

Wrap your arms behind his neck, pull him close, and kiss him.

There was a sound outside the door, and I gasped.

Is someone coming in here?

The door handle twisted, and my body was still trying to decide if it wanted to go into fight, flight, or freeze mode when Hunter tugged on my arm and pulled me into the tiny storage space beside us.

The light switched on just as we slipped out of sight and footsteps sounded on the floor. Hunter slipped his arms around my waist to pull me close, my back flushed with his chest as he leaned against the cupboards.

The footsteps were light as they tread across the room. I tried to get my breathing under control, sure that whoever had joined us would hear each inhale and exhale.

A chair screeched on the floor, and a few seconds later, there was the sound of keys clacking on a keyboard.

I turned my head to the side and whispered, "What should we do?"

"Probably just hide here until they leave," Hunter whispered back.

Which could take, how long?

I looked around, wishing our school was a magical castle with secret passageways that appeared when you needed them. But all we had close by was a solid brick wall with a few low cupboards and a wooden countertop.

So waiting it was.

I sighed and closed my eyes, leaning my head back to rest against Hunter's shoulder. As long as whoever was in here didn't check the storage space, maybe being forced so close against Hunter wouldn't be so bad.

He did smell really nice today. And he was warm.

We stood there for a couple of minutes, listening to the clacking of keyboard keys. I was starting to get bored of just standing there when Hunter bent his head down and pressed a kiss to my neck.

My eyes fluttered open, surprised at the soft touch of his lips to the tender skin. And all I wanted was to ask him to do it again. Because even though it was only the slightest touch, the electricity shooting from my head down to my toes felt so good.

His face nuzzled into my neck, his breath warm on my skin as he whispered, "I miss being so close to you." His hot breath moved up my neck and toward my ear, sending chills racing everywhere. "You always smell so good."

I wanted to say something, to break the tension mounting inside of me, but the sound of the printer whirring to life reminded me we weren't alone.

As our "intruder" walked to the printer, I hoped they'd retrieve their paper and leave, but a few seconds later, they walked back to their chair and turned on some rock music.

"Sounds like they're still not done yet," I whispered, glad that the music would at least leave more of a buffer to any sounds we made.

"I guess not." He pressed a slow kiss to my temple and then my cheek. "But I kind of don't mind being stuck back here."

"Me either..." I closed my eyes and leaned my head against his shoulder again.

He brushed my hair to the side and pulled the collar of my shirt away to trail slow kisses down the curve of my neck, sending tingles all the way down to my toes. And all I could think was that he was *really* good at this non-verbal communication thing. He was taking my breath away.

His hands slipped down my sides and across my waist. After mumbling something about my blazer being in the way, he undid the button and slipped it off my shoulders and down my arms, letting it quietly drop to the floor.

He slid his hands across the thin fabric at my stomach, making my ab muscles tighten and twist in an unfamiliar way.

And as he ran his fingertips lightly up my arms, I briefly wondered if I was even allowed to feel this good. Like, was it okay to feel this kind of heat in my veins? Or this churning in my belly?

I wasn't sure anymore. I wasn't sure where the line should be.

I wanted to think that it was fine, because it felt so good and I was pretty sure Hunter wouldn't try to push me further than I wanted—even if his limits may have changed in the past few months.

So when Hunter, who seemed to have sensed my thoughts, quietly asked, "Is this okay?" I decided to just be honest and said, "Yes."

Because if I was just talking about what was happening in this moment right here, everything he was doing—the way he was holding me—was okay with me.

Better than okay.

It was like being transported onto another plane and finding myself in heaven.

His fingers slipped down my sides, and I was just raising my arms to reach back and tangle my fingers in his hair when chair legs screeched across the floor and the music was turned off.

Had they heard us?

I held my breath, hoping whoever was in here with us wouldn't suddenly appear around the corner. But the person walked to the door and flicked off the lights, pitching us into darkness once more.

"That was close." I sighed after the door clicked shut.

"Yes, it was," Hunter mumbled. "And now that we're alone..."

He turned me around in his arms to face him, right before he pulled my lips to his.

I gasped, surprised for a second to be kissing him again, but as soon as my mind caught on to what he was doing, I allowed him to coax my mouth to move with his.

We'd been shy when we'd first come in here, but there was no shyness between us now. Because the instant our lips met, it was like another switch had been flipped, my insides lighting up like the Rockefeller Center Christmas Tree.

Hunter wrapped his powerful arms behind my lower back, pulling my hips more snugly against his. And even though I'd spent the past ten minutes in his arms, him erasing just that little bit of space between us completely swept me away.

My hands started exploring along his sides, and just as he hadn't liked how bulky my blazer had been, I didn't like the barrier his blazer put between my hands and those chiseled abs I knew he had.

So while he kissed his way across my jaw, I fumbled with the buttons on his blazer. Once they were all undone, I pushed it open in the front and slipped my hands inside.

"Are you warm?" I asked when I noticed how hot his skin felt through his button-up.

"A little," he mumbled, barely breaking the lock he had on my lips.

So to help him out, my hands slid up his chest and pushed the blazer over his shoulders before dragging it down his muscular arms and tossing it onto the counter behind him.

"Better?" I asked.

"Much better."

And this time, when he pulled me to him, he lifted me in the air and turned me around, setting me down on the counter.

"Figured I'd give your legs a break," he said when he saw my surprise.

"Thanks." I sighed.

He chuckled and rubbed his hands along the sides of my thighs as he leaned into the space between my knees and said, "No. Thank *you*," before pulling my lips to his again.

Our kisses were quick and frantic, like we were both afraid this moment might end suddenly. As if we both understood the reality that there was still so much stacked against us but wanted to ignore all those things for this stolen moment and pretend like the outside world and circumstances didn't exist.

His fingers tangled in my hair, slid across my shoulders, and smoothed down my back, like he wanted to feel everything. He pulled me closer, with his hands low on my hips, and when he slid them down over my skirt, mumbling, "Closer," I obeyed and wrapped my legs around his waist.

He sucked in a quick breath, his posture stiffening momentarily like he hadn't actually expected me to do that, but then his shoulders relaxed again and he leaned even more into me.

"You feel so good, Scarlett," he whispered against my lips. "So freaking good."

"You feel good, too." I moved my hands along his muscled back. "Somehow even better than I remembered."

When we'd kissed outside my house last month, we'd both been wearing bulky coats, so I hadn't been able to feel as much of the more muscular frame that he'd built this year. But wow, the weight training he'd done with the guys this fall to get ready for basketball season had really done amazing things to his body.

This past year, I'd stared at him enough to know that he'd

filled out in ways that were very visually appealing to me, but my imagination hadn't done his body the justice it deserved.

"I think the senior class may have gotten the senior favorites wrong," I said as I smoothed my hands up his perfectly sculpted chest. "Because you clearly should have won Best Physique."

I felt his lips curl up at the sides. "I'm glad you think so." He chuckled. "But Asher seems pretty happy with that title."

"He probably rigged the vote," I said.

"I think his biceps did the heavy lifting with that."

"Well, that's just because he wears those tight shirts all the time." I traced my fingers over Hunter's biceps, noticing how tightly the woven fabric of his white shirt strained against it. "But your arms are far superior in my book."

"Which is why yours is the only book I care about," he said before kissing me again.

34

HUNTER

SCARLETT AND I KISSED FAST. We kissed slow. And when she tugged on my bottom lip before slipping her tongue in my mouth, my heart skittered because it just felt way too good.

If this is a dream, I don't ever want to wake up, I thought as our tongues danced together, the movement sending waves of warmth coursing over me. *Because this feels incredible.*

So incredibly good.

But even though my mind was completely blissed out right now and floating away to cloud nine where there was only plea-sure and happy feelings, I knew that if I had to keep myself upright for much longer, I might just collapse. My legs were becoming so weak from Scarlett's kisses and from leaning against the cupboard for so long.

We needed a couch.

Or a bed.

Okay, so it would be weird to have a bed in the journalism room, but it would be so much easier to just relax into the kiss if we were both on a soft bed right now.

I should have suggested she meet me in my room instead of in here.

Or her room.

I wasn't picky.

We hadn't ever actually made out while lying on a bed before, so I couldn't be one hundred percent sure what it would feel like. But I did have a pretty good imagination. I bet that laying Scarlett down on a soft mattress and covering her body fully with mine would feel amazing.

Transcendent.

I let my mind wander down that path for a moment, thinking about some other things I'd like to try with Scarlett someday before pulling my mind out of that thought pattern and bringing it back to the present.

Just because I've been rethinking where I might draw the line in a physical relationship doesn't mean Scarlett is okay doing the same.

And since she was someone I wanted to be with for a long time—my feelings for her were definitely not the fleeting kind— I needed to be respectful and keep things within the boundaries that she had.

I wouldn't even try to push things further.

Even if it would feel nice...

Stop thinking about that.

Scarlett tugged on my tie, and after undoing the top two buttons, she opened the collar of my shirt and kissed me there, too.

And with her hot kisses on my neck, my knees buckled.

"What are you doing to me?" I growled, having to use my hands to brace myself against the counter.

"Just what I've wanted to do to you all year," she said. "Showing you how I feel and being selfish at the same time."

"If this is you being selfish, then please be selfish all the time," I mumbled back.

She kissed her way down my neck, sucking briefly on the tender skin there before taking the sides of my face in her hands and guiding my lips to her own neck, saying, "Kiss me here, Hunter."

And when she arched into me as I explored her neck and collarbones, all my hazy mind could think about was how there couldn't be a better way to spend an afternoon than showing my dream girl how I felt about her.

When she'd sent me those texts during my presentation, I hadn't expected for her to actually follow through with what she was messaging me.

I had initially thought when the first one came through that it had simply been a test—a way to see if I could concentrate on my presentation while she distracted me.

And maybe it had started as something teasing like that. But those flirty texts had broken the barrier we'd needed to tear down for quite some time—giving us a chance to stop thinking so much about the obstacles in our way and just act on what we actually wanted for a change.

No matter how reckless those feelings might be, she had still chosen to come here to be with me now.

I continued to kiss Scarlett, letting my hands run along the sides of her legs and enjoying her smooth skin as I nuzzled my face into the perfume at her neck.

She smelled so good. Felt so good.

But I must have let my hands graze a little too high for her comfort because she covered my hands with hers, stopping their progression, and said, "Hey...h-hold on." She swallowed. "I know things might have changed for you. But I—I'm still saving certain things for marriage."

"Oh. Sorry." I shook my head and lifted my hands up from

where they'd gone mid-way up her legs. "O-of course. I didn't mean..."

"It's okay." She touched my chest. "Like..." She looked down briefly. "I'm tempted too... Part of me really wants to..." She looked back at me in the darkness, and from the wanting in her eyes, I sensed that she might be feeling exactly the same way I did in that moment. "But I don't want to go further than kissing."

I nodded and swallowed. "Yes. I—I wasn't actually planning to go any further..." I tried to think, but my brain wasn't really working right now. "I just got a little carried away." I took a step back, knowing I probably looked super turned on right now.

She slipped off the counter, readjusting her skirt so it rested more modestly around her legs. "It just seems to be how it is with us. Getting carried away."

"Yeah..." I agreed, my voice sounding froggy. "It does."

And almost as if on cue, her watch started glowing in the dimly lit room with an alarm.

"Looks like it's time for our study session." She silenced the vibration on her wrist. "Everyone will probably wonder where we've been if we don't get there soon."

"You're probably right," I said, even though I really didn't care if anyone knew what we were doing.

It would actually be kind of nice to shout from the rooftops about how much I was in love with my best friend.

But since we still had so much uncertainty in our path, I would be fine keeping this just between us.

For now.

"Do you know if there's a light over here?" Scarlett asked.

"Yeah," I said, taking a few steps to the right. "Pretty sure there's one right here."

I felt around the wall for a second until I found the switch that lit the storage area. After my eyes adjusted to the unfamiliar brightness, I grabbed my blazer and slipped it on.

Scarlett picked up her blazer, too. But instead of putting it on, she set it down on the counter and said, "Looks like I messed up your hair."

And I loved that instead of letting me try to fix it, she stepped close to me again and tamed it herself.

"What about me?" she asked when she was done with my hair. "Do I look okay?"

"You look beautiful," I said, not needing to look at her to know that.

Her eyes sparkled with my compliment, but then she said, "Seriously though, is my hair okay? Or does it look like I was just ravaged by a beast in here?"

"It's not quite beast level." I chuckled as I smoothed her hair back down. "But it definitely looks like an eighteen-year-old guy may have had a little fun kissing you."

"I guess that's fair since I had fun kissing him, too," she said, and my heart flipped when I met her gaze because it looked like she really meant those words.

We grabbed our backpacks, and after I switched off the storage area's light, we walked to the door. Before we could leave, I briefly wondered how things would go after we stepped back into the hall.

Would they go back to normal? The way they'd been most of the year?

Would she regret the past thirty minutes when she was reminded of all the differences we had between us?

I didn't think I could take that happening again.

I couldn't keep getting my hopes up only to have them crash and burn every time.

I didn't know if she could somehow sense my thoughts or

what, but instead of reaching for the doorknob, Scarlett turned back to me and pressed a soft kiss to my cheek.

"We'll find a way to make this work, okay?" she said, searching my face.

"You think it's possible?" I asked, my voice sounding way more vulnerable than I'd planned.

She nodded. "It has to be. We wouldn't be so perfect for each other if there wasn't a way, right?"

"I hope so."

I really hoped so.

When I opened the door for us to leave the journalism room, I looked back to let her pass. As we walked out into the hall, she slipped her hand into mine.

It was the tiniest thing, to walk around the school holding hands.

But today, for me at least, it was everything.

HUNTER

THE NEXT WEEK and a half went really well for Scarlett and me. We spent most of our free time together. We talked, we held hands, we laughed, we studied, we kissed—we did all the normal things you'd expect two eighteen-year-olds to do when dating at a private boarding school.

The only thing we didn't really do was talk about The Fold and where each of us stood with it.

She still went to all her meetings, of course. And I still enjoyed doing other things on Sundays...but I knew it was only a matter of time before it came up again. Important things like that didn't just stay swept under the rug forever.

Which was why I had been trying to figure out if I was up to attending the service this Sunday. Just to see how it felt.

I didn't expect I'd ever really be able to believe in it like I used to, but perhaps it was possible to look past the issues I knew were there and only take the good parts.

Or in the very least, attend just enough meetings that Scarlett would feel okay taking a risk staying with a guy who could be physically in the church but mentally out. To look like I was at least a lukewarm member to the rest of the congregation, since appearances were important to be kept up in The Fold, but remain a non-believer in my head.

It wasn't ideal, of course, and pretending felt icky. But I wanted a future with Scarlett, so it was something I needed to at least try.

If it went okay and it was what Scarlett needed from me, it would also mean that I'd have to get re-baptized in order to look the part. There was a whole interview process that I'd have to pass in order to jump through those hoops, so that was a little daunting.

But I'd listened to podcasts about how to rephrase your answers in such a way that you could still be true to yourself while giving the church leaders what they wanted.

I still wasn't sure I could do any of that...but it was definitely something I'd been thinking about.

Though, the question was, should I tell Scarlett that I wanted to tag along with her this week and possibly get her hopes up? Or should I just sneak into the back of the chapel, test it out, and only tell her about it later if I thought I could commit to staying in?

"Do you think Xander is still hoping to see you at church?" I asked Scarlett as we rode the train back to Manhattan on Friday afternoon.

"Probably." She shrugged. "He texted me again yesterday about how excited he was to listen to the High Priest's talk on Sunday."

"The High Priest is visiting this Sunday?" I asked, surprised she hadn't mentioned anything about it before now— having the High Priest in your congregation was a huge deal to members of The Fold. He was like the king or president of the entire church and was seen as God's mouthpiece on Earth.

"Yeah." She tucked her hair behind her ear, as if uncomfortable talking too much about church things with me. "He's going to be talking the last half of the meeting, I guess. My dad has been excited for weeks since it's such an honor. And he even has a special interview with him before church."

"A special interview?" I raised my eyebrows, knowing what a big deal it was to get one-on-one time alone with someone of his status.

She nodded. "I'm not sure what it's for. My dad hasn't said a lot about it. But I'm kind of wondering if my dad might be asked to be an Elder or something like that."

"An Elder?" I asked. "Wow! That would be huge for him."

She nodded. "He's worked hard his whole life for something like that, so it would be really cool if it happened."

"I bet." Even if I didn't agree with mortal men believing they had special authority over anyone else, I knew what a big deal it was to believers.

"And if that happens, it would make sense for why he has been spending so much extra time training Xander this year," Scarlett said. "Like God was putting everything in place for my dad's replacement without us even knowing."

"Would Xander be able to take on the role of pastor while he's still a student?" I asked. "I thought he still had another year at Yale."

"I think they'd be able to work something out. Maybe ease their way into the transition."

"And you think they might announce this on Sunday?" I asked.

"Maybe." She shrugged. "If that's even what's going on. I mean, my dad hasn't been super forthcoming with why the High Priest is visiting, but it might happen."

"I guess you'll find out on Sunday, anyway."

"Yep."

I looked out the train window in front of us, thinking about whether I should say what I was thinking about saying or not.

If I was going to make an attempt at returning to The Fold, going to church this weekend would probably be the most impactful since the High Priest would be speaking. If anyone could convince me to come back, it would be their most holy leader, right? He was the one steering the boat.

"What are you thinking about?" Scarlett asked quietly as the train passed the sign that said we'd be arriving at Grand Central in ten minutes. "Am I upsetting you by talking about the church?"

"No." I shook my head. "I'm the one who brought it up when I asked about Xander." I paused and swallowed before adding, "I was actually just thinking about going to the meetings on Sunday." I dared to look at her. "Just to see how it feels after all this time."

She gasped, and her whole face lit up when she realized what I'd just said. "You want to come to church with me?"

"Just this week," I said, not wanting to get her hopes up in case it didn't go well. "Just to check it out."

But she didn't seem to care that I was trying to be cautious about this because she just hugged me and said, "I'm so happy. This is all I've wanted all year. Just for you to give it another chance."

"I'm not making any promises that I'll be going next week though, okay?" I said, worried that I might have offered too much of my olive branch out to her. "Like, if I can't do it, I don't want things to get all weird between us again."

"Okay." She sat up straight again, her voice cautious once more. "I get that. I'll try not to make this a big deal or anything." She sighed, and I could tell she was trying really hard not to be too excited over the prospect of me coming back to church with her. "But I'm just glad that you're willing to try it. It means a lot."

"Just remember that it's just a trial. I can't make any promises about how I'll feel afterward." I put my arm around her shoulders and pulled her closer. "But since I really want things to work with us, I figure I should at least give it one more shot."

"Thank you." She put her palm on my cheek and turned my face toward her. "Seriously, Hunter. Thank you. It really means so much."

"You're worth it, Scarlett," I whispered before kissing her on the forehead.

36

HUNTER

SCARLETT: **Let me know when you get here. I'll meet you at the gate so we can go inside together.**

I looked at the text Scarlett had sent me a few minutes ago as I paced the sidewalk just outside the church gates.

When I'd told Scarlett that I wanted to join her for church today, I'd meant it. I'd wanted to show her I cared enough about her that I would be willing to try church out again and see if it felt better after almost a year away.

I'd assumed it would be a pretty simple endeavor. That I could just pretend like it was any other meeting I had in my schedule for the week. Just something I was going to be trying on for size.

What I hadn't expected was the upset stomach I'd been fighting all morning or the tight ball of nerves that had my heart pounding harder with each minute that ticked the clock closer to ten a.m.

But here I was, ten minutes until the Sunday service would begin, feeling like I was just about to betray myself for the girl I loved.

I pushed the thought away.

It was just one meeting.

One hour out of the rest of my day.

I didn't need to put so much weight on something that would be over in the same amount of time it took me to write *The Confidant*'s column this morning.

I drew in a deep breath and texted Scarlett back.

Me: **I just got here.**

Then I slipped my phone into the interior pocket of my suit coat, closed my eyes, and drew in a few deep breaths.

It's only sixty minutes.

But when I opened my eyes again and looked up at the large church behind the blossom-covered trees, an overall sense of unease filled me again.

The last time I'd been inside the church was for my interview with Pastor Caldwell—the one where he'd disfellowshipped me and labeled me as a threat to the church.

And while I'd hoped that the painful feelings might have lessened more since then, they were still raw and real.

Could I even stand to be in the same room as him again? Could I look him in the eyes and smile, knowing that he thought what had happened in that room was just him holding a "court of love" and that the verdict he'd chosen based on his own biases was "for my greater good." When to me, it had felt more like a slap in the face and a shove out the door.

This is probably a mistake.

I clenched my jaw and tried to think about what to do next. Should I continue with the plan and sit through another meeting?

Or should I just text Scarlett my apologies and tell her that we'd have to find a different compromise? One that didn't involve me going inside that church building ever again.

But before I could pull out my phone and tell Scarlett

anything, she appeared at the gate wearing a blue dress I hadn't seen before, along with a huge smile on her face.

She was so hopeful that this would be the answer to our problem.

Maybe it will actually feel fine to go inside again. Maybe you're just feeding into your anxiety and making this a bigger deal than it really is.

"Ready to go?" she asked breathlessly, like she'd skipped here in her excitement to see me.

And even though I didn't know if I was, I slipped a smile on my lips and said, "Yeah, let's go."

We walked side by side down the sidewalk that led to the front doors, and I took some more deep breaths as we did.

"My dad still assumes we're just friends," Scarlett said when we were about fifteen feet away. "So I don't think it would be a good idea to hold hands or anything like that while we're in here."

"Makes sense," I said.

"But if this goes well today, I was thinking that we might be able to break the news about us being back together to him soon." She looked up at me. "What do you think?"

"Let's just see how today goes first, and then we can make a plan after that."

"Of course." She nodded, like she was just remembering that me being here wasn't supposed to be a promise yet. "Let's just see how it goes. No need to rush anything before we're ready."

When we reached the main doors of the church, Scarlett must have noticed my hesitation because she stepped closer, rubbed my arm, and said, "It's going to be okay. We'll just sit, listen, and then leave. And if this doesn't work, we'll figure something else out."

"Really?" I asked, not realizing how much I needed to hear those words until she said them.

She nodded. "If nothing else, I'm just thankful you even dared try. It can't be easy to come back here after everything you and your family went through. After all the rumors..."

"Yeah." I sighed. Somehow, I'd completely forgotten about those rumors since I'd been away at school while most of them had been flying.

She checked her watch. "But it's about to start, so let's go."

I nodded and followed her inside the first set of double doors. When she opened the second set of doors that led into the church's foyer, I came face to face with Scarlett's dad.

Pastor Caldwell's brown eyes widened momentarily, and he staggered back a little when I stepped inside. But he recovered quickly and said, "Welcome to church, Hunter." Then he offered me his hand like he'd done every time I'd come to church growing up, and added, "It's good to have you back in our presence, son."

"Thanks. It's good to see you, too," I said robotically as I shook his hand.

Did he know that I'd removed my name from the church records after our last conversation?

Was he thinking about that right now?

"Come on, let's go find a seat," Scarlett said when her father and I just stared at each other wordlessly.

So I released Pastor Caldwell's hand and said, "Okay, let's go."

Scarlett led the way into the chapel, and as soon as I entered, a sudden silence fell over the crowd.

For a second, I wondered if the High Priest had entered the room. But after a quick sweep of the chapel, I realized everyone's eyes were actually on Scarlett and me.

Or rather, they were mostly looking at me. Like I was some

sort of prodigal son who had finally found his way back to Jehovah's fold.

"They're just happy to see you," Scarlett whispered between clenched teeth as she smiled and waved at the members looking our way.

I doubted that they'd really missed me at all, since not a single person had even reached out to me when I'd stopped attending—none of my old Bible class teachers, or the kids in my age group—aside from Scarlett, of course. But if she wanted to tell herself that they cared about me, I'd let her.

Just as we were taking our seats on a pew near the front of the chapel, a little boy two rows back whispered in a voice I could hear, "Look, Daddy. It's the guy you said was on Satan's team."

"*Zachary!*" The woman beside him, whom I assumed to be his mother, instantly pulled him onto her lap and covered his mouth with her hand to silence him.

And as the boy's mother gave him a lesson about not saying rude things out loud, my gaze went to the man beside her who was none other than one of my favorite Bible class teachers.

Which I assumed meant that Brother Anchor had told his children I was one of Satan's besties.

Nice.

"I'm so sorry," Scarlett said, leaning close and setting her hand on my leg. "I can't believe he just said that."

"It's okay," I said. "He's just a kid."

Out of the mouth of babes, right?

"Still..." She sighed. "I'm sorry."

I looked straight ahead, just ready for this meeting to get over with. Or for the High Priest to at least walk onto the stand and distract everyone from the apostate among them.

But instead of the High Priest, it was Xander who appeared at the front chapel doors next.

He smiled and waved at everyone as he walked inside. Then after doing a double take at seeing me, he sauntered over to greet Scarlett.

"Hello, Scarlett," he said, all smiles as he looked at my best friend. "It's good to see you again."

"Good to see you, too," she said.

"I was just chatting with the High Priest a few minutes ago, and I think we're all in for a real treat today."

"He met with you?" she asked, her voice sounding surprised. "What about?"

"Just a few things he wanted to follow up on with me." He waved his hand. "I can't really talk about it now, but I'm sure you'll be hearing about it from your dad soon."

Was Xander going to be the new pastor then? Were Scarlett's suspicions about her dad being promoted to Elder actually spot on?

"I guess I'll look forward to hearing more soon," Scarlett said with a smile.

"I'll be very interested in hearing your thoughts on what's been revealed," he said. Then making a point of looking down at where Scarlett's hand rested on my leg, he added, "It's definitely going to mix things up."

I was suddenly reminded of something that I'd thought of recently. The coincidence of him seeing Scarlett and me together just the day before her dad found out and made her break up with me.

Would Xander report this comforting gesture to his buddy Pastor Caldwell?

Xander didn't say anything about it, though. He just said he'd catch up more with her later before going to sit on the front row, right smack in front of the pulpit.

As we listened to the organist play the prelude music, I was briefly reminded of the sermon Scarlett's dad gave a long time ago about "front-row Joes" and how the place you sit in church and whether you show up early, on time, or late reflects your dedication to where you want to sit in heaven.

Which meant, I should probably be sitting at the very back.

A hush fell upon the whole room a moment later, the sudden reverence given to the High Priest who had just walked into the chapel.

As Scarlett's dad led the eighty-nine-year-old man with white hair toward the stand, where he would be sitting in the seat reserved for the highest ranking member in attendance that day, everyone in the congregation got to their feet as a sign of respect.

And even though the High Priest wasn't like a living God to me anymore—The Fold had four deities they worshipped: God, Jehovah, Samuel Williams, and the man who currently held the position of High Priest—I stood next to Scarlett as well.

The High Priest shuffled to his seat with the help of his bodyguard, and when he gestured for everyone to be seated, Pastor Caldwell went to the pulpit to announce the opening hymn and who would be saying the invocation.

As the congregation sang their songs and said their prayers, instead of feeling like I had come back home after spending an extended period of time away, it just felt like I was witnessing another culture's spiritual practice.

One that didn't belong to me anymore.

Which made me feel sadder than I expected.

Because even with the betrayal I'd felt the past year, most of the memories I had from my time in The Fold were positive. It had been nice belonging to something and worshipping in a community with people who were really good and kind for the most part.

Which was why choosing to leave had been so complicated.

A few minutes later, it was time for the Lord's Supper to be passed to the congregation. When the man in charge of the section Scarlett and I were sitting in approached our pew, my heart started pounding.

What was I supposed to do?

Should I just go along with what everyone was doing and take it when it was offered to me?

It didn't have the same meaning to me now, but should I just go with the flow and take a piece of bread before passing the tray on to Scarlett?

To an outsider, communion was probably a seemingly little thing. Like a little snack in the middle of a long, boring meeting.

But to the members of The Fold, this was one of the holiest parts of their entire day—the time where they renewed the promises they'd made with their God to live their lives in the way the church had directed them.

It was considered a privilege to partake of and something they could strip you of if they didn't consider you to be in good standing with the church.

Pastor Caldwell had forbidden me from taking communion during our last meeting, after all. Saying I wasn't allowed to receive the blessings it offered until I humbled myself and repented of my disbelief.

I couldn't take it until *he* deemed me worthy again.

The man carrying the tray reached the row right in front of me, and I instinctively looked at Scarlett's father, just to see if he was watching me at all.

And sure enough, he was looking at me with a stern expression. Probably waiting to see if I would disobey his directive from months earlier and take a piece of bread.

When the tray was offered to me, I could feel all eyes on me, as if everyone in the congregation was waiting to see if I would take it. I considered doing it—just as an act of rebellion against Pastor Caldwell and the system he represented.

But then, I felt Scarlett lean against me. And when it seemed like she was holding her breath and waiting to see what I did, I was suddenly reminded of what this moment meant to her.

She didn't know about my meeting with her father, and so to her, whether I chose to take it or not would be a signal to how worthy I felt I was to take it. It was a way for her to get an insight into what "sins" I might have committed that she didn't know about.

Which were none.

There weren't any actions I felt I needed to repent of.

So if that was the only thing going on here, I could partake of it without a second thought since I still considered myself to be extremely *worthy*. I had zero guilt or shame about anything I'd done or the way I lived my life now.

Plus, seeing me take the small piece of bread would make Scarlett happy and also reassure everyone watching me that I hadn't completely jumped on Satan's bandwagon while I'd been away.

I could still be a safe person.

One of them.

But if I'd originally stepped away from The Fold because I couldn't play pretend anymore, why would I pretend now?

Which I guess gave me the answer I'd been searching for when I'd decided to come here in the first place.

I couldn't live a lie.

Not even for a second.

So I passed the tray on to Scarlett without taking a piece and tried not to focus too much on the way her shoulders drooped with disappointment.

Disappointment in me.

She ate her own piece of bread, passing the tray back to the church official standing beside me. When the official moved to the row behind us, I leaned close to Scarlett's ear and whispered in a shaky voice, "It's not because I'm not worthy, okay? I'm not—" I sighed and pinched my eyes shut briefly, hating the way this felt—like I had to prove I was still a good person to keep her from leaving me. I opened my eyes again. "I'm not, like, secretly doing anything immoral or living a double life, or anything like that." I paused, and then added, "I just don't feel right pretending."

Her posture went stiff again, but she nodded. When I pulled away and studied her face, it looked like she was fighting back tears.

Like the reminder that things actually were different now was just crashing over her all over again.

And my disbelief was breaking her heart.

I reached over and took her hand in mine, giving it a squeeze—silently pleading for her not to give up on me.

She squeezed my hand back, which reassured me. I could at least breathe again.

Out of the corner of my eye, I noticed Xander watching us intently. And all I could think was, *Move on, dude. She's still in high school.*

Pastor Caldwell went to the podium a short time later and said, "I had a different topic planned for my message today but was moved by the spirit this morning to talk to you about eternal families and the importance of aligning yourself with people who hold the same values when you're considering dating and marriage."

Of course.

He'd seen Scarlett with me and had decided it was time to remind his daughter that she shouldn't get any wild thoughts about a future with a heathen like me.

He went on to talk about the importance of having your marriage blessed by one of the church leaders in a sacred ceremony. And the more he talked about how our souls became lost without the blessings of the gospel and how we needed to humble ourselves and repent of any misdeeds, the more triggered I became.

So I did what I usually did when I became triggered and needed to tune out of The Fold's jargon. I pulled out my phone to scroll through ExFold Reddit.

I needed to hear from other people who had been through a faith transition so that I wouldn't feel so alone.

I was just scrolling through a few funny memes when one popped up with a likeness of Samuel Williams. Two different women were sitting on his lap with another four behind him, and his first wife Melissa crying in the corner with the words "Seven Brides for ONE Brother" written above their heads.

Scarlett noticed that I'd disconnected from the meeting at the exact wrong moment—before I could scroll past the meme making fun of the man whom she considered to be one of the Lord's anointed, she looked down at my phone and quietly gasped.

"Sorry," I said, looking up and feeling my cheeks heat as I closed the app. "I didn't plan for you to see that."

"Did you think that was funny?" Scarlett asked under her breath.

"Not really," I said.

Part of me still squirmed a little when I saw the harsher posts on ExFold Reddit. I still wasn't used to the way some of the people bashed the church.

But I understood why people did it, because sometimes, part of the grieving process involved making light of the things that were painful and caused you trauma. Finding out you'd been lied to your whole life about something you'd held so dear was extremely painful, and everyone coped with their pain differently.

Scarlett sighed. "I'm guessing that having you come here wasn't the best idea then."

"I'm sorry. I just..." I slipped my phone back into my jacket. "I guess I'm a lot different now. And...your dad's sermon... It's just kind of triggering."

"Triggering?" She furrowed her brow like she was so confused about how any of this could be difficult for me to hear. "My dad is just talking about how beautiful it is that we can be saved and live with our families in the next life if we follow the teachings Samuel Williams revealed."

"I know." But then I shrugged and added, "I guess it's just the whole idea that I need saving in the first place that's the problem."

"What?" She pulled her head back, like it was a foreign concept.

The organist started playing the intermediate hymn then, so Scarlett pulled out a gray hymn book from the pew and turned the page to hymn 301.

As everyone started singing, I leaned closer to Scarlett's ear and whispered, "I just..." I stopped, trying to think of how to word it in a way that she'd understand. "I only ever believed I was broken and in need of saving because of what the church told me."

Her eyes narrowed, but I continued, "I only ever thought I needed forgiveness for being a normal human who makes normal human mistakes because I'd been taught that." She glanced sideways at me, and from the look in her eyes, I knew what I was saying was making her upset. So to try and finish up quickly, I said, "I just don't believe this life is a test to see if you can follow a set of rules that some man wrote down a couple of centuries ago."

"He was a High Priest of God. Not just '*some man*,'" Scarlett said curtly, correcting me.

Yes, that's what he called himself and got other people to believe about him.

"To me, I just—" I put my arm behind her shoulders and leaned closer so no one around us could hear over the singing. "I guess I like what Mack told me his mom said to him before she died. That the purpose of life is simply to live. To experience it, learn from our experiences and from those around us, and just do our best with the knowledge and understanding that we have. And if we make some not-so-great choices, we'll suffer enough here in this life already that the suffering doesn't need to continue in some eternal afterlife once I'm gone. Like, I don't think me going on hikes or to The Brew on Sunday mornings is going to keep me out of heaven...if it even exists."

"You don't believe in heaven anymore?" She stared at me like I was speaking blasphemy.

"I don't know what I believe in right now," I said. "Sure, I hope there's something after this life. Something good. But...I can't say that I *know* it exists like I used to." I glanced behind me and noticed we were drawing the attention of the people behind us. So I hurried to finish with, "And I don't think I necessarily *need* to know or understand that in order to lead a good, fulfilling life."

Scarlett sat there completely frozen for a moment with her mouth hanging open in shock. Meanwhile, Pastor Caldwell glared at me, as if to warn me that I needed to stop making a scene.

I cleared my throat and turned back to Scarlett. "I should probably just leave now. Sorry if I ruined this special day for you."

"Okay." She sounded distant, like she was still in shock over everything I'd said.

I stood and buttoned my suit coat and walked out of the room, feeling so disheartened and disappointed.

Would Scarlett be done with me now? Did the differences in our beliefs actually make a relationship with her doomed?

I was just about to exit the building and walk into the courtyard when Scarlett's voice called, "Hunter, wait."

I turned around to see her walking toward me. Before I could do anything, she was wrapping her arms around me and saying, "I'm sorry if it seemed like I was judging you. I just..." She pulled back and looked me in the eyes. "It's just hard for me to understand how things could change so much so quickly."

"I know." I looked down at my feet, the turmoil I felt inside threatening to knock me to the ground.

She put a hand to my cheek, and in a gentle voice, she said, "But I want to try to understand."

"You do?" I lifted my gaze, not daring to hope.

She nodded. "You're still an amazing person even if you don't believe the same as me or want to go to church anymore."

I took her hands in mine and fought a smile. I wondered what she would think if I said the same but opposite to her. That she was an amazing person...even if she went to church.

Would having that caveat placed on her make her see how the two sides had been pitted against each other for so long? That the division of what we did or didn't believe kept us from being able to just see the person in front of us for who they really were—a human who was just doing their best with the experience and information that they had.

Until you've actually been on both sides, it's hard to understand the other perspective.

Not to say I was perfect at it. I still had my obvious bias and had chosen the side that made the most sense to me.

But I wasn't completely anti-religion or anything like that.

If people found happiness in their beliefs and they didn't cause anyone else any harm or didn't feel the need to force their beliefs on someone else—that was great.

I just saw a lot of harm from my previous religion that came in the forms of guilt and shame and anxiety over being valiant enough to earn an eternal reward. And the fact that it was based on the lies of a conman with a talent for manipulation just made it a no-go for me.

But it was nice that Scarlett was at least trying to understand, which was far better than I could have hoped for a month ago.

The High Priest's voice sounded through the speakers in the foyer a moment later. Since I knew she'd want to get back to the meeting, I said, "I'm going to go, okay? We'll catch up later."

She nodded. "I'll call you."

I was about to lean close and kiss her cheek before leaving but stopped when Xander walked into the foyer. When he saw how close we were standing together, he got a warning look in his eyes.

Like he was silently telling me to keep my apostate hands off of her.

And if Pastor Caldwell hadn't guessed that Scarlett and I were trying to work things out from what he'd seen earlier today, I had a feeling he was about to.

Our cover was officially blown.

37

SCARLETT

"SCARLETT," my dad said, walking up to where I was standing outside the chapel after church. "Can I have a word with you in my office?"

"S-sure," I said, my stomach flipping with nerves over what he might want to talk to me about.

Whenever I was visiting home, he usually skipped the after-church interviews since he would just ask me about everything during dinner. So the only reason I could think of why he was pulling me into his office now was that it had something to do with Hunter and me.

Please don't tell me to break up with him.

I was eighteen now. I deserved the space to figure things out myself.

I followed my dad through the hall where people were scattered about, chatting about various things. When we made it to his office on the north side of the building, he gestured for me to walk inside before coming in and closing the door behind him.

I took one of the cushioned seats in front of his desk while he sat on the big chair on the other side.

After scooting close to the desk, he folded his hands together and said, "I know we usually have our little chats at dinner when you're home, but I needed to talk to you about something of a private nature."

"Okay." I swallowed, curious and confused.

He looked down at his hands, like he wasn't sure how to begin. But after clearing his throat, he said, "As you know, I had a meeting with the High Priest this morning. A meeting where he reminded me of something we talked about several months ago."

"Yeah?" I asked, not understanding what he was talking about but relieved it didn't seem to be about Hunter and me.

He nodded. But instead of looking like he was excited about his meeting with the High Priest, he almost seemed distraught.

Which had never happened before. Usually, he was glowing after these special meetings since any moment spent alone with the leader of our church was such an honor. Not something that most people ever got to experience.

"Did he give you a new position?" I asked. Had he been asked to be an Elder and he was simply overwhelmed at the prospect of traveling more to fulfill the higher position?

But he shook his head and said, "It's about a revelation."

"A revelation?" My ears perked up. A new revelation could be exciting.

But then he said, "It's one that I should have informed you of when it was first given to me."

There was a revelation *I* was supposed to know about?

"I've been trying to put it off. To let things work out naturally, since I didn't know there was such a distinct timeframe for this." He sighed heavily. "Until this morning, I thought we had more time."

"You thought *we* had more time?" *What is he talking about?*

He nodded. "I wanted things to be different for you, Scarlett."

"What are you talking about?" What did he want to be different?

But instead of answering my question, he just looked at the painting of Jehovah on his wall—the one with Jehovah sitting on a hill surrounded by the children he was teaching.

"What is this revelation that you were supposed to tell me about?" I asked. *Just tell me because you're really scaring me right now.*

"I've been pleading with the Lord for it not to be you." He turned back to me, his eyes haunted in a way. "You're still so young."

"What's going on?" I asked, anxiety suddenly pulsing through my veins at the way he said that.

"You know how I've been trying to set you up with Xander since last fall?"

"Yes..."

"I'm sure you probably found it out of character for me, since I've never been too keen on you seriously dating anyone in high school. You're still my baby girl, and I remember what it's like to be a teenage boy." He ran a hand through his graying hair. "But this past fall, I had an interesting experience with the High Priest where he told me about a practice that I hadn't heard of before in all of my studying of the scriptures."

No... I frowned as a sense of dread washed over me.

"It's the practice that Samuel Williams was commanded to begin back in the days of the early church..." He looked at me carefully. "The one you said you recently learned about."

Dad swallowed nervously as he opened his desk drawer, revealing two faded journals inside—one of which looked almost identical to the journal Xander had shown me in his dorm. For a second, my dad hesitated to pick up the journals, as if he didn't really want to touch them. But after glancing at me once more, he lifted them in his hands and set them down on his desk.

He cleared his throat. "I think you've seen at least one of these journals before."

"Yes." I swallowed hard as I nodded. "The maroon one looks like the journal Xander tried to show me."

"So as I said, the High Priest spoke to me about this revelation several months ago, telling me some things I'd never heard of before..." He stopped, as if to rethink the direction he was going. Then he gave his head a slight shake and said, "What the High Priest told me is that shortly after the church was founded, Samuel Williams was commanded to take on spiritual partners to help build the Kingdom of God on Earth. And well..." He swallowed like he didn't want to actually continue.

Which made sense, since talking about our beloved High Priest having intimate relationships with multiple women was an uncomfortable subject—especially for a man like my father who had never discussed anything to do with the birds and bees with me outside of asking whether I kept my oath of chastity during my biannual worthiness interviews.

So to make things less awkward, I hurried to say, "I read enough to know that he had children with many of the women."

"You did?" He pulled his head back and frowned.

"Yes." Before he could think I had moved my research to unapproved sources, I added, "An essay on the church's website talked about it."

"Oh." His shoulders relaxed.

"Did you read the essay about it, too?" I asked, curious since Hunter had mentioned that when he'd brought up some of the issues he had with the church to my dad, it hadn't seemed like he'd known much about them.

"I haven't really looked very far into those." My dad glanced down at the journals. "You know me. I hate reading on a screen and much prefer learning from books that I can hold in my hands."

"That makes sense."

My dad had never really caught on to technology. He'd been older when I was born. Got his news from the newspaper. All his other reading was from *Visitations with Jehovah*, The Bible, or the church magazines and books.

He probably didn't really know what social media was. He didn't watch any of the popular TV shows or movies.

He was basically living in a time warp. The few times my stepmom was able to convince him to watch something with her, it was always the tried-and-true Rodgers and Hammerstein musicals from the 1950's and 1960's since the shows of these days were too worldly and inappropriate, according to him.

Yes...I'd be in big trouble if he found out I had been watching PG-13 movies with my friends since sophomore year.

"Anyway," Dad said, "the spiritual practice was used to ensure that the bloodline of our beloved High Priest could grow. Much of it was done in secret as you probably read, since it wasn't accepted by the government back then. There were many children born to his spiritual partners during that time. And when the practice had sufficiently served its purpose, it was eventually stopped." He paused and looked like he was preparing himself to say something that might be even more shocking than what we'd already discussed. With a bewildered look in his eyes, he sighed and said, "But it turns out, the practice didn't completely die."

"What?" I gasped, not sure I'd heard him right. "The spiritual partnerships didn't stop?"

He nodded. "The High Priest told me in our initial meeting

that the practice was actually continued by one of Samuel's family lines and is still in practice today."

My dad looked down at the maroon journal and leafed through a few pages. Then, carefully turning the book on the table so it was right side up for me, he pushed it across the desk so I could read it. He said, "This passage here is where Samuel wrote that his oldest son, Jethro, was to continue to take spiritual partners in secret."

"He what?" I asked, feeling like I was just repeating that same question over and over during this conversation.

"It was very confidential, and only those parties involved actually knew about it." He pointed to a paragraph in the journal, written in an old-fashioned scrawl. "They were forbidden from even discussing the sacred ceremony except for in a special place in the church."

The sacred ceremony?

"In fact," he continued, "I probably wouldn't have even heard anything about the sacred ceremony if the new revelation didn't involve you."

"How does it involve me, Dad?" I asked, hoping it wasn't anything like what was currently formulating in my mind.

His eyes darted away, and my whole body filled with dread. "You see," he said, letting out a long sigh. "The High Priest received a new revelation this past September about the man who will be the High Priest when Jehovah and Samuel Williams return to take us with them to heaven."

"He has?" I asked, a thrill of excitement flashing through me briefly at the prospect of there being more information regarding the second coming of Jehovah and Samuel Williams —something I often wondered about.

"We've known it was coming soon," he said. "That we are in the last days and need to be prepared. But until this revelation, there wasn't a firm timeline."

I sat forward in my chair, all ears now. "So, is it happening soon?"

Were we on the cusp of welcoming our beloved leaders back to Earth? Was the current High Priest the *Chosen One?*

"I think we still have many years to prepare," Dad said, seeing how I was growing excited. "But it was revealed that the Chosen One will be conceived soon. That the ceremony prophesied to bring about his eventual birth is to take place on the Friday before Easter."

"Really?" I asked, shocked it was so soon. "So in just two weeks, he could be conceived?"

"Yes." Dad nodded, a grave look on his face.

That was when I realized what he'd been working up to say this whole time. He'd said the revelation had something to do with me.

"I just thought we'd have more time, Scarlett," he said, noticing the realization dawning on my face.

"Are you trying to say that, I—?" I paused, trying to process, "—that I'm going to be part of this ceremony?"

"I didn't know about the timeline until recently," he said quickly. "Which is why I was trying to let things develop slowly. You're still so young and—"

"What are you trying to say, Dad?" I asked, my head feeling like I had a swarm of bees buzzing around it. "What exactly does this revelation have to do with me?"

"The High Priest revealed that you're the chosen vessel for the future High Priest, Scarlett."

"What do you mean by 'chosen vessel?'" I asked.

"Just like Mary was the maiden chosen to carry Jehovah, you have been chosen to carry our future High Priest."

"No." I shook my head, scooting my chair back. "I-I can't be. I'm o-only eighteen."

"That's what I told the High Priest." Dad stood and walked

around his desk. "I told him it must be a mistake and that there must be another girl. Someone a little older. Someone ready to be a wife and mother."

"Yeah, it can't be me. I'm just a regular girl. I—I'm not like..." I shook my head, trying to think through the scattered thoughts flooding my mind. "I'm not like this special, perfect girl."

I always did my best to stay on the right path. But I didn't keep all of the commandments perfectly all of the time. I wasn't anything close to what someone would call "chosen" or "special."

Not special enough for something as huge as this.

"I tried to argue with the High Priest." Dad bent down in front of me so that we were eye to eye. "Not because I didn't believe you to be worthy of such a role. But just because you're still in high school, and I didn't think you needed to carry such a huge responsibility." He took my hands in his. "I tried to ask him if the chosen vessel could be another chosen daughter of God. But as it turns out, the revelation was extremely specific about who could be the chosen vessel."

"What do you mean?"

"The revelation revealed that she would be of age at the time of the ceremony—which now that you're eighteen, I suppose you are that. She was also to be born in the first month of the year, with fair skin and hair of scarlet—the same color of the Son of God's blood that was spilt on the cross. She would be a prize among women—pure, smart, exceptional in every way."

"But—" I scooted my chair back farther so I could stand. "There are lots of girls who were born in January and have red hair." I took a few steps back as I tried to figure out a way to explain that it had to be someone else. "Lots of girls who are older than me. More mature. More ready and better prepared for something like this. I mean..." I pressed my back against the large mahogany bookshelf. "Surely this is just a misinterpretation and the chosen vessel is some other girl who did well in school and chose to stay chaste until marriage. I mean, the church has, like, two million members. I can't be the only one who fits that description."

Just because my dad was well known in the church, which had made me more familiar with the High Priest than a regular member of The Fold would, it didn't have to mean it was me.

"I know," he said, pain evident in his eyes. "I tried to tell the High Priest that it had to be some other girl. Someone older. Someone who wasn't you." He shrugged. "But then he showed me the revelation that had been written down in Samuel Williams' own hand." He went back to his desk and opened the second journal to another page. "And it somehow had your exact birthday written down—the day and year. It also described the chosen vessel as a pastor's daughter who grew up in the same congregation as Samuel William's descendant—the descendant who will also be part of the special ceremony."

"Wait, what?" I asked, not knowing what he meant by that last part.

"The revelation doesn't just mention you. One of Samuel's descendants is also part of it—since he is the man who carries the bloodline of the High Priest."

"The bloodline of the High Priest?" I shook my head, none of this making sense.

I leaned over the desk to look at the section my dad was pointing at. As I let my gaze travel over the section of Samuel's revelation that was supposed to point directly at me, I saw exactly what he was talking about. It had my exact birthday, January seventh, written in old-fashioned handwriting, and went into even further detail, saying that the chosen vessel would be in her last year of school when the ceremony was to take place. And to further identify her, she would have a birth-mark on the back of her left arm in the shape of a heart.

When my dad saw me checking the back of my arm for the birthmark we both knew was there, he nodded solemnly and said, "It isn't a coincidence, Scarlett. You were destined for this special role from before your birth."

"But I just..." I sighed, feeling helpless as I stared the facts straight in the face.

My dad studied me carefully for a moment, possibly waiting for me to say more, but when I didn't, he just nodded and gently turned the next page of the journal. Pointing at a paragraph in the middle of the page, he said, "This is the section that reveals the name of the man who will help with the ceremony."

I narrowed my eyes and read the section.

And it shall come to pass that the seed of the Great High Priest will come through the loins of Jethro Alexander Williams—the eldest son of Samuel Williams, the great High Priest of the restoration. This descendant will share Jethro's first two given names, his hair will be the color of honey with eyes as blue as the ocean waves. He will be born on the twenty-fourth day of August to goodly and righteous parents. When he is of age, he will be a student of the pastor in the heart of New York—a mighty warrior for our Lord. And together, he and the pastor's daughter—the chosen maiden—will bring forth the leader of the last days.

So let it be written.

I frowned, my heart beating so fast and hard that I could feel it in my temples.

So this revelation was saying I was basically going to have to perform the ceremony with some guy I didn't even know...?

My stomach curdled. *I'm going to throw up.*

This couldn't be right. There was no way that this could actually be a real thing.

Like, didn't Mary, the mother of Jehovah, have some sort of premonition that she would be used as a chosen vessel?

Or had it felt like this when the angel visited her?

And if this was a similar situation, was this ceremony my dad mentioned more like a spiritual sort of ceremony? One where I could still remain a virgin and not have to follow the laws of science in order to carry the Chosen One?

Could the seed of this baby somehow be miraculously planted in me or something? Jehovah and God would have the power to do something like that, right? Especially in the case of creating someone as special as the Chosen One.

Or maybe this ceremony looked a lot like IVF or artificial insemination, or something like that? Was that how it had happened with Mary? Or...

Surely I wouldn't have to... I shook my head, not wanting to even think the word. Not wanting to think about the act.

I pinched my eyes shut.

Surely God doesn't expect me to have marital relations with a guy I don't know. A guy I don't love or want to marry.

My mind whirled with all kinds of questions. But the one that came out of my mouth first was, "Do you know who this revelation is talking about? This descendant of Jethro Williams? Is it someone I know?"

Or was it a complete stranger?

Was it some older guy? Would it be similar to how Samuel Williams had been commanded to form his partnerships with girls twenty years younger than him?

My dad had had many associate pastors whom he'd taught through the years. Pastor Marcus—a man who was probably in his sixties now—had always paid extra special attention to me during his time in our congregation. Was it him?

Another wave of nausea passed over me.

"It's Xander," Dad said gently, putting a hand on my shoulder. "The revelation says that you're meant to become spiritual partners with Jethro Alexander Pierce." He sighed. "Xander, for short. He is the one the Lord commanded you to perform the ceremony with."

"It's Xander?" My mind calmed for a second, because at least Xander was familiar. Close to my age. Safe...

But then something else occurred to me.

"Is that why you've been trying to set me up with him all year?" A sense of betrayal filled my whole body.

My dad had known this was coming this whole time and hadn't even tried to clue me in!

Sure he said that he thought there would be more time, and he didn't know that there was a specific timeline until this morning. But if he'd told me what he did know all those months ago, I would have had at least *some* time to prepare.

But I only had two weeks?

Two weeks to perform some ceremony that may or may not include an act I'd been saving for my future husband—for the man I loved and wanted to share my life with.

Not someone who might be nice and seemed like a good-enough guy but wasn't someone I was even close to feeling comfortable doing that with.

"So...do I have to marry Xander then?" I asked. "Is that what's happening here?"

"It's what I think would be right," Dad said. "Spiritual partnerships worked differently in the past. The act of consummation joined them spiritually, but not necessarily legally. But since the gospel teaches that sex outside of the bonds of marriage is a sin and the church has progressed since then, I don't see why you two wouldn't be married. Xander says that he's willing to marry you."

Xander was *willing* to marry me.

That wasn't exactly the way I imagined my future husband would feel about the prospect of spending our lives together. I'd imagined words more like *excited* and *anticipating* and *eager*, *thrilled*, *exhilarated*, or *delighted* would be how my future husband would feel about marrying me.

But *willing*? It just made it sound forced.

Which...I guess was how it kind of was in this situation. Predestined since before we were even born.

"So Xander already knows?" I asked.

"He knew before I did," Dad said solemnly. "The knowledge was passed down through his family." He gestured to the journals on his desk. "The journals are his."

Was that why Xander had tried telling me about spiritual partners a couple of weeks ago? Why he'd offered to let me read that journal?

Because he knew exactly why we were being set up and wanted to give me a heads-up?

Dad continued, "Xander has known about his part since he was young, but he wasn't sure who he'd be performing the ceremony with until he started his internship with me last summer. It wasn't until after that when he had a vision of you two standing across the altar from each other."

"He had a vision?" My eyebrows shot up. I'd never actually heard of anyone I knew having a vision—not in modern days, anyway. Not since Samuel Williams died.

Visions were things that only happened in the olden days as far as the stories I'd heard.

"Xander told me that in his vision, you were both dressed in ceremonial clothing and standing in the Holy Room of the church." Dad sat on the edge of his desk. "When he first told me about it, he said he didn't want to believe it because you two barely knew each other and he knew how protective I am of you. But then he remembered reading this passage a few years ago when he was researching Samuel Williams and realized that you did fit all the descriptors of the revelation." He shrugged. "And the High Priest confirmed it."

The High Priest confirmed it? That almost made it sound like the High Priest hadn't known about the revelation until Xander talked to him about the journals and his vision.

How was it fair that Xander was able to receive a vision and have almost a full year to prepare...while I got nothing?

Nothing but a meeting with my dad, a peek into a journal, and a ticking time bomb hanging over my head.

I had less than two weeks before I was supposed to give up all my plans for the future in order to give birth to some special baby.

This couldn't be right. This had to be some sort of twisted joke.

Or could this be a test to see if I was willing to follow God's plan for me?

Like when Abraham was told to sacrifice Isaac only for God to stop him at the last moment, saying, "Never mind, I was just testing you to see if you actually had enough faith to follow me."

Maybe I had entered an alternate universe. Or had fallen asleep during the High Priest's sermon and this was just a nightmare...

I pinched myself to see if this was real. But sadly, it felt like I was actually awake.

Was this how those girls I'd read about in that essay had felt when Samuel Williams approached them?

Because if so, it was no wonder a few of them had refused

him at first—no wonder why the Lord had to send his angels to
threaten Samuel into following the commandment.

Because right now, I was feeling like I didn't have nearly
enough proof of divine revelation to convince me that this was
actually part of the Lord's plan for me and my life.

It just...it just couldn't be...

My dad must have seen my thoughts written on my face
because he held his hands out at his sides. In a somber voice, he
said, "I know this is shocking and not something you expected. It's
not what I expected, either. But I've prayed and fasted about it for
months, and the spirit witnessed to me again this morning during
the High Priest's sermon that it was true. And when I looked
down at you and Xander, both of your countenances were so
bright." He shrugged. "I *know* this is God's will for both of you."

"But there are only two weeks, Dad!" I said, sudden
hysteria coming over me at witnessing my dad's acceptance of
this whole thing. "I don't even know what this ceremony is like!
I don't have any of the details. Like, can you just walk me
through the ceremony step by step so I know what I'm agreeing
to? Maybe that will help me feel better about this."

But instead of softening and explaining what I needed to
know, my dad shook his head and got a stern look on his face.

"The ceremony is sacred, Scarlett," he said, like I should
know better than to ask such a question. "You know that the
sacred ceremonies and rituals can't be discussed outside the
Holy Room. They must be protected from outsiders who might
use them for dark purposes. But the ceremony is straight from
God, and you will be blessed for your obedience to his
command. Our whole family will be blessed. Our eternal salvation will be secured if you do this. Even your mother, who has
waffled in her acceptance of Jehovah, will be saved because of
your faithfulness. The High Priest promised it."

His words made me catch my breath. *My mom would be saved?*

My mom, who was a good person but had never been strong in the faith, could still live with me in heaven if I did this?

"The High Priest actually said that our salvation and Mom's salvation will be secured if I do this?" I asked, needing to have this confirmed. "You're not just saying that?"

"That's what he told me," my dad said. "He promised that all of your family will be blessed and their exaltation would be ensured if you obeyed."

And suddenly, a new feeling started to fill me.

A lightness I hadn't felt ever since learning that non-believers couldn't make it into the highest kingdom of heaven and I had worried over my mom's soul.

For the first time, I felt lightness and hope.

Hope that after all of these years of praying for my mom to accept Jehovah and return to The Fold, it was actually promised that there was a way for me to save her.

If I could just do this one special ceremony.

But could I sacrifice my own will to ensure the everlasting happiness of those around me? Could I give up the future I'd dreamed of, for the greater good of my family?

I didn't know if I was strong or selfless enough to do that.

"The High Priest has commanded me to do what I can to make sure this happens," Dad said. "He's counting on me. Counting on you and Xander to make sure that this special baby can come during this promised time." He took a few steps closer. "Even if this revelation seems odd to our modern eyes, the Lord wouldn't allow a fallen man to lead the church wrongly. He would be taken from the earth if he tried to lead us astray."

I nodded, though there was still a war going on inside my mind.

"I know you're probably confused and shocked right now. But I know that if you pray and fast about it, with an open heart, the truthfulness of this will be revealed to you as well." He took my shoulders in his hands, and with his brown eyes boring into mine, he spoke in his intense pastor's voice, saying, "It's God's will, Scarlett. And you need to follow it. Just think of how much you will be blessed for this and what an honor it will be to raise the chosen High Priest of the last days."

38

SCARLETT

I LEFT my dad's office feeling numb and in shock as I walked across the courtyard to the parsonage. When I got upstairs to my room, I changed out of my new dress and into my comfiest pajamas. Then I lay in my bed, crying on and off for the next hour as I thought about what was being asked of me.

If this revelation was truly from God, did that mean I'd be tied to Xander forever?

Or would it be like the spiritual partners thing where some of the women had other husbands but were just part-time wives?

Could I still be with Hunter like ninety-five percent of the time and just have Xander be more like a co-parent to the son we were supposed to raise? We would get married in two weeks, perform the spiritual ceremony that I still didn't know any details about, and then once I was pregnant, we could get divorced and raise this Chosen One together?

I sighed. Would Hunter still want me after doing something like that?

Would he be okay being a stepfather to the Chosen One of a church he didn't even believe in anymore?

Probably not.

And Xander probably wouldn't be okay with something like that, either.

Why would God command me to be with Xander? Why did I have to be the chosen vessel?

I rubbed on the birthmark, wishing I could wipe it away. Because instead of being something special now, it just felt like a death sentence.

Sure, Xander was a good guy, and if Hunter wasn't there, I might be interested in him.

But the fact was that Hunter was still here. I still wanted him, and if this stupid revelation didn't exist, I was sure we would have eventually found a way to make things work.

If free will was a real thing, why did it feel like I was having all of my choices taken away from me?

Why had I ever been allowed to believe that I'd have any sort of choice about my future in the first place?

I was on hour two of crying when my phone buzzed with a text from Hunter.

Is now a good time to talk about things?

It took me a moment to realize what he wanted to talk about since the events after church had taken me so far from the worries I'd had this morning.

Me: **I'm actually not feeling very well. I think I caught the stomach bug or something and just need to rest.**

I had certainly been on the verge of vomiting for the past couple of hours.

Hunter: **I'm sorry to hear that. I'm guessing**

you're probably not up to riding back to school tonight?

Me: **Probably not...**

I was pretty sure I'd be feeling sick for a while.

Hunter: **Want me to see if my parents' driver can take us tomorrow morning?**

Me: **That would be great.**

I just lay there, looking at my phone screen for a few minutes as I waited for him to update me, not having the energy to do anything else.

Then another text came through. **It's all set. We can leave at 6:30 and just have breakfast in the car.**

Me: **Thank you.**

I started to type out "I love you," but just looking at those words on the screen made my eyes fill with tears and a sob stretch my throat.

Because if everything my dad said was true, I might never actually get to say those words to Hunter ever again.

The future I'd dreamed of and been fighting for with Hunter had never even had a chance at existing.

39

HUNTER

SCARLETT WAS much quieter than normal as we rode back to school together early Monday morning.

I'd brought her favorite coffee—a white chocolate mocha along with her favorite custard-filled donut. But instead of smiling from ear to ear when she saw me waiting outside the church gates with it like she usually did, she'd barely managed to even smile at all.

Even now, she just seemed to barely be here. When I'd asked her if she was still sick and if she needed to stay back an extra day, she said she was fine.

But she didn't look fine. She looked like she was half-dead.

The usual vibrancy in her eyes was gone.

And when I reached for her hand where it rested limply on her leg, she seemed to hesitate for a second before letting me hold it.

"Is there something going on that I need to know about?" I asked, scared that what happened with me at church yesterday was causing her to pull away.

She'd told me before I left that she wanted to find a way to make things work out. But maybe as the day had gone on, she'd realized that it would be too hard.

She looked at me with tired eyes. "I just had a really bad day yesterday."

"Is it because of me?" I rubbed my thumb over her knuckle. "Did me leaving church ruin everything?"

Her eyes filled with tears and her lips started trembling, like she was fighting back huge emotions, but she said, "No. It's —" She released a shaky breath. "It's just something my dad talked to me about. And... I don't know. It's just, I'm confused now."

Had Pastor Caldwell told her to break up with me again? Had Xander said something about us, and he decided we had crossed the line?

I wanted to press Scarlett for more information about what exactly had happened with her dad, but I could tell she was in enough pain already that I shouldn't press her.

So I squeezed her hand instead before pulling her close. As the sun began to rise over the horizon, I kissed the top of her head and just held her as tears silently streamed down her cheeks.

SCARLETT CONTINUED to be withdrawn over the next few days. She wasn't present in any of our classes. Didn't seem to really care about our study sessions.

It was like she was in shock or numb, or something.

It actually reminded me of how I felt when I got the initial shock of finding that The Fold wasn't what I'd thought it was.

Was that what had happened to her? Had something in her meeting with her dad cracked her faith?

Or was it something completely different? Maybe a sick relative? Her grandparents were well into their eighties now, so maybe something happened to one of them?

"Do you want to talk about anything?" I asked her when we were hanging out in the common room together Thursday evening. "Is there anything on your mind?"

"I'm just thinking a lot about life after high school and what it will look like for me," she said with a shrug.

"Yeah?" I asked, wondering if she still saw me in any of those future plans of hers.

She nodded. "Like, I just—I'm not sure it is going to be exactly how I imagined."

"Really?" My voice came out higher pitched than normal.

Was she going to break up with me then?

Had I just opened up the conversation for her to do that?

She bit her lip and said, "I—"

But she didn't finish her thought because her phone lit up with a text. And even though I knew her texts were none of my business, when I saw the name at the beginning of the notification, I couldn't help but read it along with her.

Xander: **Still on for dinner at Jacob's Steakhouse tomorrow so we can talk about everything?**

She seemed to finish reading the text at the same time as me, and when she met my gaze, her expression looked guilty.

"You're meeting Xander for dinner tomorrow?" I asked, deciding to just nip whatever this thing was in the bud.

"I am..."

"Is it like a date?" I asked, trying to keep my voice even. "Is that why you've been distant? Why you've been off all week?"

Because you're seeing him behind my back, and you feel guilty about it?

"It's just dinner," she rushed to say. "I promise."

"Why, though?" I asked, not understanding why she'd be

having dinner with another guy when I'd thought she was dating me. "Why are you meeting Xander for dinner?"

I knew we hadn't officially put a label on what we were to each other. But I thought it was understood that we were basically together.

Or would be, if her dad wasn't an issue.

"It's just..." she started to say, "it's complicated."

"Does it have anything to do with what your dad talked to you about on Sunday?"

"Yes."

I waited for her to say more, but when she didn't, I asked, "What did he talk to you about, Scarlett?"

"It's something that you wouldn't understand."

"Why?" I knew I sounded frustrated, but if she was planning to dump me because of something her dad had said, it was better for me to know now versus next week or in a month, or whenever she got around to telling me that Pastor Caldwell had poisoned her against me.

She studied my face for a moment, like she was trying to decide if she would tell me what was going on or not. After releasing a heavy sigh, she said, "It has to do with The Fold. And a new revelation." She glanced out the window at a bird that had dropped onto a bare branch. "Something that involves Xander and me."

"What?" I furrowed my brow. "A revelation that involves you and Xander?"

Since when did the High Priest have revelations involving specific people? Usually, any direction he'd heard of was for the church as a whole.

She must have sensed that I knew it was odd for the High Priest to have revelations about specific members because her eyes widened, seeming fearful.

And I was suddenly nervous for Scarlett.

"You'd tell me if there was something serious going on, right?" I asked.

She nodded, but the look in her eyes told me she was lying.

And now I was truly scared.

40

SCARLETT

"I'LL BE BACK in a couple of hours," I told Hunter on Friday night after seeing the text from Xander that said he had just pulled up to the school. "And then we can hang out."

"Okay," he said, a wary look in his eyes, like he knew it was more than just dinner with a friend. "Just hurry back, okay?"

I nodded. "See you soon."

Even though all I wanted to do was cling to Hunter and beg him to somehow make this scary path ahead of me disappear, I made myself walk out of the common room.

As I headed toward the front entrance of the school where Xander was waiting, all I could think about was the fact that I only had one week until I was supposed to marry a near stranger.

There was just one week until I performed a special, secret ceremony to get pregnant with the Chosen One.

I'd been praying all week for clarity. For a sign from above that this was actually what I should be doing. But so far, despite praying in earnest, there had only been silence on the other end of the line.

Absolute silence.

And it scared me. Because I'd never felt the absolute silence before.

Was this silence God's way of punishing me for being resistant to his commandment? Was this God's more modern way of throwing me into the belly of a big fish because I didn't want to obey and follow his plan for me?

I didn't know, but the silence was deafening and made it impossible to feel any sort of comfort.

I'd even been desperate enough for some advice that I emailed *The Confidant* two nights ago since *The Confidant* always seemed to know exactly what to do in tricky situations.

But *The Confidant* hadn't messaged me back, either. Which I probably should have known would happen.

I wasn't supposed to talk about this situation with anyone, so God had probably intercepted the communication and made sure my email was lost in the sea of other high school students looking for advice.

So after spending several days with my thoughts on a continuous anxious loop, I'd texted Xander to see how he'd felt about everything. To see if it felt as wrong and invasive to him as it did to me. But as we'd texted back and forth, he seemed to be on board with it. Like he had already found peace with being told exactly who he needed to marry and was just waiting patiently for me to come along for the ride with him.

Maybe I should be flattered that he didn't mind the idea of marrying me...but all I could think about was the fact that we still barely knew anything about each other. Definitely not enough to want to spend the rest of your life raising a special kid with someone.

But maybe it was different for him. He was four years older than me and had more experience dating. So maybe he felt like he'd already spent enough time fishing for the best fish in the sea and was completely content with the one the revelation had chosen for him.

Or maybe it had nothing to do with me and he just really liked the idea of raising the future High Priest.

My dad certainly seemed honored that he would be the grandfather of the Chosen One.

Either way, Xander had suggested we have dinner together to talk things over, saying he might have some insights that would help me feel more at peace.

I just hoped I'd have more clarity by the end of the night.

XANDER WAS WAITING for me in the school lobby when I got there, and when he saw me, a big smile spread across his lips. Like he was actually happy to see me and looking forward to a future together.

"You look beautiful tonight," he said, appraising me from head to toe.

"Thanks," I said even though I was pretty sure I only looked okay. I hadn't wanted to raise any alarms to Hunter, so I'd done the bare minimum to get ready for dinner at a fancy restaurant—putting on a nice dress and doing my hair and makeup just enough that it wouldn't be too obvious how I really didn't want anything to do with the future that had been written out for me.

Xander gave me a hug, and for a second it looked like he wanted to take my hand. But he seemed to realize that I wasn't ready for that kind of familiarity right now, so he instead walked slightly ahead of me and opened the passenger door of his Bugatti to help me in.

Before taking my seat, out of instinct, I looked up at the large windows that belonged to the common room. There was a

Hunter-shaped shadow standing there, and I felt immediately guilty for keeping him in the dark about what was going on.

And from the way he stepped away from the window when he noticed me looking up at him, I could tell he probably felt like my dinner with Xander was all about betraying him and all the plans he'd been making for the future.

Xander and I pulled into Jacob's Steakhouse, one of Eden Falls more upscale restaurants, about ten minutes later. The hostess led us to a private room in the back.

"I figured it would be good to have some privacy," Xander said as he helped me into my seat. "Just because of the sacredness of this situation."

The *sacredness*? Did he really see this whole situation as a special, sacred opportunity then?

Did that mean I was a bad person for seeing it more as a punishment?

We ordered our food. After the waitress brought our drinks —wine for him, water with lemon for me—Xander asked, "So, how are you liking your classes? Are you excited for the last two months of your senior year?"

I took a sip of my water before saying, "I actually haven't been in the zone with all that as much lately." I set the glass back on the table. "I've been a little preoccupied with other things this week."

If I was going to be fully honest, it actually felt like my senior year had been stolen from me the moment my dad pulled me into his office and told me I'd be getting married on Easter weekend.

I couldn't think. Couldn't concentrate on anything. Ever since Sunday afternoon, I'd basically been in full adrenaline mode all the time. It was so exhausting.

And yet, even as tired as I was, I still couldn't sleep. Couldn't settle down at all.

Which was why I hoped to find some semblance of peace after our dinner. I really wanted to sleep through the night again.

Xander seemed to sense how much I was struggling because he set his hand on my knee and said, "I'm sure you've been shocked by everything. It's a lot to take in. Especially since the time for the ceremony is approaching fast." He gave me a sympathetic look. "I wish your dad would have explained everything sooner."

"Me too." I drew in a deep breath, wishing it would calm me. "I'm guessing you started telling me about the spiritual partner thing in your dorm room that day because you were hoping to give me a heads-up."

He nodded. "I didn't want you to be completely blind-sided." He removed his hand from my knee. "I expected your dad to mention at least something about it to you several months ago since I've had so much longer to consider everything. I just hope that once the shock wears off, you'll be okay marrying me." The look of calm he'd been exuding so far slipped momentarily, like he was also nervous over me accepting him. "But I promise to be a good husband to you and a good father to our son."

Our son.

Another flash of dread passed through me. All I could think about was how a huge part of me wanted to beg Xander to use some of his dad's billions to have me placed in a medically induced coma for the next several months while my body did whatever it needed to do to get the Chosen One here.

I was sure that whatever the sacred ceremony entailed would be handled in all of the best ways. That Xander would be a complete gentleman through everything and do his best to make me comfortable with whatever happened.

But since the only person I could even imagine being

comfortable with enough to kiss, let alone do anything else with, was named Hunter and not Xander, I just didn't want to mentally or emotionally participate in any of it.

Xander seemed like a great guy and all. He was someone I would have probably been fine dating—if things were different and Hunter hadn't already stolen my heart. But as things were now, I just didn't see him like that.

And I doubted I'd see him in that way seven days from now, either.

"I saw how you were with Hunter last week," Xander said, almost as if he could read my mind. "Is that also causing some hesitation?"

Was I supposed to answer that honestly? Because, of course, me being in love with another guy would make it difficult to pledge myself to Xander.

He must have noticed the way my face burned because he added, "It's okay, if it is. I wouldn't expect you to turn off your feelings for him instantly. But..." He swallowed and looked like he was trying to tread carefully when he said, "But I wonder if you see things working out in the long run. Your dad mentioned Hunter has struggled with his faith and I—" He sighed and lifted his shoulders in a shrug. "I just know what kind of a woman you are, and it's hard for me to see things working out between the two of you in the long run."

My hands clenched in fists on my lap because I really didn't like the way he said that.

Like he was suggesting Hunter wasn't good enough for me.

"You're just such a special girl—one of the Lord's elect. The future mother of the *Chosen One*." He picked up his wine glass. "You deserve to be with someone who can give you the most important things. Someone who can help you build a life that aligns with God's plan—a life on the covenant path."

I hated how conflicted I felt because I knew it was what I

was supposed to want. Since until recently, it was what I'd always wanted—to marry someone within the covenant. Someone who could support me in raising a family in the gospel.

And as much as I wanted, Hunter couldn't give me that.

"No matter how much you think you like your friend," Xander continued, "you are on different paths now, and no amount of loving and caring about each other will change that."

The waitress brought the plates with our food. After smiling and thanking her, Xander picked up his fork and knife to cut his steak. He said, "And you should probably find a way to break things off sooner rather than later so you can focus on the future with me."

He said it like it should be easy.

To just drop Hunter and move on with him. As if he was so ready to just run with this revelation.

But I guess none of this was new or sudden to Xander. He'd been going along with everything and trying to date me, hadn't he? He'd never been half-in or trying to figure things out with his best friend on the side like I had been.

Because unlike me, Xander had known about this revelation for close to a year. He hadn't been completely overwhelmed with the information and crazy timeline all at once.

I started poking at my fettuccine alfredo, trying to decide if I'd be able to even keep any food down when my stomach was so upset.

As I put tiny bites of food in my mouth, Xander started painting a picture of what our future could be like. Talking about which holidays we'd be spending with each of our families and all the perks I'd have as the wife to a billionaire heir. But I could only half concentrate on the things he was saying because the more he talked, the more I realized that I really did need to end things with Hunter. Probably this weekend.

Everything was moving so fast, and even though Xander seemed excited about everything, I wasn't ready to hear about Christmas at his family's cabin in Vail, Colorado. Or summers at their beach house in Nantucket.

He was probably saying it to give me something to look forward to, but all I felt was a spiraling—I needed some air before I suffocated.

I just needed time to slow down.

But the time seemed to be disappearing faster than ever because I only had one week left.

One week before I became a handmaiden of the Lord and a wife to Xander.

There were only a few days until I would perform the secret ceremony that would put me on the path to giving birth to the Chosen One.

41

SCARLETT

"I'LL SEE YOU ON SUNDAY," Xander said when he dropped me back at the school around nine p.m. "Thanks for coming to dinner."

"Thanks," I said, bending over to wave before I shut the passenger door. "Have a good night."

I waited on the sidewalk for him to drive away before heading inside, finally letting my shoulders droop after pretending for the past two hours like my life wasn't completely over.

I pulled out my phone to see if I'd missed any messages while I'd been out and saw that Ava had texted me.

We're just about to take off. I hope you have a better week this next week. Remember, spring break is supposed to be fun. I'll see you next Sunday!

Ava was flying on the Hastings' private jet, so I didn't know if she'd have any sort of cell reception. But I texted her,

Thanks. Have a fabulous week, before slipping my phone back into my bag.

I had a feeling my friends would be having a much different—and much more normal—spring break than I would.

The Hastings family had jetted off to Guatemala to work at an orphanage they sponsored—Mack and Ava joining them for the fun. Elyse had slipped away with her mom for an adventure in London where they would be seeing all the sights and catching a few plays. Asher was headed back to his aunt and uncle's house for a week of fun with his twin cousins. And even though Hunter had planned to hang out with me tonight and ride the train together back to Manhattan tomorrow, he would be heading down to Florida on Sunday morning for a few days on the beach with his parents.

I hadn't heard of Addison and Evan having any plans to leave town—they never visited their family, for some reason—so I assumed they'd be hanging out at the school while everyone was away.

But even just staying at the school for a week sounded like heaven compared to what I'd be doing: Getting married and somehow getting pregnant.

I pushed the thoughts away and headed to the dorms, hoping that if I stopped thinking about everything all my problems would magically go away.

When I got to the common room, Hunter was sitting on one of the leather couches, looking like he'd just been waiting for me the whole time.

When he noticed me, he sat up straighter and turned off the TV. "How was dinner?"

Terrible.

"It was fine," I lied. Then to get the conversation off of me, I asked, "Did you eat anything good?"

"They had pizza in the great hall so I had a couple of slices."

"Cool."

We looked at each other awkwardly, and I knew he wanted me to say more about my dinner with Xander. But when I didn't say anything about it, he asked, "Anything exciting happen at your dinner?"

"Not really." I shrugged.

"Anything you need to tell me?"

I'm being forced to marry Xander next week.

"Not really," I said again.

"You sure? Because it seems like you've had a lot on your mind lately," he said, obviously trying another route to get me to talk about the things I wasn't allowed to talk about.

"Yes. I have had some things on my mind."

"But you don't want to talk about these things with me?"

"I can't," I said, hoping it would get him to stop pressing for information I couldn't give.

"Can't?" His eyebrows knitted together. "Or won't?"

"Can't."

His frown deepened. And I wanted to tell him everything. To explain what was going on and making me act so weird.

But I had literally been forbidden to talk about it with anyone. By my dad *and* the High Priest.

As far as I knew, going against the High Priest's command was basically just asking to be struck down like all those people in the Bible.

"I actually don't really want to think about it," I said, hoping it would show Hunter that I didn't like what was going on, either. My hands were just tied.

Plus, I could at least wait to think about everything until tomorrow, couldn't I? Save it for when I was back in New York. Because for tonight, I just wanted to have one last night with my best friend. One more night where I could pretend things were different.

"I think I'm actually going to go change out of these clothes," I said.

"Okay." He gave me a disappointed look, like he thought that was my way of saying goodnight.

But since that was actually the last thing I wanted right now, I asked, "Do you want to come hang out with me in my room?"

"Oh, yeah..." His eyes lit up in surprise. "Sure. We have a couple of hours before curfew."

"That's what I was thinking," I said. It was the weekend, so we had until midnight before it was lights out.

We walked up the stairs to the girls' dorm together and stopped at Heather's door to let her know that Hunter would be hanging out in my room for a while. But after standing there for a few seconds and hearing Heather laughing about something with one of her friends, Hunter and I gave each other a look like this was our chance to be sneaky and break the rules. So we headed down to my hall without checking in.

I unlocked my door with my ID badge, and we both slipped inside. Instead of leaving the door open a crack like we were supposed to do when we had boys over, I decided to continue my rebellion against the rules and shut the door all the way so we could have some privacy.

"Should I step outside while you change?" Hunter asked when he noticed me pull my pajamas out of my dresser drawer.

When I looked back at him, he was still hovering right by the door as if he didn't want to cross some sort of line. But this was my last night of freedom and I wanted to push as many boundaries as I could, so I peeked at him through my lashes and said, "You can just turn around. I trust you..."

He turned to face the corner, and I took a few steps closer

to my closet and started the process of changing out of my dress. I was leaving my bra and underwear on, so it wasn't like Hunter would see everything if he happened to take a peek, but it did feel somewhat dangerous doing this.

Changing in the same room with the guy I liked.

I started unzipping the back of my dress. The sound seemed to do something to Hunter because as soon as he heard it, he cleared his throat and started to make small talk—like he was trying not to think about the fact that I was undressing. And just the thought of him having a reaction to any of this made my entire body flush with heat because the devil in me wanted him to look.

Because even with everything going on, I still wanted Hunter to want me like that.

"My parents are excited to take us to the Brooklyn Botanic Garden," he said, talking about our plans for the next day. "Then I was thinking we could stop at that bookstore you like and have dinner at that diner on the corner that you love."

"That sounds nice," I said, pulling my pajama shirt over my head.

But even though it sounded like the perfect day, I was overcome with sadness because I realized that once I was married—in, like, a week—I wouldn't be able to have Saturdays like that with him anymore.

I'd be spending my Saturdays with someone else.

I quickly pulled my pajama shorts on and turned around to see that, like the true gentleman that I knew Hunter was, he was still facing the corner.

"I'm decent now," I said.

I watched him turn around slowly. After taking in my pajamas with little pink cats all over them, he smiled and got a look in his eyes that said he thought I was beautiful. And I was instantly sad that tonight was probably the last night he'd ever look at me like that.

I want him to look at me like that forever.

Meeting my eyes, Hunter asked, "What do you want to do now?"

Without thinking about anything else anymore, I walked across the carpeted floor and into his arms. And after kissing him, I whispered in his ear, "This, Hunter. This is all I want to do."

42

HUNTER

CHILLS RACED across my skin with Scarlett's words, and it took me a moment to catch up to what was happening. But once I realized what she was saying she wanted to do with me this evening, I didn't hesitate to wrap my arms around her waist and pull her closer.

While part of me knew I should be worried about why she'd been acting differently all week, it was hard to concentrate on any of that because having her in my arms as she trailed hot kisses from my mouth and all along my jawline just felt so good.

So incredibly good.

And even though she'd kissed me before, this kiss seemed different from our other kisses in a way.

More urgent.

Almost like we were in a race against time, and she thought this might be our last kiss.

But that was a crazy thought, wasn't it? Because we were just at the beginning of our relationship and not the end. Even if something did go wrong with whatever she couldn't talk to me about, I knew we could fix it.

Because that was what you did when you loved each other the way we did. You fought for each other and made things work.

"Mind if we lie down on the bed?" Scarlett asked, pulling her lips from mine for a second and dragging in a shallow breath. "Just this once."

She wants to kiss me on her bed? A thrill of excitement passed through me at the thought.

"You want to lie down together?" I asked, not sure I'd actually heard her right.

"Yes," she said. "Just to kiss..." She sighed again like she was having a really hard time catching her breath. "I just want to kiss you on my bed at least once."

If I'd been in a clearer headspace, I probably would have noticed the way she'd made it sound like this might be the only chance for us to kiss on a bed. But since my brain cells only wanted to think about covering her body with mine and kissing her until her lips were swollen and we were gasping for air, I didn't register everything that might be going on.

So when I nodded, letting her know it was more than fine with me, she sat down and scooted herself back on her bed until her head rested on her quilt, her auburn hair splaying out like a crown above her head.

For a split second, I thought about doing exactly what I wanted—to put all my weight on her and see just how close we could get. But I didn't want to risk scaring her away with how much I wanted her right now, so I settled next to her instead.

She tangled her fingers in my hair to pull me closer. And when her lips captured mine in a long exchange, my veins throbbed, my heart threatening to explode because she felt and tasted and smelled so unbelievably good. And when she arched into me, pressing her chest and hips somehow closer, I was instantly drunk on her.

Not that I'd ever actually been drunk. But it seemed like it would probably feel like this.

All warm and fuzzy and happy.

Addicting.

Yes, I could definitely see myself getting addicted to this feeling and always looking forward to my next Scarlett fix.

"How does this feel so good every time?" I asked, pulling away for a second to take in a gasp of air.

"I don't know," she said, just as breathlessly. "But I like it."

"I like it, too."

I nuzzled my face into her neck and inhaled her shampoo and the extra scent that was just *her*. It was the most delicious scent I could ever imagine, and I wanted to breathe her, lick her, drink her in.

I wanted to do everything there was to do with Scarlett.

Someday, at least.

Her hands brushed down my sides, and when she slipped them under my T-shirt, my stomach muscles quivered. I couldn't remember if she'd ever touched me like this before— her hands directly on my abdomen—but I liked it. I loved the feeling of her warm hands on my skin. It was electric and brought all my nerve endings to life.

"Your heart is beating so fast," she said when her hands had slipped up to my chest.

"I know," I said, my voice sounding rough and deep. "You do it to me."

"Want to feel mine?" she asked.

"Um..." I swallowed, not sure I should say yes since her heart was way too close to other parts of her body that I shouldn't be allowed to touch right now.

But instead of waiting for me to answer her question, she

took my hand in hers and pressed it to her neck like she'd done on Presidents' Day weekend.

"Can you feel it?" she asked.

It took me a moment to concentrate enough to register her pulse with all the other things going on in my head, but I felt the steady beat a moment later and managed to croak out a, "Yeah. I can feel it."

"What about here?" she asked. Then watching me carefully, like she was waiting to see what I would do, she slowly moved my hand lower, slipping it just inside the collar of her pajama shirt until it rested over her heart. Her skin was slightly clammy, like our kisses had made her warm, but she was also so soft there.

I shook the thought away and forced my concentration away from all things soft and focused back to what she was trying to show me. Her heartbeat.

"Your heart is beating fast, too," I managed to say.

Probably just as fast as mine.

She met my eyes, her gaze tender as she said, "It always beats that fast when I'm with you."

Our lips met again, and when our tongues tangled and danced together, a delicious warmth spread all over my body.

When Scarlett rolled back against her soft mattress, I followed—instinctively covering her body with mine. As the weight of my body on hers crushed her against the bed, I realized that having her body fully beneath mine felt somehow even better than all the times I'd imagined it.

"That's nice," she whispered between kisses, her eyes darting down to our bodies and indicating how we were pressed together now.

"I know." I sighed. "You feel so good, Scarlett."

43

SCARLETT

HOW HAVE I *known Hunter for all these years and never allowed us to be this close before?* I was sure we were probably really close to that line I wasn't supposed to cross before marriage, but instead of feeling guilty or scared, all I felt was warm and happy and exhilarated.

Being in his arms like this with his lips weaving a magic spell over my mind was about as good as life could get as far as I knew. I didn't know how anything could feel better than this. It was all encompassing. And though my lips were swollen, and the slightest bit of stubble that he had was rough against my sensitive skin, I didn't care—it showed me that this moment was actually real, and we were really doing this together and making each other feel so good.

He felt wonderful. I knew we were already so close, but when his hands smoothed down my sides and my hands slipped across his back, all I wanted was more of this. More of him.

I wanted to feel more of his skin against mine.

I slid my hands across his back again. Noticing that his shirt had already ridden halfway up his torso from our kissing and touching, I decided to push it farther up his sides to help him out of it.

If this was going to be one of the last times I got to kiss Hunter, I was going to make it count.

Hunter went still for a second when he realized I was trying to take his shirt off, like he hadn't expected me to do it. "Is this okay?" I asked, making sure I wasn't pushing a boundary he didn't want to cross.

His eyes were black when he looked at me, but he nodded and said, "Of course it's fine."

To help assist me, he pushed himself up so that he was kneeling on the bed. Since I didn't want him taking off his shirt without me, I got to my knees as well and helped tug it over his head, tossing it onto the nightstand beside my bed.

He pulled me against him, and we kissed like that for a few minutes before he scooted back against my headboard and pillows. With him in an inclined position, which made his abs look somehow even better, he pulled me onto his lap, my legs straddling his hips.

His hands went to my waist and smoothed down my legs. After I took in his bare torso and admired his amazing physique, I lifted my eyes to his for a moment of intense eye contact.

It was so hot—the way he was looking at me. It was like I was the only thing he'd ever wanted in his whole life. Like I was beautiful and sexy, and he *wanted* me in all the ways a man would want a woman he loved.

He slid his hands back up my legs, his fingertips just barely grazing the skin under the hem of my shorts before pushing them along my hips and across my back, setting me on fire everywhere he touched.

I gently grazed my fingertips along his forearms, loving how

I could feel his prominent veins. His arms were so sexy—the kind that inspired sonnets. They were also strong and comforting, and every time I was in them, they made me feel safe. And with his biceps bulging from the way his arms were bent, I couldn't help but think about how I wanted to lust after and be in his arms forever.

But when I couldn't take the tension mounting between us any longer, I bent over to kiss him again. As I relaxed my body against his, he tangled his fingers in my hair and whispered, "You're so beautiful, Scarlett," before pulling me somehow closer so my body was flushed with his.

With one hand gently combing through the hair at the base of my scalp and making me release a sound somewhere between a gasp and a moan, he moved his other hand along my shoulder and down my arm. He kissed me deeply, letting his tongue flick against mine in a way that awoke a stirring feeling deep within my belly. Then he was kissing along my jawline and laying me on my back so he could press kisses down my neck and along my collarbone. And all I could do was look at the ceiling and try to catch my breath because everything felt so amazing.

His hand smoothed over my hip and gently grazed beneath my shirt to spread across my stomach. I'd never been touched like this before but his calloused hand against my smooth skin made my nervous system go haywire as my stomach trembled and squeezed.

"Is this okay?" he asked when he noticed how still I went. "Am I pushing things too far?"

If it were with any other guy, I might have been worried that it was. But this was Hunter, and he knew me better than anyone else. I knew he was safe. I could trust him. So I said, "It's not too far."

But we were most definitely tiptoeing up to the line now.

It was like our three-kisses rule from last year all over again. Where we knew we had to stick within certain boundaries but were really good at finding loopholes in order to get what we wanted. The boundaries were on our side and an enemy at the same time, and just like an enemy would poke against every side and corner, checking for a weakness, we were really good at pushing things just to the edge of where everything would come tumbling down.

Our kisses eventually slowed, and the frenzy of the past hour subsided as we fell into a more gentle and secure pace. And when the wave of passion turned into a gentle ebb and flow, we pulled away and turned on our sides so we could breathe. We rested our foreheads together and just stared into each other's eyes as we waited for our heart rates to slow back down.

Hunter brushed some hair away from my face, tucking it behind my ear. Looking somber, he traced his thumb across my cheekbone and whispered, "I love you, Scarlett," making my heart swell and my whole body feel tingly.

Because I knew he truly meant it.

Hunter loved me fully—all of me—in a way that I didn't think anyone else ever could.

And even though the words would never be able to capture all the things I felt for my best friend, I gave him a gentle smile and said, "I love you too, Hunter."

44

SCARLETT

I WOKE the next morning and smiled when I saw Hunter lying by my side, looking at me in a way that said he'd been awake for a while just watching me as I slept.

"Good morning," he said, placing a gentle kiss on my forehead when he realized I was awake.

"Good morning," I replied, leaning closer to him.

We'd fallen asleep together and it had been so nice. We'd only kissed last night, nothing more than that. But it had been amazing, and I was pretty sure I could be very content just kissing and holding Hunter for a very long time.

"You'd think that after being friends for so long I'd know everything there was to know about you," Hunter said in a tired, mumbly voice against my hair. "But I learned something new last night."

"You did?" I asked, curious what he may have learned. "What is it?"

"That you talk in your sleep."

"I do?" I asked, surprised by this fact because I'd never had anyone tell me this before.

He nodded.

"What did I say?" I asked, hoping it hadn't been anything embarrassing.

Or something I was forbidden to say.

"Just something about how attractive you think I am and how you're obsessed with me."

I rolled my eyes and patted his chest playfully. "And now I know you're lying."

"You don't think you'd say those things in your sleep?" He pushed his lips down into a dramatic, pouty face.

"Well, since I'm pretty sure I was dreaming about going to Hogwarts and trying to beat Hermione at everything, I don't think I necessarily had the guy I'm obsessed with on my brain."

"At least you can admit that you're obsessed with me," he said, kissing my forehead again. "Because I'm pretty obsessed with you."

I snuggled closer and thought about just going back to sleep when he said, "Are you planning to sleep all day then?"

"Maybe."

It was still early, right? But then I remembered we were supposed to take the nine o'clock train back to Manhattan.

I looked at my watch to see what time it was, but since I'd fallen asleep without putting it on the charger last night, it was completely dead.

"Do you know what time it is?" I asked.

Hunter lifted his arm from around me and angled it so we could both see the watch face. "It's eight forty-seven."

"Crap," I said. "We're going to miss the train."

"I think the next one leaves at ten-fifteen. We could try to make that one instead."

I thought about it. Taking the train would mean going back to my dad's house. And when I got there, my stepmom Megan was going to take me to be fitted for the special ceremonial clothing I was supposed to wear on Friday night.

I hugged myself closer to Hunter and rested my head against his bare chest. "I actually think I might want to just stay here all week instead of going home for spring break." I angled my head back to meet his eyes. "Wouldn't that be fun? Having our own little staycation?"

"As nice as that sounds," he said, his chest rumbling against my ear, "I'm pretty sure our parents would come find us. Mine are pretty set on taking me to Florida for a few days at least."

I sighed. "You're probably right."

My dad would definitely send out a search party if he thought I was going to miss my special appointment with Xander and the High Priest.

And even though for the past several hours I'd been trying not to think about what was coming for me, a sense of panic set in.

Was I actually going to get married to Xander next weekend?

After everything last night, could I really make myself break up with Hunter so I could go and spend my life with someone else?

Raise a special baby with someone else?

I really didn't see me feeling any better about that situation a week from now than I did today.

I couldn't marry someone else when I was in love with Hunter, could I?

Not even if it was what God wanted...

"If we're going to make the next train, I should probably get out of here so you can get ready," Hunter said, grabbing his shirt from where I'd thrown it on my nightstand last night.

"Okay." I scooted to the edge of my bed and stood.

I watched him pull his shirt over his head, and before he

could slip out the door and try not to get caught by Heather, I pulled him in for one last hug.

"You okay?" He looked down at me with concern as he held me in his arms. "You seem like you're worried about something."

"I'm just missing you already," I said. "That's all."

"I'll see you in, like, fifteen minutes." He chuckled lightly, smoothing his hands along my back in a comforting way. "Then we'll still get to spend the whole day together before I fly out tomorrow."

I nodded. "I'm just proving how obsessed I am with you."

"I think you just like smelling the cologne you gave me last year." He winked.

"I do have really good taste."

He smiled. "You really do."

He gave me a quick kiss goodbye. Then after opening the door and poking his head out to see if the coast was clear, he slipped into the hall and disappeared around the corner.

I closed my door again and pressed my back against it. I thought about everything coming up and everything that had happened last night.

I wanted last night to be the *first* time I fell asleep in Hunter's arms and not the *last*.

Living with just memories of kissing him goodnight and being held in his arms wouldn't be enough. Not when I actually wanted a lifetime of those moments with him.

A lifetime of smiles and kisses and laughs and long, late-night talks and inside jokes.

I wanted decades and not just days of building memories with my best friend.

Any sort of heaven wouldn't be worth having if Hunter wasn't there with me.

And if he didn't want to be there with me, then I didn't want to be there, either. I wanted to be wherever he was.

A life and eternity without Hunter would be its own kind of hell.

Surely God would forgive me for not being able to be the chosen vessel. Other people had found forgiveness and healing after disobeying God's commandments. That was what God's grace was for anyway, right? The space given to us to be human.

I just wasn't strong enough to follow this commandment right now. It had long been said that the Lord's work couldn't be stopped. That he would always find a path forward.

It would just need to be a path that didn't involve me.

Xander was the one who carried the bloodline of Samuel Williams, anyway. Not me. I was only the vessel for it. Surely he could find someone else. Someone who could actually love him like he deserved to be loved.

He was a good guy. Sweet, good-looking, and a *billionaire*.

It shouldn't be too difficult to find another girl who was up to the task of raising the Chosen One with him.

I sighed, feeling the pressure in my chest relax for the first time since my dad had pulled me into his office. I knew what I was going to do.

I was going to tell my dad that I couldn't go through with the ceremony.

And if he or the High Priest had a problem with it, I might just need to run away with Hunter and hide until they could cool off.

Because for once, I was going to put myself first instead of God.

Yes, I was choosing Hunter.

But I was also choosing *me*.

45

SCARLETT

I TALKED to my dad on Saturday night after spending the day with Hunter and his parents. He was disappointed and sad that I wouldn't be fulfilling my part of the revelation, but he admitted that he was also a little relieved because he hadn't felt completely right about asking that of me, either.

"I'll let the High Priest know about the change of plans," he said, pulling me into a hug when our conversation was over. "The Lord will just have to provide another way."

"Thank you for understanding," I said, feeling relieved and so much better. Like I actually had a future I could look forward to again.

I spent the next several days catching up on assignments I'd been too depressed to do the week before and playing a lot of board games with my dad and Megan.

Hunter texted me a bunch of photos of him hanging out on the beach, and I sent him a few, much less exciting photos of me reading books or trying out the chai latte from the coffee shop down the street that he promised had the best house-brewed chai lattes I could ever have.

Even though it was a bit spicy the first few sips, by the end of my first cup, I had a feeling I'd be visiting this coffee shop a lot more when I went to Columbia next year.

Because yep, I'd officially decided to study at Columbia with Hunter and Mack next year.

College was going to be amazing.

Hunter got back from Florida on Friday afternoon and took me out to dinner that night, saying he wanted to take his *girlfriend* out on a date.

Squeal!

Yes, Hunter Blackwell was officially my boyfriend. And once I found the courage to break the news to my dad that I was dating a non-believer, I would be shouting it from the rooftops.

"You seem a lot happier than you were before spring break," Hunter said as we walked hand in hand down the sidewalk back to my house after dinner. "Were you just having a bad few days?"

A 'bad few days' would be an understatement!

"I was worried about a service position the High Priest had revealed that Xander and I needed to fulfill," I said. This was the simplest way to explain what had actually been going on. "But I turned it down, so it's all good now."

"You turned down a position?" Hunter raised his eyebrows in surprise. Which I got—no one turned down special positions, especially when they came directly from the High Priest.

But I shrugged and said, "Yes, I did."

"Were they asking you to teach the nursery kids together or something?" He asked like it was a joke. "Because I've heard they can be quite the handful."

"Not quite." I laughed. "I think I probably would have actually enjoyed that one because toddlers are so cute. But yeah, I definitely didn't feel up to this one." I sighed and looked up at his tall frame. "I mean, I went as far as emailing *The Confidant* to see if she could give me advice on what to do."

He furrowed his brow. "You did?"

I nodded. "I mean, I would have asked you for advice if I was allowed to..." I said, worried that he'd be offended I'd emailed *The Confidant* when I'd told him that I couldn't talk about it. "It was a different kind of service position though, so I needed anonymity for it."

He narrowed his eyes, like he was concerned about what exactly my special role would have been.

But I said, "It's all behind me now though, so it's not something you need to worry about."

"Okay." He pressed his lips together. Then squeezing my hand tighter in his, he added, "I just don't want you to find yourself in a dangerous situation because something is supposed to be secret. I've read about some interesting things happening with church leaders, and I know things can sometimes get tricky when we believe someone has authority over us."

I didn't love that he was basically saying that some church leaders use their power to do bad things, since most of the leaders I knew were really good people...but I understood that sometimes a few bad apples did rot the entire barrel.

Since I knew he was only saying it because he cared about me, I said, "I know. If anything bad was to happen, I'd definitely let you know."

We walked inside the church gates, and he pulled me to the bench where we made out all those weeks ago.

I wondered if he was going to start kissing me, but he gestured for me to sit next to him instead. "There's actually something I need to tell you about." He scrunched up his nose. "I just hope you won't be mad when you find out."

"What is it?" I searched his eyes as I worried what it might be.

He wiped his hand across his forehead and let out a long breath before meeting my gaze with wary eyes. "I'm *The Confidant.*"

I went completely still for a moment as my mind tried to understand what he'd just said. Then, confused, I asked him, "I'm sorry. What did you just say?"

He bit his lip and scrunched up his face again. "I'm the person who created and writes under the pseudonym of *The Confidant.*"

So I had heard him right.

I gasped. "Are you serious? You're—" I shook my head, my brain still having a hard time forming the new connections it needed to make with what he'd just said. "You're telling me that *The Confidant* isn't a girl and that it's actually you?" My voice went up an octave at the end.

"Yeah..." He leaned back as if worried I might smack him, holding his hands up in front of him. "Please don't be mad."

"I'm not mad..." I said, still trying to figure out how Hunter —my best friend whom I practically did everything with— could be the creative genius I'd been jealously obsessed with for the better part of a year. "I'm just...shocked." I shook my head. "And kind of feel like an idiot for never guessing it when it should have been so obvious all along."

I mean, when any of our friends needed advice, Hunter was always the best person to ask. And when I'd decided to set up *Dear Eliza*, he had known exactly what to do.

All those times I'd noticed him on his phone and thought he had a secret Internet girlfriend, I should have realized he was typing way too many words for it to be a believable text thread with a flirty girl—I was pretty sure those types of messages involved way more photos versus big walls of text.

And when he'd helped me with most of those emails for *Dear Eliza* after the state basketball tournament, he'd taken everything to the next level. Several students had even commented a few times about how *Dear Eliza* was going to give *The Confidant* a run for her money if she kept things up.

I shook my head. "You probably had a good laugh to yourself every time I talked about *The Confidant* and my guesses for who she—" I shook my head. "I mean, who *he* could be."

"It was quite entertaining to see you making those lists of suspects." He laughed.

"You dork." I shoved his shoulder. Then I gasped when something else occurred to me. "I bet you loved it when I emailed you for advice about how to fix things with my best friend. Because you had to know it was me."

"I did hope it was you," he said, more seriously this time. "But only because I wanted to fix things with you so badly myself."

"And yet you didn't respond to my second email."

"I really thought I did." He held his hands up defensively. "But I must have forgotten to press send or something when you walked in the library and almost caught me emailing you back."

"That's two emails from me that you didn't respond to." I tsked and pretended to be disappointed. "It's almost like *Dear Eliza* really is better than *The Confidant*." I narrowed my gaze and gave him a wicked grin.

He rolled his eyes. "Since they're basically the same person right now."

"Yeah...I guess you're right." I shrugged. "No wonder you missed a few emails. Keeping up two secret identities must be hard."

"I might be looking forward to retiring from *Dear Eliza* when the school year ends, just a little."

"We can probably just shut that column down," I said, feeling guilty for having him keep up with something that I started. "We could just make a note in the next issue about how *Dear Eliza* has had a good run, but *The Confidant* really is the queen of advice and that they should just look there."

"*Queen* of advice?"

"We have to keep the mystery going somehow, right?" I said. "Calling *The Confidant* a king would just make it obvious that it's you, since you're the only guy in the whole school who could believably be him."

"And yet you never figured it out." He smirked. "I think I may need to report that oversight to the valedictorian committee."

"Did you really just go there?" My mouth dropped open.

"I totally did." He chuckled. "Though, Carter and Elyse didn't figure it out either, so I guess you might still deserve it."

"I've worked my butt off for those grades, so I'm pretty sure I do."

"Fine, you've still got my vote."

A slow breeze blew a few blossoms from the trees, and I watched them float through the air until they fell to the ground.

But then a new question came to mind, so I turned back to Hunter and said, "So you're, like, making a lot of money as *The Confidant*, aren't you?"

He seemed to debate on whether to answer my question. With a shrug, he said, "I do okay."

He did okay? "Which means...?" I raised my eyebrows, waiting for him to expound.

"Let me just preface it by saying that I only reached this income level out of pure desperation. My parents were going to cut me off after high school, and since I didn't want to live on the streets of New York, I had to get scrappy."

"You know I wouldn't have let that happen."

He raised an eyebrow, unconvinced.

"Okay, so I might not have reacted well when I found out what was going on with you and all the church stuff," I said. "But...if you were starving and living on the streets this summer, I would have invited you to the soup kitchen and made sure you were fed."

"The soup kitchen?" His eyes widened. "But not your actual house?"

"They serve pretty good food there," I said. "And I really don't know how to cook, so it's probably a safer bet than anything I could whip up on my own..."

He chuckled. "Well, I appreciate that you'd at least serve me some of the soup kitchen's food."

"So...how much does *The Confidant* make each month?" I asked, so curious after all the buildup.

He looked like he was fighting a smile, probably proud of whatever he'd been able to make so far. So I knew it had to be pretty good.

"With all of the special monthly memberships, it's around five figures a month," he finally said.

"Five figures a month?!" My jaw dropped. "Daaaang."

That was some serious cash.

I knew most of the students at our school had parents who brought in five or even six figures a month—my mom being one of them—so that wasn't an unheard-of monthly income. But man, that was an awful *lot* of money for a high school student to be making on his own.

"I got lucky." He shrugged like it was no biggie.

"No, Hunter. That's actually really amazing." I put my hand on his knee. "Like, I'm kind of in awe of you right now."

He got all bashful, his cheeks flushing at my compliment. Seeing his humility just reminded me of the fact that Hunter Blackwell really was the cutest and sweetest guy I'd ever met.

Man, I love him so much.

"So you're not mad at me for keeping *The Confidant* a secret?" he asked, like he was worried I might feel betrayed.

"I'm a bit bummed that you didn't tell me, just because it would have been fun to know. But I get that we all have things we keep to ourselves."

"I promise I don't have any other secrets," he said. "No other secret identities or secret Internet girlfriends."

"Well, that's good because I don't have any of those things, either."

I just wouldn't tell him how close I'd been to almost having a husband tonight.

Yikes! That would have been insane!

Should I tell him about that? Or just let him look up my email if he got curious?

I didn't have a chance to decide because my dad and Archie stepped out of the parsonage a moment later.

When my dad noticed Hunter and me sitting close on the bench, I worried for a moment that he might tell me to stay away from him because Hunter was an apostate. But he simply sighed, like he was tired and it was out of his hands now. My dad called out, "It's probably time for you to head to bed, Scarlett."

"Okay," I called back. "I'll be right in."

I turned to Hunter, and he said, "I better let you go then."

I nodded. "Thanks for dinner."

"Anytime." He bent forward and kissed my cheek. "Thanks for coming with me."

I stood from the bench to give him a hug, but when I did, my phone fell out of the pocket of my skirt.

Hunter bent over to pick it up. When he was handing it to me, we both seemed to notice at the same time that I had missed a text from Xander a few minutes ago.

"Xander's still texting you?" Hunter asked, his gaze darting down at my phone again as I took it from his hand.

"I guess?" I said. "I mean, I haven't heard anything from him this week, but apparently, I have a text from him so... yeah..."

What did he want? He hadn't reached out to me ever since I told my dad I couldn't go through with the ceremony. I didn't know how he had reacted to the news that he'd have to wait for the High Priest to reveal another girl to fulfill the role.

I swiped my thumb across the screen and read the latest text.

Xander: **Hey, Scarlett. Sorry to bother you. I know it's late, but I've been looking all over for my backpack. It's got my notes for a test I'm supposed to study for. I think I might have left it at the church when I was there with your dad today. I'd ask him to check but I know he goes to bed early. Would you be able to run over real quick and look?**

I relayed the text to Hunter with a shrug.

"Want me to help you look?" Hunter asked.

"No, I should be fine," I said. "But I'll walk you to the gate."

"Sounds good."

I hurried inside my dad's house and grabbed the church key he had hanging on a hook just inside the door. After slipping the key into the back pocket of my crossbody bag, I walked Hunter to the gate.

"I'll see you tomorrow," I said when we reached the brick archway.

"See you then." He pulled me close for a moment, giving me a kiss.

And even though I still didn't want to say goodbye to him after spending several hours together, I pulled away and waved goodbye, watching him saunter down the sidewalk toward his penthouse.

When he disappeared in the darkness, I shut the gate and then turned back to go inside the church.

I texted Xander back. **I'm going to the church right now. What does your backpack look like? Any idea where you may have left it?**

His text came right through, like he'd been watching his phone for my response.

Xander: **It's black. Green water bottle in the side pocket. I might have left it by the organ...**

Me: **Okay, I'll let you know if I find it.**

Xander: **Thanks. You're a lifesaver.**

I opened the door with my key and stepped inside. It was dark in the foyer, and even though I'd practically grown up here, the church was always a little creepy at night. I switched on the lights and rushed toward the chapel doors.

But when I made it to the organ, I didn't find anything.

I pulled out my phone and texted Xander back: **I don't see a backpack anywhere in here.**

I was about to ask if he may have left it somewhere else in the church, when his reply came through.

Xander: **Your dad also took me to the top level since I'd never been up there before. Maybe that's where it is?**

I frowned.

Why had my dad taken Xander up there?

No one ever went up to the top floor unless the High Priest was here or there was a special ceremony. But maybe he'd asked to see it since we were supposed to perform that ceremony in there today?

I put my phone in my bag since it would just fall out of my skirt pocket as I dashed up the stairs.

Then switching on the lights for the staircase, I ran up the wooden steps as quickly as I could. Maybe it was the fact that I could see the full moon streaming right through the center of one of the huge windows ahead of me, but it just felt extra creepy for some reason.

Which was probably a weird thing to feel when I'd grown up running through the halls and up and down these stairs. But the big church always felt a little different at night.

I made it to the top of the stairs and saw the black backpack Xander had described sitting next to the wall. But I also saw that the door to the Holy Room was open.

I frowned. I'd never seen that door open before. Ever.

It was always locked.

But I was so curious what might be in the room where the sacred ceremonies took place and where the High Priest had his visitations with Jehovah.

Just taking a quick peek wouldn't be bad, right?

So I took the octagonal-shaped glass knob in my hands and cracked the door open just enough for me to slip inside. I felt around the wall for the light switch, but just then, the door suddenly slammed shut behind me.

I jumped and screamed. And after a few seconds where I wondered if a gust of wind had blown the door shut, an old-fashioned lamp in the corner was switched on, blinding me for a second. With my heart beating fast, I squinted at the apparition a few yards in front of me—it looked like a guy who belonged in the early eighteen-hundreds, wearing a blue waistcoat with a cream-colored vest and a pair of brown trousers; the kind of clothes that Samuel Williams was depicted to wear in the church paintings.

I froze as terror swept over me.

Was I looking at the ghost of Samuel Williams right now? Had I just walked into a special visitation?

Was this a special meeting where I would be rebuked for not following through with the ceremony and breaking my promise to obey all of God's commandments?

But then the man took a step closer, and my eyes adjusted at the same time he smiled. And I realized I was looking at Xander.

46

HUNTER

AS THE ELEVATOR climbed to the top floor, taking me to my parents' penthouse, I fished my phone out of my pocket to open *The Confidant*'s email app.

I searched for the email address Scarlett had used previously, futurevaledictorian@awesomemail.com, and saw an unopened email with the words **I can't talk to anyone else about this** in the subject line.

I tapped on my screen to open it, my eyes quickly scanning over what she'd said.

Dear Confidant,

This email might be a little weird, but I don't really have anyone else I can talk to about it. But since you always have such great advice, I figured I might as well try.

So I'm in a pretty strict religion. I love it and it's my whole life, but I just found out about a revelation that is making me struggle a little. It's just kind of surprising and different from any of the revelations I've learned about at church before.

It's hard to explain, but basically, my dad told me last

week that there was a revelation many years ago about the girl
—or woman, I guess—who would be the mother of the High
Priest in the second coming of Jehovah and Samuel Williams—
the Chosen One. (If you don't know what the High Priest in
my church is, he is basically like what the Pope is in the
Catholic church. But since my church is the one true church, I
guess he's a bit higher than that because he's actually the High
Priest of the entire world and not just the church...)

Anyway, I basically found out that I am supposed to
marry this other guy from my congregation, and we are
supposed to perform some ceremony that will make me get
pregnant with this future High Priest. (I know just writing
that sounds crazy, right?)

I know the guy I'm supposed to perform the ceremony
with, and he seems nice enough, but it's just so sudden and a
little weird, and I'm really confused at what I should do. Especially since I am already in love with someone else.

Do you have any advice? Or a way that I can figure this
out fast? (I only have another week!)

I've tried praying about it, but I'm not getting the right
answers.

I'm planning to meet up with the guy tomorrow so maybe
that will help give me more clarity on where to go from here,
but I just don't want to make the wrong choice and possibly
mess up my future and disappoint God.

Thank you,
Your confused friend.

P.S. Please don't post this on your website since I'm pretty sure
my best friend will figure out that it's me and he won't
understand.

I was shaking when I finished reading the email.

What in the actual heck is going on? Was Mr. Caldwell actually fine with basically sacrificing his daughter and her future for some stupid made-up revelation? Because what kind of crazy pills was he taking?

And what was the High Priest taking, too?

This was, like, early-church-and-Samuel Williams-level crazy.

"Are you coming in?" Bash's voice called from the kitchen, and I realized that the elevator door was open.

"Yeah..." I said, looking back down at my phone, completely dumbfounded.

Scarlett had called this off though, right?

That was what she'd been telling me tonight, hadn't she? There couldn't have been some other revelation about a special service position for her and Xander that she'd decided to turn down.

I ran my hand through my hair as I walked into the entryway of our home and sat down on one of the couches in the living room.

As I laid my head back, my thoughts wandered down another path.

If Scarlett had been the one to turn down this "special role," did that mean that Xander had been fine going along with it? Was that why he was always texting her and trying to hang out with her, because he was just fine going along with it all and just wanted to get to know her better?

Because that was just weird. And so similar to all the stories I'd read about Samuel Williams and his spiritual partners.

Should I be thankful that the High Priest had at least picked a girl who was eighteen instead of fourteen this time?

Bash walked into the living room with a bowl of ice cream a minute later. Leaning against the wall, he asked, "What do you look so disgusted about?"

I shook my head and held up my phone. "I just found out that Pastor Caldwell and the High Priest tried marrying Scarlett off to Xander."

"What?" Sebastian's dark eyebrows rose behind his glasses.

I shook my head, still not believing what I'd read in Scarlett's email. "Apparently, there was some revelation that said how Scarlett was supposed to be spiritual partners with Xander and have his baby."

"Hold up." Sebastian crossed the room and held his hand out for my phone. "You said Xander? As in Xander Pierce?"

"Yeah..."

And as he scanned Scarlett's email, I realized Sebastian didn't look nearly as shocked as he should. When he was done, he pointed at my phone and said, "That guy needs to be put behind bars."

"Who? Xander?"

Bash nodded. "He's a nut job." When I just frowned in confusion, he added, "When my friend Paxton was roommates with him at Yale, he said Xander had this weird thing for younger girls going on."

"Younger girls?" I frowned. "What do you mean by that?"

"Like, he had this weird obsession with high school girls. Paxton told me that Xander didn't go to any of the college parties like everyone else in their dorm. Instead, he was always dating girls that were still in high school."

"Really?" I mean, if he was a college freshman, he couldn't have been that much older than the high school girls...but it was still a little weird that he was seeking them out. Especially when he had gone to college in a new city, and it wasn't like he was just visiting his old friends from high school.

"At first, Paxton assumed it was maybe because Xander was just more at their level...like maybe he wasn't mature enough to date the college-aged girls." Bash released a low breath and gave me a serious look. "But then it came out that he convinced a sixteen-year-old girl to run off with him and get married."

"Wait, he got married?" My voice raised an octave.

"Yeah..." Bash nodded. "I don't think it was legal. It later came out that he had done the same thing with, like, two other girls... But yeah, he's a creep."

"But—" I shook my head, not believing what I was hearing. "How is that even possible? Like, how is this not public knowledge?"

Bash rubbed his thumb against his fingers in the "money" gesture. "You can bury a lot of skeletons when your family is loaded."

"Why didn't you say anything until now?"

"It happened, like, three years ago, and after he got caught, I honestly thought it stopped." Bash held up his hands. "And I thought that the people who knew him had been warned. I thought for sure that the High Priest had even disfellowshipped him for a while." Bash rubbed his cheek. "But I guess that was actually right before the old High Priest died, so maybe no one else knew about it."

That was the fun thing with The Fold's policies. A lot of them relied on their leader's "personal revelation," and if they chose not to report things, they would claim it fit under a clergy exemption. Having "church royalty" like the Pierces involved in a scandal would bring negative attention to the church. And if there was anything The Fold cared about most, it was their image.

Bash sighed and leaned back against the couch. "In the church's eyes, he was probably just continuing God's work—since they have that hidden doctrine about Samuel Williams' posterity continuing the spiritual partners thing. So they probably figured it was all good as long as he didn't get caught by anyone."

I shook my head. "That crap is so messed up."

He nodded. "And if this kind of stuff is still happening, you really need to find a way to get Scarlett out of it."

"I know." I sighed.

Had any of this caused any cracks in Scarlett's beliefs? Or did she see it as being fine...but just not for her personally?

I shook my head as I pictured her and Xander standing together in the church.

And as soon as that image clicked into place, a cold feeling of horror washed over me because I realized that Scarlett was actually in the church tonight because of Xander asking her to go look for his backpack.

No!

I pulled out my phone and told Siri to dial Scarlett's number as I jumped to my feet.

"What's going on?" Sebastian sat up straighter, setting his ice cream bowl down on the cocktail table.

"I think Scarlett is in the church with Xander right now."

"What? Seriously?"

"Yes." I put my phone to my ear and prayed that Scarlett would pick up and tell me she was fine. But when it just rang and rang, I started running toward the elevator.

47

SCARLETT

"GLAD YOU COULD JOIN me after all," Xander said as I frantically turned around and tried to open the door.

Please, please open.

But even though I could turn the glass knob, the door wouldn't budge. Because the deadbolt had been locked.

With a key.

Why in the world did the Holy Room have a way to lock someone inside?

"What are you doing here?" I turned back around to face Xander again, a sense of panic rising in my chest. "And why did you lock the door?"

"I'm here to fulfill the Lord's commandment." He took a step closer, a sinister smile I'd never seen before on his lips. "I'm here to ensure that the work we were chosen for is completed."

"But I told my dad that I couldn't be the chosen vessel," I said, even though I was sure that Xander probably already knew it.

Hence the covert plan to get me here, and the reason why he thought he'd need a locked door to keep me from running.

"I know you wanted to ignore the role you were given," he said. "But even if your faith is weak, your body is still capable of bringing forth the birth of the Chosen One and ensuring that the bloodline of Jehovah continues."

My faith was weak, but my body was capable?

Was he planning to force me to perform the ceremony?

I turned back around and tried the door again, but when it still didn't budge, Xander chuckled and said, "The Lord's work cannot be stopped, Scarlett. Jehovah's bloodline will continue."

He keeps saying that.

If I wasn't in the throes of a panic attack, I might ask him what he meant by Jehovah's bloodline continuing, but my heart and mind were racing so fast that I couldn't really form words when I needed to figure out how to get the heck out of here.

Where had he put the key? Did he have a pocket somewhere in that Samuel Williams' costume he was wearing? I scanned his waistcoat and trousers, looking for some sort of pocket in the old-fashioned material.

He cleared his throat. "Just as I don't advertise that I come from the bloodline of Samuel Williams, I also don't speak about the even bigger family secret." He stepped close enough that I was forced to press my back against the wall. Then, looking down and studying me for a moment—seeming to enjoy the look of terror on my face—he bent close to my ear and whispered, "I'm actually a direct descendant of Jehovah."

All I wanted to do was push him away and scream, but I knew that if I was freaking out, it would make it harder for me to find a way out of this room.

He was so much bigger than me, and though I was pretty strong for a girl, if this turned physical, I would easily be overpowered by his tall frame.

Maybe if I feigned interest in whatever weird story he had

to tell, he'd get distracted enough that I could slip my phone out of my bag and call 9-1-1 without him noticing.

The service was always spotty in the church, but maybe from the top floor it would work.

So to buy myself time, I asked, "Are you saying you're a descendant of the actual Jehovah? Like, *the Son of God,* Jehovah?"

"Yes."

"But Jehovah didn't have any children," I said. "The Bible never said anything about it."

"That's because it happened later." His eyes smiled, like he was so thrilled to share this shocking story with me. *"Much later."*

An eerie chill raced down my spine.

"You were supposed to learn this story tonight," Xander said. "Every worthy member of The Fold learns about it when they come to have their marriage blessed."

"So my dad knows about this?"

"Of course."

"Then why has no one ever mentioned Jehovah's posterity before?"

"Some revelations can only be spoken in the holiest of places," he said, gesturing to the curtain on my left, like he was speaking of this room being that specific place. "Talking about the sacred traditions in the outside world could lead to grave consequences. The serpent is always looking to confuse and lead Jehovah's disciples astray."

My dad had said that the sacred ceremony was something he couldn't speak about, so maybe some of what Xander was saying was true?

I shook my head. That would be so weird, though. To have some sort of hidden doctrine that only certain members knew about.

"As you know, God has to work by the laws of science," Xander continued, thankfully taking a step back so I could breathe. "But when Samuel Williams was eighteen, his mother told him that the man who raised him wasn't Samuel's biological father after all. That just like Jehovah wasn't Joseph of Nazareth's biological son, Samuel was conceived in a similar manner. His mom was Jehovah's spiritual partner—a chosen vessel just like Mary." Xander moved to the wall on my left. Opening a keypad next to the curtain, he said, "Samuel Williams was the literal son of Jehovah, which is why he was able to restore the true church and priesthood here on earth."

Okay, Xander had to be suffering from some sort of delusion right now. Because this almost sounded like the plot for Dan Brown's *Da Vinci Code*, with all the secret ceremonies and talk of Jehovah fathering children no one had heard of before.

Or maybe Xander had truly lost his mind. I'd learned in Psychology that certain mental illnesses could be triggered during our twenties after suffering a big stress. When I said that I wouldn't be able to fulfill my part of the ceremony, did it stress out Xander so much that it sent him into some sort of mania?

While he was distracted with the keypad that would do who knew what, I tugged on the zipper of my bag, attempting to discreetly open it so I could reach inside.

But as soon as Xander heard the zipping noise, he looked back at me.

I thought for sure he would snatch my bag away, but instead, he simply said, "Just a few moments, and all will be revealed to you, Scarlett."

Is there anything here that I could use as a weapon? I wondered, looking at the other end of the room. There was a high back chair in the corner with a side table, as well as the lamp that he'd turned on after he'd first locked the door.

I could probably use the lamp as a weapon...if I could somehow sneak up behind him.

I didn't love the idea of trying to knock him out with it—it was likely that I might not do it right and only make him more volatile. But if he tried attacking me or doing anything else, it might be my only hope.

I looked around for something else that might be helpful, knowing that he must be planning to move onto the next phase of his plan if he was using the keypad that would make some unknown thing happen.

But the only other thing besides the curtain and the basic furniture was a window, so there was literally nothing else for me to use.

In all my imaginings of what could be behind the mysterious, permanently locked door, I'd never pictured something so minimalistic for the High Priest to use when Jehovah visited him. Or so small. It was barely the size of my bedroom at the parsonage.

But people got married and did other ceremonies up on this floor of the church, right? So there had to be another room up here somewhere.

Just as I had the thought, the white curtain started to slowly part, revealing a large wooden door that was curved at the top. And once the curtain was fully in the open position, the door slowly started to swing open, revealing a short, dimly lit walkway that led to what looked like a much larger room.

With a smile on his face, Xander gestured to the secret hallway and said, "Welcome to the Holy of Holies, my love. As you can see, everything is ready for you."

48

SCARLETT

I DIDN'T WANT to walk into the next room, but since the only exit I'd seen so far was locked, I followed Xander down the short hallway with hopes there would be a different door in the next room that could be my way out.

Organ music wafted in the air, lending an eerie vibe. But with Xander's back to me for the first time and with the music covering any other noise, I took the chance to quickly unzip my bag the rest of the way. After turning the volume of my phone all the way down, I held down the two side buttons that would make the emergency S.O.S call.

Please have service.

Please send help.

"Here we are." Xander turned around to look at me just as I'd zipped my bag back up. "Welcome to the holiest place on earth. The place where the veil between mortal men and God is the thinnest."

With my heart pulsing through my whole body, I took in everything there was to see. This second room was much larger than the first—about half the size of a basketball court. And while everything in the last room had been completely white, this reminded me of the medieval churches that I'd seen in movies.

The walls were made of gray stone. The main lighting came from sconces that resembled old-fashioned torches on the walls. To my left were several rows of dark, wooden pews—which I assumed meant that whatever ceremonies took place in here often had multiple people in attendance.

And at the very back of the room, in the center of the wall behind the pews, was a door.

Should I run for it now?

Would it be locked, too?

Xander must have seen me looking at the door because he said, "Don't worry, Scarlett. That door has been secured as well. No one else will stumble into the sacred ceremony we're about to perform. Privacy is not an issue."

A cold chill raced down my spine and the hairs on my arms raised.

He thought I was worried about someone coming in?

Did he actually think I would go along with his crazy plan once I saw this weird room?

I drew in a deep breath, hoping to calm myself enough to think. Maybe there was something in here that I could use to get away from him.

I moved my attention to what must be the front of the room, and if I'd been delusional enough to think that it would hold something better...I was wrong.

Because from what I saw, I was starting to wonder if my roommate during freshman year had been right all along and that I actually had been raised in a freaky, secret cult without knowing it.

My breathing became shallow, my heart racing, as I took in the stone steps that led up to a large platform that was about three feet off the ground. In the center of the platform was what I could only describe as a really big altar covered in a gold, satin cloth with red rose petals scattered around the edges.

Surrounding the altar were hundreds of flameless candles of varying height and width. And right behind the altar and candles was a huge, stained-glass window that I had never seen from the outside of the building before.

But even though I knew there had to be a solid wall behind the stained glass—there was no way I wouldn't have noticed something like this from the outside—there had to be some sort of artificial lighting between the glass and the wall to make it look like it was backlit by the light of the full moon.

Xander gestured at the stained glass and said, "It's beautiful, isn't it?"

Though I felt like I might throw up from seeing all the candles and the altar the size of a bed, I knew that if I continued to engage him in conversation, the longer it would be before he could follow through with whatever ceremony he'd prepared for.

Hopefully, my S.O.S. went through.

Hopefully, the GPS system would lead the police right to me.

"It is beautiful," I said, trying to sound like I was in awe instead of weirded out by the scene it was depicting. "But what is it?"

It didn't look like any of the church art I'd seen before—paintings of Jehovah during his life in Israel or other important people from the Bible.

Instead, the stained glass featured a young woman in a white Regency-era nightgown, sitting on a large bed and looking up at a man dressed in white robes.

A man who, from his beard and long hair, I assumed must be the resurrected Jehovah.

"The stained glass represents the night Samuel Williams was conceived," Xander said, glancing up at the artwork in awe. "The night Jehovah visited Anna Williams in her bedroom while her husband was away."

Wait...? So Xander didn't actually make that story up?

It was actually real enough for the church to commission someone to create this massive piece of art to show what had apparently happened over two hundred years ago.

But if that was the case, why had I never heard of it? Why had no one—not even my dad—ever uttered a single word to me about Samuel Williams being a descendant of Jehovah?

"If you had come to our scheduled appointment tonight," Xander said as he walked up the steps to the platform, "you would've had everything revealed to you through a special ceremony. You would've been washed and cleansed before being dressed in your special ceremonial clothing and taught the sacred practices of Jehovah." He sighed and picked up a folded piece of white fabric from the corner of the altar. "But since you were disobedient to the Lord's command, there are no helpers or witnesses to assist with the ceremony this evening. You will simply have to make do with me acting the part of Jehovah and the angels tonight."

He would be acting the part of Jehovah and angels?

"D-do angels usually visit this room?" I croaked out, my face and hands feeling clammy with sweat.

"In the flesh? No." Xander said. "But God does have his special servants who are called to act as proxy for his angels. I think Brother and Sister Morris were the ones scheduled to assist with this ceremony tonight."

Brother and Sister Morris? I pictured the older couple from our congregation. My dad and Megan had gone to visit them on Presidents' Day weekend, mentioning something about Sister Morris being sick and needing a blessing.

But if everything that went on in here was so secretive, did it possibly mean that instead of going to their house, they'd actually all been here?

Performing another ceremony?

"Do many people have this ceremony performed?" I asked, wondering if what he was talking about was special just for the revelation of the Chosen One, or if it was part of the marriage ceremony.

"All those worthy to have their marriage blessed in the Holy of Holies perform the first ceremony we will be experiencing tonight." He took a step down and then another from the raised platform. "The second ceremony—the one that needs to be performed under the light of the full moon—is at another level of sacredness. It's something that only the two of us will have the honor of performing on the altar."

Was that his flowery way of saying he planned to have sex with me on the altar?

Was that what everything would lead up to?

He stepped off the platform, and when he offered the white cloth to me, I suddenly couldn't breathe.

I had tried to stall and give the police enough time to get here—but they should have been here by now if they were coming, right?

Was that why Xander hadn't taken my bag from me? He'd probably known any calls for help would go unanswered because the cell service was somehow blocked in the Holy of Holies.

I darted my gaze around the room, desperate for another door to appear. For a key. For a paper with a secret code written on it that would make another hidden exit open.

I needed some sort of miracle to help me escape before Xander could force me into doing something I had already told my dad that I just couldn't do.

When I looked back at Xander, he was unfolding the fabric he'd offered me. And when he shook it out to reveal its full length, I saw that it was an old-fashioned nightgown almost identical to the one Anna Williams was wearing in the stained-glass image.

"If you could just put this on, my love, we can get started," Xander said, offering the nightgown to me again.

And I knew I needed to at least try that door at the back, just to see if it was magically not locked. So I took one step back and then another, but when Xander saw that I was about to run, he let out a deep chuckle and said, "If you're not interested in making this easy and dressing yourself, I will happily assist you in that part."

49

HUNTER

"SHE'S STILL NOT ANSWERING?" Bash asked while putting on his shoes. When he'd seen the panicked expression on my face as I'd run out of the living room, he'd grabbed his shoes and jumped into the elevator with me.

"Not yet," I said, shaking my head and dialing her number again. "What if he's got her?"

"Then we'll make sure he spends a lot of time in jail," Bash said. But when he saw the look on my face, he seemed to realize I was actually more worried about how much trauma Xander was going to leave Scarlett versus what would happen to him afterward.

Bash shook his head. "If we hurry, he hopefully won't have gotten very far. From what I heard, he was really theatrical with his conquests in the past. So if this is supposed to be like one of the ceremonies they perform in the Holy of Holies, I don't think he'll skip any of the steps. He seems the type to be thorough in following that kind of ritual to a T."

I exhaled an anxious breath. "Hopefully, she just lost her

phone and isn't even alone with him," I said before pressing the button to call Scarlett again.

After Bash finished tying his shoes, he said he was calling the police.

But as my own phone rang, instead of hearing Scarlett's lovely voice telling me that she was okay and safe in her bed, I only got her pre-recorded voicemail saying to leave a message.

"Please call me back, Scarlett," I said after the beep, my body tense with anxiety, sweat dripping down my forehead. "I read your email, and I'm worried that Xander might be dangerous. Whatever you do, don't go anywhere near him. If you're okay, please at least text me. Either way though, Bash is talking to the police right now, and they're on their way to the church."

The elevator finally made it to the main level. As soon as the doors opened, Bash and I darted out and sprinted toward the church down the street.

And even though I hadn't prayed to any sort of god or deity all year, I found myself pleading to anyone that might be listening: *Please let Scarlett be unharmed. Please don't let her suffer the trauma that so many other people have gone through.*

A minute later, the church came into view. There was a faint light coming from one of the windows where the staircase was.

Someone was still in there.

Please be okay.

I pushed myself to run even harder, my heart feeling like it would burst inside my chest any second.

Why had I let her go into that church alone? Why hadn't I told her about the Holy of Holies or the rituals and blood oaths they performed in there when I'd first read about them?

If I'd ignored her father and just told her everything I knew, she would have known that the revelation the High Priest claimed came from God was just the writings of someone with ulterior motives.

I made it to the wrought-iron fence that marked the perimeter of the church property, having left Bash several paces behind me. As soon as I made it to the archway, I pushed the gate open and ran straight for the main entrance of the church.

Please be unlocked still.

I grabbed the door handle and yanked it open, but it didn't budge.

"NO!" I banged on the door with my fists. "Open up, Xander!"

But when it still didn't budge, I raced down the steps to try a different set of doors. There were three other entrances that I knew of, so there was still a chance of getting inside if Scarlett happened to have just used a different door this time.

Deciding that she might have chosen the one closest to the parsonage, I ran to the west entrance. But once again, it was locked.

If the other sets of doors were locked, I might need to break through a window.

I was just running toward the opposite side of the building when the doors of the main entrance suddenly burst open. An instant later, Scarlett was running down the steps.

"SCARLETT!" I pivoted my direction and started sprinting toward her, relief coursing through my veins.

When she registered that someone was out here with her, she turned her head in my direction and gasped, "Hunter!"

A second later, she was falling into my arms, clinging to me tightly, and I was frantically asking, "What happened? Are you okay? What did he do to you?"

"I'm okay," she said between sobs, burying her face into my neck. "I got away before he could do anything."

And with those few words, my whole body went weak with relief.

She'd gotten away in time.

He hadn't hurt her.

We both collapsed to the ground as my knees gave out from the strain of the run and the relief of finding Scarlett. I started to inspect her face and her body for any signs of a struggle while Bash ran onto the church grounds.

"Is he still up there?" he asked breathlessly when he noticed Scarlett clinging to me on the grass.

"I think so," I said. "I didn't see him come out."

"He's on the top floor." Scarlett pointed toward the doors she'd just run out of. "In the Holy of Holies."

He'd taken her in there?

Bash's face flashed with the same alarm I felt at Scarlett's mention of the secret room where the most cult-like rituals took place. But after hesitating for only a second longer, my brother ran into the church to find Xander.

Sirens sounded in the distance, and soon the streets were lined with police cars, a firetruck, and an ambulance.

Several first responders arrived on the church property. When I pointed toward the church doors, five police officers ran inside with their guns ready.

The lights to the parsonage switched on shortly after that, and Scarlett's dog, Archie, bolted out the door to see what the commotion was about, followed by her dad who was dressed in a gray bathrobe.

"What the heck is going on here?" he called when he saw Scarlett and me in the middle of the chaos.

Even though I wasn't sure exactly what had happened in the church, when the clouds parted and the light of the full moon allowed me a closer look at Scarlett's clothes, I noticed they were torn and turned askew.

As if Xander had tried ripping them off of her.

My eyes flashed with red, and I felt like barfing. Because while Scarlett said she'd gotten away before Xander could harm her, it looked like it had only been just barely.

When Pastor Caldwell was only a few feet away and able to take in his daughter's appearance, I said, "It looks like your buddy Xander tried to rape your daughter."

And when Scarlett's sobs got louder at hearing my words, I knew that what I'd assumed was true.

50

HUNTER

"CAN Hunter ride back home with us?" Scarlett asked her mom when it was time to leave the police station.

After the police found Xander and Bash in the Holy of Holies, they'd arrested Xander and taken everyone else connected to the incident—Scarlett, Pastor Caldwell, Scarlett's stepmom Megan, Bash, and me—to the closest police station to be questioned on our versions of what had happened tonight.

It had taken a few hours for the police to release us—everyone but Xander who had been officially taken into their custody.

We'd all been questioned separately, so I still wasn't sure what exactly had happened in the church since Scarlett had been pretty quiet, crying off and on as we'd sat in the waiting area.

I didn't expect her to tell me everything tonight because I knew she was still in shock and understandably emotional about everything that happened.

But I hoped she'd be okay.

"Of course Hunter can ride with us," Scarlett's mom said, looking at me in a way that said she'd do anything to make Scarlett feel safe and comfortable right now. "We'll do anything you want."

Scarlett nodded. "Thanks."

We walked out of the police station together. I wasn't sure how much physical space Scarlett would need after going through what she had tonight, but when we climbed into the back of the cab and buckled in, she scooted right up against my side and had me put my arms around her, like she wanted to burrow away from everything that had happened in the church.

When we got back to the building that her mom and my parents lived in, Scarlett asked if I could stay and watch a movie with her until she fell asleep. Since I would literally do anything—anything at all—to make her feel safe, I followed Scarlett into her mom's apartment and sat next to her as *You've Got Mail* played on the big TV in the living room.

But instead of paying attention to the movie, Scarlett started telling me about what had happened in the church. About the locked doors, the secret rooms, the weird costume Xander wore, and the creepy stained-glass window.

"I didn't think I'd get out of there," she said. "It was so scary."

"How did you get away?" I asked. "If all the doors were locked, how did you escape?"

Because if there had been some sort of holy intervention or miracle that saved her, I might need to rethink my current agnostic state and start believing there actually was a Higher Power that intervened in our lives.

But instead of giving credit to anything like that, she said, "I forgot that I had it in my bag, since I basically put it in there and forgot all about it after my birthday, but..." She sighed and looked up at me with her big brown eyes. "When I was pulling out my phone to try and call 9-1-1 again, I saw the pepper spray my dad gave me and was able to spray it in Xander's eyes. While he was on the ground and trying to wipe the pepper spray away with his clothes, the key fell out of his pocket and I used it to unlock the first door."

"I'm so glad you noticed it."

She nodded. "Me too. I think it literally saved my life. I don't know if Xander would have ever let me out of there."

She shivered, like she was reliving the most intense moments. I pulled her close, kissed the top of her head and said, "I'm so sorry you had to go through this. So sorry you were ever put in contact with that guy."

She leaned closer. "I just can't believe that no one knew he was dangerous. How does someone like that slip through the cracks? How was he ever considered eligible to be an associate pastor?" She shook her head. "Like, I'm pretty sure he's met with the High Priest at least a few times. Shouldn't the High Priest have sensed something was off in their meetings? Shouldn't his special gift of discernment have tipped him off that something was wrong with Xander?"

That was certainly the kind of thing we'd been taught would happen. That the Lord's servants had some kind of almost supernatural power to bless people's lives or to figure out things like this—like having a special sixth sense.

And even though I wasn't sure how Scarlett would react to my skeptical thoughts on the subject, I knew that staying silent on things might only keep her at risk for being preyed on by other wolves in sheep's clothing. So I said, "Do you think it's possible that the High Priest is just as susceptible to human error and oversight as the rest of us?" I swallowed and licked my lips. "That maybe Xander was able to slip through the cracks because we're all human and perhaps a little too trusting when someone claims to have special inspiration from God?"

Scarlett went still, and when her brow furrowed, I worried that I had upset her further with my skeptical thoughts.

But after a few heart-pounding seconds, she said, "I guess that's something I might need to think about."

51

SCARLETT

I FELL ASLEEP CUDDLED up to Hunter on my mom's couch but awoke in a panic a little after two, my mind racing with nightmares of locked rooms and stained-glass windows and all the questions the events of last night had spurred within me.

Even though I didn't want to think that what Hunter suggested about the High Priest having no more discernment than the rest of us could be true, I couldn't get the thought out of my mind.

Or the other questions that came with it.

Because if there was some sort of flaw in the High Priest's power as a seer for our time—if he could get things so wrong with Xander and that revelation—what other things could he or any of the other High Priests of the past gotten wrong?

Had any of the teachings I'd been raised to believe in actually been inspired by God and Jehovah?

Or were they just the workings of man? Men who may be doing their best, but were nonetheless, still just men.

I glanced at Hunter sleeping in the corner of the couch. I

knew I wouldn't be falling asleep again until I'd done something about these new thoughts and questions I had, so I grabbed my phone from where it had fallen to the floor earlier and opened up an Internet browser.

With my fingers trembling only slightly as I typed in the URL I'd visited once before, I hit the search button and let the "Questions for the High Priest" load.

Then instead of listening to the voice I'd been conditioned to hear when looking into anti-Fold material, I scooted closer to the light of the lamp bookending the other end of the couch and started reading.

Once I started, I literally couldn't get myself to stop. Just as Hunter had said had happened to him, the more I read, the more questions I had.

Because how the heck had Samuel Williams created such a tangled web of lies and turned it into a religion that still preyed on good people today?

How had I never been taught any of these stories in Bible class?

And how had Hunter resisted telling me everything he'd studied?

I WAS JUST cross-referencing some of the things I'd read on the website with some of the church history essays when Hunter woke up. His lids were heavy as he looked in my direction. After wiping some of the sleep from his eyes, he sat up straighter and asked, "Couldn't sleep?"

"I had a nightmare," I said.

"Really?" Concern was etched in his eyes. "You should have woken me up."

"It's okay." I shook my head. "It gave me time to catch up on some reading."

"You're doing homework?" Hunter raised his eyebrows, like he assumed that the reading I was doing was for school.

"I'm not reading for a class," I said, pushing myself away from the corner of the couch I'd sunken into over the past four hours. I sat on the cushion next to him. "I started reading that essay you told me about a while back—the essay that Pastor wrote after finding a lot of problems in his church history research."

Hunter's eyes grew wide. Glancing at my phone in my hand, he asked, "You're reading the 'Questions for the High Priest?'"

"I finished that about an hour ago." I nodded. "Now I'm going through the church history essays so I can cross-examine everything." I was still feeling shocked about how much information had been packed into one document. "But my mind is kind of blown."

"It is?" He narrowed his gaze, like he wasn't sure how I meant that. After studying my face for a second, he asked, "Do you think any of what the essay says is true?"

I thought about his question and tried to figure out how I felt about all of the things I'd been reading.

"I'm not really sure what to think or believe right now," I said. "It's just so crazy. All the things it said Samuel Williams did—the ways he'd manipulated and swindled people...the real reason why he'd taken so many teen brides..." I closed my eyes briefly, feeling the pain of betrayal creeping in as my brain formed new connections to everything I'd learned so far.

Because when you looked at the stories separately, just story by story, they could be interpreted in whatever inspiring way you wanted to see them. There was a lot of wiggle room.

But when you actually took a step back and looked at all

the stories in the actual context of what was happening during that time period, you could see the true motivations for when certain revelations came about.

It made everything look completely different.

And after seeing it that way, I couldn't help but worry that I'd been lied to my entire life.

Was it possible that Hunter had actually been right all along? That the church I loved was just something a man in the 1800's had made up because he'd seen how easily he could convince people of anything? Because he loved power and knew that turning himself into a god could be a lucrative career move?

He'd been so untouchable.

He'd had so much power, and when anyone spoke against him, he'd used that power to threaten and silence them...or expel them out of the community altogether.

Once the naysayers were all gone, the ugly truths were easier to keep buried since he owned a printing press and could control the narrative.

Plus, the Internet wasn't a thing back then, and people were afraid of what might happen to their families if they spoke up about the things this powerful man did behind the scenes. The real truth only came to light when someone noticed the puzzle piece that didn't quite fit and started looking into things with the chance that it might blow up their whole world.

I swallowed, my eyes pricking with tears. If I came away from the research rabbit hole I had dove into and decided that I had been brainwashed my entire life, would I ever be okay again?

Would I become another person for the members of The Fold to look down on? Someone they'd write off as being weak-minded or never having enough faith in the first place?

Would my dad feel that way about me?

A wave of nausea came over me as I wondered if I was already on my way to becoming a permanent disappointment to my dad if I did step away.

The church was literally his whole life.

"Are you okay?" Hunter asked in a gentle voice when I must have seemed lost in my thoughts for too long. "Do you need me to do something?"

"I don't know if I'm going to be okay," I said in a wobbly voice. "All my life, I've been told that Samuel Williams was this amazing man. That he was basically at the same level as God and Jehovah because of all the miraculous things he supposedly did." I wiped at the corners of my eyes. "I was told that if I ever did hear someone speaking evil against the Lord's anointed, then I needed to ignore it because it was just Satan trying to persuade us away from the straight and narrow path because his greatest goal was to confuse us." I drew in a shaky breath as I tried to push back the overwhelming emotions: Sadness. Hurt. Anger. Confusion. Betrayal.

I shrugged. "I'm just wondering if now that I know more of his background, if maybe there were actually legitimate reasons for him to have so many enemies. If maybe instead of being a hero, he was actually the villain. But because he was a master manipulator, he was able to use those skills to pull the wool over our ancestors' eyes and use his own paintbrush to smudge a few brush strokes here and there and paint himself as the good guy. Because even villains want to be the heroes of their own stories."

"It is definitely something to consider," Hunter said, like he was trying to be as unbiased as he could and give me the support and space I needed to figure out my feelings and all the thoughts running through my head.

"I just don't understand," I said, "that there can be so much out there—on the church's own website—that most faithful members don't even know about. Don't even think to look into."

———————

I DID MORE research over the next day and a half—choosing to skip church because just the thought of stepping onto church property after my traumatic experience made me feel sick to my stomach.

But after reading until my eyes hurt, and I had a crick in my neck from hunching over my phone and books for so long, I had to catch my ride back to Eden Falls with Hunter and get back to real life.

"How did you not just read this stuff twenty-four seven?" I asked Hunter as his parents' driver drove us back to the school Sunday night. "Because there's still so much for me to read that I don't know how I'm going to concentrate on my classes or do any of my homework this week."

"It was pretty all-consuming," Hunter said. "But since I started my research at the end of the school year, I was able to do my most intense reading over the summer."

"How long did it take you to decide you were done?" I asked. Over the past two days, I had already gone back and forth on what I wanted to do about a dozen times.

One minute I was sure the church was a load of crap, and then the next, I was back to hoping that if I just found the right piece of information, everything would magically be okay again and I could go back to believing it was true.

"It was a few months before I felt like I had enough information to leave," Hunter said. "But it's definitely different for everyone. My parents were fine leaving after just a few weeks."

"That's so fast."

"It was," he said. "I was shocked when they told me

because they'd been members for so much longer than me. But we're all different." He reached over and took my hand in his. "And I think it's good to remember that there isn't a certain deadline for you to decide by. You can go as fast or as slow as you need. You can take a break from the church and see how it feels to just be a regular human living a more secular life. Or..." He squeezed my hand. "You can continue attending all your meetings if that makes you happier while you figure things out. You could even try something in-between."

It made sense that Hunter would say that. He had always been more of the "take things slow and figure out all the details before jumping into things" personality while I'd been the "jump in headfirst, and then figure it out as I go" type.

"And what if I decided to stay?" I asked. "Would you think any less of me?"

"I would have questions," he said. "Just because I care about you and always want to know what you're thinking. But if you really thought The Fold was more of a positive force in your life than negative, then I would hope that I could be okay with us being on different spiritual paths."

I didn't know why, but just hearing that I wouldn't lose him if I came to a different conclusion than him in the end took a huge weight off my chest.

"What about you?" he asked. "If you decide to stay, do you think you could be okay dating someone who doesn't want anything to do with religion right now? Would that be a deal-breaker for you like it was before?"

I thought about it and everything we'd been through together the past few months.

But I only had to consider his question for a few seconds because I knew my answer. I'd known it since I'd woken up in my dorm room a little over a week ago and found him smiling at me.

So I said, "As long as that person is you, I don't care what you believe. Because I know your intentions and what an amazing person you already are. And I just want to be with you."

"Well, that's good to hear." He gave me a gentle smile and pulled me closer. "Because I just want to be with you, too."

52

SCARLETT

THE NEXT FEW weeks were busy as the end of the school year approached and I prepared for all of my final exams.

I'd taken Hunter's advice and decided to take some of the pressure off from figuring out my beliefs and where I thought I fit into the universe. I knew I couldn't forget the things I'd experienced in the Holy of Holies with Xander or the ways my dad and the High Priest had been manipulated into believing there was an actual revelation that said I was predestined to be with someone like him.

But it was nice to know that I didn't need to have all the answers *right now*.

I had time.

And Hunter was so great to support me as I worked to figure things out for myself. He was a safe person to talk things out with, as well as a great listening ear when I just needed to vent. And the more I learned—the more bombshells that seemed to be dropped on me—the more empathy I had for him because he'd had to do so much of this on his own.

I hadn't been there for him when he had to wrestle through

his own dark night of the soul.

But when I tried to apologize to him for not being *his* safe person last year, he just told me not to beat myself up over it. Because he understood what it was like to be a true believer and that I'd just been doing what I'd been raised to believe was right at the time.

At the end of May, just a week before graduation, it came out that Xander had actually been the mastermind behind the revelation regarding the Chosen One's conception all along.

That while he had found Samuel Williams' journals in his dad's personal library, he'd taken the one with the "revelation" to a document forger and had him create the pages for the made-up journal entry and then had it bound right into the book.

When I asked my attorney why Xander had chosen me to be his victim in the first place, she explained that Xander admitted to developing an obsession with me when he'd interned with my dad last summer. Xander's office at the church had given him the perfect view into my bedroom, and he had become infatuated with me after watching me through the window several nights.

"But why go through the trouble of creating the whole revelation in the first place?" I asked. "Wouldn't most stalkers just try to seduce me the normal way?"

To which my attorney replied very matter-of-factly, "From what our source said, Xander noticed what a tight leash your dad kept on your dating life, and being the religious zealot that he is, he decided to seduce you using the spiritual language that your father speaks fluently."

So yeah, Xander had basically just taken great notes from his hero and ancestor, Samuel Williams, and figured it could be an exciting way to manipulate young girls into sleeping with him.

Which, as it turned out, was something Xander had done a few times before, according to the handful of other women who came forward to tell the experiences they'd had with him in the past after the story broke.

And while I felt terrible that Xander had preyed on so many other girls, some who had been younger than me at the time of the abuse, I was glad that it just gave the court more ammo to use against him.

Hopefully, he wouldn't be able to hurt anyone else again.

"HOW'S THE VALEDICTORIAN SPEECH COMING?" Hunter asked as he brought our chai lattes to the table after Kiara had called his name. "Have you found the right inspirational quote to open with yet?"

"Not quite," I said, taking a sip from my drink after he handed it to me. "But I'm sure I'll figure it out."

"You always do." Hunter took his seat next to me and opened his laptop.

It was the Sunday before graduation, and we were both working at a corner table in the local coffee shop that Hunter had always snuck away to on Sunday mornings.

When he'd invited me to come with him a couple of weeks ago, I'd thought for sure we'd get in a car accident on our way here because I'd always been taught it was such a huge sin to shop or visit places like this on the Lord's day.

But after coming here three weekends in a row and not being in any sort of mortal peril, I found myself looking forward to the more laidback Sunday mornings and hoped that we would continue the tradition when we were back in New York.

My dad didn't love that I had decided to take a sabbatical from The Fold to see how I felt without it in my life.

But he did understand why I needed space after everything that had happened with Xander. He too had been shocked that the High Priest hadn't been able to use his special spiritual gifts to see the wolf living among us, but after having his own doubts for a few weeks, my dad seemed to separate that experience from all the other positive experiences he'd had with The Fold. I doubted he'd ever choose to leave his faith.

Which was understandable. He found a lot of fulfillment in his beliefs. And if I was going to expect him to respect my own spiritual journey, I would respect his.

We all deserved to live life on our own terms and in the way that made the most sense to us.

But if the next few months continued the way this past month had, I was starting to think I may never go back. My faith in The Fold being the right path for me had been shattered, which I still sometimes cried about because it had been such a big part of my life. But this starting with a clean slate and seeing what the universe showed me it had to offer was more freeing than I would have thought. Plus, with Hunter there to support me as I figured things out, I knew I would be okay.

"Do you think Elyse and Carter know you're the one who will be receiving the award and giving the speech?" Hunter asked, breaking me from my thoughts.

"I don't know if the committee has officially reached out and told them they didn't win." I set my cup on the table between our laptops. "But they knew the valedictorian would be notified right after the final grades were tallied last night, so I'm pretty sure they've already figured it out."

"Hopefully, we won't find them in the middle of egging your car when we get back to the school," Hunter said with mirth in his green eyes.

I laughed. "If anyone is doing that, I'd put my money on Asher."

"Yeah, that's probably more likely," Hunter agreed with a grin. "He definitely seems the type to avenge his girlfriend's honor by doing something like that."

"That he does." I took another sip from my drink and leaned back in my chair. "So, did you figure out which emails *The Confidant* is answering for next week's column?"

"Not yet," he said. "I got too distracted by reading the comments on today's column."

"Are there a lot?" I sat up again and leaned closer to look at his computer screen.

I hadn't had a chance to read the column yet myself, so I was curious which question and Hunter's subsequent answer had spurred so many comments.

Hunter angled his computer so I could look at the screen better and said, "Have a look for yourself."

So I started reading the first few emails he'd answered. And while the advice was at the typical quality that Hunter's columns were always at, I didn't see why they'd receive more feedback than previous weeks.

"Did I pass it already?" I furrowed my brow and glanced at Hunter who was watching me as I read.

But he just shook his head and said, "Keep going."

I finished the fourth question, and when I got to the last email from someone who called herself, *Pining for my mega-hot best friend,* I smiled. "This looks like it might be something you have a little experience with."

"Because I think you're mega-hot?" He smirked.

"No..." I felt a blush rise to my cheeks. "I was thinking more 'the pining for your best friend' part, but I'll definitely take that compliment, too."

"You better, because it's true..." He chuckled, and with a

wink, he added, "But yeah, I might have just a little experience with the pining part, too."

"Yet another thing we have in common," I said before letting my gaze scan through the email.

Dear Confidant,

I'm in a bit of a tricky situation that I'm not quite sure what to do about. You see, I have a major crush on one of my close friends and have no idea what to do about it. We've known each other for years, since he was friends with my older brother first, but it wasn't until this past year that we became close enough for me to consider us best friends.

Anyway, he's really awesome, and the more time we spend together, the more desperate I am to get out of the friend zone. I mean, I went as far as asking another guy out to make him jealous.

Dumb...I know. Especially since the other guy was totally into someone else.

Anyway, I'm worried that if I tell him about my feelings and he doesn't feel the same, it will make things really weird. Especially since we'll literally be living in the same house next year—as roommates.

Like, how am I supposed to live across the hall from him and not make it obvious that I think he's the most beautiful and amazing human to ever exist?

Ugh. I know that sounds dramatic, but I really don't know what to do.

Do I just pretend like I'm not in love with him and hope he makes the first move? Or do I tell him how I feel and hope that by some miracle he feels the same, and we can start living the life of my daydreams soon?

Help!

-Pining for my mega-hot best friend.

"Well, that sounds amazingly familiar," I said when I'd finished reading.

"I know, right?" he said. "I could have basically written the same email last year... And again this year, too."

"Me too," I said. "You know, except for the roommates part. Now *that* sounds exciting."

"What...you mean you sleeping in the girls' dorm and me in the boys' dorm but sharing the same common room doesn't count as living in the same place?" Hunter raised an eyebrow. "Because I'm pretty sure we've basically been roommates since freshman year."

"Fine. I'll just tell my dad that I've been roommates with my boyfriend for four years." I grinned. "I'm sure that would make him feel even more warm and cozy towards you."

I watched Hunter's life flash before his eyes at the prospect of me telling my dad something like that. After stumbling to speak, he said, "Okay, m-maybe it's a little different than that. We definitely don't need to give your dad even more reasons to worry about the path of darkness I'm leading you down."

"Yeah...probably keep our semi-roommate status just between us," I agreed with a smile. Then looking back to the column he'd written, I asked, "So what advice did you give this girl? Anything good?"

"I think it's pretty good. But you should probably read it yourself."

Dear Pining for my mega-hot best friend,

Sounds like you are in a very tricky situation indeed. One that may surprise our readers to discover that I, myself, have actually been in for several years because I have been in love with my own best friend since my freshman year.

It took me a long time to figure out how to get out of the friend zone—and she actually helped me out with it quite a bit because she is braver than me—but I just wanted to tell you that from my own experience, it can be so rewarding to put yourself out there and tell the person you care about exactly how you feel.

There is always the risk that your friend won't reciprocate your feelings, and things might become awkward for a little while. But like you already mentioned, confessing your feelings may also be just what you need to start an amazing new journey with your best friend—something possibly even better than what you've dreamed of having.

I know that for me, falling in love with my best friend and pushing through the difficult times has been one of the best decisions I've ever made. And if I had to do it again, I would. Because she is simply everything to me and I would literally do anything for her.

So basically, my advice is to put yourself out there—even if you need to start with one of those social media "kissing your best friend challenges."

If it goes well, you might have a fun first-kiss story to tell your family and friends about. And if it doesn't, you can always pass it off as just jumping on the trend with hopes of going viral and nothing more.

It's up to you, of course, but that's totally what I was going to do before my best friend beat me to it.

"You were planning to do that best-friend-kissing challenge with me?" I gasped.

"I was." He got a bashful look on his face. "Ever since I saw one of the videos during sophomore year, I'd been trying to get up the nerve to do it."

"Really?" My voice raised in pitch because Hunter was basically the sweetest guy in the whole world.

He nodded.

So I had to say, "Well that's kind of funny because I wanted to do it back then, too."

"You did?"

I nodded.

"Well," Hunter said. "It certainly took us long enough."

"And yet, it all worked out just the way it was supposed to."

"Yes, it did." He bent close and gave me a tender kiss that made my stomach flutter.

When he pulled back and his gorgeous green eyes met mine, it felt like my heart might burst because I still couldn't believe he was mine and I was his.

Even when we were old and gray, I was pretty sure I'd feel like the luckiest girl in the world to have won the heart of the man of my dreams.

When the door to the coffee shop opened, I looked back at Hunter's computer and asked, "So what are all those comments you were reading about, anyway?"

"Just some people being excited for us." He got a half-smile on his lips. "People saying they wished a guy would talk about them the way I talk about my girlfriend."

"You did say some really sweet things."

"It's easy to say when they're all true."

Gah! I had to cover my heart with my hand because Hunter really was getting me all up in my feelings this morning.

But then he got an amused smile on his lips, and I knew there was more to the comments than what he'd said so far.

So I asked, "What else are people saying? Did they figure out who you are?" Because there weren't too many people at our school who had recently started dating their best friend.

He just grinned and pointed at a particular comment thread and said, "No one has guessed who I am yet, but I'm

guessing it's because a lot of people are excited to find out that
The Confidant is part of the LGBTQ+ community."

"What?" I frowned, so confused at how they would have
gotten to that assumption. "How did you dating your best
friend make your readers jump to those conclusions about your
sexual orientation?"

"Because just like you assumed yourself, it appears that
most of my readers don't think that *The Confidant* could ever
be written by a guy." He chuckled, like he got a huge kick out of
misleading so many people with his pseudonym. Pointing to a
specific comment, he said, "Like this one here that says, 'I'm so
excited that *The Confidant* finally got *her* happily ever after,
too.'"

"Well, that's sweet that everyone is so excited for you..." I
said, unable to contain my grin. "Even if they filled in a few of
the details wrong."

"It is fun." He took my hand in his, giving it a squeeze. "But
it was even more fun having a chance to brag a little about you."

I squeezed his hand back. "Just let me know when you're
ready to come out of the writer's closet so I can finally brag
about how I'm the lucky girl who's dating *The Confidant*."

"I will," he said. "For now though, you'll just have to settle
for dating Hunter Blackwell."

"Which, since he's mega-hot and amazing, is pretty brag-
worthy all on its own."

"I thought you were the one who was mega-hot, though."

I shrugged. "Pretty sure it's both of us."

He grinned. "Then it looks like we are the perfect match."

I chuckled, and before leaning in to give him a quick kiss, I
whispered, "I really think that we are."

EPILOGUE
KIARA

"I SEE that you've done an even better job of confusing your fans about who *The Confidant* might actually be," I said to Hunter as I brought the breakfast sandwiches he and his girlfriend had ordered to their table.

"You noticed the comments, too?" Hunter chuckled.

"I've told you I'm a fan," I said.

"Wait—" his girlfriend, Scarlett, asked, a confused expression on her face. "You know he's the..." She glanced around the coffee shop, like she was worried people were listening. Then after assuring herself that the only other person in here besides us was too far to overhear, she said, "You know that Hunter is *The Confidant*?"

"I figured it out a few months ago."

When Scarlett's mouth dropped open in shock, Hunter just smiled and said, "Apparently, Kiara is a much better detective than you." Then with a teasing smirk, he added, "Maybe we should tell the committee that they should give the valedictorian award to the true brains of Eden Falls."

"But she doesn't even go to our school." Scarlett lightly

smacked Hunter's arm. She looked up at me apologetically and said, "I mean, I'm sure you are amazing and would have given me a run for my money...but—"

"It's fine." I laughed, enjoying the teasing vibe these two had together. "I've got a solid B average, so I think your award would have been safe."

"But you're a senior?" Scarlett asked.

"Yeah," I said. "I graduate in just a few days, too."

"That's cool." She held out her hand. "I'm Scarlett, by the way."

"Kiara." I shook her hand. "Nice to meet you."

Hunter sat up straighter, and after clearing his throat, he said, "Remember when we went rappelling and saw that girl at the cottage on the Hastings' property? That was Kiara."

"Really?" Recognition dawned on Scarlett's face. "So you know the Hastings?"

"A little," I admitted. "My mom works for them so I see them from time to time."

"Well, that's cool," Scarlett said. "Hunter and I are close friends with Carter, Cambrielle, and Nash, so we're over there all the time."

The bell on the coffee shop door jingled. After Scarlett and Hunter looked in the direction of who had just walked in, Hunter said, "Speaking of the Hastings..."

When I glanced to see who had come in, my heart did a little flip-flop because standing with his siblings, with the sunlight making his dirty-blond hair streak with gold, was Nash.

He wore jeans and a blue shirt that I knew would bring out the color of his amazing blue eyes, and when he looked in my direction, I felt my entire body buzz with electricity.

Was he looking at me?

Had he recognized me?

A slow smile spread across his lips, like he was happy to see me. And when he started walking toward me, I swallowed and worried I might have a heart attack because this could not be happening.

After being basically invisible to him for the past three years, did he actually notice me?

But then he got a little closer, and I realized he was actually walking to say hi to Hunter and Scarlett.

Because *they* were his friends.

Not me.

I sighed. While Nash was giving Hunter a high five, I turned to Scarlett and said, "Looks like I have some orders to take. It was nice meeting you."

Scarlett smiled, thankfully not seeming to notice how jittery I was around Nash. "Nice meeting you, too."

I went to the counter, and as soon as I stepped up to the register, Cambrielle and Carter Hastings were ready with their orders.

I put in their drink and breakfast orders. Then Carter, seeming to realize that Nash was too busy chatting with Hunter and Scarlett to order his food, called to his brother, "You want the Green Eggs and Ham sandwich and mango smoothie like usual?"

Nash nodded and said, "Yep," before going back to his conversation.

I totaled their order, and after they paid, I printed off the ticket to get started on their drinks.

As I listened to the group of friends chat and laugh while I frothed the milk for Cambrielle's cappuccino, I couldn't help but be a little envious of the close friendship that they all seemed to have.

I finished making the drinks and was about to call out

Carter's name for the pick-up when I looked up and saw Nash standing just on the other side of the counter.

"Are those ours?" he asked.

"Y-yeah," I said, a flash of heat rushing over me.

And just like always, I was immediately caught off guard by how blue his eyes were up close. They reminded me of the ocean back home, and all I wanted to do was swim in them.

"Perfect." He took the cups in his hands, balancing his smoothie in the crook of his arm. Then he said, "Thanks," before turning and walking back to his table.

I let out a low sigh as I watched his retreating back, wondering, not for the first time, when I would get over my stupid crush and move on to liking someone more attainable.

Because if he was ever going to notice me, it should have happened by now.

But since I was really good at holding onto the unrequited-love thing, instead of going to the other end of the counter and starting the sandwiches for the Hastings' siblings, I pulled out my phone and opened my email app to my drafts folder and clicked on the email I'd been thinking about sending for a few months.

I read over what I'd typed.

Dear Confidant,

What do you do when the guy you like doesn't seem to realize you exist?

-Kiara

PS: Remember how you said you owe me one for keeping your secret?

Yep...I was still just as pathetic as I had been back in February when I'd written this.

But I knew nothing would change if I didn't do something about it, so I pressed the button to send the email.

And just as I was pulling out the bread to make Nash's breakfast sandwich and telling myself not to freak out, I saw Hunter pull his phone out from his back pocket, like he'd just felt the email notification push through.

Crap! I probably shouldn't have sent that when Nash was sitting right next to him.

Hunter furrowed his brow at me, like he was curious why I would email *The Confidant* when I could just walk over and talk to him—I'd opted to use my regular email account kiara-matheson@awesomemail.com so he knew it was from me.

Just read it, I mouthed, my heartbeat pulsing in my temples.

So he looked back at his phone and seemed to scan the email while everyone at his table was too wrapped up in their conversation to notice.

He looked up again when he'd finished. I could see he was wondering who I had written to him about, so I decided to just make everything really obvious and eyed Nash.

Hunter looked at Nash, too, and seeming to make all the connections in his head, he started typing something on his phone.

A moment later, my phone buzzed with a new email that said, *Want me to play matchmaker?*

BONUS EPILOGUE
HUNTER

NINE YEARS LATER

"WHERE'S MY BEST FRIEND?" Scarlett's dad, Jeremiah, called in a singsong voice after stepping into the entryway of our home. "Does my best friend, Levi, live here?"

"Grandpa's here!" the voice of my three-year-old son Levi squealed from the kitchen at the sound of his grandpa's voice. And a few seconds later, my son with auburn curls came running around the corner and into his grandpa's arms.

"You came!" he said. "I so excited!"

"I'm so excited to see you, too," Jeremiah said, hugging Levi tight. "I heard you just got a new scooter. Can you show me?"

"Yes!" Levi jumped out of his grandpa's arms and immediately started running toward the garage where his scooter was stored. "It's over here, Grandpa!"

After getting back up to his feet, which was surprisingly fast for a man in his seventies, Jeremiah went after Levi.

"Well, that looks fun," Megan said. "But I was wondering if my sweet Avery might be awake from her nap?" She took a few steps toward the kitchen, looking like she was trying to peek around the corner for signs of a baby bouncer near Scarlett's feet.

"She just woke up." I chuckled. If Jeremiah was Levi's best friend, Megan was definitely Avery's biggest fan. "And I'm sure Scarlett would love for you to take her off her hands for a bit."

"Oh good." Megan's eyes lit up, like the whole reason she and her husband had decided to make the hour drive over here was for the baby snuggles and had nothing to do with Scarlett and me.

Which, since our kids were the cutest little gremlins, I couldn't really blame them.

"She's just this way." I led Megan into the kitchen where my beautiful wife was just pulling a batch of chocolate chip cookies out of the oven, our cute five-month-old daughter sitting in the bouncer a few feet away.

"Mind if I take her outside to watch Levi and Grandpa?" Megan asked after lifting Avery from the bouncer.

"Please do," Scarlett said, brushing some hair out of her eyes with her arm. "Levi always loves an audience for his tricks."

"We'll come out once we get these cookies on the cooling rack," I added, looking at the warm and gooey cookies that Scarlett and I were taking to her new church's social this evening. I didn't always attend the church socials with her, but since she was in charge of the fishing booth tonight, I thought it would be fun to tag along and take a trip down memory lane.

Megan and Avery slipped outside, and I went to the other side of the island to be near my wife.

She had just pulled the apron over her head and set it on the countertop when I pulled her against me and whispered in her ear, "Or maybe instead of going outside, we should head to our room. I'm sure Levi can keep everyone distracted for at least thirty minutes."

"Hunter!" Scarlett gasped, her mouth dropping open. "You know we can't do that while my dad is right outside."

"He'll never know." I mumbled close to her ear before kissing her neck in the way I knew she loved.

She relaxed into me, and I was starting to think that I might have convinced her to sneak down the hall when Levi's giggle sounded through the window. She pulled back and said, "Later, okay?"

"Is that a promise?" I asked, getting my hopes right up again. "Because it sounds a lot like a promise."

And I knew that even though she liked to play hard to get, from the way she was fighting a smile, she was totally making plans for tonight in her head. Then she said, "Only if you promise to take baby duty tonight. I have a surgery with Dr. Aarden tomorrow, and I can't be sleep-deprived for that."

Did I mention that my wife was in her second year of residency at the hospital where Mack's dad was a neurosurgeon?

Because yeah...in case it wasn't already obvious, my wife was freaking amazing.

Once she'd deconstructed some of the hard and fast rules that The Fold had taught her, Scarlett had realized that it would be okay for her to have a more demanding career that she loved, versus looking only for things she could do from home while raising kids. And with more options than she'd previously thought she'd had, she'd fallen in love with medicine.

It was demanding and medical school had been intense, but since I was able to be more flexible with my work—The Confidant was still going strong and I had even ventured into writing a few non-fiction books—we'd been able to find a balance that worked for us.

"I don't know," I said, rubbing my chin like I needed to think about her bargain. "The books can't be written if I'm sleep-deprived."

"Then I guess we'll just have to try again some other time." Scarlett shrugged like it was no biggie and she didn't want some adult play time just as much as me.

She grabbed a spatula from a drawer and started scooping the cookies onto the cooling rack.

But since I was still addicted to my wife after all these years, I stepped up behind her, wrapped my arms around her waist, and said, "You know it's fun." I kissed her neck, her jawline, and then her cheek. "Totally worth staying up late for."

"Hunter..." She said it more like a sigh than actual words. "My dad and Megan are just out..."

But she didn't finish her sentence because she was turning around in my arms and pulling me to her.

"So maybe you don't want to wait until tonight after all?" I chuckled.

"Just kiss me, okay?"

Not needing to be told twice, I pressed my body into hers and kissed her in exactly the way I knew she liked.

We only kissed for a few minutes before I made myself pull away. Because even if Scarlett's dad had warmed back up to me by the time Scarlett and I started college, he didn't need a visual reminder of how his grandkids had gotten here.

"So you're on baby duty tonight?" Scarlett smoothed her hair back down as we both tried to catch our breath.

"Of course," I said, combing out a tangle at the back of her head with my fingers. "You know I can never say no to you."

"And apparently, I can never say no to you, either."

I smiled, loving that we were still so obsessed with each other after all this time. Loved that with all the curveballs life threw our way, we always came away stronger. "Should we go outside to watch our adorable children?"

She slipped her hand in mine and tugged me toward the front door. "Yes, let's go."

DEAR READER,

Thank you so much for going on this crazy journey with Scarlett and Hunter. When I decided to write about characters going through faith transitions, I knew I was probably a little crazy. Most contemporary romance authors wouldn't touch the subject with a ten-foot pole. But after having this story nag at me for several years, I knew I needed to just write it down so these characters would stop bugging me and I could move back to my regularly scheduled, slightly less controversial, romances. 😉

As you may have guessed, I went through something similar to my characters in 2018 and since I know that there are so many people going through faith transitions—people who feel alone and like no one in their life understands their choices—I wanted to write this book with hopes that it would make them feel seen as well as to shed light on what the process can actually be like.

Not everyone's story is the same, so this was definitely not meant to be a catch all, but Hunter's experiences were similar to my journey in many ways. (Xander was definitely fictional though!)

I purposely did not explicitly say where Hunter and Scarlett ended up on the spirituality/religious spectrum. I wanted to leave that more open-ended since this story wasn't about what exactly my characters believed in, but more about their relationship and how they learned to hold space for each other's journeys and love each other because of who they were and not what religion they may or may not belong to.

I like to think that we're all just doing our best with the knowledge and experiences that we have and as long as our beliefs/spiritual practices don't cause us or anyone else harm, then that's awesome.

I have had a few early readers try to figure out what religion(s) "The Fold" was based on, since it seemed so realistic. But I promise, I really did try to create my own cult-like church in my head. Of course, with my personal experience with religion, it is likely that certain things unconsciously slipped through, but it was definitely not my intention to shine a spotlight on a specific belief system.

Any relation to another Christian denomination is there only because many religions have so much in common, just like most cults have similar practices and tendencies. And while I wanted The Fold to be more extreme, I also wanted it to feel realistic and not obviously cult-like at first glance. (Because where's the fun of having secret rituals and weird revelations if you know about them from the beginning of the book?)

I chose the 1800s specifically for Samuel Williams to be born because I'm familiar with that time period and it's also when a lot of religions were created (even if many of them died out long before now.) And since many of those religions also had founders who had heavenly visions and wrote books about them (Ann Lee, Emanuel Swedenborg, Joseph Smith, Joanna Southcott, Mary Baker Eddy) I thought that would be a great tie-in for Samuel Williams too. Plus...it was really fun to have Xander dress up in the 1800s clothing in his final scenes and show just how crazy he really was.

Also, having him dress up as a figure Scarlett trusted really helped with the Little Red Riding Hood vibe I was going for. (Did you pick up on the connection between Scarlett and

Hunter's names, her red coat and the references to the "wolf" in sheep's clothing??)

I could probably nerd out on all the different things that influenced this book. But I will just end here by saying thank you so much for taking a chance on Scarlett and Hunter's story. I really loved hanging out with them during the past few months and I'm excited for them to pop up here and there in the upcoming books in the series.

If you want to stay in the know about my upcoming releases and other special behind-the-scenes news, sign up for my newsletter, join Judy Corry's Crew on Facebook or follow me on Instagram!

Also, if you enjoyed The Confidant, please consider leaving a review and telling a friend!

Always grateful,

Judy

Nash and Kiara's story is next. Make sure to pre-order your copy here: https://authorjudycorry.com/products/the-confession

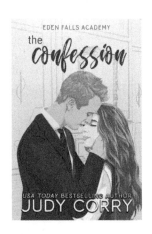

STAY CONNECTED!

I hope you enjoyed THE CONFIDANT! If you haven't already, please sign up for my newsletter so you can stay up to date on my latest book news. https://subscribepage.com/judycorry

Join the Corry Crew on Facebook: https://www.facebook.com/groups/judycorrycrew/

Follow me on Instagram: @judycorry

ACKNOWLEDGMENTS

Even though my name is on the front of the book, there are some people that I need to thank for helping me along the way.

First, I need to thank my amazing editor, Precy Larkins, for taking on such a beast of a book. (And for putting up with the crazy schedule and deadline I had for it!) I'm always super insecure when I first share my work with someone and I was particularly terrified to share this manuscript. But Precy was so generous to spend extra time on Scarlett and Hunter's story and helped me get it to a place where I felt safe sharing it with the world. She really is the best editor I could ask for and I feel so lucky to have found her with my first book!

I also need to thank my beta readers Melanie Yu, Kera Butler, Jordan Truex and Sofia Simpson for helping me see this book from a different angle than I may have on my own. Your thoughts and reactions were so insightful and pushed me to make this story stronger than I might have otherwise.

Thank you to Wastoki for your amazing cover illustration. I have loved working with you on so many of my books.

Thank you to the readers, bookstagrammers, booktokers, bloggers and reviewers who read my books and share them everywhere. I appreciate all the care you put into your posts and reviews. It truly means so much to me.

Thank you to James, Janelle, Jonah and Jade for being such awesome kids and for letting me talk about my books with you. The past few months have been crazy, but you have all been so wonderful and I'm the luckiest mom in the world to have each of you.

Lastly, I need to thank my husband Jared, who has been holding my hand and encouraging me all along the way. Thank you for being such a great sounding board and letting me talk through the scenes when I needed a listening ear. Things can get intense in my head when my anxiety is at an all-time high and I appreciate him being there for me in the ways that I needed when I was terrified to share this book.

And if you made it this far, I just wanted to say thank you, dear reader, for taking a chance on The Confidant. I know it was a tricky storyline and you probably just got way more insight into my state of mind than you wanted...but I really appreciate you putting your trust in me to take you on an emotional journey with the characters I made up in my head. I couldn't do what I love without your support.

Also By Judy Corry

<u>Eden Falls Academy Series:</u>

<u>The Charade</u> (Ava and Carter)

<u>The Facade</u> (Cambrielle and Mack)

<u>The Ruse</u> (Elyse and Asher)

<u>The Confidant</u> (Scarlett and Hunter)

<u>The Confession</u> (Kiara and Nash)

<u>Kings of Eden Falls:</u>

<u>Hide Away With You</u> (Addie and Evan)

<u>Rich and Famous Series:</u>

<u>Assisting My Brother's Best Friend</u> (Kate and Drew)

<u>Hollywood and Ivy</u> (Ivy and Justin)

<u>Her Football Star Ex</u> (Emerson and Vincent)

<u>Friend Zone to End Zone</u> (Arianna and Cole)

<u>Stolen Kisses from a Rock Star</u> (Maya and Landon)

<u>Ridgewater High Series:</u>

<u>When We Began</u> (Cassie and Liam)

<u>Meet Me There</u> (Ashlyn and Luke)

<u>Don't Forget Me</u> (Eliana and Jess)

<u>It Was Always You</u> (Lexi and Noah)

<u>My Second Chance</u> (Juliette and Easton)

<u>My Mistletoe Mix-Up</u> (Raven and Logan)

<u>Forever Yours</u> (Alyssa and Jace)

Standalones:

<u>Protect My Heart</u> (Emma and Arie)

<u>Kissing The Boy Next Door</u> (Lauren and Wes)

ABOUT THE AUTHOR

Judy Corry is the Amazon Top 12 and *USA Today* Bestselling Author of Contemporary and YA Romance. She writes romance because she can't get enough of the feeling of falling in love. She's known for writing heart-pounding kisses, endearing characters, and hard-won happily ever afters.

She lives in Southern Utah with the boy who took her to Prom, their four awesome kids, and two dogs. She's addicted to love stories, dark chocolate and chai lattes.